PHOENIX RISING

ALSO BY EDEN HART

The complete *Girl on Fire* Series:

Girl on Fire Book 1

Ashes Falling Book 2

Embers Burning Book 3

Phoenix Rising Book 4

PHOENIX RISING

EDEN HART

PHOENIX FLAME
PRESS

To readers, the explorers of imagination

To librarians, the guardians of books

To booksellers, the merchants of wonder

1

DAY 593—July 9

NEW YORK

INVASION.

The four of us raced along Columbus Avenue, dodging blackened pieces of metal on the road. Fires raged in nearby buildings, billowing thick smoke that fouled the air.

Our trawler, *DeepSea*, had arrived from Florida an hour ago—and our world had changed in a minute.

Lynxx's terrifying words echoed in my mind like a death knell.

The Chi'az are destroying our satellites.

"I need to contact the others." Asher paused at a corner, switched on his radio and heard static.

Lynxx, Nila, and I tried our radios. More static.

"Maybe the Chi'az have jammed our signals," I cried.

"Doubtful," Lynxx said. "I think the falling satellites have interfered with the reception. It's probably just temporary."

"Cripes, I hope Willow and Harl are okay." Asher frowned, as though visualizing his ex-girlfriend and his friend lying burned and dead. Then, shaking off his fears, he crossed to a line of abandoned cars. With our Templar destroyed by a flaming chunk of metal, we needed another vehicle to get back to Weston Tower. "Let's check these out, guys."

The Chi'az are preparing for the Final Wave.

I scanned the sky. Nothing. No more pieces of burning satellites. No spacecraft. Despite the plumes of smoke, the sky seemed peaceful and innocent—except for its pale red color.

"They're not invading yet, Kassia," Lynxx softly told me.

"I know. But you just said they'll be coming in a few months." I turned to Nila. "What do you think they're planning to do?"

"I'm a Sphere hybrid, not an Outrider hybrid," the middle-aged woman reminded me. "We're enemies of the Chi'az. They don't share their plans with us."

"Do you agree with Lynxx, though?" I persisted. "Do you think the invasion will be in a few months?"

"Probably."

Invasion.

Dread pressed on me like an iron anvil.

We hurried along the parked cars, searching for a usable one. Many had been damaged by the falling satellite pieces. Others were buried beneath terra vines.

Finally, after inspecting two dozen vehicles, Asher peered under the hood of an SUV. "This one might be okay." He dosed the fuel tank with a small bottle of ReVive, used his Mini-Charger on the battery, then revved the engine.

The rest of us swept mounds of decomposition dust from the cabin before piling inside.

As Asher drove down the street, I asked Nila, "What about the others in your group from Florida? Are any of them hybrids too?"

"They're all human. They don't know I'm a hybrid. It's safer that way."

"For who? You? Them?"

"Everyone."

A low rumble came from a concrete canyon up ahead, a strange sound in a city usually swathed in silence. I tensed. *The Chi'az invasion?* Surely not. They wouldn't mobilize the same day they destroyed our satellites, would they?

A herd of elephants and rhinos thundered from a side street and stampeded toward us. The ground trembled. Trunks flailed in terror. Animals screamed. Squealed. Trumpeted.

What were they running from?

"Buckle up!" Asher swung the steering wheel into a U-turn. Too late.

A wild-eyed elephant headbutted the side of our SUV, flipping the vehicle over. It landed upside down with a shuddering crash that jarred my bones. Glass shattered. Metal crumbled. Stunned, we hung from our seatbelts as leathery animal feet pounded past our smashed windows.

A rhino horn slammed through a passenger door, its sharp tip skimming my upper arm. Biting back a cry of pain, I grabbed my arm and felt warm blood trickling through my fingers.

"Are you okay, Kassia?" cried Lynxx.

"I'll live."

"Shh!" Asher ordered as the thundering feet barreled down the street. "Those animals are terrified. Something's hunting them. Don't move or talk, guys."

The four of us hung upside down, silent, trapped by our straining seatbelts. We weren't meals *on* wheels, I thought apprehensively, but meals *under* wheels. Prime prey for the oncoming ... what?

A soft patter of feet approached the SUV.

Holding my breath, I willed my heart to stop pounding like a drum. I listened.

Multiple footsteps. Running. Chasing.

A stream of ugly feet raced past my shattered window, uncaring of the hot concrete. Long segmented toes. Clawed toenails. Corpse-gray skin. I glimpsed the tops of wooden poles and sticks ... no, the *bottoms*. The world outside the SUV was upside down, and I hung in my seat, confused and afraid—yet certain of one thing.

Those strange feet were death.

No one moved in the upturned vehicle.

Seconds later, the footsteps faded away.

Silence.

An animal squealed.

More silence.

Finally, we released our seatbelts and crawled from the wrecked vehicle.

"What were they?" Nila murmured, staring down the deserted street.

"Not human, that's for sure," I said as Lynxx helped me wrap a bandage around my bleeding arm.

For a long minute, we stood beside the crushed SUV, scanning for movement in the shadows. Two more squeals rang out. Sharp. Pain-filled. Close.

Asher turned to me, withdrawing his sword. "Kass, we need to find another vehicle ASAP. Splitting up is the fastest way. I'll protect Nila. You protect Lynxx."

"Hey," Lynxx snapped, his golden eyes flashing with male indignation. "I can protect myself."

Asher ignored him, his gaze focused on me. "Nila and I will head west. You and Lynxx go east. Try to find something in good condition. Make sure the tires are okay and the engine works. We'll use our walkie-talkies to stay in contact, but keep the volume low."

I nodded. "Got it."

"Stay alert and stay alive."

"You too."

Lynxx and I moved down the block, scanning cars, buses, and vans. All were damaged or overgrown with terras.

We paused at a corner.

Across the street loomed a very different Central Park from the one I'd loved for years. Its lush groves of trees had vanished, leaving skeletal black silhouettes. Statues wore leafy gray clothes. White angel-vine terras draped park benches like old sheets.

A tan delivery van stood in the middle of a field, intact and free of terras. As we hurried toward it, Lynxx glanced around. "Isn't this Sheep Meadow?"

"Yes." A sharp memory pierced me. My cousin and I had celebrated my sixteenth birthday here, just hours before the Night of the Red Mist. It had been Thanksgiving, and my parents, sister, and cousin had all been alive.

That day, I'd kissed Loner-Lynxx on a birthday dare, and I still remembered how the heat of his body had blazed through my own as though we were both on fire. My future had stretched excitingly before me, rich with dreams and hopes and possibilities.

Now, my family and eight billion people were dead—and our world was being terraformed by a non-terrestrial species.

Somewhere in Central Park, an animal screamed.

I licked my dry lips, nervous. "What's going on?"

"Nothing good."

We moved behind a thick bush. Through my binoculars, I studied the tan delivery van, noting its undamaged exterior. Around it, a field of dazzling flowers gleamed in the sunlight. The saucer-sized flowers resembled lotus blossoms that glowed as though lit by internal lights. They sprawled in a riot of sapphire blues, iridescent golds, glittering reds and greens and violets.

Glow-lotus terras. Beautiful. And deadly.

Lynxx pointed to a small dead deer pinned down by the lethal flowers. "We can forget about getting to that delivery van. Too dangerous."

He was right. The second we stepped on those flowers, our feet would be impaled by the terra's nail-sharp stamens and—

Footsteps thudded behind us.

2

Screaming, a black rhinoceros thundered across the grass like an enormous battering ram. Foam flecks flew from its mouth, and its padded toes flung up chunks of dirt.

Lynxx pulled me further behind the thick bush and we crouched together, peering through its leaves.

A pack of gray animals raced from the rear of an overgrown building. About four feet tall, they moved upright on two legs. Hideous bat-like faces. Huge black eyes. Pointed ears on top of large misshapen heads.

Lynxx and I exchanged stunned glances.

Krols. Gray, not black like the ones in Florida.

Shrieking and waving long sticks, the pack chased the rhino into the patch of glow-lotus terras.

To my surprise, the krols stopped at the edge of the flowers, not stepping on a single petal.

My gaze dropped to their gray-skinned feet, segmented toes, and clawed toenails. *Oh no.* These looked like the xanimals that had chased the elephants and rhinos past our overturned SUV earlier.

The frightened rhino lumbered across the glowing plants. A few steps in, dozens of needle-sharp stamens shot up and impaled its feet. Squealing, the animal crumpled to its leathery knees, then crashed onto the terras. After a final violent convulsion, it fell silent and still.

Moments later, a layer of bright flowers sprouted from its body.

A krol stepped forward from the pack. Its snout bore a jagged red scar, and its pointed ears were tattered. This scar-snouted krol uttered a sharp bark as it raised a stick.

Another krol scurried from behind the overgrown building, holding a large metal lid like a tray. On it, a pile of smoldering ashes exhaled wisps of smoke.

Scar Snout shoved the pointed end of its stick into the ashes and waited until bright flames licked the end. Then it stalked to the edge of the glow-lotus terras and swept the flames across several plants. The rest of the krols also lit their sticks and ignited other parts of the field. Within moments, Sheep Meadow blazed with multicolored flames.

I huddled with Lynxx behind the shrub, my nose crinkling at the pungent smoke that gushed from the burning terras. As the brilliant flames spread across the flowers and the dead rhino and deer, I braced myself. Sure enough, the flowers exploded with little screams. Dozens, then hundreds, of these sharp cries filled the air, like lost souls mourning their deaths.

The walkie-talkie on my belt vibrated.

"Hello?" I whispered. "Speak softly."

"Where are you?" Asher asked in a low voice. "What's that racket?"

"We're in Central Park, hiding from a pack of krols."

"What? Krols in New York?"

"Gray ones, not black like the ones down south. Just as savage, though." I wiped a bead of sweat off my forehead, trying to ignore the blazing sun.

"Do you need help?"

"No, I think they'll be gone soon."

"Be careful."

"Count on it."

"Good," he said. "Nila and I have found a working car. We'll wait for you and Lynxx at the corner of West Sixty-Fourth Street and Central Park West."

"Roger."

I relayed the conversation to Lynxx. He nodded absently, his focus still on the krols as he murmured, "That's alarming."

"What? That there are krols in New York? Yeah, really bad news."

"No, alarming that they're using fire as a tool. No Earth animal has ever done that—except humans. These krols are smarter than we thought."

A few minutes later, the glow-lotus terras' screams faded, the flames sizzled into oblivion, and the wafting smoke dispersed. Most of the krols ran to the scorched rhinoceros, their clawed feet crunching across the burned flowers. After tying a rope around the rhino's neck and shoulders, they dragged the heavy animal over the blackened plants and toward the road.

Scar Snout strode at the front of the pack, the small dead deer slung around its muscular shoulders like a shawl. The krol carrying the lid of smoldering ashes followed behind.

As they left the park, Lynxx watched them, his golden eyes worried. "Normally, when animals bring down large prey like a rhino, they'll feed on it where it fell. But these krols suppressed their savage instinct. Instead, they used rope—another tool—to drag it away."

"Yeah. I saw that."

"They also used self-control and worked cooperatively. Even worse, they strategized. They drove that rhino into the glow-lotus terras, knowing the plants would kill it. Then they burned the flowers so they could recover their prey without impaling themselves."

"Maybe they're not that smart. The rhino will rot long before that pack of krols can finish eating it."

"That's the most worrying part of this whole thing."

"Why?"

"If those krols had just wanted a meal," he said, "they would've fed on the rhino back in the burned field. Later, they would've returned to feed on the carcass again."

"Like lions do."

"Exactly. However, these krols are dragging the rhino carcass away to their lair or den or whatever. It wasn't killed to feed a mere dozen animals."

"You mean—?"

"Yes," he said. "There's a large colony of krols living in Manhattan. And until the Chi'az arrive, they've just become our most dangerous enemy."

3

IN A GLOOMY SILENCE, we drove toward Weston Tower.

Asher and Nila had picked us up in an old Toyota that rattled down the empty streets. We passed scores of damaged buildings and pieces of burned debris from the satellite, but we didn't see any gray krols.

However, we knew they were around. Possibly hiding. Definitely dangerous.

Asher turned onto the street leading to our garrison. "Commander Powell won't be happy to learn about the krols." He slowed the car and leaned over the steering wheel. "Or maybe he already knows."

A pair of tall metal gates led into Weston Tower's massive courtyard. On either side, high concrete walls surrounded the four buildings of the one-block garrison. As usual, armed soldiers stood guard on the concrete walls—along with something new and terrible.

Along the top of the walls, three barrel-chested bodies were spread-eagled on upright wooden Xs.

Krols.

Skinned.

Their raw elongated limbs were splayed wide, with their wrists and ankles tied to the ends of the beams. Large heads with fearsome snouts lolled to the side, their black eyes glaring even in death.

"Gross," I gasped. "Why would the commander do this?"

"The bodies must be a warning." Asher accelerated again. "Something like: *if you try to attack this garrison, you'll die too.*"

Lynxx added, "Remember the skinned bodies we saw on our way to Miami? They were probably warnings too."

The soldiers hurriedly opened the gates and waved us inside—

—to a scene of chaos.

Last year, when I'd first joined the garrison, the courtyard had contained an assortment of working vehicles. Today, the helicopter had smashed blades from the fallen satellites, and half of the cars and trucks were damaged.

The fire engine, still intact and working, had its ladder stretched up the wall of Weston Tower, our one-hundred-story home. Men and women shouted over the roaring flames as they trained their hoses inside. People rushed between spot fires on the ground, hastily extinguishing them.

In the courtyard, books and toys lay scattered among guns, crossbows, and swords from toppled tables. Twisted pieces of metal littered the pavers, along with chunks of concrete from gaping holes in the tower. Dark smoke trailed from dozens of smashed windows that stared blindly at the destruction, and somewhere a baby cried.

Despite the chaos and damage, I was relieved to be back at Weston Tower. We'd spent weeks driving down to Miami, battling terras and xans, and losing friends and teammates. After a slow sea voyage in a stinking trawler, we were finally home. I had missed the garrison's sense of community, plus its practical benefits of wind-and-solar-generated electricity, hot showers, and fresh food.

Asher stopped our rattling Toyota next to an old man with wild gray hair. "Hey, Einstein."

"Welcome back, Asher," the head chef said fondly. As usual, he wore a white apron around his plump middle, and his shirt sleeves were dusted with flour. "Good to have you home, son."

"Good to be back. Is everyone from the trawler okay?"

"Most. They're still waiting for one ambulance to return."

"Those guys didn't make it." Asher threw Nila a regretful glance.

Einstein hastily crossed himself. "May they rest in peace."

"Have you seen Harl and a blond teenage girl, very beautiful?"

I kept my face expressionless. *Very beautiful.* Asher was merely stating a fact. Despite the struggles to survive after the Mist, Willow was still more beautiful in real life than in her movies and TV show. Her fringed violet eyes were stunning, her thick blond hair fell in glossy waves to her waist, and her face was a perfection of delicate features.

"Harlem's helping Soo-Yun with the sick and injured." The old man's face crinkled in a soft smile. "And your Willow is inside too."

Your Willow. Sharp pain flashed through me.

Asher threw me a guilty glance. "She's not my Willow anymore, Einstein. Anyway, how did you know who she was?"

"She was a famous movie star long before the Mist, son. Even I knew who Willow Grace was."

"Where is she?"

"In the infirmary."

Asher drew in a sharp breath. "Is she hurt?"

"Not a scratch. She's helping out. They've been swamped with injuries today." Chef Einstein glanced at his watch, then winced as he flexed his arthritis-gnarled fingers. "Let's catch up later, son. Right now, I need to make a stack of lunches and rustle up some bottles of water. Those poor soldiers on the walls are doing double duty today." With an apologetic nod, he hurried off.

The other vehicles from the convoy were parked nearby, most bearing only superficial dings and dents. Asher pulled alongside them and switched off the Toyota's engine, quoting, "Be it ever so humble, there's no place like—"

Soldiers wrenched open the doors. Rough hands dragged us out.

I struggled against the man pinning my arms behind my back. "What are you doing, Wilcott?"

Sergeant Thorne stalked across.

"What's going on?" Asher cried.

The sergeant jerked his head at Private Wilcott and the other soldiers holding Asher and me. "Let them both go." He turned his beady eyes on Lynxx and Nila. "Put these two with the others."

Guns drawn, the men forced Lynxx and Nila across the courtyard. Asher and I hurried behind, demanding answers, receiving none. The soldiers shoved Lynxx and Nila into an enclosure behind a razor wire fence, where the refugees from Florida sat on the hot ground, hands on their heads as they endured the scorching sun. Backpacks and luggage lay outside the wire, beyond their reach.

"What are my people doing here?" Nila snapped. "Some need medical treatment. And where's Dr. Tran?"

"Shut up and sit down," Sergeant Thorne ground out. "Put your hands on your head, lady. No talking." When Lynxx protested, Thorne pointed his rifle at him. "Just give me an excuse, you hybrid scum." Spittle sprayed from a thin mouth twisted with hatred.

I wasn't surprised at Thorne's behavior. During our trip to Miami, he'd been openly hostile to Lynxx on discovering he was a hybrid. While most of our team had eventually accepted Lynxx's origin, the sergeant had clearly remained suspicious and angry.

Fortunately, he had no idea that Nila was a hybrid too.

"Do as he says," Asher told Lynxx and Nila. "I'll try to sort this out." He turned to Sergeant Thorne. "Where's the commander?"

"Gone. He's checking on the horses stabled outside the garrison."

"When will he be back?"

"No idea. Apparently he's an hour overdue."

Asher ran an agitated hand through his sun-streaked hair. "Has Lieutenant Wu sent out a search team for him?"

"Wu and Sergeant Bowen are with Commander Powell."

"Then I'll take out a team."

"Forget it. I'm in charge until they get back, Weston," Thorne said sharply. "I already have four men gearing up for a search. Meanwhile, you need to stay at the garrison. It's safer here."

"I won't sit on my thumbs while the commander—"

"*Open the gates.*" The cry came from a soldier on the front wall.

An exhausted and filthy Commander Powell staggered past the creaking gates, half carrying Lieutenant Wu. The latter's shirt hung open and bloodied bandages wrapped his chest.

People rushed over and eased Wu onto a stretcher.

"Commander, where's Sergeant Bowen?" asked Thorne.

"Dead."

Thorne swore, then turned to the stretcher-bearers. "Get Wu up to the infirmary. Have that new doc, Tran, help him."

I glared at the sergeant. "So you've imprisoned everyone in Nila's group except Dr. Tran?"

"We've got injured people," Thorne shot back. "Anyway, I've assigned a soldier to watch Tran every second, in case he's a hybrid too."

Powell sank onto a wooden bench, wiping smears of blood off his face.

"Sir," Asher said to the black man, "you need to see the doctor."

"The blood's not mine, son. It belongs to Sergeant Bowen."

My stomach knotted. I had liked Wade Bowen. He'd been a tough instructor but fair.

"What happened, Commander?" I asked, half-suspecting the answer.

Please don't say it. Please don't say it.

But he did.

4

"Krols." Powell's brow knotted in anger. "Vicious things. They killed Bowen and almost killed Wu and me. But then that meteor shower hit. It scattered the creatures like cockroaches." He glared at the battered courtyard and the holes in Weston Tower. "Shoot! The meteors really pummeled the garrison."

Asher drew in a deep breath. "Sir, we need to talk about those 'meteors' and Nila—"

"Nila? Isn't she the leader of that group in Florida?"

"Yes, sir. She wants to talk to you urgently."

"Son, I'm relieved you're home in one piece." The man wearily surveyed the debris everywhere. "Even though home isn't exactly in one piece. We'll talk later. First, I need a sit-rep from Sergeant Thorne." Sighing, he waved the officer across.

Thorne gave him the bad news. Four dead. Twenty-two injured. Fires on three floors, all now extinguished. The rooftop garden partially destroyed. Dozens of broken windows. Fifteen vehicles damaged. Helicopter out of action.

The commander remained silent as the list went on. When Thorne finished, he asked questions, issued orders, then pointed to the crowd behind the razor wire fence. "Is that the group from Florida, Sergeant?"

"Yes, sir."

"Why are they being detained?"

"There could be hybrids among them, Commander," said Thorne, spitting out the words. "On our way to Miami, we met this old guy, Xavian—a hybrid. He told us there's no way to tell hybrids from humans. That thing about black marks on their earlobes is garbage. A myth."

Powell groaned. "I suspected as much."

"Anyway, until we can vet these strangers, we need to keep them under guard. We can't let a bunch of hybrids snoop around Weston Tower, learning our weaknesses and plotting ways to breach our defenses."

Powell gestured to the detainees. "Why's Lynxx in there?"

Sergeant Thorne puffed out his chest, eager to drop the bombshell. "He's a hybrid."

"*What?*"

"He—*it*—confessed to being a hybrid during our mission to Florida."

Asher stepped forward. "Lynxx voluntarily revealed his identity, Commander. That says something about him, doesn't it? He didn't want to keep lying to us."

"Really?" Powell said, expression stony. "Yet it was okay for him to lie to us for months?"

"Maybe he was afraid, sir," I suggested. "Many people believe all hybrids are evil and should be killed."

"You don't agree, Miss Madison?"

Miss Madison. The commander's formal use of my last name was a rebuke. Even after a year, he still hadn't fully accepted me.

"No, I don't agree, sir," I replied. "Remember that hybrid Bone up on the skyweb months ago? He admitted there were two groups of hybrids: the Outriders, who are loyal to the Chi'az and want us dead; and the humanized ones—the Sphere—who want to live in peace with us. Lynxx is one of the humanized hybrids."

Sergeant Thorne glared at me, then addressed the commander. "What are your orders for the Florida detainees, sir? And Lynxx?"

"Leave them in the enclosure for now. We have other things to deal with."

Thorne threw me a smug smile.

Although annoyed, I understood Powell's caution. On the Night of the Blue Meteors, he had discovered that one of his most trusted men, our helicopter pilot, was an Outrider spy. Since then, the commander had been wary around newcomers, slow to trust and quick to suspect.

Asher and I trailed Powell around the courtyard as he surveyed the damage and spoke to people.

Softly, I asked Asher, "Why didn't you tell Powell that Nila's a hybrid?"

"Because Sergeant Thorne's been really jumpy lately."

"You think he's ready to snap?"

"Yes. If Thorne found out that Nila was a hybrid, he'd probably shoot her on the spot."

"And then we'd never know what proposal she's bringing from the Sphere, right?"

"Exactly." Asher glanced around, ensuring Sergeant Thorne was out of earshot. "First chance I get, I'll tell the commander about her."

"Good."

We continued trailing Powell.

Further along the garrison walls, six more skinned krols were spread-eagled on giant Xs. Some bodies were a dull black, as though they'd been on display for days. A couple had glistening red muscles and sinews, as if freshly skinned. One was almost bones. At each body, crows pecked and tore at the dead flesh, small crabben xans ripped off pieces with their claws, and rats scurried over the splayed limbs.

Gruesome.

Eight-year-old Zoey, rescued from a cruise ship a few months ago, joined two little girls who were tossing stones into a smoking crater in the courtyard. We peered in the hole and saw a huge lump glowing on the bottom.

"That's one big chunk of meteor," Commander Powell said, voice strained.

"Glad it didn't hit Weston Tower." I paused. Now wasn't the time to explain that the "meteors" were actually pieces of Earth's satellites. "What do—?"

"Kass!" Asher yanked me back as bits of wood and plaster waterfalled from the damaged tower above. They thudded onto the ground, just missing me.

Harlem poked his head through a window. "Watch out below."

"Are you okay?" Asher asked me. When I nodded, he looked up and yelled, "Next time, shout a warning *before* you throw out stuff, Harl, not after."

"Oops," Harlem called sheepishly. "My bad. Sorry, guys."

We moved on.

At the razor wire enclosure, Powell paused.

The detainees no longer had their hands on their heads. However, they remained seated on the ground, faces anxious and worried—except for Nila and Lynxx. Nila sat among her people, coolly watching Commander Powell and making no attempt to talk to him. Wise decision, I thought. The nearby soldiers were on edge. If Nila disobeyed their orders by approaching them, they could shoot first and ask questions later.

Lynxx sat at the back of the group, leaning against the concrete wall, hands in his lap, eyes closed.

Uh-oh.

He appeared asleep, but I knew better.

The air suddenly felt weighted with foreboding. Lynxx would never risk mind-blending in the open unless something was wrong. Very wrong.

Worried, I glanced around, wondering what threat he was investigating.

People cleaned debris from the damaged grounds. Soldiers patrolled the walls, ignoring the skinned krols. Black smoke wafted from the holes in Weston Tower.

A few feet away, a rat sniffed at a squashed tomato. "Lynxx?" I whispered, peering closer. Nope. Its eyes were black, not silver. The rat wasn't mind-blended with a hybrid.

What was Lynxx looking for? Where was the danger coming from?

A janitor joined us, unrolling a large plan of the plumbing. "Excuse me, Commander." As the two men conferred about toilets and other damaged pipes, I scrutinized Lynxx's slumped form again.

He was still mentally absent.

A lizard scurried from a hole near the concrete wall, and a squirrel rummaged through the contents of a toppled trash can. I dismissed both animals. If danger was coming, Lynxx would need to move quickly and efficiently. He'd need wings.

A pigeon fluttered onto the razor wire near me, and I edged closer to it. *Lynxx?* Cooing, it rustled its feathers and peered around with black eyes.

Wrong again.

The janitor left, taking his plumbing diagram with him.

Commander Powell turned to Asher. "I'm surprised about Lynxx being a hybrid."

"I was too. Still, you should release him, sir."

Powell's brows shot up. "You've always been fiercely opposed to everything non-terrestrial."

"Sir, if it hadn't been for Xavian—the old hybrid that Sergeant Thorne mentioned—Willow would be dead." He pointed to a slender blonde hurrying across the courtyard.

"Willow?" Powell asked, puzzled.

"*Ash.*" She flung her arms around her ex-boyfriend's neck. "You're alive!"

I struggled to keep my expression neutral as Asher hugged her back. When he saw me watching, he quickly released her.

Commander Powell gaped in astonishment. "This is Willow, Asher? Your Willow?"

Your Willow.

Chef Einstein had used the same words.

How could two words hurt so much?

Flustered, Asher said, "As I was saying, sir, Willow is alive today because of a humanized hybrid."

"Xavian," added Willow, tears welling in her lovely violet eyes.

Powell folded his arms. "So you were friends with a hybrid, Miss Grace." Accusation tinted his comment.

"I was." Willow lifted her chin and firmly went on, "And even though Xavian was a hybrid, he was the kindest, most compassionate *man* I've ever known. He was good and I loved him like a father. He died protecting me."

I nodded in agreement. During our mission to Miami, the Outrider hybrid, Bone, had used a crop duster to spray us with a beta version of the Threads. Although weakened by cancer, Xavian had ridden his motorcycle straight into the airborne virus, determined to rescue Willow—and condemning himself to death.

"It's true, sir," Asher agreed. "Xavian died trying to protect Willow."

"You saw this for yourself, son?"

"We all did. And in Lynxx's case, sir, he's always been a big asset. His research and information on the terras and xans have been invaluable. Dozens of people at the garrison are alive because of him. He's proven he's trustworthy and loyal to us, sir."

Commander Powell unfolded his arms. He shifted his gaze from Willow to Asher, then across to the detainees. "Very well. Thorne, release Lynxx."

Scowling, the sergeant stomped to the razor wire enclosure. Lynxx remained slumped against the back concrete wall, eyes closed, mind elsewhere.

My heart started pounding. He was about to be exposed.

Maybe Commander Powell, Asher, and the others could accept "humanized" hybrids if they weren't seen as a threat. But if they learned about the hybrids' mental powers—their ability to mind-blend, remote-push, and remote-kill—everything would change. Most people would feel threatened by the hybrids, and many would respond with fear and violence.

Frantic, I stepped forward, desperately trying to think of a distraction. "Sir, I—"

Lynxx stirred, opening his eyes. He pointed to the sky and shouted a warning that chilled my blood.

"Tumbleweeds!"

5

Five dark spots floated high in the smoke-hazed sky.

A siren shrilled, its shriek rising and falling in panic.

"Tumbleweeds!" The word ricocheted around the courtyard from multiple throats. Adults and children shouted and scrambled for the safety of Weston Tower.

In the razor wire enclosure, Nila jumped to her feet. Ignoring the soldiers with their raised weapons, she cried, "Let us out, Commander! We're sitting ducks in here." She turned to me. "Bring me the black-striped backpack. Hurry!"

I ran to the luggage piled outside the razor wire fence.

Powell squinted at the oncoming tumbleweeds, then shouted to his soldiers, "Release them. Now."

The moment the fence was dragged apart, the detainees grabbed their children and the injured, and they bolted toward Weston Tower.

As I shoved the black-striped backpack at Nila, I glanced up. The tumbleweeds were dropping with alarming speed. Not everyone would make it indoors in time.

Nila shoved a fat orange gun into the commander's hands and thrust another at Asher.

"Shoot the flares in the same direction." She handed out cartridges. "It'll distract the tumbleweeds. Hurry." Quickly, she loaded a third flare gun.

A child's terrified scream came from behind us.

A gray-brown tumbleweed was arrowing toward the three little girls who'd been tossing stones into the crater.

Nila shoved her flare gun into Lynxx's hands. "Shoot the flares. Now."

She ran toward the children.

I dashed after her as the tumbleweed dipped closer. "Nila, remote-push the tumbleweed away!"

A series of bangs sounded. Overhead, red lines arced across the sky, followed by brilliant explosions. Four of the tumbleweeds raced toward the red starbursts.

However, the gray-brown tumbleweed, big as a car, continued targeting the children.

Running, I again cried, "Push it away, Nila."

Ignoring me, she shouted, "Girls, get inside the building!"

More flares boomed through the afternoon sky, trailing bright red lines.

The three girls started running toward the Tower, but Zoey stumbled on a chunk of concrete and fell.

"Get the others to safety, Nila," I yelled. "I'll get Zoey." When the woman hesitated, I cried, "Go. Hurry!"

The tumbleweed dropped toward Zoey, its branches opening like a mouth.

Desperately, I mentally remote-pushed it. The terra bounced along the pavers for a few yards, then stopped. Clattering, it rolled forward, straight for Zoey, who was scrabbling to her feet.

I lunged at the skinny outstretched branches as they snagged the child's pink top. The woody sticks felt creepy in my hands, and their thorns punctured my palms in multiple places, drawing blood.

Angrily, I remote-pushed the outstretched sticks, cracking them into bits like kindling. They fell away, releasing Zoey. Again I remote-pushed, so hard that sparks flashed before my eyes.

The gray-brown tumbleweed shot into the air, trailing a wake of broken woody bits.

"You're okay, Zoey." I gathered the whimpering child into my arms and raced to the tower. Lynxx, Asher, and the commander followed.

In the lobby, Zoey gave me a quick hug—"Thanks, Kass"—and scurried off to join the two girls saved by Nila. The other members of the Florida group were gathered in the marble lobby, guarded by Sergeant Thorne and his men.

Outside, all five tumbleweeds chased the red starbursts across the sky, while on the concrete walls, soldiers warily emerged from their emergency shelters.

Nila stood alone at the glass wall that overlooked the courtyard. Joining her, I quietly asked, "Why didn't you remote-push that tumbleweed away from the girls?"

"I couldn't."

"I thought all hybrids could remote-push."

"They can. But I can't do it while I'm here in Manhattan. I'll explain later."

We fell silent as Powell crossed to us.

"Are you okay, Miss Madison?" he asked me.

"Yes, sir."

"You got lucky out there with that tumbleweed today."

"Yes, sir."

Powell turned to Nila. Sweat beaded on his forehead as he studied the olive-skinned woman. "Nila, isn't it?" When she nodded, he said, "You raced toward a tumbleweed terra, trying to save three little girls. You're either incredibly brave or incredibly stupid."

She remained silent, her eyes fixed on his face, watching him intently.

"So, which one are you?" he demanded. "Brave or stupid?"

"I'm not in the habit of standing by while tumbleweeds snatch up helpless children."

"Obviously you know how dangerous they are."

"We had them down in Florida."

"I see." Powell winced as he gingerly touched his left side. "It was a good idea using the flares to distract them."

"I guess that means I'm not stupid," Nila said with the barest hint of a smile. "Oh, and you're welcome."

"For what?"

"No need to thank me for saving two of the kids, Commander. Although Kass here might appreciate a thank-you for saving the third child."

Powell blinked, surprised at her cool tone. Had he expected Nila to grovel a shaky thanks for releasing her people from the razor wire enclosure? Instead, this strong, confident woman was quietly insisting that she be treated as an equal.

He regarded her silently, then turned and spoke with Asher in a low voice. Nila waited nearby, still watching the commander.

I joined Lynxx, who stood apart from the others.

"What did you mind-blend with?" I murmured.

"A red-tailed hawk, *Buteo jamaicensis*," he whispered. "Fast flier. Sharp eyesight."

"What alerted you to the tumbleweeds?"

"A flock of birds overhead. When they abruptly changed direction, I guessed something was coming."

"You risked exposing yourself by mind-blending in the open."

"No choice. You saw the courtyard today. People were wandering around dazed, confused, frightened—all prime pickings. I needed to identify the oncoming threat."

Commander Powell ordered Thorne and four soldiers to escort the sick and injured from Nila's group to the infirmary. The rest were to be taken to the community hall on the second floor, with soldiers posted at the doors.

Powell wiped his sweating brow and returned to Nila. "Asher said you need to speak to me urgently. What do you—?"

He staggered and almost fell.

Nila darted forward, catching him. "He's injured," she said, lowering him to the marble tiles.

Finally, I understood why Nila had been watching the commander so closely. She'd noticed his sweating brow, the twinges of pain that had flickered across his face, his slow movements—and she'd realized that he wasn't weary but hurt.

Asher opened the commander's dark jacket and shirt, revealing a wad of blood-soaked bandages on his left side. "Get a stretcher." When it arrived, he accompanied the unconscious man to the infirmary.

Lynxx watched them hurry away. "Why didn't Powell tell anyone he was hurt?"

"Because he's a good leader," Nila said. "He wanted to make sure that everyone else was okay before dealing with his own injuries."

A soldier approached her. "You're to join the rest of your group in the community hall, ma'am."

"Very well." She left.

6

Commander Powell's wound was stitched, treated with some precious antibiotic powder, and bandaged.

After spending the night in the infirmary, he awoke at dawn, impatient and restless. Ignoring Dr. Tran's orders to rest, he insisted on inspecting the local damage from yesterday's aerial bombardment. Numerous streets were riddled with debris, making driving impossible, so fourteen horses were brought from the stables.

Escorted by six soldiers, the commander and Nila rode from the garrison, followed by Liberty Team. We formed a long line, our mounts picking their way down a mixture of damaged and intact streets.

On the long city blocks, shadows reigned in the early morning. They swathed the sides of buildings, clung to the roads, and gathered in corners. As movement flickered in a nearby patch of darkness, I sensed unseen eyes watching us.

Every so often, I glanced up at the pale red sky, watching for tumbleweeds—and more falling satellites.

Asher summarized for Powell the events of our trip to Florida: The crop duster's cloud of Threads, spread by the gaunt-faced Bone. The deaths of some team members. The rescue of Willow and Xavian. The new terras and xans we'd encountered. Our problems with the krols. And the falling satellites back in Manhattan.

Powell's eyebrows rose. "They weren't meteors, son?"

"No, sir. Lynxx thinks the Chi'az destroyed our satellites to clear the way for their invasion, possibly in a few months."

Commander Powell unleashed a torrent of swear words.

Asher's place was then taken by Nila. She and the commander rode side by side as they quietly spoke, and I wished I could mind-blend with her horse so I could hear their conversation. Yesterday, she'd revealed to Asher, Lynxx, and me that she was a Sphere hybrid. Today, I guessed she was sharing this revelation with the commander—along with other things.

What was the vitally important project she needed to discuss with Powell? Why was it a secret?

Patience had never been one of my virtues, and I shifted restlessly in my saddle.

"Sore, Kass?" asked Asher from his stallion beside me.

"A bit." I jerked my chin toward the pair riding ahead of us. "Can you hear what Nila is saying to the commander?"

"No. I'm sure he'll fill us in when he can."

Asher's faith was greater than mine. I'd learned that people didn't share their secrets unless they absolutely had to. Lynxx and I were perfect examples of that.

In the distance, the bellow of a buffalo echoed in a city block. Vultures circled overhead, scanning for dead or dying animals. A breeze stirred the green terra leaves on the nearby buildings, setting them nodding and rustling.

I wished I were back at the garrison, fast asleep, lost in dreams of another world ... another life.

Asher looked around, making sure no one was close enough to hear our conversation. "How are you doing?"

"Fine. Why do you ask?"

Awkwardly, he replied, "Because of your ... you know."

"Leukemia? It's not a dirty word."

"Isn't it a secret?"

"Maybe not for much longer. I haven't needed any Lazarus tonic for the past sixteen days."

"Really? Don't you have to drink it every week?"

"I used to, but Lynxx thinks my leukemia might be cured. We'll be more certain in a few weeks. Right now, I feel fine."

Relaxing, he beamed at me. "That's fantastic news."

I should've been excited and relieved at the thought of finally beating my disease. However it was hard to rejoice when so many buildings had been damaged by yesterday's fallen satellites. The destruction throughout the city was a clear indication of the oncoming invasion.

If the Chi'az conquered Earth, humanity was doomed. My life—and everyone else's—could be measured in months.

On horseback, we rounded a corner. The street extended before us, free of potholes and craters and burned metal.

However, a strange object lay on the road further ahead.

We halted as two soldiers investigated.

They returned, grim-faced. One man spoke in a low, urgent tone to the commander, who listened, then shook his head. "We're not going back," he told them. "We all need to see what we're facing. Ignorance is not bliss. It's dangerous."

We started riding toward the strange object, but halfway there, the horses sniffed the air, then snorted and flicked their ears in agitation. When they stopped and refused to proceed, we dismounted and tied their reins to lampposts. As my mount yanked at its tether, I murmured soft words, petted Bluebell's neck—and gently remote-soothed the animal. Relaxing, Bluebell nibbled on some Earth weeds that grew in the pavement.

The six soldiers spread out, semiautomatic rifles raised, ready for trouble.

Liberty Team scoured the area for dangerous terras or xans. Between us, we had a comforting array of weapons, including flamethrowers, nets, guns, and swords. After we gave the all clear, Asher and I accompanied Commander Powell and Nila to the strange object.

A large X had been drawn on the road, each line about five feet long and a foot wide, and colored with white chalk.

Carefully laid along this chalk X was a human skeleton. Every bone had been separated and stripped of flesh. The skeleton's arms and legs were dotted along the cross, with a rib cage and pelvis in the center and a skull at the top.

Powell groaned. "It's Sergeant Bowen." The soldier who'd been killed by the krols yesterday.

"Are you sure, sir?" I asked, distress welling within me.

"Positive." He pointed to a grisly object on the skull.

I recognized the tight orange curls on the bloodied flap of skin. It was the sergeant's scalp.

Sickened, I turned away.

Sergeant Bowen had trained me in sword fighting, his sharp instructions woven with snippets of praise. He'd patiently taught the older children how to dismantle and clean the guns. And he'd spent hours grooming the horses in the stables, inspecting their feed and exercising them so they didn't get fat and bored. He'd loved those horses—and he'd loved life, even in a post-apocalyptic world.

Crouching, Asher examined the bones. "They have scratches on them."

I peered at a femur covered in dozens of faint nicks. "Teeth marks?"

"I think so."

Powell's dark eyes narrowed, and he struggled to speak through his fury. "We need to find these creatures' den and kill them all."

"What creatures?" Nila asked.

"Krols."

She shook her head. "The positioning of these bones isn't perfect, Commander. But it's pretty close. I can't believe any animal or xan is intelligent enough to reassemble this skeleton. Humans did this."

"Who? Wilders?"

"Who are they?"

Powell told her about the gang of bikers who lived in Manhattan. Since the coming of the Mist, the Wilders had attacked Weston Tower a few times, eager to plunder our indoor farms, stores, weapons, and equipment.

"The thing is, we've had a truce with them for over a year," he went on. "Besides, Wilders aren't cannibals. They don't dismember humans and gnaw on their bones. This is the work of savages. Krols."

"Maybe," Nila said. "But we still need to focus on the Chi'az, not the krols."

"The Chi'az aren't killing my people."

"They will. Like I said, I believe they're preparing to invade within months." She gestured to the burned objects protruding from the walls of tall buildings. "Those pieces of satellites are proof that the Final Wave is coming."

"And when the Chi'az get here, we'll fight them. But to fight, we need to be alive."

"Exactly. That's why Bone and some other Outrider hybrids are working on their Threads. If they succeed, they'll wipe out the remaining humans before the Chi'az arrive. We have to stop them. I came to the Weston Garrison for one reason: I need a safe place to finish my work. I don't have time for distractions."

My ears sharpened.

What was Nila's work?

And how did it relate to the Chi'az and the Outriders?

7

STANDING BESIDE THE DISMANTLED skeleton, Powell said, "You'll get your lab and equipment, Nila, and as many assistants as you need. Plus all the detainees from Florida will be released and integrated into the Weston Battalion."

"Fine."

"However, I still plan on wiping out these krols."

I frowned. What equipment did Nila need? And why?

The woman was a humanized hybrid who'd saved my life back in the trawler when a krol had attacked me. And yesterday she'd helped save some little girls from a tumbleweed. She claimed to have done everything she could to protect her small group of humans back in Florida.

But what if she had inserted herself into the Florida group so she could hide among humans? Had people died because of her?

Were some people in the Weston Battalion going to die because she was now hiding among us?

Four crabben xans emerged from a crack in the pavement. Clawed front legs raised, they scurried across Bowen's skeleton in search of scraps. Repulsed, I remote-shoved them off his rib cage, and they tumbled along the road, then skittered away. Too late, I guiltily glanced around. Had anyone witnessed the crabbens' abrupt flight?

Nila gave me a faint nod, but the others hadn't noticed anything.

The woman had made no attempt to remote-push the crabbens off Bowen's skeleton, I noted. She'd told me that she couldn't—or wouldn't—use her mental powers while in Manhattan. Clearly, she was determined not to draw attention to herself.

Nila folded her arms. "We shouldn't waste time on the krols, Commander. I'm concerned about our joint survival. If the Outriders wipe out humanity, they'll focus on the Sphere next. And I'll be at the top of their list of Sphere hybrids to destroy."

Good. She'd already told Powell that she was a hybrid.

She continued, "Sphere hybrids and humans need to work together if we want to survive."

A wind swept across Bowen's skeleton, rattling the bones.

"We need to survive the Chi'az *and* the krols," Powell firmly told her. "There are a dozen skinned krols on wooden crosses around our garrison. The ones that killed Sergeant Bowen are angry. Instead of just eating him, they cut him into pieces, ate his flesh, then crudely reassembled his bones on this chalk cross." He gestured to the displayed skeleton. "This is a deliberate message: *you kill us, we kill you.*"

"The krols aren't as important as the Chi'az," she insisted. "They're just animals."

I stepped forward, months of Lynxx's lectures echoing in my head.

"Please don't underestimate these krols, Nila," I said. "Since their arrival, the terra plants and xanimals have sought food and mates, and they've bred. In this way, they've been acting like Earth plants and animals. For thousands of years, the smartest species on our planet has been humans. Now, these krols are the second-smartest species."

Asher shook his head. "These krols aren't as smart as humans, Kass."

"Of course not. But they're much smarter than any Earth animal or any of the other xanimals we've seen. Plus they're far more dangerous."

"I agree." Powell looked at Asher and me. "Apart from Lynxx and the three of us, no one knows that Nila is a hybrid. Have either of you told anyone else?"

I blinked at the abrupt change in conversation. "No."

"No one," Asher added.

"Good," Powell said. "No one else is to know that Nila's a hybrid."

"Why not?" I asked, tired of secrets. "She's Sphere, not an Outrider. She's humanized."

"That wouldn't matter to some people."

Remembering Sergeant Thorne's hostility yesterday, I slowly nodded. He had been enraged at the thought of more hybrids joining our garrison. Powell was right. Others could react like Thorne—or worse.

"We've got a lot going on at the moment," the commander continued, "with far worse problems on our horizon. Sometimes a leader needs to withhold certain information which might cause friction among his troops."

"I understand, sir," I said. "Does that mean you're not going to tell the Weston Battalion about the oncoming Chi'az invasion?"

"That's different. They absolutely have to know about the invasion. We need to be prepared."

With a rustle of wings, a black vulture landed on Bowen's skull and snatched up the bloodied scalp.

"Get away," Powell snapped, kicking out. He missed and the bird flew away, Bowen's orange hair dangling from its talons. "Foul creature," he cried, then winced in pain. Gingerly, he touched his injured side, and his fingertips came away red.

Nila frowned. "You've broken some stitches, Lincoln."

My eyebrows rose at her use of the commander's first name.

Powell seemed too sore to object to Nila's subtle claim for equality. "I'm fine." He drew in a shaky breath. "Still, let's go back to the garrison. I want to arrange some teams for search-and-destroy missions on the krols."

She sniffed. "After Dr. Tran stitches up your wound again."

"Very well."

"What do we do about Bowen, sir?" Asher pointed at the skeleton.

"I'll dispatch a squad later to gather the bones for burial."

As we rode toward the garrison, Asher and I dropped back to speak to the commander privately.

"Sir," Asher quietly said, "yesterday Nila told us she had something important to discuss with you. What's going on?"

Powell surveyed the shadowy street. "We can't talk out here, son."

"Maybe some broad brushstrokes, sir?"

When Powell hesitated, I quietly said, "Nila's hiding from the Outriders, isn't she?"

"Yes."

"And we're going to help her, aren't we?"

"Yes."

Asher exhaled in shock. "If we help Nila, won't we be putting the entire Weston Battalion at risk?"

Exactly what I'd been thinking a little while ago.

"Yes," Powell admitted. "But we have to take the risk. Wars aren't bloodless."

We rode on, Powell's words heavy in the air.

Wars aren't bloodless.

8

AT WESTON TOWER, THE news that Lynxx was a good, humanized hybrid was met with mixed reactions.

Some people were angry. Others were afraid of him. However, most were okay with the revelation, remembering the many people he'd saved with his research on dangerous terras.

Almost everyone, though, was stunned and frightened when Powell announced a possible Chi'az invasion. But the black man's strong leadership and confident speeches turned anxiety to determination and fear to strength.

"The Chi'az invasion isn't certain," he declared in a general meeting. "We don't have an invasion date. It might be in a few weeks, months, or even years. But whenever it happens—*if* it happens—we'll be prepared, folks. We'll be ready to fight. And we'll survive."

People rallied. They stockpiled food, water, equipment, weapons, vehicles. Our farms across Manhattan were moved to buildings inside the Weston Garrison, and even the horses and livestock were relocated to hastily erected barns down the back.

The garrison's walls were reinforced, and the guards increased. As soon as our equipment worked again, we used radios and Morse code operators to spread warnings around the world of a possible Chi'az invasion.

Teams made rough repairs to Weston Tower, patching smashed windows and holes in the walls. Thankfully, most of the tower remained intact, and we still had water and electricity.

Each morning, dozens of extra teams left the garrison. Half of them cleared debris from the main streets that we used. Several teams gathered building materials for the repairs to Weston Tower, while others searched for the science equipment that Nila needed.

Liberty Team and the other resistance teams accompanied as many workers around the city as possible, protecting them from dangerous terras and xans.

Four squads of heavily armed soldiers hunted the krols, killing every one they found and destroying their lairs. Finally, Commander Powell announced that the main krol lair—inhabited by eighty-three creatures—had been obliterated.

The krol threat was under control.

"There are still a few stragglers around," he warned. "Exercise care when outside the garrison. Always go out in pairs or teams."

The victory over the krols was met with cheers, relief, and celebrations.

Three weeks later, I stood on the rooftop of Weston Tower, stretching out a kink in my back.

I wished I could get rid of my fear as easily as the kink in my muscles, but I couldn't.

At dinner last night, when I'd heard the rumors about an upcoming E-Day, my appetite had vanished. Later, I'd tossed and turned in my bed until dawn.

Glumly, I surveyed the rooftop.

I had a rare morning off before heading out with Liberty Team this afternoon. Instead of doing something pleasant or relaxing, I had decided to spend it working in the rooftop gardens, digging in the dirt and repotting plants.

Technically, I didn't need to be here. Commander Powell had already assigned teams to fix the damaged gardens. Many of the clear plexiglass sheets that soared overhead had been smashed by the fallen satellites, along with the transparent walls erected as windbreaks. At least half the crops had been destroyed, plus most of the vertical gardens on the tall wire trellises.

Across the rooftop, four men assembled a new garden bed. Our elderly chef, Einstein, weeded a large vegetable patch, aided by Isabel, who now looked fit and well. The old woman's arrival in a light airplane had triggered our mission to Florida, plus the retrieval of Dr. Tran, Nila, and the others. From what I'd heard, Isabel and Einstein had become a couple, and their happiness was a small light amid all the anxiety.

In my case, my own personal relationships were in tatters.

My friend Pepper was dead and I missed her.

I hardly saw Asher outside of work and Liberty Team missions; I'd expected this after our recent breakup, when I'd admitted to Asher that I'd been keeping Lynxx's hybrid identity a secret.

Things also remained unsettled between Lynxx and me. When he had still been at Weston Tower three weeks after returning from Florida, I'd confronted him in the rooftop gardens a few minutes ago.

"I thought you were going back to your penthouse apartment at the Ferguson Complex."

"I'm thinking of remaining at the garrison."

My mind had flashed to our kiss behind the trawler's lifeboats. "Oh?"

"Look, I know you and Asher have broken up. That's not why I'm staying. I'm not interested in being anyone's second choice. Ever."

"I didn't ... I wasn't ..."

"You and I are just friends, Kassia. That's all." His firm words had held an unmistakable resolve, as though he'd closed his heart to me. "But things have gotten worse in Manhattan. We've got krols in our city, and an oncoming Chi'az invasion. Now is not the time to be living alone."

"I agree."

"Then you're okay with me staying at the garrison?"

"Totally."

After Lynxx had left to get some bags of fertilizer, I'd crossed to the rooftop parapet.

Still stretching out the kink in my back, I gazed at Manhattan. The patchwork of terras now covered more than half of the city. In a few years, the buildings and streets of New York would be buried beneath a thick jungle.

Plumes of black smoke no longer dotted the view. The buildings set alight by the burned and broken satellites had eventually collapsed into rubble.

After the Sat-Fall—our nickname for The Day of the Fallen Satellites—firefighters from Weston Tower had put out blazes in the Chrysler Building, Trinity Church, and the New York Public Library; since we only had one working fire engine left, Commander Powell's policy was to save important landmarks and to let office buildings burn themselves out.

I moved away from the parapet, my thoughts turning to another somber topic.

Yesterday afternoon, Dr. Tran had shared some news with Nurse Ortiz. She'd passed it onto Soo-Yun, who'd told Harlem.

By dinner, the rumor about E-Day had spread throughout the garrison. Many newcomers refused to believe it was true.

But I knew better. I'd been down this path before.

Euthanasia Day existed.

9

THIS TIME TEN PEOPLE were marked for death. No one could stop the killings.

Except me ... maybe.

During the Sat-Fall, twenty-two people had been injured. Most had recovered, but seven had developed serious infections. In addition, Nila's group from Florida contained three critically ill patients: one woman had terminal cancer, a middle-aged man had severe diabetic complications, and a grandfather with emphysema struggled to breathe.

All had been admitted to the Weston Garrison's infirmary. None had responded to the limited drugs available to treat them.

When Willow had heard the E-Day rumors last night, she'd been at dinner with Asher and me. Her beautiful face had paled, and her violet eyes had widened with horror.

"The commander's a monster," she'd cried. "If Xavian had survived the Threads from that crop duster, Powell would've had him killed because of his terminal cancer." Tears rolling down her cheeks, she'd fled the mess hall, with Asher following her.

On the rooftop parapet, a morning breeze fanned the hair around my face, and I brushed it back with a distracted hand.

Was Commander Powell a monster? I wondered. I'd certainly thought so last year when I'd begged for my cousin's life.

Charlotte—CJ—had become a quadriplegic following a terrible fall, and after thirty days Powell had her euthanized. Later, he'd said to me, *I can't waste precious drugs or treatments on people with incurable conditions.*

Tomorrow was E-Day.

Ten people were going to be killed.

Maybe I can do it, I told myself, unconvinced. *Maybe I can save them.*

If I couldn't, this would be my last day in the Weston Battalion.

The doors of the elevator hissed open and Commander Powell stepped onto the roof.

My heart raced.

Eleven o'clock. Right on time.

Since the Sat-Fall, the commander had spent a few minutes every morning at the rooftop's telescope. Before the Mist, tourists had used them to peer at the view. These days, Powell scoured the skies for Chi'az ships, searched for krols, surveyed the spread of the terras, and watched Manhattan's slow deterioration into a massive jungle.

Heart still racing, I hurried over. "Excuse me, sir."

Face hardening, Powell said, "I've already heard pleas from numerous people, Miss Madison."

"But—"

"My position hasn't changed since your cousin CJ died. Sometimes we have to make harsh decisions. I hate it as much as you do, but it's a fact of our new world. Those ten sick people will need long-term medical treatment, which we can't provide. That's why we offer them a kinder option."

"You're going to put them to sleep like old pets, sir. I'm suggesting we treat them instead."

"With what? Nonexistent drugs? They'll just get sicker, be in more pain, and end up dying miserable deaths. At least tomorrow we can give each of them a gentle passing."

I winced at Powell's euphemisms.

Kinder option? Gentle passing?

Had Charlotte regarded her oncoming death as either of those things? In an attempt to save her life, Lynxx and I had gathered bags of Lazarus leaves from Feral Tower, a place that had lived up to its nickname with its vicious hyenas and other wild dangers. However, by the time I'd returned to the garrison, my cousin had already been euthanized.

I'd been unable to save Charlotte all those months ago, but maybe I could save the people scheduled to die tomorrow.

"I'm not here to plead for their lives, sir," I said. "I'm here to confess something."

The commander folded his arms and waited.

I drew in a shaky breath. "For a year, I've been drinking a tonic each week made from Lazarus-vine terras. I think it's cured my leukemia."

"Kassia!" Lynxx's shocked voice came from behind me. "What are you doing?" Dropping his bags of fertilizer, he hurried forward. "She didn't mean it, Commander. She must have a fever. Or she's exhausted from working long hours every day for the past few weeks. We're all tired and saying things we don't mean."

"Please, Lynxx," I said sharply, "this has nothing to do with you." I would never mention his involvement with the tonic.

"Is this true, Miss Madison?" demanded Powell. "You had leukemia? And you think you've been cured by drinking a tonic made from terras?"

Uh-oh. From Powell's tone, this wasn't going the way I hoped. I glanced at the cityscape. At least I'd have thousands of empty buildings to choose from when I was banished from the garrison.

"Kassia—" Lynxx beseeched.

I silenced him with a wave of my hand as I answered Powell. "Yes, sir. I know I've broken your rules, and if that means I'm thrown out of the Weston Battalion, then so be it."

"If Kassia is forced to leave," Lynxx said firmly, "then I'm going too."

"Keep out of this," I told him. "You had nothing to do with my terra tonics." I hoped my angry lie sounded convincing.

Suspicious, Powell studied Lynxx. "Did you know that she was drinking these terra tonics?"

Lynxx raised his chin, defiant. "Know? Who do you think brewed the tonic for her each week? And by the way, Commander, remember when you were shot during the assassination of Samuel Preston, the secretary of state? Your wound became severely infected and you should've died. I didn't let you. I snuck into the infirmary one night and injected you with a liquid made from eye-wing terras; they contained a super antibiotic that saved your life."

"You did that?"

"Yes."

"You injected me with a terra solution?"

"Yes."

I braced myself for the explosion about to erupt.

For a long minute, Powell remained silent. Then, quietly, he said, "Thank you."

I gaped at him. "Excuse me?"

"Euthanasia sickens me but it's a necessary evil. If we can find other ways to save our seriously ill or injured people, well, count me in. The world has changed. To survive, we need to change too. If the choice comes down to using medicinal terras or killing people, I vote for the former." He looked at Lynxx with a dawning expression of hope. "Do you have any more of those eye-wing terras or Lazarus plants?"

"I'm growing both species in a greenhouse back at my old apartment. They were seedlings when I left for Florida. By now, most should be mature. Hopefully, they weren't damaged in the Sat-Fall."

Commander Powell gestured for Lynxx to walk with him. "Tell me more about these medicinal terras."

Staring after them, I breathed a trembling sigh of relief.

10

OVER THE FOLLOWING DAYS, an unlikely hero emerged at the garrison.

E-Day was postponed as the ten people marked for death were treated with Lynxx's medicinal terras. Eight recovered. The woman with terminal cancer remained in agony and she chose the "kinder option," as did the old man with emphysema.

When news spread that Lynxx's terra drugs had healed most of the doomed people, he was regarded as a hero by nearly everyone in the Weston Battalion. Sergeant Thorne and a few others continued to grumble, but even their hostility fell silent as more and more people were healed by the terra drugs.

Teams scoured the city for eye-wings and Lazarus-vine terras, and Lynxx taught a group of volunteers how to make his terra medicines.

Anyone seriously injured or ill was given a choice: multiple doses of terra drugs or a single dose of conventional drugs. All chose the terras. Longtime sufferers of arthritis, asthma, and other chronic diseases also requested the drugs and were either cured or saw a tremendous improvement in their conditions.

Three days later, I watched Chef Einstein briskly stride across the courtyard to where Liberty Team was gearing up for a mission.

"I'll arrange a late lunch for your team," he told Asher, who was helping me sort through our weapons.

"Thanks." Asher smiled at him. "How's your arthritis these days?"

"What arthritis?" Beaming, Einstein held out his hands. They were still old and wrinkled, but the arthritic lumps had disappeared. His fingers flexed and moved with the ease of a young man. "Isabel's arthritis has completely disappeared too. And other people's aches and pains. Lynxx deserves a medal."

"I totally agree," Asher said.

"He's changed people's lives," I added.

"And he's saved many lives." Einstein fixed his stare on Asher. "Just like you, lad." When Asher shrugged modestly, Einstein went on, "There's more than one way to be a hero. You and Lynxx are both heroic, each in your own way. But he's more ..."

"More what?" I asked.

"Lynxx is more cautious. Level-headed. Focused."

Asher raised a brow. "And I'm not?"

"No, lad. You're brave, no doubt about it. You're also impulsive and, on occasion, you're rash. It could get you killed one day."

Asher grinned. "Next time, I'll try to look before I leap."

"Good idea." Einstein clasped the boy warmly on the shoulder. "The world needs both you and Lynxx. And personally, I'd be mighty sorry to lose a friend like you."

As the days passed, people continued to prepare for battle. They trained with firearms and swords, lifted weights, ran circuits, practiced martial arts. More food was stockpiled. More reinforcements were erected.

Nila set up a lab in the Tower and added a new potted zap terra, replacing the one lost in the Sat-Fall. She and her assistants worked long hours on her mysterious special project, while Lynxx and his assistants produced a variety of terra meds.

Everyone wanted to be as prepared as possible, including me.

Whenever I saw Zoey playing in the courtyard, I remembered that she was alive because of my mental powers. If I hadn't stopped that tumbleweed from scooping her up that day, she would've faced a hideous death.

That realization lingered in my thoughts.

Early one morning, I visited Lynxx in his lab at Weston Tower. We hadn't spoken since our conversation with the commander on the rooftop. Lynxx was still angry that I'd revealed my secret to Powell—my weekly drinking of terra tonics.

And Lynxx was right. Since he was the one who'd secretly brewed these forbidden tonics, I should've discussed my decision with him.

But there'd been no time.

This morning, he was alone in his lab, so I got straight to the point. "I want to continue developing my mental powers."

He paused, an empty beaker in hand. "What?"

"We need every advantage we can get in the upcoming battle with the Chi'az."

"True."

"Will you start training me again?"

He hesitated, then nodded. "When?"

"How about tomorrow? I have the afternoon off."

"Fine."

"We'll need somewhere private," I said, irritated at his short, one-word responses.

"Okay."

"That rules out the garrison."

"Yeah."

Enough with the curt replies. "Do you know a place where we can train in private?"

Finally, his answer was longer than four letters. "There's a spot a few miles from here." As a faint smile lightened his face, I realized he had finally forgiven me. "It's extraordinary."

11

THE NEXT DAY LYNXX and I drove to Washington Square Park.

In the ten-acre landmark, green velvet-vine terras covered the famous arch to the north and the fountain in the center. A scattering of yellow terra trees grew among the maples and oaks.

We paused at an overgrown bench. A short distance away, four giraffes—father, mother, twin calves—dined on hanging blue vines. Near them, a family of elephants chomped on tall orange weeds, the parents protectively flanking their baby.

I smiled at the peaceful scene.

Every day our world was changing. Buildings and streets were becoming terra jungles. Xans were now as common as dogs, cats, and pigeons had once been. Our lands and oceans were being targeted by a hostile non-terrestrial species called the Chi'az.

Despite all this, many Earth animals continued to thrive, and I was comforted by the survival of these elephants and giraffes.

Hopefully, humanity would survive as well.

"Where are we going, Lynxx?"

"Look up."

In the treetops, a skyweb terra stretched overhead.

It was smaller than the skyweb our helicopter had flown over last year. I shuddered, remembering the huge tumbleweeds up on that thing, and our battle with the Outrider hybrid, Bone.

Lynxx pulled a folding rope ladder from his backpack and threw its hooked end over a high branch.

Gesturing to the dangling ladder, he asked, "Do you want me to go first?"

I studied the terra that shaded the park. "I hate skywebs. I still have nightmares about that one we were on with Bone and Professor Doylen."

"It wasn't much fun," he admitted.

"We both almost died up there. It was creepy, too. All those animal skeletons. The tumbleweeds digesting their prey. Oh, and let's not forget the black mamba that slithered around the place, plus—bonus nightmare—the great white shark that lunged at us from a tumbleweed." I backed away from the ladder. "I'm not climbing up there."

"It's a cloudweb terra. They're similar to skywebs, only much nicer. I've been on this one a few times. It's safe." Lynxx looked at me earnestly. "Do you trust me, Kassia?"

Déjà vu flashed through me.

Months ago, Lynxx and I had been dining in a conservatory filled with lush Earth plants, and he'd brought out a bag of floating Mozart flowers to light the room. That evening, noticing my wariness, he had asked, *Do you trust me, Kassia?* My answer had been blunt and truthful: *Mostly. I don't trust anyone completely.*

Now, standing beneath the cloudweb terra, Lynxx again asked, "Do you trust me, Kassia?"

"Completely," I replied, meaning it.

He smiled, and I felt as if I'd been warmed by sunshine.

We scaled the rope ladder, which he hauled up after us. "We don't want any uninvited guests."

I followed him further up the tree, climbing from branch to branch. Emerging through a hole in the cloudweb, I cautiously stepped onto the web, which dipped and swayed like the mat of a trampoline.

I gazed around in wonder. "Incredible!"

The cloudweb extended across most of the park's ten acres and was as high as some of the surrounding buildings. The skyweb last year had been brown and sparse and ugly. This one was covered in white flowers that felt soft and fluffy beneath my feet, like walking on an enormous cloud. Here and there, the leafy tops of yellow terra trees poked through the web.

Overhead, clouds blocked the sunlight, shading the web and surrounding buildings.

Lynxx pointed to a distant treetop covered with bright yellow leaves. "We'll start our training at that Helios-tree. It's harmless."

"Why's it called Helios?"

"It's named after the sun god in Greek mythology."

As we walked toward the treetop, I peered at the web more closely. The fluffy white flowers looked familiar, and fragrant petals floated up with each step we took.

"Are these Mozart flowers?"

He nodded. "This is where I gathered the ones for our dinner in the conservatory ages ago. They love growing on cloudwebs."

"But these flowers aren't giving off colored waves."

"They will if birds start singing or if we play music. However, we'll skip the music today. We don't want to draw attention."

"From what?"

"Anything that's in the park below us. Straggler krols, lions, hyenas, Outriders, Wilders. Take your pick."

"I'll pass, thanks."

Colorful parrots and toucans flitted among the white Mozart flowers, along with squirrels, chipmunks, and lizards.

"They're feeding on the honey-like sap that the terras produce, Kassia."

Overhead, the clouds suddenly parted. As sunlight touched the white Mozart flowers, they changed. Some turned blue, others became red, gold, green, or purple, until the entire field of flowers appeared drenched in colors from an exploded rainbow.

He smiled. "I was hoping the sun would come out."

"It's incredible," I breathed. After weeks of bleakness, this place of peace and beauty lifted my spirit—and for the first time in ages, I felt happy.

Further in the city, gunshots broke the afternoon silence.

Automatically, I reached for the pistol in my belt, and Lynxx checked his revolver. Although we both had enhanced mental powers, our physical weapons were still useful.

My happiness evaporated. "Have you heard the rumor? The Wilders are getting restless. Our truce is in danger of being broken."

"Not surprising. Wilders have radios, so they've probably heard about the upcoming Chi'az invasion. Plus they've lost people to the krols. Weston Tower must seem highly appealing to them at the moment. I can't understand why they haven't already joined our cell."

"They're still refusing to accept Commander Powell's rules."

"Most unwise."

"There are rumors of the Wilders planning an attack on the garrison. They've tried it before, you know."

"Desperate people do desperate things."

We rounded the Helios terra treetop—

—and I jerked to a halt.

12

A FEW YARDS AWAY, a large tumbleweed lay on the cloudweb, almost hidden by the yellow Helios leaves.

Instinctively, I remote-pushed it. Hard.

The thing bounced up a foot, then fell down again.

"What the heck?" I stared at the three ropes that tied the curved branches to the web.

Lynxx hurried forward. "Sorry. I meant to warn you. It's dead. Promise." He kicked the tumbleweed once, twice. The curved branches didn't widen into a mouth, and it didn't rattle and clatter. It was as lifeless as a tombstone.

I glared at the thing. Gray-brown. Large as a car. Skinny broken branches. "This looks like the terra that tried to swallow Zoey in the garrison courtyard a few weeks ago. What's it doing here? Why's it tied to the web?"

"So it can't get blown away."

"Who cares?"

"I would if I'm inside it," he replied. "I've used this tumbleweed a few times over the past three weeks. It's the perfect spot to leave my body when I'm mind-blending. People avoid cloudwebs, but even if someone came up here, they'd never approach a tumbleweed."

"Yeah, most people are sane," I muttered.

He bit back a smile. Then he gestured to some squirrels on the nearby branches. "I thought you could practice your remote-soothing on them."

"I've already practiced remote-soothing a dozen times on the horses in the stable and also on Harlem's cat, Fluffy."

"Okay, how about some remote-pulling? It's where you draw an animal toward you."

"Why would I do that?" I asked, aghast. "If I'm attacked by an animal or xan, I'd remote-push the thing *away* from me, not pull it closer. Right?"

"Yes, but—"

"Have you ever used remote-pulling to defend yourself?"

"Well, no," he admitted. Then, sighing, he suggested, "Okay, how about practicing some more remote-pushing?"

"I already know how to do that."

"So what do you want to do?"

I hesitated, gathering my courage.

During my mind-blend with the frog, Hopalong, I'd been snatched up by a clicker xan that had tried to feed frog-me to its hatchlings.

The clicker grasped one of my frog-legs with a pincer claw and squeezed. My leg bone snapped. Agony flared through frog-me, hot as fire.

What if something went wrong today? What if I got hurt again? Or killed?

One of my father's quotes flowed through my fears. *Courage doesn't mean you don't get afraid, Kass. Courage means you don't let fear stop you.*

The words rushed from my lips. "I want to practice mind-blending."

"What? Why? You hate it."

"Sure, I was terrified the first time I tried it as Hopalong. But when I mind-blended on the trawler with that albatross, Wings, I was only scared; I was more terrified that *you* were going to die, Lynxx."

He fell silent. "I understand," he finally said. "However, why don't we focus on remote-pulling today—"

"Or skip that and go straight to mind-blending," I insisted. "I have to learn to control it."

"Okay. Okay. But this time I'm coming with you. If you get into trouble again, I'll be there. I'll mind-hop into whatever's attacking you and force it to back off."

"Good idea," I said, relieved. "What will we blend with? The squirrels?"

"No. We need an animal that's harder to see and far less tasty to falcons and hawks." He pointed to a branch in the Helios-tree. "Like them."

I peered through the yellow leaves. After several moments, I saw four lizard-like creatures almost blended into the brown branch. Each was about a foot long, with a large bumpy head, sucker feet, and a short, fat tail that resembled a dead leaf.

"You want us to mind-blend with xans? Is that even possible?"

"They're not xans. They're Earth animals. Leaf-tailed geckos from Madagascar, genus *Uroplatus*." He paused, thinking. "Actually, I'm not even sure if we *can* blend with xans. I've never tried it. But I've blended with these little Earth geckos." He pointed to a nearby pair. One had a large dark spot on its knobby head. "You go with the spotted one. I'll take the light brown one."

"What do we do with our bodies?"

He gestured to the gray tumbleweed. "That's the safest place."

"Are you sure it's dead?"

"One hundred percent."

Reluctantly, I followed him into the center of the tumbleweed, wincing as he remote-pushed the branches shut behind us. We lay on a thick blanket that cushioned us from the thorns. Around us, the curved branches were tightly woven, except at the spot where I'd broken them during Zoey's rescue. Through this thinner spot, I peered at the two geckos, which were almost invisible on the branch outside.

Leaning on one elbow, Lynxx said, "You need to know a little about the reptile you're blending with. For a start, leaf-tailed geckos are usually only active at night." He went on, giving me a quick lesson on their basic behavior and physiology. Then he repeated the instructions he'd given me for mind-blending with Hopalong.

When he finished, I told him, "Got it."

"Are you sure you want to do this?"

"Positive." And yet I found myself nervously reaching for his hand.

Gently, he squeezed my fingers as we lay down in the tumbleweed.

"Ready," I whispered.

Focusing on the spotted gecko, I narrowed my eyes and threw my mind forward.

I flew past gold starbursts. Plunged through a gray wall. Landed in something spongy and alien. Felt a moment's suffocation in the other mind. Another push and then *I* was there. Centered. In the gecko. Peering through huge bulging eyes.

A giant wet tongue slimed across my left eye, then my right one.

Freaking heck! What was that?

Oh. It was me. Or, rather, gecko-me. Lynxx had mentioned that, since most geckos didn't have eyelids, they licked their eyes to keep them moist.

Where was he?

I looked around. Hundreds of yellow shields hung from thick lengths of wood. No, not shields. They were yellow leaves, and the thick lengths of wood were branches.

Everything I saw was vividly colored. The leaves weren't a single yellow; they were multiple shades, even on the same branch. The yellow of sand on a tropical beach. Yellow as the sun. A pat of butter. Daffodils. Lemons. Lynxx had explained that geckos were hypersensitive to colors and could even see color in the dark.

A light brown gecko clung to my gnarled branch, watching me with silver eyes.

Lynxx?

It lifted a front foot and moved it back and forth, fat toes outspread.

Lynxx was waving at me from the brown gecko's body.

Gecko-me hurried toward him. *Whoa!* What was that rasping sound? Glancing back, I saw my leaf-shaped tail scraping along the branch. Gecko-me lifted it a little and I set off again, quietly this time.

As I trailed gecko-Lynxx onto the green trunk of the Helios-tree, a tingle rippled my body from head to tail. I watched my front legs change from brown to a bright green that matched the Helios's trunk. *What the—? Oh, that's right.* Geckos were like chameleons; they could change color to match their surroundings, but the changes were usually slow and limited in color range. "For some reason," Lynxx had told me, "these particular geckos can change color quickly and dramatically. It's possible their ability has been enhanced after a year of eating Helios-tree leaves."

Lynxx, his gecko body now also green, headed down the trunk. I followed. At first it felt weird walking down the side of the tree, but my sticky toes handled the vertical descent with ease. Not once did I feel in danger of slipping or falling. Apparently, geckos could stick to almost every surface, except dry Teflon.

At a distant sound in the park, Lynxx lifted a lizard hand in a familiar gesture. *Stop. Wait here.* He scurried off to investigate.

Gecko-me waited patiently. I studied my green leafy tail. Very attractive. Licked my eyes again. *Still gross.* Sniffed an ocean of smells that I could somehow identify, including elephant dung, rotting vulture, skunk.

A fat fly, big as a cat, buzzed past my face.

With lightning speed, my tongue darted out, grabbed the insect, and thrust it into my mouth. Instinctively I gulped it down.

Gecko-me just ate a huge fly. Dis-gus-ting!

A chirp came from the end of the branch. Gecko-Lynxx lifted a front hand and waved me forward. I joined him at the end of a branch and stared down.

Two horses clopped into view. Harlem and Soo-Yun had started riding lessons shortly after the elimination of the krols in Manhattan. They paused their mounts beneath the Helios-tree terra, close enough for gecko-me to hear them chatting about the grazing giraffes and elephants.

Excitement coursed through me as one of my childhood dreams came true. I was virtually invisible. I could sit on this branch, listening and watching—and they'd never know I was there.

Was this how the Invisible Man felt? *Great fun.*

Harlem and Soo-Yun flicked their reins. Disappointed, I watched them ride away.

I perked up at the sound of more riders approaching. Good. More people to practice my "invisibility" on. My gecko-host didn't seem to care that another mind was sharing its brain. Perhaps it was full from that disgusting fat fly and was content to let me control it.

A girl's musical laugh drifted in the air. Two new riders stopped their horses beneath the Helios-tree, and I gazed down at a cascade of blond hair that gleamed in the sunlight.

Willow. With Asher.

13

As GECKO-LYNXX TURNED TO me, I was glad he couldn't read the pain on my gecko-face.

"Look at the elephants and giraffes, Ash," cried Willow, her lovely face glowing with happiness. "Aren't they incredible?"

"Amazing," he said, one hand resting on his holstered gun. "We're so close, yet they don't seem worried about us."

Grief and regret pierced me like arrows, and my hold on the gecko slipped. As its brain quivered, I quickly tightened my control.

After Asher and I had decided upon a break, Willow had offered me her sympathy. Then she'd quickly stepped into my spot—or perhaps she saw it as resuming her rightful place at her former boyfriend's side.

Since then, Asher had treated Willow with affection but not as a full-on girlfriend. He was clearly holding back from her. Was it because he was overloaded with work at the Weston Garrison? Or cautious after our own rocky romance?

Of course, I had no idea how Asher behaved with Willow in private.

Maybe today in my "invisible" state, I'd get a better glimpse of their relationship. Did he miss me as much as I missed him? Or was he drifting back to the girl he had called "the love of his life"?

Gecko-me sniffed the air. Perfume. *Sheesh.* I glared down at Willow. What kind of girl bothered with perfume these days?

Asher said, "We'd better catch up with Harl and Soo-Yun." They rode on.

I stared after them, filled with a strange emptiness.

Gecko-Lynxx's sharp chirp cut through my pain. Time to focus on today's lesson.

Numbly, I ran through the routine we'd agreed on earlier. Gecko-me scampered up and down the trunk, chomped on dry Helios leaves, and even hung effortlessly upside down from a branch. I should've been excited at the control I had over the gecko, but I wasn't. I didn't even care about being invisible anymore—

—until a gang of eight Wilders on foot stopped to stare at the wild elephants and giraffes.

Gecko-Lynxx and I crept onto a lower branch, my lizard body tingling as I changed color to blend with the brown wood.

The Wilders were dressed in their usual jeans, shirts, vests, and boots. Most of them had long oily hair, greasy beards, and bandaged injuries. All carried guns and knives.

"How about some roast giraffe tonight, boys?" a man said, his skinny body twitching. He licked a pair of thin lips and wiped his sweaty neck with a rag.

Another man snorted. His bald head was covered with a huge swastika tattoo. More tattoos covered his neck and arms, and a long scar divided his forehead. It was the Wilder that Lynxx and I had rescued from some strangler terras last year. *Fang.*

"Forget the roast giraffe," Fang said with the authority of a leader. "It's too tough to chew. My jaw's still aching from the last one. We don't need no stinkin' giraffe meat, anyway. Soon we'll be chowing down on the hundreds of steaks stuffed into them freezers at the Weston Garrison."

Gecko-Lynxx and I stiffened, listening.

Fang's men babbled in excitement.

"I heard they got bison."

"Venison."

"Fish."

"Eggs."

Fang growled, "Plus enough canned goods to last us for years."

"That's if we win," snarled another man.

"We'll win," Fang said grimly. "We have to. Otherwise them krols will keep picking us off until we're all gnawed bones."

"They got Stinko Jon yesterday. Snatched him right off his Hog."

"What a moron! I told you all not to ride your Hogs around this stinkin' area. They're magnets for them krols."

Gecko-Lynxx and I glanced at each other. The commander had been right about some stray krols remaining in the city.

"Anyway," Fang continued, "them control freaks at the garrison won't be expecting our attack. Them skinned krols on their walls may scare away the xans, but they don't scare us off none."

"Yeah," a man said, his Adam's apple bobbing in his dirty neck. "Plus we got some powerful weapons they ain't got."

Gecko-Lynxx and I exchanged alarmed glances.

What weapons?

"It's *our* turn to have Weston Tower," Fang snarled. "Remember, everyone in there dies. No prisoners, except for the pretty ones."

Muttering and nodding their agreement, the gang of bikers moved off in the opposite direction to the riders on horseback.

Lynxx and I scurried back to our bodies.

The Wilders were planning to attack the garrison.

But when?

And what were their "powerful weapons"?

14

At dawn the next morning, fifty of us assembled in the garrison courtyard.

Liberty and Trident Teams were fully armed. We also had half of the Weston Battalion's soldiers, plus most of its security personnel. Medical teams loaded supplies into two ambulances. A convoy of empty Hummers waited in front of the steel gates.

I snuck a sideways glance at Willow, hoping she was ready for this.

Since joining the garrison, she'd worked hard to be a part of Liberty Team. Already an accomplished sword fighter, she had spent hours every day training with firearms and practicing martial arts.

While I admired her dedication, lately I thought I'd detected a faint ... *something* ... in her. A change. After my breakup with Asher, she'd been hyper happy, unnaturally so. But recently that had faded to a kind of brittleness. Was she hiding her fears behind a facade of confidence?

Frowning, she stood beside me in the assembly, lips tight.

"Stay near Asher or me," I whispered. "We're both experienced at fighting dangerous terras."

"I'll be fine." Her long blond hair was braided and pinned up, and her hand rested on the hilt of her sword as she straightened her shoulders. "I may not have chosen this destiny, but I accept my duty."

I looked at her curiously. "Isn't that a line from *Pandora*?" In between her movies, Willow had starred in the super-popular TV series for three years. She'd played Pandora, a brave and feisty teen who had battled the supernatural evils she'd accidentally released from a wooden box.

Willow remained silent, staring into the distance, lost in thought.

I sighed, once again missing the camaraderie of my friend Pepper.

Clad in camouflage gear, Commander Powell strode onto a makeshift platform. He addressed the gathering in a firm, authoritative voice.

"Everyone knows their role in today's mission. The soldiers and security forces will engage the enemy. Liberty and Trident Teams will handle any dangerous terras and xans. The medical teams will wait nearby, just in case." The commander paused, then said, "Let's do this. Good luck, everyone."

He headed for the lead Hummer, followed by half a dozen soldiers. As the rest of us climbed into the other armored vehicles, I glanced at the entrance to Weston Tower. Lynxx lifted a hand in farewell, clearly unhappy at being banned by the commander from today's mission: "You're too valuable to risk on the battlefield."

Our convoy drove through the deserted streets of Manhattan. Guilt-ridden, I stared through the window. How many people were going to die today?

Yesterday afternoon, Lynxx and I had told the commander about the conversation we'd overheard in Washington Square Park—leaving out the part where we'd been mind-blended with geckos. Powell had checked and double-checked what the Wilders had said, then dismissed us. Half an hour later, he'd called for a meeting with Lieutenant Wu, Sergeant Thorne, and the council.

I had thought Powell would increase the number of soldiers on the walls and order further reinforcements around the garrison.

To my shock, he'd ordered preparations for an attack on the Wilder encampment. His mandate was hard and clear. *Kill every biker.*

"They're like tumors," he had told the council. "For too long we've tried living with them, but they still want us dead. We'll lose if we try to fight a war on two fronts: the Chi'az and the Wilders. We need to eradicate the Wilders first. Then we can focus on the Chi'az."

We drove past a large cathedral-dome terra in the sidewalk, its leafy branches arched like an open umbrella. In this early-morning sunlight, its brilliant leaves again reminded me of the stained glass windows of churches.

Willow peered through the Hummer window, murmuring, "Xavian loved cathedral-domes." Grief shaded her face. "I miss him so much."

Asher patted her hand. "He seemed like a decent guy."

I noted his use of the word *guy* instead of *hybrid*. Progress!

"He was like a father to me." Tears gleamed in her violet eyes as she leaned on his shoulder, her lower lip trembling. "Thank goodness we finally found each other again, Ash. When I'm with you, breathing the air you breathe and feeling the warmth of your skin, I feel alive again."

I sighed. More well-known lines from *Pandora*.

At the steering wheel, Booker glanced back at Willow, his eyes puzzled behind his wire-rimmed spectacles. The others in the Hummer also looked at her in surprise.

I tried to hide my concern. Most of the time, Willow seemed strong and confident. Other times, she appeared emotionally weak and vulnerable. Her dead guardian, Xavian, had once told me that she was both as strong as hardwood and as fragile as butterfly wings.

Alert for trouble, Asher kept scanning the streets and sidewalks, not noticing Willow's erratic behavior.

A block from the Wilders' location, a series of gunshots broke the early-morning hush. The convoy slowed and Powell's voice crackled from our radio. "Proceed with caution. I repeat, proceed with caution."

Our vehicles parked near the Edge Complex. The two ambulances and their crews waited behind as the rest of us crept toward our target. By the time we reached the end of the block, we could hear shouting, more gunshots, and familiar screeches and snarls.

A pair of old buses were parked across the road, restricting access to the plaza beyond. Suspicious, Commander Powell sent two men forward; when they signaled that the vehicles were empty, we crept to the buses and peered through their windows.

The bikers had turned the large Edge Plaza into a combined kitchen and living room. Half a dozen extinguished campfires dotted the area, each straddled by a metal spit. Tattered couches and chairs ringed the ashes. An axe lay next to a pile of split logs. Pieces of burned metal and trash littered the pavers—along with a couple of dozen bodies, mostly Wilders plus a few krols.

A battle was raging in the plaza.

Men crouched behind the scattered couches, shooting and shouting. Gray krols hurled wooden spears and, incredibly, carried makeshift metal shields. Two creatures leaped at a bearded biker who slumped to the ground amid a blitz of claws and sharp teeth.

There were at least thirty krols here—more than just the few "stragglers" presumed left in Manhattan. I wondered if a second pack had been living in the city. Or was this a new pack, recently arrived from the countryside?

Sergeant Thorne turned to Commander Powell and Asher. "Those krols are doing our job for us."

Powell nodded grimly. "We'll wait until the Wilders are all dead. Then we'll go in and finish off the remaining krols."

I wasn't surprised at the commander's attitude. From the first day I'd met him, he'd made his goal clear: the survival of the Weston Battalion. He would only risk his troops if he had no other choice.

Today, he would leave the Wilders to their fate.

I peered through the bus window again. "Commander, there aren't any dangerous terras in the plaza—"

"Good."

"—but there are women and kids."

15

ON THE LEFT OF the battlefield, three pregnant women and four children huddled behind a row of wooden barrels.

A short distance away, a pink-haired teenager crawled toward the group, one bloodied hand clutching her stomach. Shrieking, some krols pointed their spears at the defenseless civilians.

"Change of plans!" Powell switched on his radio and ordered his men to attack the krols, adding, "The Wilders are no longer our targets. Repeat, the Wilders are no longer our targets." He turned to Asher. "Get those women and children to safety."

Led by Commander Powell, our soldiers and security forces charged into the battle. The Wilders were startled by our arrival, but at our shouts—"We're here to help you!"—they turned their weapons back on the krols.

Liberty and Trident Teams rushed to the wooden barrels and began shepherding the pregnant women and children to safety. A Wilder youth with a sword ran to join Asher and Booker, and together the trio fought off some attacking krols.

I hurried to the pink-haired teenager who'd been crawling across the ground. She lay facedown in a growing pool of blood, and as I gently turned her over, she clutched at her slashed abdomen. *Oh no. She's holding in her intestines.*

I didn't reach for my first aid kit. No point. I'd seen these injuries on the battlefield before.

"You'll be okay," I lied to the dying girl.

She clutched my arm. "Please don't leave me. Don't want to be alone."

I glanced around. The battle was ongoing in the plaza, away from us.

"I won't leave you." The girl was clearly in pain, and for her sake I hoped it'd be over soon. Trying to distract her, I asked, "What's your name?"

"Tammy."

"I'm Kass. Were you being held prisoner by these Wilders?"

Weakly, she shook her head. She pointed at the women and children being hustled from the area by our teams. "We all joined them. Had to. Safer with Wilders ... than on streets alone." Her hand tightened on my arm, as though afraid I'd desert her.

"Why didn't you come to the Weston Battalion?"

"Couldn't. My brother joined Wilders." She looked at a youth sprawled on a tattered couch. His throat had been slashed by claws, and his dead eyes stared at eternity. "He ... only family left. Couldn't leave him."

And for the first time, I realized that not every Wilder was a thug. Some people were just desperate or made poor choices.

If Asher hadn't found me after I'd left the subway bunker, or if I'd been banished from the Weston Battalion, I would've been alone. Weak and sick, would I have eventually joined the Wilders? Would I have seen them as my only hope of survival in this post-apocalyptic city?

Perhaps.

But I'd been lucky.

And I'd never been alone. Lynxx had always been in the background, helping me, protecting me, loving me.

The girl's fingers loosened on my arm as her eyes dimmed.

"You'll be okay, Tammy," I whispered, stroking her forehead. "You'll be okay."

Her hand slipped off her abdomen, and her intestines bulged out in glittering red coils.

I felt for a pulse. Nothing.

Tammy still wasn't alone. She had joined her brother in death.

At a shout, I looked around. Numbly, my brain registered snippets of the battle:

The crumpled bodies of four krols lying nearby.

Booker dragging a bleeding Wilder youth away.

No signs of the women and children.

A gray krol swinging its clawed hand down—

—as Asher crumpled to the ground, bleeding from his neck. The gray krol stood over him, raising its clawed hand again, about to deliver a death blow.

Noooo! I'm too far away to remote-push it!

Desperately I reached for the gun in my holster—

—and watched the krol jerk in a death dance as bullets riddled its body.

Holstering his revolver, Commander Powell darted across to Asher. "You'll be okay, son. You'll be okay."

I'd just uttered that same lie to a dying girl.

I rushed to join them, unzipping my backpack.

Asher clutched at his neck with blood-covered fingers.

"You'll be okay," I lied as I pulled his hand away. Three slashes exposed the tendons and muscles in his neck, and I shoved a pad of bandages over them, trying to stop the bleeding.

The commander yelled for help, then barked orders into his radio.

As Asher's eyes slowly closed, I cried, "Stay with me, Asher. Stay awake." In one of Soo-Yun's first aid lessons, she'd told us that a conscious patient was more likely to survive than an unconscious one.

His eyes remained closed.

Quickly, I bandaged his wound.

Further away, the fighting continued. Krols attacked humans. Gunshots blasted. Fangs and claws slashed flesh, opening abdomens and throats. Swords battled spears. Bullets pinged off metal shields.

In the middle of the fighting, I glimpsed a familiar eagle with silver eyes swoop down, claw a krol with its taloned feet, then dart away.

WindLord-Lynxx.

I should've guessed that Lynxx wouldn't obey the commander's orders to stay at Weston Tower, safe from harm.

Amid all the bedlam, the commander and Sergeant Thorne grabbed Asher's limp body. As they carried him away, Powell called back to me, "What the heck is Willow doing?" He jerked his head left.

Sword in hand, Willow was fighting a pitchfork-wielding krol. Teeth bared, the beast dropped the pitchfork, grabbed an iron bar and heaved it at her. She ducked aside, the bar missing her by an inch.

I hesitated, my gaze swiveling between Asher and her.

"We'll take care of Asher, Miss Madison," the commander shouted as they turned a corner. "Help Willow."

Asher will be fine. Asher will be fine.

"Yes, sir."

The krol snatched up his pitchfork and ran into the multistory Edge Complex beside the plaza. Willow followed a few yards behind, her sword drawn.

I took off after Asher's former girlfriend.

Why was she chasing a krol into a building?

16

Inside, the lobby was covered in velvet-vine terras that released a faint lavender scent.

"Willow," I shouted.

"Here." A faint cry echoed in a stairwell.

I bolted toward the steps. No time to search for my head-lamp in my backpack. I wished I had my gecko eyes again so I could see in the dark.

In the stairwell, light streamed through gaping holes in the exterior wall, and bits of burned metal dotted the area, suggesting the building had been hit during the Sat-Fall.

"Forget about that krol, Willow," I cried. "We need to get out of here."

From above, her voice echoed down the concrete shaft. "Can't. Our mission."

"Our mission is to live, not to chase a single krol that's running away from you."

"It's not running away from me."

"What are you talking about?"

No answer. Just the sound of her boots clattering up the steps.

I pounded up flight after flight, tempted to yell out that Asher had been injured, but I couldn't risk it. For some reason, Willow felt compelled to hunt down this particular krol. If I distracted her in the middle of this pursuit, the krol could turn and kill her.

Asher will be fine.

Above, a door creaked open, and she shouted down the stairwell, "Eighth floor."

I reached it half a minute later, shoved open the metal fire door, rushed inside—and stopped.

Gun drawn, I scanned the area.

The rear wall of the office had fallen away, leaving the room open to the air. Sunlight streamed in, along with distant shouts and gunshots. Half of the floor was also missing, exposing metal beams and mangled wires in a huge hole. Green terra vines hung from the remaining walls like shredded wallpaper, and clumps of wheat terras grew in the carpet.

Clutching a bloodstained sword, Willow stood on a patch of floor a few feet from the void. The tattooed Wilder leader, Fang, was balancing on a metal beam that extended over the void, with a pale red sky behind him. Eyes bulging with fear, he stood with his arms outstretched as he tried to balance himself.

"Where's the krol?" I cried.

She pointed her dripping sword at the void. "I killed it—and I saved this innocent."

I gaped at her. "You saved—? The krol was *chasing Fang?* And you *saved* him?"

"Isn't that our mission? Save the innocents? Kill the krols?"

As the air began to quiver, I felt a strange vibration. Lynxx's words flashed through my mind: *a hybrid mind-blended with a bird or animal sometimes gives off a vibration, almost like a current in the air.*

With a flutter of wings, WindLord landed on an upturned table near the gaping wall. It—he—blinked at me with silver eyes.

Lynxx.

Calmer now, I returned my attention to Willow. "This man isn't an innocent."

Fang took a hesitant step forward, croaking, "Move, bitch. I wanna get out of here."

"Too bad," I replied. This bald, tattooed biker was a vile human. Everything about him made my skin crawl.

"Kass," said Willow, surprised. "This innocent is our mission."

"No, he's not. He's only alive because Commander Powell couldn't watch a bunch of women and kids get slaughtered by the krols. He wanted *those innocents* saved, not the Wilders. You should've let the krol kill Fang. He's a worse scumbag than those xans."

"Hey," Fang cried, the ugly scar on his forehead pale amid his furious, flushed face. "Watch your mouth, bitch, or I'll—"

"You'll what?" I demanded, holstering my gun and withdrawing my sword.

WindLord-Lynxx fluttered in agitation as I stepped onto the beam.

"You'll what, Fang?" I again asked as I walked forward, my sword pointing at him. Anger outweighed my fear of the void beneath the beam. "You'll order an attack on the garrison just so you can steal our food, our weapons, our electricity? You'll steal everything we've worked dawn to dusk for? You made your choices, Fang. You refused to join the Weston Battalion because you didn't like the commander's rules. You chose violence over discipline and work. You chose to smoke dope terras and kidnap girls and laze around with your weak pathetic followers, waiting to die."

"I'll ... I'll ..." His mouth opened and closed like a guppy.

"You'll what? Kill every person at the garrison except for the pretty ones?" I was close enough to see the shock in his beady eyes. "Yes, I know all about your plan to attack our garrison. You're a waste of air. When I gut you and throw your worthless body from this beam, no one will mourn you."

"Bitch. You won't kill me."

He was right. My job was to kill terras and xans, not people. Although I despised this thug, I couldn't simply throw him from this beam, no matter how tempting.

Still, it felt good making him sweat a little.

"Scumbags don't deserve to live." My sword touched his chest, and he grimaced as I pushed the steel tip against his dirty T-shirt. "Just a bit more pressure and—" I stopped, struck by a sudden idea. "You don't deserve it, but I'll give you a chance to save your useless life."

He exhaled in relief, his foul breath wafting across me. "What ya want?"

"Information."

"I ain't got none."

I ignored his lies. "What are the powerful weapons you were planning to use against the Weston Garrison? Where are they?"

"What? I don't have no weapons."

My patience snapped. After one small persuasive nick to Fang's neck, I had my answers.

When he finished babbling the details, I stared at him in horror. As expected, he had guns—but he also had rocket launchers.

I glanced at WindLord, then back at Fang. "You claim that your men moved the weapons to Rizmo's Warehouse. That's half a block from here, right?"

"So?"

"It's a shame someone couldn't ... go to the warehouse ... to see if you're lying or not. Perhaps enter through a broken window or door."

To my relief, WindLord-Lynxx flew away.

Puzzled, Willow asked, "Shall I go to the warehouse? Is that my new mission?"

"No. We're all going to stand here quietly while I study Fang's face. I'll figure out if he's lying or not."

Minutes later, WindLord returned to his perch on the office desk. Clutched in his right talons was a bundle of straw, which he released. As the straws floated in the breeze, he shook his feathered head. *No.*

"You're lying, Fang," I snapped. "You didn't store the weapons at Rizmo's Warehouse." I whipped the tip of my sword back to the bleeding nick on his neck. "You have one more chance. Then I'm cutting your throat as easily as you and your men would've cut mine."

"No, no," he hastened to say. "You're pretty. We would've kept you alive. Her too." He jerked his head at Willow, who stood gazing into the distance.

My anger swelled at the thought of us being their sex slaves.

"This is your last chance," I ground out. "Where are the weapons?"

"Mowel Warehouse. It's three doors down from Rizmo's Warehouse. Swear it. Now let me go."

Sword raised, I stared at his face. "First, I need to decide if you're lying or not."

WindLord-Lynxx flew off again. This time, he returned with a long bullet clenched in his claws.

I lowered my sword. "Lucky for you, Fang, you're telling the truth."

He gawked at me. "How can you tell just by looking at my face?"

"Maybe I have superpowers or something."

WindLord gave a raspy caw, perhaps an eagle-snort of amusement.

Outside, the shooting and shouting had stopped. The battle was over. Had we won?

Is Asher alive?

"Willow, time to leave," I said.

She turned her glazed gaze on me. "Did you say something?"

"Wait for me on the landing. We'll go down the stairwell together." I wouldn't tell her about Asher's injury until we were outside again. Was he still alive? His neck had been badly slashed. So much blood.

I shuddered. Pushed away my fears. *Asher will be fine.*

"Go!" I told her.

"I depart on wings of speed." Another line from *Pandora.* She left.

"Willow and I are leaving," I told the biker leader. "Count to one hundred before coming downstairs. Got it?"

"Yeah, but—"

"What?"

"Most of my guys were killed by them stinkin' krols today. I might have only a few left."

"So?"

"What am I gonna do? Where am I gonna go?"

"I don't care."

"Them krols will get me sooner or later."

Sheathing my sword, I turned away. "I hope so."

Willow and I hurried down to the plaza, now strewn with dead Wilders and krols. As Willow wandered in a daze behind me, I quietly spoke into my radio.

The news was mixed.

We'd won the battle but had lost three people. Another fifteen had broken bones, concussions, or deep slashes that needed medical treatment.

Asher's injuries were critical—

—and he hovered on the edge of death.

17

Blood. Lots of blood.

By the time we returned to Weston Tower, Asher was still clinging to life, in desperate need of blood to replace what he'd lost.

I stared at the long line of people outside the infirmary, patiently waiting to donate.

I'd forgotten how popular he was. Asher had started the Weston Battalion shortly after the Mist, offering food and shelter to scores of shell-shocked survivors in Manhattan. Since then, he'd tirelessly fought the terras and the xans.

To the people in the garrison, he was an inspiring model of determination, enthusiasm, intelligence, and kindness. He was also like a son to Commander Powell, a close friend of Harlem, the love of Willow's life, a dedicated leader of Liberty Team—

—and the boy I had once given my heart to.

Unable to donate blood, I paced the courtyard for over an hour, waiting and hoping and praying to every god in existence.

Finally, my nerves frayed, I returned to the infirmary.

"Are you here to give blood, Kass?" Willow walked from the infirmary, a small plaster on the crook of her arm.

"I can't. I just wanted to see how he is."

"Still touch and go." Her violet eyes brimmed with tears. "Dr. Tran has finished operating on him. He's in recovery now."

"At least he's alive." Thanks to Dr. Tran.

During our mission to Florida, we'd fought terras and krols and had lost several people, including my friend Pepper. The price had been high, but we'd gained a real doctor. Tran would hopefully save many lives in the future, and he was already training Nurse Ortiz and Soo-Yun, plus our new medic Juliet, in medical procedures.

"Are visitors allowed?" I asked her.

"Only Lynxx."

My heart leaped. "Lynxx?"

"He's using his medicinal terras on Ash."

Some of my panic evaporated. Time and again I'd seen the effects of Lynxx's medicinal terras. Between Dr. Tran's surgical skills and Lynxx's powders and potions, Asher had a good chance of surviving.

He'll be fine. He'll be fine.

Willow followed me into the elevator. "You can still donate. They need all blood groups, not just O positive. Nurse Ortiz wants to build up reserves for when the Chi'az invade."

"No one would want my blood."

"Why not?"

I couldn't tell her about my hybrid-infected blood, so I told her another truth. "I used to have leukemia, a disease of the blood."

"Used to?"

"I don't think I have it anymore." It had been thirty-five days since my last dose of the Lazarus tonic, and I still felt healthy. Lynxx believed I was cured, but I was more cautious. Leukemia was a sneaky killer, and I couldn't relax until a few more weeks passed with no symptoms.

I gave Willow a sideways glance. This morning, she'd been distant and distracted and had laced her conversation with lines from *Pandora*. At the moment, she seemed normal again.

As we exited the elevator into the lobby, she asked, "What do we do now?"

"Excuse me?"

"Will Liberty Team be sidelined until Ash recovers?"

"No such luck. We'll be back at work tomorrow."

"Without Ash?"

"Powell will appoint a temporary team leader, probably Booker."

Poor Booker. The twenty-year-old was an avid reader who preferred novels to battles. He would hate all the stresses involved in being team leader. He wouldn't be interested in strategizing upcoming missions, anticipating potential problems, sorting out personnel issues, and scheduling training sessions. It was a full-on job that would leave little time for his reading ...

... or, I realized, for worrying about Asher.

In the courtyard, Commander Powell was inspecting the barrel of a dismantled gun. He handed it back to the preteen weapons cleaner—"Good job, Emma"—then looked around as we approached. "Ahh, Willow. Is Asher awake yet?"

Willow. The commander had used her first name, even though she'd only been in the Weston Battalion for a few weeks.

"No, sir," she replied.

His face fell, disappointed. "I suppose it's too soon."

I waited a beat. Should I ask him? Was this the right time? Probably not. Then again, the commander didn't like me, so there'd never be a right time.

I cleared my throat. "May I speak to you, sir?"

"What is it, Miss Madison?"

I suppressed a groan. *Miss Madison.*

"Someone needs to take over Liberty Team while Asher's recovering, sir. I'd like to volunteer for the job."

"Why should you get the promotion instead of Booker? He's been with the Weston Battalion longer than you."

"Booker's a good fighter and he'd be a competent leader. But you need someone who's more than competent, someone who'll throw themselves into the job and work morning to night to succeed. That's not Booker. That's me."

For a long minute he remained silent, his brow furrowing. I quailed inside. Had I gone too far?

Finally, he spoke. "I've watched you since you joined the Weston Battalion. Watched all the mistakes you made in the beginning. Watched you struggle day after day to become a better fighter. At first, Asher's reports on you were mixed, and I didn't believe you'd make it. Yet somehow you kept improving. You worked hard and never gave up."

He paused as a member of the council handed him some papers to sign. Then he continued, "In the past few days, you've provided valuable intel. You and Lynxx warned us about the impending Wilder attack, a fact confirmed by the three pregnant Wilder women we saved. Also, my soldiers have verified the stash of weapons in the Mowel Warehouse. Good work."

"Thank you, sir."

"I was also impressed with the way you treated Asher's injuries under battle conditions this morning. You probably saved his life, Miss Madison." I remained silent, sensing a big *but* coming from the commander. "When Asher first brought you into the garrison, I argued against you joining the Weston Battalion. I thought you were hiding how sick you really were. And recently you admitted that I'd been right. You'd had leukemia."

He looked at me sharply, awaiting my response.

"Yes, sir. I had leukemia. But I got better because of Lynxx's Lazarus tonic. He's helped me a lot. And not just me. He doesn't go around advertising it, but he's helped lots of other people too."

"I agree. Besides Asher, we had fifteen injured during this morning's battle. With Dr. Tran's skills and Lynxx's medicinal terras, it looks like they're all going to make it. Lynxx is a valuable asset to the Weston Battalion." Powell paused. "I have a feeling that you'll make a good team leader."

I blushed in surprise. "Thank you, sir." The commander had actually paid me a compliment.

"Congratulations, Kass. You're in charge of Liberty Team while Asher's in the infirmary."

"Thank you, sir." Somehow, I managed to sound calm. But inside I was doing cartwheels.

Finally, the commander had called me *Kass*.

18

POWELL MOVED AWAY TO answer his crackling radio.

In an overbright voice, Willow told me, "Congratulations." She stared into the distance again, a wistful smile on her lovely face.

Was she remembering her years as a famous movie and TV star? Was she reliving the flash of cameras at press conferences, the cheers of adoring crowds, the glamour of Hollywood parties?

Powell turned back to us, smiling. "Asher's waking up. He's asking for you."

Willow snapped back to the present. "At last." She started to hurry off.

"Not you, Willow," he said. "Asher's asking for Kass."

She stared at me in shock.

Nila joined us. "Lincoln, I need to talk to you. It's urgent." Her voice had an edge sharp enough to cut glass.

"Go ahead, Kass." Powell waved me on. "I'll be up to see Asher as soon as I can."

I glanced over my shoulder as I hurried into Weston Tower. Commander Powell and Nila were huddled together, talking softly. What new problem was rearing its ugly head? *Not my concern.* At the moment, Asher was my priority.

When I reached his private room, I waited outside as Soo-Yun finished taking his blood pressure.

Through the open doorway, I could see Asher lying in bed, eyes closed, bandages encircling his neck. The usual hospital smells were drowned out by a familiar scent of turpentine from the Lazarus terra paste beneath his bandages.

He'll be fine. He'll be fine.

The room was thick with dark memories. A year ago, I'd been in here with my cousin, stunned to find Charlotte alive—and devastated that she'd become a quadriplegic.

A few hours later, she'd been euthanized.

Grieving, I had lain on Charlotte's empty bed, so sick from my leukemia that Death's shadow had weighed me down. Miserable and desperate, I'd injected myself with the Lazarus solution that Lynxx had made for my cousin. The purple liquid had saved me—and changed my life.

Now, Asher lay in Charlotte's former bed, also pale and weak but alive. He rested a hand on Harlem's tuxedo cat, Fluffy, who lay curled against his side, purring loudly.

Soo-Yun nodded to me. "Much pain med finally working. Keep visit short. Five minute, okay?"

"Sure." As she left, I hurried to Asher. "How are you feeling?"

With a weak smile, he gestured to his neck, then gave me a shaky thumbs-up.

Lynxx entered the room, medical chart in hand. "He's much better, Kassia."

"Will he be okay?"

"I believe so. Dr. Tran stitched up his wound and treated it with medicinal terras." Neither of us mentioned the irony of this situation. Asher had always opposed ingesting terras, and yet they were the things helping to save his life. "He won't be able to speak for a couple of days."

"The commander said he was asking for me. If he can't speak, how did he ask?"

Lynxx pointed to a yellow notepad and pen on the nightstand. One word was written in Asher's handwriting: *Kass*.

Quietly I asked Asher, "Why did you want to see me?"

Bewildered, he looked at me, head tilted. Then he shrugged. On the yellow notepad, he wrote two words: *can't remember.*

"That's not uncommon," Lynxx told me, reading the notepad over my shoulder. "People often have some amnesia following an operation. A kangaroo could hop across the room while they're in recovery, and they wouldn't remember it."

"Do you think he'll eventually remember why he wanted to see me?"

"Sorry. Probably not."

I didn't know whether to be relieved or disappointed.

Lynxx glanced at his watch. "I need to get back to my lab." After hooking the chart over the end of the bed, he left.

I sat with Asher, telling him of my temporary promotion to team leader and the earlier incident with the Wilder leader, Fang, at the Edge Complex. I kept my comments factual, not mentioning my concerns about Willow's semi-strange behavior. Maybe I'd imagined things. Besides, she seemed okay again.

Asher struggled to listen, but the painkillers were strong and he drifted off to sleep. *Good. Sleep will help him heal.* With a last pet of Fluffy's furry head, I left.

Willow was waiting in the main infirmary. "What did Ash say, Kass? Why did he ask for you?"

"He couldn't remember. He's groggy from painkillers, plus he can't talk until his neck heals some more."

"Oh. Well, I'm sure he wants to see me." She hurried down the hallway to his room.

I returned to the courtyard, now bustling with activity. Almost a dozen newcomers were scattered among various groups.

After this morning's battle at the Edge Complex, Fang had abandoned his gang and fled. The five surviving Wilder males had asked—*heck, they'd begged*—to join the Weston Battalion. All had been accepted under strict conditions. Now, two Wilder men were helping another man change the windshield of a damaged Hummer. A Wilder youth picked up trash from the pavers. Another transferred wooden boards from a pickup truck into the tower.

A short distance away, Zoey sat cross-legged on the pavers. The little girl wore a pink plastic tiara on her head, and she giggled as she tossed pieces of a Twinkie to three pigeons.

Smiling, I watched her.

The child lifted a toy wand and waved it at the pigeons.

One bird strutted forward, its wings outstretched. Pausing, it bowed to Zoey. When she clapped her hands in delight, the pigeon fluttered back to the other cooing birds.

Hurriedly, I joined her. "What ... what are you doing?"

She grinned. "Did you see the bird bow to me? I'm their princess."

"How did you train it to bow?"

"I just think it and they do it. I'm magic."

"No!" came a soft voice from behind. Nila gaped at the child. "She can't do that out here." Agitated, her gaze swept the courtyard. "They could be watching!"

"I don't think anyone noticed, Nila."

"Get her inside. Quickly. Then come and see me, Kass. I'll be in my lab." Nila rushed away.

I scribbled a note and gave it to Zoey. Excited, she ran inside Weston Tower.

When I arrived at Nila's lab, she was alone and pacing the floor. "Is Zoey inside?"

"Yes. I called in a favor. She's watching a Cinderella DVD in the children's play area."

"Good." She paused beside a potted zap terra on a lab bench.

"She's a hybrid, isn't she?"

"Yes, but not a pure hybrid from two hybrid parents. She's a cross." I nodded. Xavian had already told us that a human and a hybrid could have children. She continued, "I met Zoey and her parents a few months before the Mist. Nice couple. Carson was a Sphere hybrid. Diane was human. The other week, when that tumbleweed rolled toward the three girls in the courtyard, I recognized Zoey."

"So Zoey's able to mind-blend?"

"Not yet. She'll develop that power when she's a teenager. Until then, she'll just be able to do basic remote-pushing."

"She thinks she's doing magic."

"I'll talk to her. Explain that she can't remote-push in front of humans, especially out in the open. If humans find out that hybrids have enhanced mental powers, they'll fear us even more than they do now."

"Hiding that secret isn't the answer," I said, aware of the secrets I'd kept over the last year.

"Eventually we'll have to reveal our powers," she agreed. "But not now. We have much bigger battles to fight and survive, like the Chi'az and the Outriders."

"You're right." I glanced at the potted zap terra beside her. Its long gold leaves arched like a fountain of frozen water. "You must really like these terras."

"Not particularly. Every time I grasp a leaf, it zaps me—and it hurts."

"Um, so don't touch them?"

"I have to." She glanced around, making sure we were still alone. "The terra's electrical shocks temporarily enhance my mental powers."

"Excuse me?"

"That's how I'm able to make such fast progress with my work. Ten seconds pain for almost an hour of superintelligence."

"Are you serious?"

"Totally. But I can't hold the leaves for longer than ten seconds. If I get too big a shock, I could die."

Gingerly, she gripped a long gold leaf with her hand. Glittering gold sparks shot out, sizzling and crackling like steaks on a hot grill. Ten seconds later, she released the plant and staggered back. Sweat trickled down her forehead—into brown eyes that glinted with an unnatural brightness. "The effect only lasts an hour. Without the zap terra, I'd be weeks away from finishing my work."

"How many times a day do you zap yourself?"

"Three. That seems to be my limit."

Footsteps sounded in the hall.

We fell silent as Commander Powell entered the lab. "I thought I'd find you here, Nila."

"How's Asher, Lincoln?" she asked, lowering her unnaturally bright gaze to some papers on her desk.

"Getting better. He's asleep right now. Willow's sitting by his bedside, waiting for him to wake up."

Of course she was, I thought.

Powell leaned against a metal lab table. "Any questions, Kass, about your first mission as Liberty Team leader?"

When I blinked in confusion, Nila stepped forward, still averting her eyes from the commander. "Sorry. I haven't told her yet. We got sidetracked."

"What's the mission?" I asked.

They fell silent.

Uh-oh.

As Powell's pager vibrated, he said, "I need to go. Nila can fill you in, Kass. Everything she's about to tell you is in the strictest confidence. You can't discuss it with anyone. Understood?"

"Yes, sir."

I must've looked worried because he added, "Liberty Team will join Lieutenant Wu's squad tomorrow. It's a simple retrieval mission, that's all. Nothing to worry about. No pressure."

Ten minutes later, as Nila finished talking, I sat in shock.

Hopefully this joint mission would be as simple as the commander claimed.

But if it failed, every last person on Earth could die.

No pressure.

19

The next morning, a dawn mist layered the narrow river in Upper Manhattan.

Four soldiers straddled the inflatable sides of our black Zodiac, quietly pulling their paddles through the mist-veiled waters. Lieutenant Wu rested a hand near the rear motor, ready to switch it on at a moment's notice.

A thick silence surrounded us. No birds sang on the shore. No seagulls screeched overhead. No one spoke in the Zodiac.

Holding a paper map, I sat in the front of the boat and scanned the shoreline again.

We were a mile from our destination.

On the left, a wide road had once separated the water from the park beyond. These days, the road was buried beneath terra vines, and the park was almost a terra jungle.

I glanced at the three members of my team.

Natalie and Yuki gazed around with wide eyes; both were new to Liberty Team, replacing Pepper and Rusty, who'd died on the Florida mission. Booker had reluctantly pocketed his paperback when the engine was cut and the paddling began; now, he pushed his glasses up his nose and sighed, as though unhappy at swapping his wonderful fantasy novel for an ugly and bleak reality.

So far, our mission had gone well, although I wished we'd been able to park closer to the pickup point. But the no-go Red

Zone had grown from Washington Heights into a band across Manhattan Island.

Lieutenant Wu, fully recovered from his injuries, had left our armored Hummer near the southern edge of the Red Zone, and we'd continued up the river in the Zodiac.

As the mist began to dissolve, patches of the pale red sky appeared. The river was smooth and still, its surface only disturbed by the dip and pull of our paddles. No signs of dangerous terras or xans.

All conditions were good for our mission.

Hopefully, no one would die today.

Yesterday afternoon, I had listened in shock as Nila detailed the background to this mission.

Last year, after the Red Fever had failed to eradicate the human race, the Outrider hybrids had begun working on a more virulent virus to finish the job. During our recent mission to Florida, Bone had piloted a crop duster that had sprayed us with a black substance called the Threads 1.0. Fortunately, it had only made us sick.

"What about a vaccine?" I had asked Nila yesterday. "Didn't the Sphere have a vaccine against the Threads 1.0?" In fact, Lynxx and I had shared a dose.

"Yes, we had one. Trouble is, that earlier vaccine won't protect against the new Threads 2.0 that they're developing. We need the Outriders' latest vaccine."

"Do you have any of it?"

She shook her head. "It won't be ready until the Threads 2.0 is ready. Once their new virus is finished, the Outriders will finish their vaccine, administer it to their hybrid colleagues, and then release their latest Threads. I doubt we'll be able to steal a sample of their new vaccine in time to reverse engineer it. All the Sphere hybrids will be vulnerable to the Threads 2.0."

I knew how intensely the humanized Sphere hybrids wanted to destroy the Outriders and prevent the arrival of the Final Wave—the Chi'az invasion.

But how could this brilliant Sphere scientist, Nila, forget one very important fact?

"Plus every human," I reminded her sharply. "Every human is also vulnerable to the Threads 2.0, Nila."

"Of course. Of course."

"So how do we win?"

"By releasing my secret weapon first. I call it the Shimmer."

On the riverbank, a high-pitched cackle split the early-morning air.

In the Zodiac, people tensed. The soldiers stopped paddling, and Lieutenant Wu's hand tightened on his gun.

I pointed to a large cream-and-brown bird in a tree. "Just a kookaburra," I said, voice low. A *laughing jackass* as Lynxx had once called the Australian bird.

People relaxed a little and the boat moved forward again.

I peered through the thinning mist at the trees and sky, searching for a familiar golden eagle. Then I remembered and my shoulders slumped.

No WindLord-Lynxx was watching out for me today.

No Asher was leading Liberty Team; he was still in the infirmary, recovering from his injuries.

No Pepper was sharing the mission with me; my friend was dead.

I had even left Willow back at the garrison, unsure of her fitness for this mission. I'd assigned her to fetch coffee and food for Lynxx and Nila, who were working on Nila's formula for the Shimmer.

Today, I was on my own.

Yesterday Nila had explained to me, "My Shimmer is a self-replicating gas that can spread around the world in a matter of hours. It'll kill terra plants, xans, and unvaccinated hybrids."

"Is the Shimmer gas dangerous to humans?" I'd asked.

"Completely harmless to humans, Earth animals, and Earth plants."

"What about the Outrider hybrids?"

"They're only vaccinated against their Threads. The Shimmer will kill them."

"So it's a race. If the Shimmer is released first, we win and the Outriders die."

"Yes, Kass. And if the Threads 2.0 is released first, they win and we die."

Our Zodiac entered a strange section of the river. Fifty feet from the bank, hundreds of terra trees grew in the shallow waters, in a line parallel to the riverbank. This long leafy "wall" stretched into the distance.

We had two options.

We could keep our Zodiac to the right of the "wall." However, the trees would block our view of the bank, and we could go straight past our target, Ethan Steel, without realizing it.

Or we could take the Zodiac along the fifty-foot-wide section of water between the bank and the line of terra trees in the water. From there, we'd be able to see Steel at the pickup point.

Option Two was the logical choice.

Lieutenant Wu looked at me, his face tight with a silent question. *Are those terra trees in the water safe, Kass?*

I peered at them through my binoculars. Long curving branches that soared overhead. Masses of skinny leaves resembling green ribbons. Gray bumpy trunks. Small white flowers.

They were harmless ribbon terras. However, I couldn't guarantee that there was nothing dangerous living *in* the trees.

Frowning, I gave Lieutenant Wu a thumbs-up—followed by an open-handed rocking motion.

Safe. Probably.

When the Outriders had learned of the Sphere's plans, they had tried to stop the development of the Shimmer. They'd started by killing every Sphere hybrid they could find.

"That's why I came to New York," Nila told me in her lab yesterday afternoon. "I needed a place where I could finish developing the Shimmer in safety. But even here in the garrison, I can't relax."

"Why not?"

"I'm worried there might be Outrider spies in the Weston Battalion. As you know, hybrids look like humans. Since my arrival in New York, I've been extra careful. Bone has been searching for me for months. He almost found me in Florida. If I use my hybrid mental powers here in New York, I could attract the attention of an Outrider spy nearby—and if they find me, they'll kill me."

"Are there any spies in our garrison?"

"I honestly don't know. That's why it's important we keep this Shimmer a secret from most people here."

In silence, the soldiers paddled the Zodiac along the narrow channel created by the wall of ribbon terras.

The mist had been replaced by shadows from the branches overhead. Bees darted among the white flowers. Ribbon leaves floated on the water, releasing a familiar vomit-like stink. My nose crinkled. A dab of peppermint oil on my upper lip would've drowned out the stench, but I couldn't use it. As team leader, my priority was to keep my teammates alive, and smells were an important part of identifying terras.

To the left of the Zodiac, the water rippled.

My eyes narrowed. Were these ripples caused by the rise and fall of our paddles? No. They were too far away. Gone now.

Seconds later, a dark shape arrowed through the water, toward the Zodiac.

"Watch out!" I warned, voice low and urgent.

A scaly eel-like head darted from the water and lunged at a soldier peering over the Zodiac's side. The xan's mouth gaped, its fangs ready to clamp onto—

I remote-pushed. *Hard.*

The eel xan flew backward. Its neck twisted in midair with a loud snap, and the creature sank below the surface, bubbles marking its grave.

My colleagues glanced at each other, shocked at the close encounter and bewildered by the creature's abrupt death.

Stunned, I stared at the spot where the eel xan had disappeared. I'd only meant to remote-push the thing away. Instead, I'd remote-killed it.

Weeks ago in a huge onion terra, Willow's elderly guardian, Xavian, had remote-killed a huge diamondback rattlesnake. He'd done it deliberately.

My remote-killing today had been accidental. Unexpected. And frightening.

I needed to get control of my powers before I hurt someone.

Unnerved, I again scanned the overhanging ribbon terras and the nearby bank, hoping to see WindLord.

Nothing, of course. Lynxx was still back at the garrison, helping Nila in her lab.

There were eight other people in the Zodiac with me.

And yet I felt utterly alone.

According to Nila, the Shimmer was almost finished. All they needed was one last piece of the formula.

"I just found out," Nila told me yesterday, "that a Sphere mole in the Brethren has discovered the final piece. But he wants to be picked up from Upper Manhattan before he'll share it with us."

"So Bone and the Brethren are back in New York?"

"Yes."

"Why doesn't your mole just give you the rest of the formula?"

"It's his bargaining chip. Ethan Steel has lived among the Brethren for over a year. I guess he's become as suspicious and mistrusting as they are."

"So we have to rescue this Ethan Steel before he'll give you the final piece?"

"Exactly, Kass. He'll be at Casper Point at 9 a.m. tomorrow, waiting to be picked up."

I lowered my map. Casper Point—and the Sphere hybrid, Ethan Steel—were just around the bend in the river.

As soon as we returned to the garrison with the last piece, the formula would be finished. And the Shimmer gas would be prepared for release.

The prospect of reclaiming our planet was intoxicating. I almost felt lightheaded at the thought of walking the streets, seeing only Earth plants and Earth animals. I imagined waking up unburdened each morning, no longer worried about terras and xans and Outrider hybrids—or a Chi'az invasion.

Could these dreams come true?

Maybe.

If we could pick up Ethan Steel without alerting the nearby Brethren camp. *If* the hybrid actually had the final piece of the formula. And *if* the Sphere's Shimmer gas worked.

A lot of *ifs*.

Step one was to pick up Ethan Steel.

A simple retrieval mission, Commander Powell had told me yesterday.

I hoped he was right. This was my first time as team leader, and I longed to show the commander that I was worthy of his trust.

The splash of paddles ceased, and a couple of the soldiers softly swore. Our Zodiac had stopped at the bend in the channel. Here, a clump of ribbon terras stretched from the leafy "wall" to the shore, blocking our progress.

Lieutenant Wu rolled his eyes in frustration, then directed the boat to a clearing on the bank.

Leaving a guard with the moored vessel, we set off on foot.

20

LIEUTENANT WU AND I led the way, watching for dangerous terras. Twice, Liberty Team had to slash a path through some patches of strangler terras; other times, we detoured around them.

A quarter of a mile from the meeting point, we heard a noise that swelled louder and louder as we entered a grove of trees. High-pitched clicks. Everywhere. They merged into a racket that drilled through my eardrums and into my brain.

Click xans.

Masses of the critters clung to the branches of the surrounding trees. Their spiderlike bodies were covered in short black spikes, and each of their eight segmented legs had pincer claws. Although the venom in their pointed tails was only lethal to small creatures, it could sicken a human for days.

I shuddered, remembering the click xan that had grabbed me when I was mind-blended with a small frog, Hopalong.

Lieutenant Wu held up a hand, signaling caution.

Further in the grove of trees, something moved. Peering through my binoculars, I saw six gray krols hacking chunks of flesh from a dead antelope.

We crept onward, keeping to the shadows while moving as quietly as possible. The click xans' racket drowned out our footsteps, and the gray krols didn't notice us. A few minutes later, we left the noisy grove and the krols behind, to my immense relief.

Wincing, I shook my head, wondering if the racket had deafened me.

Overhead, two seagulls screeched. A twig cracked underfoot. Squirrels chattered on a branch.

I relaxed a little. Hearing intact.

As a man stepped out from behind a large boulder terra, my hand darted to my gun.

Six-foot tall. Middle-aged. Crew cut. Black-rimmed glasses. Gray pants, gray shirt, red armband. He matched Nila's description of the Sphere mole who'd been living with the Brethren for the past year.

Lieutenant Wu raised his rifle. "Identify yourself."

The man glanced around, nervous. "Ethan Steel."

"Password."

"Alaska." He shifted restlessly from foot to foot. "We need to leave right away. Stone and six recruits are overnighting in a building only a couple of miles away. They're loading the final canisters of chemicals. If Stone discovers I'm missing, he won't be happy." A tremor racked his body, and behind his thick glasses his eyes glittered with fear.

"Who's Stone?" Lieutenant Wu asked.

"Bone's second-in-command. A hybrid."

The name Stone fit with something Lynxx had told me a while back. *As a baby, every hybrid is named after a hard, inanimate object like steel, gun, blade, and so on.*

I stepped forward, Nila's instructions fresh in my thoughts. "Do you have the final piece of the formula, Steel?"

"Yes."

"Show us."

Ethan Steel tapped his head. "It's in here."

"Where's your backup copy? On a piece of paper somewhere?"

"Negative. I memorized it, then destroyed all physical copies. Safer this way."

"For who?" I asked, hiding my dismay.

"Me. If you want the formula, get me to Nila in one piece. The sooner the better." He scanned the forest behind him, still nervous. "The clock's ticking."

"What are you talking about?" I asked.

"The Outriders are making steady progress with their latest biological weapon. We need to release our Shimmer gas before they release their Threads 2.0."

I shuddered, remembering the ugly black threads that had gushed from Bone's crop duster. Long and sticky, they'd clung to our skin like poisonous black worms.

"What's the Brethren's location?" Lieutenant Wu asked Steel.

"They were working in that building I just mentioned, the one a couple of miles from here. But last night they loaded up their equipment. I think they're setting up a new lab somewhere else today."

"Where?"

"In Jersey City. That's all I know."

"How many people are in your Brethren group?"

"There are four hybrids: Bone and Stone plus two scientists. There are also twenty human recruits who do all the menial work. Twenty-four in all."

"Okay, let's move," Lieutenant Wu said to the man. "We have to go back through a patch of trees infested with click xans. Some krols may still be around, so be quiet. Stay in the middle of our group, Steel, and do exactly as instructed."

We made it through the noisy grove of trees with no problems—except for a budding headache deep in my brain. The krols were gone, possibly driven off by the brain-drilling clicks.

The commander's *simple retrieval mission* was going smoothly. So far.

We were only a hundred yards from the Zodiac when Lieutenant Wu held up a hand, halting us. He pointed at a clump of trees on our right.

Krols. Seven of them. Wooden spears clutched in clawed hands, they walked upright through the trees, their backs to us.

Breathing shallowly, I waited with the others. In a minute, the krols would be gone. We would be able to reach our boat and—

A buzzard dived from a tree. As it swooped past us, I glimpsed silver eyes.

The buzzard was mind-blended with a hybrid.

Lynxx?

I shook off the wild idea. Lynxx didn't like buzzards and would never mind-blend with one. Another hybrid was controlling this bird.

The silver-eyed buzzard circled around, flew above our group again, then gave an ear-splitting screech.

The seven krols whipped around—and saw us.

Brandishing their wooden spears, they charged.

Chaos.

Gunshots and shouts from us. Shrieks and screams from the oncoming krols.

The buzzard plunged toward the closest attacking krol. I felt a beat or something in the air. The buzzard's eyes reverted to their normal yellow color and, with an alarmed squawk, it disappeared above the treetops.

A moment ago, the closest krol's eyes had been dark. Now they flashed a hard silver.

The hybrid had mind-hopped from the buzzard into the krol.

Ethan Steel ran toward the Zodiac moored further down the riverbank. The krol with the silver eyes barreled after him. I ran after them both, revolver drawn but unable to fire in case I missed the krol and hit Steel.

If you want the formula, the man had said, *get me to Nila in one piece.*

With a savage snarl, the krol leaped at Steel and knocked him to the ground. Long claws slashed at the man's throat. Blood spurted in a red fountain. As the krol bent its fangs toward Steel's neck, I fired several shots that slammed it to the ground.

Another beat in the air. Nearby, a field mouse with silver eyes scurried away.

I dropped to my knees beside Steel, who gurgled as blood spurted from his ripped throat.

No no no no!

Even as I yanked a wad of bandages from my backpack and pressed them to his throat, I knew it was useless. The slashes were too deep and he'd lost too much blood. He'd be dead in minutes.

On the riverbank, soldiers and krols continued battling each other. I ignored them, tuning out the gunshots and shouts and cries. All that existed was this blood-soaked patch of ground and this dying man.

"I'm so sorry. Please tell me the formula. Don't let the Outriders win." As I spoke, I pressed one hand on his wad of bloodied bandages and rummaged through his pockets with the other. They were empty. "Nod if you kept a paper copy."

He stared at me with wide, pain-filled eyes. Shook his head a little.

"Ethan, tell me the missing piece of the formula."

He opened his mouth. Tried to speak. Only a gurgle came out.

I shoved a pen into his hand and placed a notepad beneath it. "Can you write it down?"

The pen fell from his weak, shaking fingers. Blood continued to seep through the bandages. His face grew paler.

He was dying.

The Outriders and the Chi'az were going to win. A new species would rule our world—and destroy it. The Threads 2.0 would wipe out the remainder of humanity.

Despair grew within me, along with an icy dagger of defeat. Everything we'd done, all our struggles to survive, had been for nothing.

Unless ...

21

Lynxx had once told me that hybrids could mind-blend with weak-minded humans.

What about a dying Sphere hybrid weakened by a severe injury? Can someone like me mind-blend with him? My heart clenched in terror at the idea. Even if I could somehow blend with Ethan Steel's hybrid mind—*no way, it's far too dangerous*—what if he died while I was in there? I'd die too.

But without that last piece of the formula, every person on Earth would die.

I sensed the man's life trickling away, the sands of his hourglass emptying.

Sick with fear, I lay on the dirt, focused on Ethan Steel—

—and threw my mind forward.

Flashes. Starbursts. A gray wall. Claustrophobia.

And then I was there.

Inside.

A midnight darkness swirled around me, totally different from Hopalong-frog's mind or Wings-albatross's mind, or even the gecko's mind. This one was acutely aware that he was dying. Grief and fear and pain crashed through me in drowning waves, along with black horror and razor-sharp regret. Was this how my sister Olivia had felt as she'd died? And my father? Charlotte? All the other people I'd loved and lost? The horror felt intense and real —and if I'd had a mouth, I would've screamed in anguish.

With a massive effort, I braced myself against the torment and mentally asked, *Ethan, can you hear me?*

His thoughts flickered weakly around me. *Y-yes.*

Tell me the formula. Quickly.

I'm dying, aren't I?

No time for lies. *Yes. But you can save countless lives. You were brave to infiltrate the Brethren for a year. Finish your mission. Tell me the formula.*

In the intense darkness, a chemical formula washed through me. It should've been as foreign and bewildering as Chinese, but it wasn't. I understood it. Imprinting the information in my mind, I felt Ethan Steel's life force evaporating like the mist earlier this morning. Desperately, I leaped from his dying mind—

—and back into my own.

Gasping, I sat up. Looked around. Saw I was in *me* again.

Thank goodness.

Ethan Steel lay nearby. The bloodied wad of bandages had slipped off his throat, revealing red slashes that gaped like silent shrieks. His eyes dimmed and his chest fell still.

Lieutenant Wu raced to us, blood streaming down his cheek from a deep cut. Beyond him, the ground was littered with krol bodies. No human fatalities, just injuries.

"He's dead, isn't he?" Wu cried. "We've lost our last hope."

"No, Lieutenant." I grabbed the pen and notebook from Steel's lifeless hand and scribbled a long line of chemical symbols across a page. "Just before he died, Steel told me the formula." I thrust the page at him. "Guard this with your life."

I began shaking so badly that I could barely stand. I longed to hide in a corner and cry from the horror and despair of my mind-blend with Ethan Steel, but I couldn't. I was still the team leader, responsible for the safety of others.

Somehow, I suppressed my shakes and held myself together. I tended to injuries. Helped our new team member, Yuki, hobble back to the Zodiac with his twisted ankle. Wrote out two more copies of the formula, just in case. Wrote up briefing notes for the commander.

By the time we reached Weston Tower, I felt as brittle as wafer-thin ice on a pond, but I couldn't break yet. Tight-faced, I forced myself to give verbal reports to people—Commander Powell, Lieutenant Wu, Nila—followed by a quick stop at the infirmary; Asher was asleep but improving. I avoided Lynxx, aware he'd know something was wrong as soon as he saw me.

Then I took an elevator to a damaged floor still closed off after the Sat-Fall. In the furthest corner of the furthest room, I sat against the wall, my knees to my chest.

Finally alone, I buried my face in my hands and allowed the horror of my mind-blend with the dying Ethan Steel to swirl through me once again.

Filled with a dark and depthless anguish, I wept.

22

THE NEXT MORNING, LYNXX approached me as I left the mess hall. "You didn't eat any breakfast."

"I wasn't hungry."

"You missed dinner last night too."

When I shrugged, he lowered his voice. "I heard yesterday's mission went bad."

"We got the formula," I replied flatly. "That makes it a success."

His anxious eyes searched my face. "Come with me."

He led me into an empty office. There, with the door closed, I quietly told him everything: The silver-eyed buzzard. The attack by the pack of krols. The hybrid-controlled krol slashing open Steel's throat. My mind-blend with Ethan Steel—

—and the black horror of being in the hybrid's mind as he lay dying. The jumble of fear, pain, grief, and regret. The chill of his death. My silent anguish.

I sat on the edge of a desk, staring sightlessly at the carpet. "All night I kept reliving the ordeal. Even now, a part of me feels back there, helpless, trapped in Ethan Steel's mind, swallowed by his darkness."

"I'm so sorry." Lynxx hesitated before gently saying, "I want to show you something."

"What?"

"You'll see."

We took the elevator to the twenty-fifth floor, closed since the Sat-Fall. Makeshift repairs sealed a wide hole in the external wall, and pieces of burned metal lay in the open office space. In a conference room, three windows were painted black; the fourth was half-open, allowing in sunlight.

"Welcome to the Aerie," Lynxx said.

I paused in the doorway.

A large nest of branches sat on a long desk. Two golden eagles stood beside the nest, sticks held in their beaks. At our appearance, they cocked their heads and studied us with solemn black eyes.

I recognized one of them. "That's WindLord."

"Right." He held out an arm and whistled. The other eagle fluttered onto it. "This is his mate, SkyLady." The female, larger than WindLord, had light brown feathers on her body and bands of white on her tail feathers.

"What are they doing here?"

"I've trained them to return to this office each day."

"Why?"

"It's much easier for me to mind-blend when I know where the eagles are. Otherwise, I have to blend with a random pigeon and fly around the city looking for them." He placed SkyLady back on the desk, and the two birds resumed weaving the sticks into their nest.

"Why not just stay blended with the pigeon?"

"Eagles are better. They're big, strong, and fast. Plus other birds don't attack them."

"True." I looked at the mass of sticks and twigs on the desk. "No eggs."

"Not yet. They just started building this aerie—eagle's nest—a few days ago. They now regard this place as home." He gave me a slow smile. "I'm sure they wouldn't object if we borrowed their bodies to go flying."

"Excuse me?"

"You take SkyLady. She's used to mind-blending and won't resist you." He pointed to a long couch in the office. "We can leave our bodies there. No one knows we're up here, so they'll be safe."

"I thought you had to help Nila with the Shimmer."

"She doesn't need me for the next couple of hours. She's still checking Steel's formula."

"So you know about yesterday's mission?"

"She told me everything after you guys got back. I wish I could've gone with you."

"Me too." I paused. "Why do you want me to go flying? I don't need to practice mind-blending. I know how to do it. I've done it with the frog Hopalong, the albatross Wings, the leaf-tailed gecko, and now Ethan Steel." I shuddered.

"Blending with a dying man was traumatic. It's left you depressed and miserable. You need some joy in your life, like flying. It'll balance out the gloom."

"I flew as Wings. It wasn't joyous."

"On that occasion, you were stressed as you searched the ocean for Owlfred-me. Today will be different. You'll love it. Trust me."

I hesitated, tempted to hide in an empty room again, but I'd done that all night, and I still felt bleak and drained. "Okay. Just for a little while, though."

Minutes later, we were outside in our eagle hosts, flying. We kept close to Weston Tower until I got used to mind-blending with SkyLady. Lynxx was right. The female eagle was compliant, and I was soon controlling her with effortless ease.

At first I flew mechanically, going through the motions to please Lynxx. But then, like ice melting, my stress and worry began to dissolve—

—and, finally, I embraced the wonder of flying.

SkyLady-me spread my wings as I soared through the air, weightless and free. A tilt of feathers, a glide of wings, the rush of wind and sunshine and life. This wasn't a frantic dash in an albatross, desperate to save Owlfred-Lynxx. This was a merging with the air that eclipsed anything I'd ever known before.

This was sheer bliss. Pure joy.

WindLord-Lynxx looked over at me, and his silver eyes seemed to hold a gentle satisfaction. *I told you so, Kassia.*

Eagle-me followed WindLord-Lynxx as we swooped down to the garrison courtyard, taking care not to get too close or attract attention. Other birds might not attack eagles—but we didn't trust Sergeant Thorne, who had deliberately shot poor Owlfred when we were on the trawler.

With the sharp vision of my eagle eyes, I quickly spied two familiar figures enjoying the sunshine. Asher wore a navy robe and had fresh bandages around his throat. He sat on a courtyard bench, chatting to people who stopped by to wish him a speedy recovery. Beside him, Willow smiled and nodded at the well-wishers with the grace of a queen, as though they were here to see her, not Asher.

My eagle eyes narrowed as I tried to calculate height and speed and trajectory. If I timed it just right, could I crown Queen Willow's head with some eagle droppings?

WindLord-Lynxx gave me a sharp whistle, as though guessing my plan. He veered off and flew along the street beyond the garrison.

Later, Willow.

I followed him.

We swept down city canyons and past buildings blurred by green terra vines, and we soared over rooftops layered in terra plants. Up, up we powered, to the warm thermals that flowed through the sky. Here, SkyLady-me spread my wings and glided next to WindLord-Lynxx on the rivers of air. Peace filled me as I surrendered to the freedom and bliss of being a part of the sky.

Too soon, WindLord-Lynxx swooped down and we returned to the office in Weston Tower.

After a quick mind-hop, we were back in our bodies, stretching. The two eagles shook their feathered heads and flew off outside.

Disappointed, I watched them leave. "Did we upset them?"

Lynxx brushed a feather off his black shirt. "They're probably getting more sticks for their nest or searching for some tasty rats."

I winced, glad SkyLady hadn't had an attack of the munchies while I was blended with her. Glancing at my watch, I said, "Were we really gone for an hour? It went so fast! When can we fly again?"

"I'm going out again later this afternoon. I want to try to find the Brethren's new lab in Jersey City. Lieutenant Wu and a squad have already started searching for it today."

I only hesitated a moment. "Count me in. What time are you leaving?"

"About 5 p.m. The eagles are usually back by then."

I did a quick calculation. This afternoon, Liberty Team's mission was to clear a patch of glow-lotus terras from the lobby of the Empire State Building. We'd be back well before 5 p.m. "See you then. And thanks for the flying. I loved it."

I headed down to the courtyard, but Asher was gone. By the time I got to the infirmary, he was asleep. His face had more color in it, his breathing was regular, and the bandages around his throat were free of bloodstains.

Soo-Yun assured me, "He all better maybe in few day. You wait for waking up? Willow here soon. She get treat for Asher from kitchen."

"Liberty Team has a mission," I said. "Please tell Asher I dropped by."

Just before five o'clock, I returned to the small office where Lynxx waited. The two eagles were there—hopefully having already eaten. Even though I was getting hungry, I didn't feel like rats for dinner.

Leaving our bodies on the couch, we mind-blended with the birds and headed for Jersey City.

23

THE TWO EAGLES WERE strong, fast fliers, and we were soon at our destination.

For over an hour we searched the southern part of Jersey City by air. Nothing except a few straggler humans. No signs of any groups. No soldiers posted outside hotels, apartments, or other buildings large enough to house twenty-four Brethren.

It was 8 p.m. by the time we reluctantly flew back to Weston Tower. Forty minutes of flight each way, plus one and a half hours of searching, added up to almost three hours away from the garrison. If we were gone any longer, someone could notice our absence.

Besides, Lynxx had warned me that three hours was the comfortable limit for mind-blending. After that, our bodies could start waking up without our minds in them—and that, he stressed, could be dangerous.

Over the next few days, Lynxx and I met in the Aerie late each afternoon, then flew to Jersey City, widening our search for the Brethren.

Finally, on the sixth day, we found them. They were in a five-story building that sported a sign partially covered with terra vines: Crendell Laboratories. Two armed men in gray coveralls guarded the front door.

WindLord-Lynxx and SkyLady-me perched on a nearby roof. From here, we saw Bone and a youth exit the rear of the building and pace an adjoining parking lot.

Bone scanned the deserted area, alert for trouble. His gaunt face looked like skin stretched over a skull, and his thin body moved with the difficulty of someone whose muscles were wasting away.

Was he sick? If so, had his illness warped his personality? Or had he always hated humans?

Although Bone and the teenage boy spoke in low voices, our eagles' sharp hearing allowed us to listen to their conversation.

"Should have killed *Sssteel* myself," Bone hissed, his gray-clothed body rigid with a quiet fury.

I tensed. *Steel.* The Sphere hybrid, Ethan Steel, had infiltrated the Brethren and discovered the last piece of the formula Nila had needed.

"His *papersss?*" Bone hissed at the boy. "Anything there?" As before, he spoke in a clipped manner, as though too tired to waste energy on unnecessary words.

"No, sir. I've spent the past few days going through boxes of his notes. The formula's gone."

The boy's voice sounded familiar. Like the armed guards, he wore the gray overalls of a recruit—a human who'd been persuaded into helping the Outriders by promises of protection and survival.

"Traitor!" Bone crushed an empty soda can between his two hands, the movement deliberate and vicious, as though visualizing crushing Ethan Steel's head. "Stone, in buzzard, clawed open Steel's throat. Good. Steel not talk to Weston Battalion now."

Eagle-me squinted at the back of the teen's head. The thick brown hair looked familiar too.

The boy turned. His face was thinner than before, his hair longer, but he still had the same handsome square jaw and dark brown eyes.

Jase Harris.

My cousin Charlotte's boyfriend. My high school crush. The boy who I had lived with for a week after the Mist, when we'd banded together for company and survival. The boy who had abandoned me when I was sick and dying, so he could join a group of survivors heading to Florida.

I should've guessed that Jase would end up working for the bad guys. He hadn't changed. He was still looking out for number one.

"Should we be worried about the Weston Battalion?" asked Jase, his voice deep and rich. Once, it had made me weak with longing; now it only made me sick with disgust.

"No," Bone replied. "Steel not know of Chi'az *ssscouts*. Not know some on Earth."

WindLord-Lynxx and I glanced at each other, shock turning our eagle eyes rounder than usual.

My bird heart pounded. *Chi'az scouts on Earth?*

Unlike the kids and teenagers who had worn colorful scout ties and badges, I knew the Chi'az scouts would have a far more sinister mission. I guessed they were gathering information for the invasion.

When had they arrived? I wondered. How many were here? What did they look like? Where were they? Did this mean the invasion was soon?

With a grim death-smile, Bone continued, "Plus Steel not know of Lightning One." He looked up, his death-smile thinning. "On time."

Above the parking lot, the air quivered and I glimpsed faint pieces of a rainbow. A bus-sized bubble emitted a soft hum as it descended. The humming ceased. The air stopped quivering. The rainbow vanished.

One moment, the weedy asphalt was empty. The next moment, a large white object was parked on it. As long and wide as a school bus, it was shaped like a white bullet with rounded edges. A strange ripple covered its surface.

My eagle beak gaped in shock.

It was a spacecraft.

24

LATER THAT EVENING, LYNXX and I told Commander Powell about the small spacecraft at Crendell Laboratories. We claimed that "Goldie," one of Lynxx's contacts, had given us the tip.

Commander Powell hurriedly called a closed-door meeting with a select group of people, including Lieutenant Wu, Sergeant Thorne, Nila, Lynxx, and me.

Asher also attended, having made a rapid recovery from his injuries.

Commander Powell clasped the boy on the shoulder. "Are you sure you're up to this, son?"

"It's been a week since my operation, sir. Dr. Tran's given me the all clear." His bare neck looked almost normal, except for a pink tinge. "Apparently Lynxx's terra meds sped up the healing."

"At least those freaking plants are useful for something," Powell growled.

Nila shifted restlessly at the conference table, as though impatient to get on with the meeting.

That evening, Operation Lightning-Threads was born. Its twin objectives were to destroy the Brethren's new lab in Jersey City and to secure the spacecraft.

Commander Powell asked Nila, "Did the Sphere know about the Chi'az scouts on Earth? And their ship?"

"Yes."

"Why didn't you tell us?"

"You couldn't have done anything," she replied with a shrug. "Hopefully you *can* do something about Bone."

Lieutenant Wu assured her, "We'll have the element of surprise, plus soldiers, planning, and weapons on our side."

"Good." Nila paused, then quietly told us, "I've finished integrating Steel's formula into my work. The Shimmer will be ready in a week, so we should increase the security outside my lab." She turned to Lynxx. "I need you to monitor things here tomorrow." Her unspoken implication was clear. She trusted Lynxx more than other people. Was it because he was a hybrid like her?

Lynxx cast me an alarmed glance, clearly worried he wouldn't be able to help out as WindLord during tomorrow's mission. I gave him a faint nod. *We'll be okay.*

"Fine," he reluctantly told Nila. "I'll stay in the lab until you return."

"Return?" Commander Powell looked at Nila. "Where are you going?"

"On the mission," she replied.

"Out of the question. You're too valuable to risk."

"I won't be in the firing line, Lincoln. I'll be with Liberty Team. They'll be entering Crendell Laboratories by the rear entrance."

"What if—?"

"According to the Sphere's intelligence, there were only two Chi'az ships on Earth. The Sphere stole the second one—Lightning Two—from Mexico a few months ago. That's the one I learned to fly."

"Where's Lightning Two now?"

"Sabotaged by an Outrider spy in our group. Since then, we've been desperate to get our hands on the remaining ship, Lightning One. But we couldn't find it. Until now."

"Why's the Sphere so eager to get a Chi'az ship?"

"Because of their hyperdrives."

"What's that?"

"It's a propulsion system capable of incredible speeds. As I just told you, the Shimmer gas will be ready for release in a week. Using the hyperdrive, we could distribute half a dozen drums of the gas around the world in a few hours."

"A few hours?" Powell gasped.

"Yes." She gave a faint smile. "The Shimmer should destroy every terra plant, xan, Outrider hybrid—and any Chi'az already here." Her smile disappeared. "Unfortunately, if the Outriders have Lightning One, they can distribute their Threads globally in a few hours too. We can't let them beat us."

"So if the Outriders have the ship," Powell said, "they win?"

"Probably," she replied "That's why I need to go on tomorrow's mission. I'm the only person in the Weston Battalion who can fly the ship back to the Weston Garrison. Plus I can figure out the safest way to destroy any canisters of Threads we find at Crendell Laboratories."

Powell hesitated, then nodded.

After the meeting, Asher took me aside. "How are you feeling? No symptoms of your previous condition?" The word *leukemia* hovered in the air.

"I feel fine," I replied, meaning it. "Completely normal."

"Good."

"*You're* looking much better, Asher."

He took my hands, his blue eyes soft. "Thanks for visiting every day. I always felt better after you stopped by the infirmary."

"You had lots of visitors," I reminded him, my heartbeat quickening at the warmth in his gaze. "Willow was constantly by your bedside."

"She's not you."

Did he still have feelings for me? Or was I misreading him?

Flustered, I changed the topic. "We should leave Willow here tomorrow."

"Why? She's a good fighter, and she'll be upset at being sidelined."

"We may be rushing her a bit."

"How?"

I was tired of dancing around the truth. Time to be blunt. "Sometimes when Willow's with Liberty Team, she's not Willow. She's Pandora, the character she played on her TV show."

"What are you talking about?"

"She acts like Pandora, she speaks dialogue from the show, and she gets this distant look on her face, like she's off in her own world."

His eyes turned cool. "Are you saying she's mentally ill?"

"No, but I think she's more fragile than she lets on." As he stiffened, I hurriedly added, "You can make up your own mind about her over the next few days, Asher. Till then, keep her in the garrison. Commander Powell trusted me with Liberty Team when you were in the infirmary. Now I'm asking you to trust me about Willow."

He huffed off, not replying.

The next morning, he assigned Willow to help Chef Einstein in the kitchen.

At 8 a.m., our fleet of silent electric vehicles headed for Crendell Laboratories. Stopping two blocks from our target, we continued on foot, keeping to the morning shadows that spilled from the buildings onto the roads.

Asher led Liberty Team, looking even fitter and healthier than last night. However, from the cool way he spoke to me, I sensed he was still upset at my comments about Willow.

We hurried down the sidewalk, scanning for terras. Lots of harmless ones. No dangerous ones. So far, so good.

A bird fluttered onto a nearby trash can. My heart leaped, then sank again. It was a falcon, not an eagle. Black eyes, not silver.

Disappointment coursed through me. Lynxx was back in the lab at Weston Tower. I had to stop expecting—*hoping*—to see WindLord during my missions.

Lieutenant Wu and a dozen soldiers waited at the corner of Crendell Laboratories as Sergeant Thorne, five soldiers, and Liberty Team headed to the rear of the building.

I took my position near the rear entrance, relieved there were no Brethren guards back here. And no sign of Lightning One. The large parking lot adjoining the building only held an old van overgrown with terra vines.

Stretched along the rear wall were two wide garage doors, both closed. Was the ship behind one of them? Or was it at another location?

My stomach roiled at the thought of the oncoming battle. Hopefully, it would be short, with low casualties.

I checked my watch. Nearly time.

Beside the parking lot, a fenced-off playground held a swing that hung as limp and empty as a fading dream. Had I ever swung back and forth on swings? Had I ever laughed and called out to my friends and family in playgrounds? Lately, my happy childhood memories were starting to feel unreal, like scenes from an old movie.

At the head of the line, Sergeant Thorne raised a hand. *Get ready.*

Gunshots erupted from the front of the building.

Lieutenant Wu and his men had engaged the enemy.

25

At the rear door, Sergeant Thorne and three soldiers sprang into action.

Raising their assault rifles, they burst into the building and barreled up the stairs. Nila, Booker, and two soldiers followed behind, hugging the wall as a shooter on an upper landing sprayed bullets down the stairs.

Asher and I headed left, the strain between us forgotten. We were united in our focus on the mission—and on our survival.

Cautiously, we entered an enormous commercial garage.

No vehicles. No Lightning One ship.

At the top of the metal garage door, sunlight streamed through four thin ventilation slots, bathing the area in hazy light. Tall metal shelves lined the walls, crammed with boxes, bottles, and cobwebs. Metal drums were piled in front of the shelves, and the high roof was dark with shadows that rustled and shifted.

Two men entered through a door on the opposite side. Both wore white lab coats with red armbands. These had to be the two Outrider scientists that Ethan Steel had mentioned.

Seeing us, they darted behind a stack of drums and began shooting.

Oh no. They were *armed* Outrider scientists.

Asher and I crouched behind some drums and returned fire.

Overhead, the darkness jittered as bats fled their roosts and, squeaking in panic, exited through the ventilation slots at the top of the garage door. Rats dropped from shelves and scampered into corners.

The garage echoed with the sound of bullets ricocheting off the metal walls and drums and—

A deafening explosion boomed as a drum on our far right burst into flames. Asher and I dived behind a stack of boxes, where he hunched over me protectively. My brow rose in surprise. Did he still care about me? Or was he just being his usual white knight self?

Smoke saturated the air with a sharp stench that scratched my throat and stung my eyes. For the first time, I read the stickers on the other drums. *Dangerous chemicals. Highly flammable.*

In the firelight, long thin shapes slithered across the floor, and I groaned in dismay. *Snakes.* I should've guessed they'd be living in here, hunting the rats and bats.

Asher shoved his gun into his belt. "This garage is a powder keg. One stray shot and the whole place could go up." On the far side of the garage, the gunfire abruptly stopped. He gave me a grim smile. "I think the guys shooting at us have reached the same conclusion."

"So what do we do?" I whispered. "Wait here for reinforcements?"

Outside, the gunfire and shouts intensified as the battle continued.

"That might be a while." He unsheathed a hunting knife with a serrated blade. "I'll circle behind the drums and take them by surprise."

"Too dangerous. It'll be two to one. I'll come with you."

"Forget it. You're not physically strong enough for hand-to-hand combat against those men."

"True." But I was mentally strong enough to use my powers against the scientists, if I got close enough. That would even the odds—

—except both of the scientists were Outrider hybrids. In that case, once Asher and I were within range, they'd use their mental powers against *us*.

Knife in hand, Asher began to move off. I grabbed his arm, tugging him back. "We need to go together."

Something thudded onto the floor a couple of yards away.

Startled, we turned.

A six-foot snake reared up, tail blurring in a rattled warning, fangs bared and ready to strike.

Gasping, I remote-pushed the rattlesnake into a distant corner.

Asher gaped after it. "What the—?"

New thuds sounded on our right as more snakes dropped near us.

"Don't move, Asher."

Desperately, I remote-pushed them away, flicking my attention from one to the other and the next: the diamondback about to strike Asher's leg, the rattler that had just missed my head as it fell, two small black snakes, a longer gray-scaled viper.

As fast as they fell, I remote-pushed the snakes behind distant boxes or into far corners. Some I slid across the floor. Others I remote-pushed through the air, uncaring of Asher's stunned expression.

"What's happening?" he cried. "Where are they coming from?"

I glanced up. "The rafters," I lied. The scientists knew they couldn't shoot because of the drums of explosive chemicals. Instead, they were remote-throwing the snakes at us, hoping we'd get bitten and die.

Clever.

I wished I'd thought of it first.

Finally the snake-fall stopped and I sagged with fatigue, my head aching. I eyed the shadowy corners. Maybe I could remote-push the snakes back toward the scientists.

Nope. Bad idea. They'd just remote-throw them at us again. Breathing heavily, I looked around for other weapons.

A large light shade crashed to the floor, missing Asher and me by inches and showering us with broken glass.

"Cripes," he whispered, pulling me away from the twisted debris. "This place is a death trap."

"Let's get out of here."

"You go. Get help, if you can. I'll wait here. I can't let those men escape."

"No way." I couldn't leave Asher alone with the Outrider scientists. He had no idea what he was up against—which was why, I suddenly realized, I would have to tell him the whole truth about hybrids and their mental powers. But not now. *Survive first. Confess later.* "I'm staying."

At the top of the garage door, I glimpsed movement.

A large jellyfish terra, big and red as a party balloon, had squeezed through a ventilation slot. It floated inside the garage, drawn by our shouts, its translucent body filled with blood from a recent feed. Tentacles waving, it glided toward the scientists.

I had an idea.

Must act quickly.

26

UNCLIPPING MY KNIFE, I threw it as hard as I could.

It arrowed through the air. Midway across the garage, I gave it a massive remote-push that sparked pain behind my eyes. Blinking it away, I watched the knife plunge into the jellyfish terra, popping it like a balloon.

Awed, Asher murmured, "Good arm!"

Blood rained on the two men below.

Shouting and swearing, they fled from their hiding spot. Frantically brushing the blood off their faces, one yelled, "It's burning."

Huh! Were the jellyfish fluids acidic?

Asher stepped out from our shield of boxes. Feet astride, he aimed his gun at the distracted scientists and pulled the trigger. Once. Twice. The shots thundered through the garage. When both men slumped to the floor, he ran across and pumped more bullets into their bodies.

Shocked, I stared at him. I'd never seen Asher kill anyone in cold blood before.

Avoiding my gaze, he rejoined me. "It was them or us. This is war."

In the neighboring garage, metal clanked as though a roll-up door was slowly rising.

Asher and I bolted outside and saw Lightning One in the next garage. For the first time, I noticed thin horizontal windows across the front and down the side of its hull. As its engine began humming, a faint rainbow flickered across the whole ship.

Bone was loading two large black canisters into the ship via an open hatch. Seeing us, he shouted to someone inside, "Take off, Stone!" He threw himself inside Lightning One, firing blindly behind him.

We hit the ground amid a hail of bullets.

"Are you okay?" Asher asked.

"Yes. You?"

"Fine."

I glanced at Lightning One. The hatch was closed and the engine hum began increasing.

"Bone is getting away," I cried as we scrambled to our feet. "Those black canisters could contain chemicals for the Threads."

And then—

—a massive explosion filled the garage. It engulfed Lightning One in a cloud of billowing black smoke and raging flames.

Asher pushed me behind him, ever the protector.

Indignant, I stepped up beside him, saying, "We're out of the blast zone."

Together, we watched the roiling fireball. Had a stray bullet struck a drum of chemicals in the garage?

Behind the garages, I heard explosions from inside Crendell Laboratories and the sound of windows shattering.

"We've lost Lightning One," I groaned.

"Maybe not. It could have a super strong hull. Or it could have a vulnerable hull that's protected by some sort of force field—"

"—that may or may not be turned on."

At the rear of the building, the billowing smoke parted as the ship emerged from the fireball. Its hull was blackened and dented, and its former engine hum was now a moan—but it lifted into the air, tilting at an awkward angle, and slowly flew away.

"Come on." Asher ran toward a tall office building on the far side of the parking lot.

I followed him up a fire escape and onto a flat rooftop that overlooked part of Jersey City. Crossing to the parapet, we focused our binoculars on Lightning One in the distance. The ship was still flying at an awkward angle, with red smoke streaming from its damaged hull like a spray of blood.

It vanished behind some tall buildings. Moments later, a loud bang sounded, followed by a plume of red smoke.

"It crashed," I cried.

"We need to get that ship before *they* do." Asher gestured to a pickup racing along the street below. A man in gray coveralls stood on the open cargo area, holding on to the cabin roof with one hand and pointing to the expanding smoke plume with the other.

My eyes narrowed. "Brethren recruits."

"Yep. They want their messiah back—and the ship."

"We have to get to Lightning One first."

"Our guys are trying." Below, two armored vehicles from the Weston Battalion were tearing along the street, trailing the recruits' pickup truck. In the distance, the red smoke had spread beyond the tall buildings, increasing the possible area of the crash. "We can't let the Outriders get it."

The needs of the many outweigh the needs of the one.

Stopping the release of the Threads was critical. It was more important than my secret mental powers. More important than my place in the Weston Battalion. And more important than my relationship with Asher.

Still, the thought of risking everything on a Hail Mary was frightening.

But I had no choice.

I had to use my mental powers right now in front of Asher—even if it meant losing him forever.

Nearby, pigeons cooed in their rooftop coops.

I drew in a deep breath. "Asher, listen carefully." When he turned to me, I lay down on the filthy concrete rooftop. "I'm about to fall unconscious—"

"What's wrong with you?"

"—but don't worry, I'm fine. I'll only be unconscious for a little while. You need to guard my body until I get back—"

"What are you talking about?"

"—however, if anything happens to me, Lynxx will explain."

"*What?*"

I focused on the biggest pigeon in a nearby coop and mind-leaped into the bird.

<h1 style="text-align:center">27</h1>

As PIGEON-ME LAUNCHED INTO the air, I glanced down.

On the rooftop, Asher was crouching beside my non-conscious body. "Kass. Kass!"

No time to worry about the cost of my decision. In some ways, I was relieved that he and the others would soon know my secret. I was tired of living a lie.

Mind-blended with the pigeon, I flew past the pickup and the two armored vehicles racing along the street below. Ahead, the red smoke from the crash had drifted across several blocks near the riverbank. I stayed high and scanned the area with my sharp bird eyes.

There.

Lightning One had crashed in the middle of a street, smoke trailing from its—

Pigeon-me glimpsed movement on my left.

A dark shape. Wings wide. Talons outstretched as it shot down.

Hawk.

Tiny heart thudding, I darted right—and the talons missed me by a feather.

Lynxx's warning echoed in my thoughts. *If a host dies while you're mind-blended with it, Kassia, you'll die too.*

Up, up I flew, frantically winging away—

—but the hawk was fast. It narrowed the distance between us. The tips of its talons started to close around my feathered body. *No!* The hawk was going to impale pigeon-me. Its claws would piece our heart and we'd both die—the pigeon and me.

No escape.

No time to think.

Desperately I pushed my mind *out*, through the starbursts, beyond the gray thickness. I plunged into another sponginess, a different mind, sharper, predatory.

I was in the hawk.

Instantly, I opened my talons. The pigeon bolted free, trailing bloodied feathers in its wake.

Within the hawk, my new host's mind struggled against me. I pushed back, almost a shove. Another shove, harder this time, and the agitated struggles simmered down.

I *was* the hawk.

I'd never mind-hopped between two creatures before. Hadn't planned on doing it today. Or ever.

No time to dwell on my fear and excitement.

Focus on Lightning One.

Hawk-me swooped down to the damaged ship. I darted through the open hatch, half-expecting Bone to slam a baseball bat into my small feathered body.

Nothing.

The interior's walls were marble-smooth, with long narrow windows on either side. Toppled boxes and tools cluttered the floor.

No sign of the two black canisters.

At the front, a stranger—probably Stone—lay slumped over a flat control panel. Blood trickled from his crushed skull, down his forehead, into his lifeless eyes. The previous groaning-humming engine now lay silent.

Both Lightning One and Stone were dead.

And Bone was gone. Had the missing canisters contained chemicals for the Threads 2.0?

I flew up and down the streets and between the vine-covered buildings, peering through broken windows, listening for noises. Nothing. Either Bone had fled the area or he was well hidden.

No time to keep searching for him. I could hear engines in the distance: the throaty growl of the Brethren pickup, followed by the higher pitch of the Weston Battalion vehicles, no longer in silent mode.

We had to secure Lightning One first.

Wings powering as fast as possible, hawk-me raced back to the rooftop.

Asher was still kneeling beside my body. Clasping one of my limp hands, he shouted into his radio, "I don't know what happened. Kass babbled some nonsense, then fell unconscious."

Huh! I don't babble. And it wasn't nonsense.

I flew down to my body and leaped from my hawk host.

"Asher, I'm okay." As I sat up, I saw pigeons bolt from their coops in a flurry of fear and scattered feathers. My hawk host pursued them, apparently fine after our mind-blend. *Go, pigeons.*

"Hang on, she's okay." He switched off his radio. "Kass. What happened? Is it your leukemia?"

"No, I'm fine." I jumped to my feet. "Radio our two vehicles. Tell them that Lightning One crashed near the docks beside the riverbank. It's behind an orange-and-black building with three flagpoles on its roof."

"What? How do you know where it is?"

"Tell them! Otherwise the Brethren could find the ship first."

At my sharp urgency, he radioed the location to our vehicles. Clicking off, he faced me. "What's going on? Why did you fall unconscious? And how could you know where the ship crashed? Those buildings are blocking our view."

"I'll explain later. Right now, reaching Lightning One first is our priority."

He hesitated, then radioed Lieutenant Wu with the crash location.

"Roger," the lieutenant responded. "My men and I will head there now."

"What about Crendell Laboratories?"

"All secure here. Out."

Asher didn't speak as we clattered down the fire escape and rushed back to the laboratory. Every time he glanced at me, I felt the pressure of his unanswered questions.

By the time we reached Crendell Laboratories, twenty-two bodies lay lined up outside. Most were Brethren recruits, along with the two hybrid scientists.

I recognized three familiar faces among the dead. Private Khan and his brother were Pakistani exchange students who'd struggled with homesickness. The third fatality, Corporal Nouwen, was Sergeant Thorne's best friend.

Other soldiers were injured, none seriously.

Asher asked a nearby soldier, "Where's Nila, Corporal?"

"She went with Lieutenant Wu to retrieve the ship, sir."

Three people in gray coveralls stood nearby, guarded by our soldiers.

"Who are they?" Asher asked Booker, who was passing bandages to Juliet, the new medic.

"Recruit prisoners, boss. There were two more, but they shot themselves rather than be taken alive. Stupid brainwashed fanatics."

My cousin's boyfriend, Jase, was one of the gray-clad prisoners. Obviously he'd chosen his own survival over the cult's ideology. Whenever I looked at him, I remembered my fear and despair as he'd walked away from me in Central Park that day.

Weak, sick, and alone, I'd considered killing myself.

Thank goodness I hadn't.

I hoped Jase was now feeling some of the fear I'd felt.

"Kass," said Asher, his eyes still heavy with questions from earlier, "we need to talk."

"Later. Not here. Not now."

Frustrated, he strode toward the brick building, where smoke drifted from broken windows. "Have it your way. I'm heading inside."

At the sound of gunshots, I jerked around.

Sergeant Thorne was standing over the bodies of two of the prisoners, his face twisted with fury. He turned toward Jase, who stood rigid with shock.

28

"STOP, SERGEANT!" I CRIED, running toward them.

Thorne ignored me and raised his weapon.

Instinctively, I remote-shoved. Thorne's gun flew from his hand and skidded across the ground. Swearing, he scurried to retrieve it.

Asher shouted, "Stand down, Sergeant Thorne!"

"These traitors killed my buddy. They deserve to die."

"Stand down! That's an order. Commander Powell will want to interrogate this recruit. He could have some useful information."

Thorne stormed off.

Frowning, Asher again strode toward Crendell Laboratories.

I noticed that Thorne hadn't commented on the gun flying from his hand. Had he dismissed it as an accident? Sometimes people ignored things they didn't understand.

I caught up with Asher. "Thorne just murdered two unarmed people."

"Unarmed doesn't mean innocent. Those *people* worked for the enemy."

"They surrendered."

"No, we beat them. We're in a fight for our very survival, Kass. We don't have the time or the resources to handle long-term prisoners." Stopping, he faced me. "We need to talk."

I glanced around. Soldiers were moving in and out of the front entrance, close enough to hear our conversation. "Later."

He opened his mouth, ready to argue, but his radio crackled into life.

Lieutenant Wu said, "We've secured the ship."

"Where was it?" Asher asked.

"Behind the building you described."

"Any survivors?"

"None," Wu replied. "There's a dead man slumped at the controls. No sign of Bone."

"What about those Brethren recruits?"

"We can hear their pickup now. They won't be a problem. We can handle them."

I moved off, eager to get away from Asher and his questions.

Jase was still under guard, and as I passed by, he called out, "Thanks, miss."

Miss? Didn't he recognize me?

"For what?" I asked, pausing.

"Saving my life." Casually, Jase stepped over the bodies of the two men who'd just been shot. "That wacko sergeant was going to kill me."

"Maybe you deserve to die."

"Why?" He scowled at me without the slightest trace of recognition on his face. "For being chosen?"

"What are you talking about?"

"Bone chose me to help him in his quest."

"You mean, to wipe out the remainder of humanity."

"Humanity was doomed anyway. We'd polluted the planet beyond belief. Clogged the air with filth. Poured sewage and trash into the oceans. Every day, more and more people were being born. But there weren't enough resources for the ones already struggling to survive." His comments sounded like rehearsed excuses to justify mass murder.

Disgusted, I asked, "Is that why you helped the enemy?"

"It's the law of the jungle. Survival of the fittest."

"More like massacre of the innocents."

"You don't understand."

"What? That you're deluded?"

He fell silent, studying me. I could almost hear the gears and levers whirring in his brain. Abruptly, his scowl disappeared and he forced his lips into a winning smile.

"You're beautiful." His voice dripped with admiration. "Perhaps we can continue our debate later. I'm always happy to spend time with a hot girl. You look really familiar. Have we met?"

I felt like slapping the smirk off his face. This boy had abandoned me when I was sick. Today, he was the one who needed help. Did he really believe he could charm me with his fake smiles and compliments?

Liberty Team's newest recruit, Natalie, poked her head from an upstairs window. "Hey, Kass, you gotta see this."

Jase's head snapped toward me, recognition finally dawning. "Kass? Kass Madison?"

I left him staring open-mouthed as I hurried into the building.

Upstairs, I joined Asher and a group of people clustered around something in the middle of the wrecked room.

A body lay among the smoking rubble, its skin blackened by the explosion that had destroyed this lab. It was about eight feet tall, with an overlarge head, no neck, four elongated limbs, and a skinny torso.

Natalie's eyes glittered with excitement. "Look!" The ex-cheerleader was bright and perky and seemed unfazed by the surrounding horror. "This might be a Chi'az scout!"

"Maybe," I replied, unconvinced.

Asher ordered two men to tie the smoldering body to the tray of a pickup parked outside. "Kass and I will drive it to the garrison."

I stifled a groan. He was making sure we were alone on the trip back to Weston Tower.

Fifteen minutes later, we headed off in the pickup, its tray laden with the strange burned body. Asher drove a couple of blocks in silence, then slowed for some "traffic." A herd of bison stretched across the street, grazing on straw-grass terras. The large animals, twenty or thirty, ignored our vehicle and only reluctantly moved aside when Asher blasted the horn.

On our left, tiny xan insects buzzed in a bush, watched by crabben xans in the straw-grass. Monkeys clambered over abandoned cars, and deer ambled down a side street.

None of these non-terrestrial creatures or wild Earth animals belonged here.

Or perhaps *humans* didn't belong here anymore.

When we were past the bison, Asher said, "Okay, Kass. No more stalling. Talk."

I hesitated. Clearly, it was important to tell people about the hybrids' ability to mind-blend, remote-push, and remote-kill, but this revelation would affect Lynxx too. Did I have the right to reveal his secret without warning him first? Which was more important? My allegiance to humans—or to Lynxx?

I sighed. In order to fight the Outrider hybrids, humanity needed to know the truth about their mental powers. Now.

Sorry, Lynxx.

There, in a battered pickup, with a tarpaulin-covered body tied to its back tray, I confessed the last of my secrets to Asher.

I reminded him of the poisonous buckshot-pod terra that had sliced my hand back in Grand Central Station. I told him again how Lynxx's hybrid blood had mixed with my own. And then I detailed the gradual development of my hybrid powers, from remote-pushing through to mind-blending.

Asher's knuckles whitened on the steering wheel. "So when you were slumped on the rooftop a little while ago, you weren't inside your body? You were flying around in a *pigeon?*"

"*Mind-blended* with a pigeon, then a hawk. My consciousness was inside the birds, in control."

"You've done this before?"

"A few times."

Shock had paled his face, highlighting the scar on his cheek. "Can Lynxx do these things too?"

"Yes. All hybrids can, once they become teenagers."

At a loud sound, I turned. In the tray, the tarpaulin was moving and flapping, and for an awful moment, I thought the burned body was struggling to break free of its ropes.

Asher glanced in his rearview mirror. "It's okay. Just the wind." He resumed our conversation. "These hybrids are more dangerous than we suspected."

"Yes."

"Can they mind-blend with humans?"

"No. Well, mostly no."

"Mostly?"

"They can blend with a person who's very sick or weak or dying. Plus they can blend with a lunatic or a baby."

"Cripes!" His eyes narrowed. "You've known about your powers for months, haven't you?"

Anxiety fluttered in my chest. I knew what was coming. "Yes."

"Yet last month, you told me—again—that you had no more secrets. You were lying, right? *Again.*"

My anxiety stiffened into self-defense. "I didn't ask for these mental powers, Asher, just as I didn't ask for leukemia. Or the Red Mist. Or to lose my family and friends ... and me."

"You? What are you talking about?"

"I'm not the same girl that I was before the Mist. Lynxx's blood has made me different. I'm not like everyone else anymore. This is definitely not who I wanted to be, but it's who I am now. And I'm okay with that."

"That's obvious. How could you deliberately hide all of this from me?"

"I was afraid you'd reject me. I'm not afraid anymore."

"Time after time, I forgave you for hiding stuff from me because I understood why you did it. But this is—"

"Unforgivable? Look, I know my lies have damaged our relationship. I haven't been fair to you, and for that I'm truly sorry. But it is what it is." After a slight pause, I softly added, "I need to step away from our relationship, Asher." The unplanned words slipped from my lips, surprising both of us.

"We're already on a temporary break."

"I think we should make it permanent." *Did I just say that?*

"Why? Despite everything, I still care about you, Kass. Deeply."

"I know you still care about me—despite my tainted hybrid blood, despite my hybrid mental powers, and despite all the secrets I've had to keep in order to survive. That's why I want to break up."

"I don't understand."

"I've changed and I finally accept that. But you don't fully accept me the way I am now."

"I'm trying."

"I don't want to be with someone who has to *try to* accept me. I want to be with someone who loves me, no matter what."

Unbidden, my thoughts flashed to Lynxx.

Once, his love for me had been unconditional. He had loved me when I was skinny, sick and dying, and living in a subway tunnel with only a pet mouse for company during the day. He had loved me when I was frightened and confused. And he had loved me when I'd become strong and independent, with extraordinary mental powers.

Once, he had loved *me*. But I'd rejected him time and again, and his feelings had changed ...

Carefully, Asher steered the pickup around a patch of tentacle terras on the road.

"I agree," he said, staring ahead. "We should break up." He sounded relieved. Was it because he could now rekindle things with Willow? Or was he relieved because our relationship had run its course and now, at last, it was over?

Within me, grief and loss twined together—along with my own sense of relief. No more lies. No more denying my nature. No more secrets.

For the rest of our drive back to Weston Tower, neither of us spoke another word.

We both knew there was nothing else to say.

29

WE DROVE THROUGH THE garrison's gateway, into a courtyard bustling with activity.

Adults were carefully unloading Lightning One from a large flatbed truck. Soldiers ordered excited children back as Nila inspected the damaged ship. Stretcher-bearers rushed wounded soldiers into the tower. Commander Powell and Lieutenant Wu rummaged through singed archive boxes taken from Crendell Laboratories.

Elsewhere, a group of armed and dirty hunters piled krol carcasses in a corner. An ex-biker from Fang's group argued with a mechanic working on a motorcycle. Two little boys brandished dead pieces of tentacle terras as they chased screaming girls around a play area. The elderly woman from Nila's community, Isabel, swept up bloodied scraps of jellyfish terras.

"Home sweet home," I muttered.

Ignoring me, Asher parked the vehicle.

The commander crossed to our pickup. "I heard you might have a Chi'az body under that tarp, son."

"Possibly, sir." Asher began unknotting the ropes. "We never saw the thing alive or unburned. We don't know what it is."

Nila joined us, staring in awe at the burned alien. "Is this a Chi'az scout?"

"No idea," Asher replied. "Have you ever seen one?"

"No."

Powell told Asher, "Take it up to Nila's lab."

Still ignoring me, Asher helped three men carry the tarp-wrapped body across the busy courtyard. People moved out of their way, staring with fascination and dread.

"I'll examine the corpse shortly, Lincoln," said Nila, "after I finish assessing Lightning One."

"Is the ship badly damaged?" he asked.

"Hard to say. With the right tools and equipment, we might be able to get it working again. I'll need lots of resources and personnel, though. Without Lightning One, we can't distribute the Shimmer gas around the world."

"We can still release the Shimmer in New York," said Powell. "That was our original plan."

"It'd be far more effective," she said, "if we release it simultaneously in multiple places around the world."

"True." The commander's eyes were dull with worry. Once again, I noticed how much he'd aged since the Night of the Blue Meteors. His hair was grayer, the lines on his face were deeper, and his military posture had become stooped, as though under the weight of the responsibilities he bore.

Nila headed back to the ship, leaving me alone with Powell. My turn.

How would he react to the news about my mental powers? Bracing myself, I stepped forward. "May I speak with you privately, sir?"

"I'm rather busy. Is it urgent?"

"No, sir. But it's important."

"Fine. Stop by my office in an hour."

Relieved, I watched him hurry off, glad my confession had been delayed for a while.

Lynxx approached me. "I see we got the ship."

"Yes." My chest tightened as I looked around. No one was nearby. "Lynxx ..."

"Yes?"

"Asher knows about my mental powers."

"*What?*"

"I had to tell him." Briefly I described the events on the rooftop earlier today.

"How did he react to your revelation?"

"Not very well. We broke up. It was my choice." When he looked skeptical, I admitted, "Well, when I suggested breaking up, he agreed."

"Do you think he'll tell anyone?"

"It doesn't matter. In an hour, I'm going to tell Commander Powell about my mental powers as well."

"You can't! We agreed to keep it a secret. It's hard enough fitting into the Weston Battalion as a hybrid. And now you want to tell everyone that we're even more different than they suspect?"

"I'm sorry, but I'm not a hybrid. I'm human. People need to know what they're facing with the Outrider hybrids and their mental powers."

"You should've discussed this with me first!"

"There wasn't time. I was with Asher when Lightning One crashed. I had to mind-blend with a pigeon in order to find the ship before the Brethren did." I gestured to the damaged ship. "And look, we got it."

"At what cost? Publicly revealing that we have enhanced mental powers is a bad idea. Very bad. People will look at us with fear and distrust. Is that what you want?"

I drew in a sharp breath. Was Lynxx right? Weston Tower was my home and its community my family. Here I'd found safety and warmth and purpose—and I was about to jeopardize it all. Maybe I shouldn't tell the commander about our powers. And if Asher told him, I could deny it. If I kept my secret, I could quietly continue my life in the Weston Battalion.

Except people needed to know.

I sighed. "I have to tell the commander. I don't think he'll turn on us. He likes Nila and he knows she's a hybrid. Also, he considers you valuable, Lynxx, despite being a hybrid. And although I have hybrid powers, I'm still human."

"It's too big a gamble, one I never agreed to."

"I'm sorry. Every person—every *human*—needs to know what we're up against."

He gazed at me, his golden eyes filled with pain. When he spoke, his voice was so low that I had to strain to hear him. "For a year and a half, I've done everything possible to keep you alive and healthy, Kassia. You were my reason for getting up each morning. And even when things were rocky between us, I always trusted you."

"Please—"

"Your decision to reveal our powers ... *your* decision, not ours, Kassia ..." He swallowed, then whispered, "It feels like a blade to my heart. A betrayal."

He turned and walked away from me.

Dismayed, I stared after him. My decision was the right one, wasn't it? *Yes.* Still, my own heart ached so badly that I thought it would split apart. I'd lost both Asher and Lynxx today. And if Lynxx was right about the commander, I could also lose my home—and the trust of everyone I cared about.

How would I bear the pain?

"Kass."

I looked around. Jase, still under guard, stood a short distance away.

Scowling, I approached him, eager for a distraction from my misery. "What?"

"I just wanted to say how amazing you look." He flashed a wide smile. "The last time I saw you, you were skinny, ill, and death-pale." He smirked. "Now you're hot."

Skinny. Ill. Death-pale.

"Save your breath," I snapped. "I used to think you were a decent guy. It turns out, you're just a weak jerk who looks for the easy way out."

His smirk vanished. "You've changed. You used to have a crush on me."

"Until I saw the real you."

"You admired me."

"That soon changed to contempt."

"I'm still the same boy you liked from high school."

"I'm not the same girl."

"No, you're beautiful, strong, and confident."

"Actually I'm smart. Too smart to be used by someone like you."

Flustered, he stood there. Obviously, I wasn't responding the way he wanted. Did he honestly believe he could manipulate me with his hollow compliments?

"We were a team, Kass. We spent over a week together looking for your sister and Charlotte."

"I found Charlotte. She was alive. In fact, she was a member of this garrison."

"Really?" His face lit up. "She's here?"

"She *was* a member. She died the day after I joined the Weston Battalion."

"What happened?"

"She'd become a quadriplegic after a bad fall. The Weston Battalion didn't have enough meds or personnel to take care of her for the rest of her life, so she was euthanized."

"What? That's barbaric."

I remembered thinking the same thing after Charlotte's death. "It's the prime law of the Weston Battalion. If you don't contribute to the community, you're out. You need to think about that."

"Why?"

"Because it'll be applied to you."

"You're just trying to scare me."

"Why would I do that?"

"Because you're still upset that I left you alone when I joined Rick's group." He didn't sound apologetic; he sounded defensive. "What are you saying? That if I don't contribute to the Weston Battalion, they'll kick me out?"

I noted his muted outrage over Charlotte's death had passed faster than a heartbeat. He was back to focusing on the most important person in his life: himself.

"You're an enemy combatant," I reminded him.

"Oh. Yeah. Well, I guess I can handle prison. At least it's three meals a day and a roof over my head."

"Prison? The Weston Battalion still doesn't have the resources or personnel to spend on people who don't contribute to the community."

"So they'll just let me go?"

"Never. You're the enemy."

For the first time, fear shadowed his face. "Then what's going to happen to me?"

"I don't know. And I don't care."

Dismissing him from my thoughts, I walked away.

30

A short while later, I entered Commander Powell's office.

As usual, he was working behind a large desk piled with papers and folders. A dismantled rifle lay on his coffee table, along with cleaning rags and a jar of grease. Maps of Manhattan covered his wall, highlighting various areas.

My gaze swept the maps. When I'd joined the garrison last year, the highlighted areas of terras had covered a quarter of the city. Now, they were over half.

Powell looked up from his paperwork. "What do you want to talk to me about, Kass?"

I hesitated, Lynxx's warnings fresh in my thoughts. Then I took a deep breath. "Sir, it's about the hybrids. And me."

"Yes?"

"They ... I ... have special powers—"

He waved his hand dismissively. "You mean their ability to mind-blend, remote-push, and so on? I already know."

I gaped at him. "You know?"

"Nila told me all about it last night. I'm planning to release the information about the hybrids' mental powers to the Weston Battalion today."

"Really?"

"You can also do those mental things, right? Didn't you develop some powers after Lynxx's blood mixed with yours?"

"Yes," I said, still unable to accept his casual attitude. "You're not angry with me?"

"Why would I be? You gained your powers by accident, right?"

"Yes."

"Okay, then. But you need to keep *your* powers a secret."

I stifled a groan. *Another secret.* "Asher already knows, sir."

"He's fine. I trust him with my life."

"I see. May I ask why you don't want to tell the Weston Battalion about my powers, sir?"

"Obviously, the Outriders know that Lynxx and Nila are hybrids and therefore have mental powers. However, it's possible the Outriders don't know that *humans* can develop these unique mental powers via hybrid blood."

"Oh. I get it. You don't want them deliberately creating armies of enhanced humans."

"Exactly. Of course, if they spread their Threads 2.0 before we release the Shimmer gas, nothing matters. We'll be dead." Powell rubbed his eyes tiredly. "Still, let's not give them any more weapons for now. Apart from Asher, Nila, and Lynxx, you can't let anyone else know."

"Of course, sir."

The commander leaned back in his chair, studying me. "I've been impressed with your work lately, Kass. You've displayed courage, quick thinking, and leadership on your missions. All these qualities, plus your enhanced mental powers, make you a valuable asset to the Weston Battalion."

At the unexpected praise, tears welled in my eyes. Quickly I blinked them away. Resistance fighters didn't cry in front of their commanders. "Thank you, sir."

Powell nodded, then returned to his paperwork.

Once I was out of the office, my stiff posture crumpled. Shaking, I leaned against a wall. For years I'd been a sickly girl. Sure, I'd been loved by my family and friends. Others, though, had dismissed me as worthless or irrelevant.

And now, the commander had paid me an incredible compliment.

I was a *valuable asset*.

Wrapped in a bubble of happiness, I hurried off to tell ...

I jerked to a halt.

... tell who?

Asher and Lynxx weren't talking to me. Willow wouldn't care. Pepper was dead. I had other friends at the garrison, but I wasn't particularly close to them.

Abruptly, my bubble burst.

I felt hollow.

Was this going to be my life from now on? Living among people—yet still alone?

31

THE NEXT MORNING, NILA summoned me to a meeting.

The moment I entered her laboratory, I felt it.

Tension. It hovered in the air like an invisible dark presence. *Uh-oh.* What was going on?

Commander Powell and Nila had their heads together, talking softly. Usually, five assistants worked in the lab, but today they were all absent. In a far corner, the burned corpse from Crendell Laboratories lay on a dissecting table, its flesh peeled back from its abdomen.

Moments later, Lynxx entered the room. When he saw me, he hesitated. Then, face expressionless, he crossed to Nila.

"What's Kassia doing here?" he asked, voice flat.

"I need you both." Her eyes were dull with fatigue and underlined with dark shadows. "I've had people working on Lightning One all night, and I think we can patch up the damaged exterior. The engine's a bigger problem, though. It needs Ceerin."

"What's that?" I asked, not looking at Lynxx.

"It's an oil made from the roots of seaweed terras," she replied. "Think of a car; it runs on fuel like gasoline, but it also needs oil. Without oil, the engine stops. It's a similar situation with Lightning One. Its fuel supply is intact, but its oil—Ceerin—leaked out when the ship was damaged. So we—"

A series of shrieks came from beyond the garrison. High-pitched. Sharp. And threatening.

"Krols," Commander Powell said grimly.

From further away, another series of shrieks answered.

Lynxx scowled. "They're communicating with each other."

"Any idea what they're saying?" Powell asked. When Lynxx and Nila shook their heads, the commander muttered, "I hope it's nothing to do with the garrison."

"I wouldn't bet on it," Nila said. "Those krols are smart and they hate us. Sooner or later, they *will* attack the garrison. That's what they did down in Florida."

"All the more reason to fix Lightning One and start spreading the Shimmer gas around the world."

"Exactly, Lincoln."

Lynxx asked her, "Why did you call this meeting?"

"I know how to make Ceerin oil." Nila avoided looking at Lynxx and me. "I just need two bags of seaweed terra roots."

Powell added, "There's a large patch of them growing in the Hudson River near the east bank."

Confused, I asked, "Doesn't Neptune Team deal with marine missions? Or are these seaweed terras dangerous?"

"They're harmless," Commander Powell replied awkwardly. "And Neptune Team already tried gathering the stuff earlier this morning." His shoulders sagged. "We lost Pablo Valdez and Rosalie Webster within ten minutes. The rest of the team barely made it out of the water alive."

Oh no. Pablo. That sweet, skinny kid had been a part of Liberty Team when I'd joined. Now he was dead.

"What happened?" I gasped.

"Sharks."

The tension in the room suddenly felt darker.

"Seaweed terras can grow over two hundred feet tall," Nila explained. "They stretch up from the bottom of the river to the surface, creating an underwater forest of leaves and pods. Swarms of fish live in those seaweed forests, and packs of sharks follow the fish."

"Can't you send down divers with spear guns?"

"All our divers were armed this morning," Powell said. "But there were dozens of bull sharks. Many were behaving aggressively. Bizarrely."

Bizarrely?

I pushed aside the questions that rose to my lips. Instead, I asked Nila, "Can you use something else to make the Ceerin?"

"Nothing else will work. That's where you two come in."

Lynxx folded his arms, clearly unhappy at being teamed up with me. However, he knew better than to object in front of the commander.

Powell shifted uncomfortably. "Nila and I have figured out a way for you two to get the seaweed terra roots." His voice held a brittle, strained quality.

Uh-oh. I wasn't going to like this.

Powell cleared his throat, drew in a deep breath, and outlined their plan. As I listened, I felt the color drain from my face. My heart slammed against my rib cage. When the commander finished, Lynxx and I exchanged a brief horrified glance.

Lynxx spoke firmly. "With respect, Commander, your plan is ..." He struggled to find some tactful words.

Forget about tact.

"It's crazy!" I cried. "A suicide mission."

Powell shook his head. "If you and Lynxx combine your mental powers, you should both survive."

Sharply, Lynxx asked him, "So you know about our mental powers? And you're okay with them?"

"Yes," Powell replied. "In fact, I'm prepared to use them in getting this Ceerin."

I returned to their insane plan. "You're asking me to ..." I staggered a step as though the floor had suddenly shifted beneath my feet. "I can't."

"You can," Nila insisted. "You have to."

Commander Powell stared intently at us. "You two are our only hope."

"When's the mission?" Lynxx croaked.

"This afternoon."

Silence filled the lab as Powell and Nila awaited our decision. I struggled to breathe through the horror now smothering me. Trapped, knowing they were right, I somehow managed to nod my assent. Nearby, Lynxx muttered a reluctant, "Okay."

The commander and Nila gave guilty sighs of relief.

Dazed, I left the lab. My stomach churned and I fought an urge to throw up—but I wasn't sick with leukemia.

I was terrified.

32

A WARM WIND KNUCKLED the surface of the Hudson River into small white tips.

Overhead, the summer sun hung in a pale red sky, and seagulls dipped and rose in streaks of cream-and-brown feathers. On the bank, green terra vines covered vans and cars. Gold terra flowers adorned benches, trash cans, and rusting poles.

Color was everywhere.

Yet the world seemed gray to me.

Or perhaps it was *me* that was gray.

Lynxx and I stood on the riverbank, our wetsuits still dripping from our second scuba diving lesson. Neither of us looked at the other. Despite the upcoming suicide mission, our relationship remained gray and chilly, and his earlier accusation lingered in my mind. *Your decision to reveal our powers ... your decision, not ours, Kassia ... It feels like a blade to my heart. A betrayal.*

Guilt gnawed at me. Even though I'd had no choice, Lynxx was right.

Nila joined us. "I heard you both aced your scuba diving lessons."

We reluctantly nodded.

She asked, "So, are you ready?"

Chest tight with apprehension, I looked around.

A rattle of chains came from a large tarpaulin-covered object further down the bank. Asher and the rest of Liberty Team retreated a few steps as the thing beneath the tarp shook and quivered, trying to escape.

But the chains held. For now.

"Why's it covered up, Nila?" I asked.

"Darkness seems to settle it down a little."

"It doesn't look settled to me."

A short distance from the shore, a massive patch of green seaweed terras grew in the water, their tips floating on the surface. Small fish swam among them, flicking diamond-bright droplets into the air as they fed. The scene looked deceptively innocent and peaceful—

—except for the sharks.

Dozens of triangular dorsal fins sliced the water, circling and weaving, disappearing and resurfacing as they fed on the fish. Every so often, a shark would suddenly attack another shark, and the water would froth and bleed scarlet.

The predators' violent behavior was unprovoked, terrifying, and bizarre.

The behavior of the yellow fish was just as weird. Why would they hang around when sharks were eating them? Were they tranquilized by something in the water? Or were they on suicide missions too—like Lynxx and me?

"Are you ready?" Nila again asked us.

Ready for what? To die?

"Yeah. Sure," I muttered.

"Can't wait," Lynxx mumbled.

Calmly, she continued, "The water's only a hundred feet deep where you're going, so you won't need to worry about dying from the bends."

Huh! I hadn't even considered that possibility. There were so many other things that could kill us on this mission.

She fell silent as two men from the Weston Battalion approached Lynxx.

"Glad you're on our side," one said to him.

"Yeah," the other added. "We need our own good hybrid to balance out those Outrider wacko-hybrids."

After giving Lynxx a thumbs-up, they moved on.

The men's behavior was common in the Weston Battalion today. The commander's recent announcement of the hybrids' heightened mental powers had sent shock waves through the garrison. However, most members were relieved that the Weston Battalion's own hybrid, Lynxx, was mentally enhanced too.

People clung to a common belief: *If the Outrider hybrids have a superweapon, we need a superweapon too.*

Sergeant Thorne and a few others remained grim-faced at the news, but they kept their hostility almost hidden.

Thankfully, no one seemed to know that Nila was a hybrid—or that I possessed heightened mental powers as well.

Asher joined us, giving me only a brief nod, obviously still upset at our breakup. My heart ached and the day turned a little grayer.

"It's under control. Sort of," he told Nila, gesturing to the object shaking and rattling beneath the tarp. "This is a terrible idea."

"Noted, Asher," she replied. "You've already expressed your disapproval three times this morning. However, it's the only way. And your commander has signed off on it."

"You can't send Kass down in that thing," he persisted. "It's crazy."

I was surprised by his passionate opposition. Did he still care about me? Or was he simply troubled that a member of his team was being sent on a suicide mission?

"I've seen sharks in a frenzy before," Asher continued. "I watched them through the glass wall of my father's yacht on the Night of the Red Mist. Some of the sharks tore each other to pieces. What do you think these bull sharks will do to Kass and Lynxx?"

"We don't have a choice."

Leaving them to their argument, I hurried across to Willow, who was reaching for some orange flowers growing on a bench.

"Don't pick them," I cried. "They're spitters." A harmless but horrible terra plant.

Hastily, she backed away. "I thought they were perfume-globes." Another harmless terra plant. Much nicer, though.

"Asher made the same mistake once," I told her. "We were investigating an abandoned cruise ship that had a patch of spitters growing inside."

"Did he—?"

"Yep. One spat huge globs of stinky orange goo in his face. He wasn't happy."

Her lips twitched, then she broke into laughter. "Xavian used to tell me to check each terra plant three times before deciding what it was." Her face shadowed with grief. "I miss Xavian so much. It's like a pain that won't go away." A sigh. "At least Ash and I have found each other again."

I wondered why Willow never mentioned missing other people besides Xavian. Had this world-famous actress been isolated from her family and friends? Had her managers and publicists sheltered her from personal conflicts and the realities of everyday life? It would certainly explain her fragility in this harsh new world.

"How are *you* doing?" she asked me.

"What do you mean?"

"Asher told me that you two have broken up."

"Oh. Yes." I searched Willow's beautiful face, but she was too good an actress—or too polite—to openly show her relief. "I'm fine, thanks."

"Really? Then why are you going on this crazy mission?"

"Lynxx can't get the seaweed terra roots by himself."

"He's got those mental powers," she said. "You don't."

Good. Asher hadn't revealed my latest secret to her. Clearly he was honoring Commander Powell's instructions to keep quiet about my powers.

"Lynxx will be flat out mentally controlling that thing," I said, gesturing to the tarp-covered object. "Someone else has to gather and bag the roots. It's a two-person job."

"Exactly. Let a guy go with Lynxx."

Seriously? Sexism in these times?

I hid my annoyance beneath an even tone. "Perhaps Asher should go instead of me. Is that what you're suggesting?"

This time, the world-famous actress couldn't hide her emotions. Alarm. Worry. Fear.

She fell silent.

"It's time, folks," Nila called out.

We all moved back as Harlem and Booker dragged the tarpaulin off the large round object. The thing shifted and quivered. The chains tethering it to the ground clinked. And its curved branches rattled like dried bones.

Tumbleweed terra.

Big enough to swallow an SUV.

Dangerous enough to impale and digest a person in hours.

Terrifying enough to give me nightmares for the rest of my life.

Numbly, I allowed people to finish outfitting me. Full face mask. Mic and earpiece so Lynxx and I could talk to each other underwater. Air tank strapped to my back. Black gloves to match my wetsuit. Speargun.

The spectators scowled at my speargun.

"... like a giant matchstick ..."

"... useless against those crazy sharks ..."

"... should give her grenades and an Uzi ..."

I knew the speargun was just for show. My real weapon would be my mental powers.

Lynxx, clad in full scuba diving gear, waddled in his flippers toward the tumbleweed. Putting on a dramatic show for the watching crowd, he waved his arms like Moses parting the waves, and people cheered as the lethal branches opened before him.

Heart thundering, I followed him into the tumbleweed, trying not to think of my previous experiences with them.

But the memories flooded back.

Pepper and I shouting as we're snatched up by a tumbleweed and stuck on the side of a skyscraper.

Me wandering around a massive skyweb terra dotted with dozens of feasting tumbleweeds.

Five tumbleweeds dropping toward the garrison courtyard. The little girl Zoey screaming. Running.

The hybrid Bone emerging from a tumbleweed and snapping Pepper's neck.

And now, today, I had actually agreed to be swallowed up by one of these hideous terras.

Lynxx and I stood together as the curved branches enclosed us in a woody embrace. My heart pounded so loudly that I didn't hear the order to undo the chains, and I gasped as the ground dropped away. Slowly, our tumbleweed rose into the air.

"It's okay, Kassia." Lynxx's voice sounded cool and remote in my earpiece. "I have Goliath under control."

"Good. Wait ... what? You named the tumbleweed?"

He didn't look at me but stared ahead through his full face mask. "I was reading an old magazine last night. It mentioned this submarine, *Goliath*, from a BBC show. This terra will be taking us to the bottom of the river, just like a submarine. So I named it Goliath."

Lynxx being whimsical? Ha! He was more human than I thought.

As the tumbleweed flew over the Hudson River, my gloved fingers tightened around my speargun. The wind rushed past, cooling patches of my bare skin. Beneath my flippered feet, bones crunched in the branches. Animal or human?

Seeking a distraction, I asked, "What was the name of that BBC show?"

"*Deep Trouble.*"

"How apt."

His voice was strained from controlling the terra. "I'll take Goliath down to the edge of the seaweed patch. We can harvest the roots there."

"Okay." The sharks were in the middle of the huge patch. Maybe we'd be able to complete our nightmare mission before they noticed us.

"Ready?" he asked.

"Not really."

"Hang on. We're going in."

<h1 style="text-align:center">33</h1>

THE TUMBLEWEED DROPPED LIKE an elevator.

I gripped a curved branch as we hit the surface and waves plumed around us. We fell through the bubbling water, past darting fish, heading for the bottom a hundred feet below. The strange underwater world was lit by sunshine; Nila had mentioned that sunbeams could penetrate six hundred feet in clear water—and this water was like liquid crystal.

On one side of us, long streamers of green seaweed terras swayed in the current. On the other side, a wrecked plane lay on the sandy bottom, a dozen skeletons scattered near the broken fuselage.

Oh no. Was this the 737 that had hit the Brooklyn Bridge while Charlotte and I were crossing it last year?

No, this wreckage was too far from that bridge, I realized. This was probably one of the planes that had crashed in the days following the Night of the Red Mist.

The tumbleweed, Goliath, landed with a bump, spraying sand and grit around us. When the water cleared, I noticed an expanse of knee-high orange plants carpeting the sand.

The edge of the seaweed terra patch was only a few feet away.

"Let's get this over with," I said into my mic as I grabbed an empty bag.

Lynxx parted the branches, and I was about to step onto the orange terra plants when he pulled me back. "Careful!"

"What's wrong?"

"Look over there."

As a bull shark swam across the orange terras, gold electrical charges flashed from the plants, zapping the shark. Dazed, it floated in the water.

I groaned. "The terra plants are giving off electrical charges."

"Yes, just like Earth's electric eels. I think these orange plants are an aquatic form of zap terras."

Long tendrils shot from the orange terras and wrapped themselves around the shark. When the bull shark struggled, a navy dye spurted into the water—and the shark fell limp. The tendrils hauled in their catch, which disappeared into the mass of orange terra plants.

"I think that navy fluid knocked out—or killed—the shark," he said.

"If I'd stepped on those plants ..." I shuddered.

"Let's find another spot." Lynxx remote-closed Goliath's branches and allowed the terra ball to rise.

We floated around the outside of the tall seaweed patch, past old sunken boats and shipping containers. My gaze lingered on the skeletons scattered across the bottom. Why hadn't they turned into decomp-dust? Then I remembered that only the people who died from the Red Fever turned to dust, not those who died in accidents.

"Those people must've died when their ships sank," I said.

Shrugging, Lynxx remained silent. Obviously he was prepared to discuss mission-related topics, but he wasn't interested in chatting with me.

I ignored his chilly attitude. *Survive first, talk later.*

We circled the seaweed terra patch, then arrived back at our starting point.

"These orange zap terras are everywhere," I said. "There's nowhere safe to land."

"Except inside the patch. I've used my aquascope, and it looks like the zap terras are scarcer the deeper you go into the patch."

"So the center might be clear?"

"Possibly."

"What about the sharks?" The breath was dry in my throat. "There are heaps of them in the middle."

"I know." Lynxx finally looked at me, his voice emotionless in my earpiece. "We can abort the mission. There's no point in harvesting terra roots if we die down here and can't get the roots to Nila."

Self-preservation was a heady temptation, but reality was harsh and cruel.

"Without the roots," I said, "Nila can't fix the ship. And without the it, she can't distribute the Shimmer gas around the world. If the Outriders release their Threads 2.0 first, humanity is finished." Asher. Soo-Yun. Harlem. The people at the garrison. Us. "We have to try."

Face tightening, he steered Goliath through the watery green jungle, toward the center of the patch. Schools of yellow fish nibbled on the seaweed terras, along with a medley of small aquatic creatures. Dark shadows swept us as sharks passed overhead.

"Here's a spot." Lynxx lowered Goliath onto a sandy area littered with broken pieces of an old trawler, but clear of the orange zap terras. "Be careful."

As he remote-pushed the branches open again, I grabbed the empty bags and swam to the streamers of seaweed terras. Behind my face mask, sweat trickled down my skin as I held a sharp knife and reached for a green steamer. Again and again, the streamer slid through my gloved grip. Frustrated, I pocketed my gloves, gripped the streamer with my bare hand, and sliced through the terra.

I worked quickly.

Cut the green streamer close to the sand. Rip out the root. Shove it in a bag. Repeat.

I filled two bags, which I passed to Lynxx. As I shoved roots into a third bag, I glimpsed something on my left. An adult skeleton lay among the plants, with crabs crawling over its rib cage.

What—?

Pain jolted up my arm. A flash of agony raged through my body, into my head. Bright lights flashed behind my eyes. My brain sizzled, as though an electrical current surged through it, and I couldn't move.

Through the sparks and frizzing in my brain, I glimpsed an orange plant among the seaweed terras. Had I accidentally grasped an aquatic zap terra?

As a cold shadow passed over me, I felt a shift in the water—

—and I sensed the approach of death.

34

A SHORT DISTANCE AWAY, two bull sharks charged at each other. Jaws wide, the predators twisted and thrashed in battle, blood streaming through the water.

I tried to move. Still couldn't.

My muscles felt as frizzled as my brain.

"Kass!" Lynxx shouted in my earpiece.

He bolted from the tumbleweed. Grabbed my limp body. Pulled me toward Goliath. Through my daze, I could see other sharks racing downward, drawn by the fresh blood. I could also see Goliath trembling and shifting as though straining to break free of Lynxx's remote control.

In a few more yards, we'd be inside.

A shark—huge and white-gray—lunged at us. Hell-black eyes. Gaping mouth. Rows of jagged teeth.

Lynxx jerked his head in a fierce remote-push. The shark shot backward, thudded against the side of the old trawler, then darted off. A large metal crate tumbled off the trawler's deck and fell onto the rear of Goliath.

Lynxx thrust me inside Goliath and closed the branches behind us.

"Go," I muttered into my mic as my sparking brain slowly began to clear.

Behind his face mask, his brow knotted in concentration. The tumbleweed quivered. Didn't move.

Again, he tried remote-pushing the terra. It shook and rattled, but remained on the spot.

We looked around. The back half of the tumbleweed lay trapped beneath the metal crate that had fallen from the sunken trawler.

"Goliath is stuck," he groaned.

"Break branches?" I suggested weakly, thinking of the gray-brown tumbleweed that had chased the little girl Zoey. I'd broken several of its skinny branches to save her.

"I could if the tumbleweed was smaller. But larger ones like this have strong, flexible branches. They tend to bend, not break."

Again and again, he tried remote-pushing the metal crate away.

Voice trembling with fatigue, he said, "Nope. Not working." He glanced at me as he snatched a few seconds' rest. "What happened out there?"

"Think I grabbed a zap terra."

"You okay?"

"Five out of ten. Getting there."

"Sorry, we can't wait until you're ten out of ten. I have an idea." He slipped off a glove and grabbed my bare hand. "Remember when Bone dragged Pepper into his tumbleweed? We had to combine our mental powers to stop him from leaving with her."

"I remember."

"Okay. We'll concentrate on moving that crate together." His grip tightened around my fingers. Hand in hand, we focused on the heavy crate that held Goliath down. My head ached and sweat beaded on my forehead, but I forced myself to endure.

Move, crate. Move. Move.

Nothing.

By now, a dozen sharks were battling each other. Thrashing tails hit Goliath, and bloodied scraps of flesh floated through the red water.

"We're not strong enough," he muttered, releasing my hand. "Sorry."

"It's not just you. I'm not at full strength either. I'm still remote-controlling Goliath's urge to swallow us, and I'm also remote-pushing away some of those sharks as well."

"Any second now, a shark could smash Goliath into pieces."

"That's it!" he cried.

"What?"

"We aren't mentally strong enough to push that crate off Goliath. But those sharks are physically strong enough." He scanned the writhing predators. "Can you control the tumbleweed by yourself?"

I nodded. "Think so. Why?"

"I'll be back in a minute."

"Where are you going?"

"See that bull shark over there?" He pointed to a gray shark that swam near our tumbleweed. Blood trailed from a bite in its side. "Bully's going to get us out of here."

Lynxx went limp. His body floated in the water.

The bull shark's black eyes flashed into silver.

Bully-Lynxx circled around and, with a flick of its tail, headed straight for Goliath—and me. Its ugly pointed face loomed closer and closer, like a scene from a horror movie. Despite its silver eyes, I thought it was going to smash the tumbleweed into pieces, then rip Lynxx's body and me apart. Frantic, I grabbed his non-conscious body and pushed him behind me.

The silver-eyed bull shark slammed into the side of the metal crate, shoving it off Goliath. The tumbleweed shook vigorously, as though jerking awake. Caught off guard, I staggered back, losing my grip on Lynxx, and he floated in Goliath's stomach among the two bags of seaweed terra roots.

With a crackle of woody stems, the tumbleweed drifted upward. Thorns popped out like claws springing from a cat's paws, and branches began contracting around Lynxx's body and me.

I rushed to remote-push the branches back, sweeping my focus from left to right. More stars flashed behind my eyes, sharp as knife stabs. Ignoring them, I grabbed Lynxx's limp arm and pulled him close. The branches stopped crackling. The thorns retracted. Still non-conscious, Lynxx's body drifted at my side.

I scanned the red water. Where was he?

Above, the silver-eyed bull shark writhed and gushed blood as a pack of sharks rushed in for the kill.

Oh no. If Bully died before Lynxx could leap free of their mind-blend, he'd die too.

Desperately, I tightened my mental grip and remote-pushed Goliath upward, toward the attacking pack. My head felt about to split apart, but somehow I managed to remote-push the thorns on the outside branches, and they popped up again. *Good.* Four inches long. Tips like scalpels. Lethal.

Protected by the thorny ball, I whammed a passage through the attacking sharks, searching the bloodied water for the silver-eyed one.

There.

Bully was a mass of ripped flesh, and its tail was barely twitching. It was dying.

"Hang on, Lynxx," I shouted, even though I knew he couldn't hear me.

I remote-pushed Goliath toward the bleeding shark—and watched its silver eyes fade to a dead black.

No! I was too late. I should've—

"I'm back," Lynxx's voice sounded in my earpiece. Looking around, I saw him sitting up, stretching his arms and flexing his fingers.

Thank goodness.

My grip on Goliath slipped. The tumbleweed shook and more thorns sprang out.

"I'll take over." Lynxx remote-pushed the thorns back into the woody stems.

I sagged against the curved wooden wall, weak with relief. He was alive. We both were. "That was way too close. If I'd lost you—"

"You would've handled Goliath and returned to the riverbank," he said, voice chilly once again.

"That's not what I meant," I said, searching for the words to dissolve the ice wall between us.

"I know. But it doesn't matter anymore. Let's just get this mission over with." His words were empty of emotion, and the ice wall between us grew a little thicker.

Powered by Lynxx, Goliath burst from the water, trailing bits of seaweed. As we flew toward the riverbank, we shoved off our masks and breathed in the fresh air. The sunshine felt warm on my face and the sky was still a cloudless pale red—yet the world seemed even grayer and colder than before.

Lynxx landed the tumbleweed on the bank, maintaining his mental grip until Liberty Team chained it down again. Then he created an opening in the branches, and we stumbled out with the two bags of terra roots.

Asher rushed across to me. "Are you okay? You were gone a long time."

"Yeah. But we got the roots. Yay us, right?" Barely holding myself together, I thrust my bag into Asher's hands.

"What happened?" he asked.

"We survived."

I staggered away, on the verge of breaking down. My nerves were shredded, my body ached, and my head pounded.

That night, my sleep was filled with nightmares of bloodied sharks, thorny tumbleweeds—and my anguish at Lynxx almost dying.

<h1 style="text-align:center">35</h1>

THREE DAYS LATER, NILA, Lynxx, and others were still working on the Ceerin oil and repairs to the Chi'az ship. Despite the process being complicated and slow, Nila was increasingly optimistic about getting Lightning One operational again.

Her autopsy of the strange burned body revealed an over-sized brain, leading her to suspect that the owner had used telepathy to communicate instead of verbal speech. This fit with the hybrids' mental powers.

To my surprise, Jase remained alive. Determined to avoid execution, he began sharing snippets of information about the Outriders with the commander. None of these snippets were particularly useful, and Powell started losing interest in their conversations.

Worried, Jase offered up his ultimate trading piece: the location of a bag of penicillin.

"Only I know where it is," he insisted. "It's hidden in a remote spot that you'll never find. I can take a team there. I guarantee I won't try to escape."

Reluctantly, Commander Powell assigned *two* teams to help Jase retrieve the precious penicillin.

"You can't trust him," I told the commander.

"I agree." He turned to Asher. "If that lowlife endangers our people in any way, son, you and Harlem have my permission to shoot him."

"Noted, sir," Asher replied grimly.

The next day, Liberty and Trident Teams—plus Soo-Yun, who had the morning off—accompanied Jase to Manhattanville.

Sinkholes riddled the area, forcing us to park our vehicles and walk the last few blocks. At the overgrown General Grant National Memorial, Jase pushed through tall weeds to an eagle statue. Shoving aside a thick velvet-vine terra, he withdrew a bulging bag from between the bird's carved legs.

Asher scowled at him. "You told us the penicillin was hidden in a remote spot that only you could find."

"I exaggerated. So what?" Jase smirked. "I needed a break from sitting in that stinking prison cell."

"You played us." Asher's scowl deepened. "You think you're smarter than everyone else, don't you?"

"What's your problem, pal? You got your bag of penicillin and I got a day out. It's a win-win."

Definitely a win-win for *him*, I realized. The commander had agreed to place Jase on probation if he delivered the penicillin—which he had. The creep would now be allowed limited freedom in the garrison.

Harlem shouted to Asher, "Hey, bro." He stood on the main walkway. "Look what I found. And it's still got air in it." He held up a soccer ball, as triumphant as an Olympian showing off a gold medal.

"Kick it to me," Natalie shouted, excited. The ex-cheerleader waved her arms in large movements as she spelled out, "L-I-B-E-R-T-Y. Yay, Liberty Team."

The two teams spread out on the cracked, weedy path as a game of soccer got underway.

"Ash," said Willow, "we should be heading back to the garrison."

"We're well ahead of schedule," he replied, "and we've already searched this area for dangerous terras and xans." He grinned at the happy soccer players. "I think it's safe for them to have some fun for a little while."

"Okay, let's you and me have some fun too." She took his hand and led him to a patch of orange flowers. "You've got to smell these, Ash. This time, I'm *sure* they're perfume-globe terras, not spitters."

I stood on the sidelines and watched the soccer game. My teammates called for me to join them, but I shook my head. For some reason, I didn't feel a desperate need to belong anymore, to be one of the guys. I knew I wasn't. My hybrid mental powers set me apart from the others, even if they didn't know about them yet.

And, surprisingly, I didn't mind being different anymore.

My powers were now a part of me and I wasn't just at peace with them. I *embraced* them.

The two teams played for fifteen minutes, then took a break.

I watched Asher and Willow flirt over the perfume-globe terras. He was relaxed, warm, and tender, and her beautiful face glowed with happiness. Once, they had been deeply in love. Clearly Willow still loved Asher.

Was he falling in love with her again?

Pain flashed through me, but I tried to ignore it. Worrying about love and loss felt trivial against the larger, darker issues that threatened us all: the Outriders and their lethal Threads.

"Penny for your thoughts." A smug Jase appeared at my side.

"Go away."

"Grumpy."

"What do you want?"

"To chat."

"Not interested."

I saw Harlem present a huge bunch of perfume-globe terras to Soo-Yun. Her face lit up and she gave him a delighted kiss. Blushing, he scuffed the ground with his sneakers.

Another pair in love. Don't they realize that we have a war to win before they can all live happily ever after?

"You've done well." Jase assessed me, calculating the right things to say. "Maybe you can put in a good word for me to Commander Powell."

"Why should he listen to me?"

"Because you're respected in the Weston Battalion."

"What?"

"I've seen the way people treat you. The commander. Nila. Asher. Others. They respect you."

I tried to hide my surprise. Was Jase right? True, lately I had noticed people asking my opinion about things. And they had actually listened to my answers—mostly. *Huh!* I'd always thought I had to blend into a group before people accepted me. Maybe I was wrong. Maybe someone different—an underdog or an odd fit—could still be part of a group. Lynxx was certainly accepted.

Jase shifted his stare to Willow, who was laughing with Asher, her eyes openly adoring him. "Even Willow respects you."

"Now you *are* lying." My dreams of belonging evaporated. Obviously, Jase was still playing games. Was he trying to ingratiate himself into the Weston Battalion by winning over a person he considered a weak link—me?

"Willow respects you. She also sees you as a rival. She's after your boyfriend, you know."

"Asher's not my boyfriend anymore," I said sharply, tired of our conversation. "Now go away or I'll remind Commander Powell of some harsh truths. How you're only out for yourself. How you joined forces with Bone, an Outrider hybrid. How you left me to die in Central Park when you took off with some other survivors. Shall I go on?"

Face darkening, he stomped away.

The soccer match resumed.

Taking a deep breath, I closed my eyes. I listened to the laughter of the soccer players, smelled the perfume-globes, felt the caress of a breeze—and for a few moments I was back there.

I'm having a picnic with my family. Mom's lying on a blanket near a scent-heavy flowerbed, revising one of her screenplays. Dad's sunning himself as he reads a book. Olivia and I are wandering around the park, dodging a casual soccer match, chatting and giggling. My whole family is healthy and happy—and alive.

Sighing, I opened my eyes.

And the real world flooded back.

A pale red sky soared overhead, dotted with circling vultures. The famous General Grant Memorial stood sad and empty, overgrown with terra vines. Weeds cracked the walkway beneath my feet. Nearby, a scattering of teenagers had put aside their weapons to play soccer, desperately trying to recapture a sliver of their pasts. Like me.

But our pasts were forever lost to the dusts of time.

All that remained was now.

Dropping my backpack, I ran across to the soccer players and joined in the fun.

36

HALF AN HOUR LATER, Asher wound up the soccer game.

Harlem's Trident Team and Soo-Yun decided to walk the few blocks to Morningside Park, where they'd been scheduled to destroy a clump of strangler terras today. Unable to stand Jase's presence any longer, I quietly arranged for him to accompany Trident Team on their mission.

"No way," Jase said when Harlem told him the news. "I hate stranglers."

"And I love them, right?" Harlem snapped, cradling his soccer ball. "You either come with us or you walk back to the garrison. Alone. No weapons. Your choice, pal."

Swearing, Jase followed Trident Team down the walkway.

"Remember, Harl," Asher called out, "shoot him if he gives you any trouble."

"Gladly."

"Maybe we'll get lucky," Asher muttered to me. "Maybe the strangler terras will do us a favor and strangle Jase."

I choked on a laugh. During our recent missions, the chill between Asher and me had thawed into an almost friendly relationship.

Now, if only Lynxx would forgive me.

Liberty Team began heading back to our Hummer. We were still a couple of blocks from the vehicle when a loud metallic creak fractured the silence.

We stopped. Listened.

In the distance, a krol uttered a series of sharp barks. Then silence.

Closer by, another metallic creak sounded.

"Something's up." Asher kept his voice low. "We could be walking into a trap."

Cautiously, we continued down the block, alert for an ambush. I scanned our surroundings. Overgrown buildings. Streets riddled with small and large sinkholes. Trash blowing across roads. Vultures wheeling overhead.

No sign of a golden eagle.

Even though Lynxx could mind-blend with any creature, lately he'd always chosen to blend with WindLord. I swallowed my disappointment, reminding myself of Lynxx's important work on Lightning One. He didn't need to constantly watch out for me or—

"*Help.*"

A faint cry, barely audible.

We paused, looking around.

"*Help.*"

We crept to the corner. Asher peered around it, then motioned Booker and me forward for a look. Our rookie members, Natalie and Yuki, stayed behind us, hopping from foot to foot, barely controlling their curiosity. Willow waited nearby, gazing into the distance.

I examined the scene. A short distance away, West 126th Street was intersected by Broadway. Soaring across the intersection was an elevated train track holding a passenger car. In front of the elevated track, a sinkhole stretched between the buildings on West 126th Street.

Booker and I pulled back from the corner, allowing Natalie and Yuki to have a quick look.

"No one's around, boss," Booker whispered. "It seems safe."

"I disagree," I murmured.

"Why?"

"Because of the buses."

Asher nodded. "I agree with Kass."

At the intersection, parked buses stood on either side of West 126th Street. They blocked anyone from turning left or right into Broadway. If we continued down West 126th Street, we'd have to skirt around the sinkhole and walk beneath the elevated train track.

"Help. Please."

"I think a guy's stuck in the sinkhole," Natalie said, her chirpy cheerleader voice subdued for once. "Shouldn't we help him?"

"Those bus barricades might be nothing," Asher said, "but I'm not risking it."

I explained to Natalie, "It could be a trap set by the Wilders or the Brethren."

"Okay, guys," Asher told us, "we're taking another route back to our vehicle."

"Help us. Please help." A louder cry this time. Clearer.

"Wait!" I swung around. "I know that voice. It's Mr. Isaac." The old hermit had lived a short distance from the subway bunker that I'd shared with my sister, Olivia.

"Are you sure?"

"Positive, Asher. I heard his voice every week for months when we were living in the tunnel. I used to bring him bags of mushrooms and meat. He would only speak to me through his closed bunker door, so I got to know his voice really well."

"Have you ever met him in person?"

"No. I swear it's his voice, though."

A brief hesitation. Then, "Okay. Proceed with caution, guys."

We hurried to the large sinkhole, which was shallower than the one that Asher and I had jumped into during our trip to Florida. This one was only thirty feet deep, and it didn't have terra roots or pipes crisscrossing it.

Two men were at the bottom. One sat clutching a leg wrapped with a dirty piece of material. Beside him stood a skinny old man with wire-rimmed glasses.

"Mr. Isaac?" I called out, unsure which man was my ex-neighbor. "Are you okay?"

The skinny old man peered up through his wire-rimmed glasses. "Is that you, Mushroom Girl?"

Awful nickname!

My friends chuckled.

"Yes, Mr. Isaac. It's me, *Kass Madison*. What happened?"

"My buddy, Raj, got too close to the sinkhole. He fell and broke his leg. I can't get him out."

A faint rumble sounded in the distance.

I glanced up at the clear sky. Was that thunder?

Booker moved toward the hole. He halted when Asher held up a hand, ordering, "Stop. Something's still not right here."

"What, boss?"

"I don't know. It's just a gut feeling. We need to be careful."

The rumble grew louder and louder, sounding almost desperate. *Terrified.*

Not thunder.

Slowly, I turned.

37

FURTHER DOWN THE STREET, a dozen bison raced toward us in a cloud of dust. They seemed to be shrieking and screaming—but as they got closer I glimpsed spear-wielding creatures behind them. *They* were the ones shrieking and screaming as they chased the bison.

Krols.

We were directly in the animals' path.

"They're on the buses too," Natalie cried. "And on the passenger car."

I swung around, confused. Bison on buses—?

No.

Krols now crouched on top of the buses that flanked the sinkhole. Others stood on the roof of the passenger car on the elevated track. Their clawed hands gripped wooden spears, and their black eyes were focused on the approaching herd. A couple of them glanced at our small group beside the sinkhole, but they made no move to attack us.

"We need to get off this street, boss." Booker wiped his fogged glasses with his shirt. "We can squeeze past the sinkhole and the buses—"

"No," Asher said. "The second we get too close to those buses, the krols will spear us."

He was right. More krols were appearing, and some were starting to focus on us instead of the oncoming bison. Glaring, they curled their lips back in pointy-toothed snarls. Were

178

they angry that humans had recently killed scores of their kind throughout Manhattan? Possibly. These creatures were smart—and dangerous.

Our Japanese team member, Yuki, scanned the place. "What about buildings alongside sinkhole? True, they have bars on windows and doors, but—"

The thunder of hooves grew closer and the ground shook. Metal creaked.

The krols leaped from the roof of the train and disappeared behind it. Moments later, the passenger car tilted forward. With a ragged metallic groan, it toppled from the elevated track and landed with a ground-shaking crash on West 126th Street. It blocked the road behind the sinkhole, forming the third side of a dead end.

Asher paled. "Those krols are working together *and* thinking strategically. They've built a trap for the bison."

Horrified, I stared at the sinkhole. The krols were displaying the intelligence and strategic behavior of primitive man.

Shrieking, the creatures jumped from the elevated track, landed on top of the fallen passenger car, and locked their gazes on the charging animals.

Liberty Team was also trapped. However, we weren't the krols' targets. Yet.

But we were right in the path of the stampeding bison. The panicked animals were closing in on us. Fear drove their muscled bodies, and their hooves struck the road in a barrage of panic.

"There." Asher pointed to the bottom of the sinkhole. A large pipe about eight feet in diameter poked from one side of the hole. "We need to get inside there. Move, everyone!"

We scrambled down the sloping sinkhole, veering around blocks of concrete and jutting steel bars. Asher and Booker scooped up the injured man, Raj, and bolted for the gaping pipe, followed by Willow. Yuki and I grabbed Mr. Isaac's arms and hustled him forward. Natalie brought up the rear.

As we hurried inside the huge concrete pipe, bats winged overhead, fleeing outside. The bottom of the pipe was lined with black pellet-like droppings and urine, and a foul stench saturated the air, forcing us to breathe through our mouths.

While the others moved further inside the dark pipe, Asher and I remained near the entrance, watching the carnage outside.

The krols drove the herd toward the sinkhole, howling gleefully as the massive beasts tumbled down the slopes. Some bison broke their legs and flailed on the debris, bellowing with pain. Others struggled to climb the loose dirt, hooves frantically digging into the soft soil.

The krols raced down the slopes and began their slaughter. Spears whizzed into foam-flecked brown bodies. Blood spurted in scarlet streams. The dying animals' squeals and bellows made me shudder, and the merciless shrieks of the krols sent icy shivers down my spine.

I remembered images of a diorama at a "Prehistoric Man" exhibition years ago. In it, the early humans had herded bison over a cliff so they could easily kill them.

In the street today, the krols had herded the bison into the sinkhole for a similar reason. They'd worked together, using strategy and a trap to achieve their goals.

I swallowed. The krols were evolving at a frightening rate.

Around us, the air stank of fear and pain and death. Finally, the last bison gasped and stopped kicking. A brief silence fell. Then, as one, the krols raised their dripping spears and shrieked a long cry of triumph that spiraled up and up.

Asher and I glanced at each other and retreated further into the darkness of the pipe. I hoped the krols were too excited by their bloodied victory to remember the humans in this pipe.

From the darkness, we watched them split into small groups of four. Grunting and straining, each group hauled a massive bison up the dirt sides and onto the road.

Finally, the krols disappeared with their catch.

Two dead bison remained in puddles of blood near our pipe. Had the krols left them behind because they had enough fresh meat? Or were they planning to get them later?

I stiffened at a worse possibility. Perhaps armed krols were guarding the sinkhole, out of sight, ready to kill us when we left the pipe.

From Asher's shallow breathing and tense posture, I sensed he had the same fears as me.

Time passed with molasses slowness. Naked-necked vultures ripped flesh from the two brown carcasses. Flies settled on the blood.

And still no sight or sound of the krols.

Asher and I edged forward to the rim of the pipe.

"They could be hiding up there, you know," he whispered to me. "Waiting for us to emerge from this tunnel."

"I know."

"We can't leave here until it's safe." He cleared his throat. "Maybe you can see if it's safe, Kass."

"What? How?"

He pointed up. Three bats had remained in their roost, hanging upside down from the pipe. "That 'blind as a bat' thing is a myth. They can see fine, even in daylight."

"You want me to mind-blend with a bat?" I fought to keep my whispered voice from squeaking in disbelief. "I thought you hated my hybrid powers."

"Not today," he replied, sounding sheepish. "Does that make me a hypocrite?"

"A bit."

A lot!

I was tempted to wait until he begged a little, but I wanted to get out of this stinking pipe too. The others were further inside, enduring the stench and filth in silence. Raj sat on the bat droppings, his broken leg outstretched; Mr. Isaac held a rag over his friend's mouth, muffling his groans. Willow and the others leaned against the curved concrete side, unwilling to sit on the filthy black floor, which crawled with insects and grubs.

"Okay," I muttered to Asher. "I'll do it. But you have to hold my non-conscious body up. Don't lay me down on that disgusting muck. Promise?"

"Promise."

Asher held my limp body to his chest as I pushed my mind into the nearest bat. As usual, I met a gray resistance. I shoved through it and merged with the bat. Then, with a flap of leathery wings, I was outside. It felt good to be flying through the sunshine, even if I was merged with an ugly-faced critter.

Bat-me flew around the sinkhole and then around the neighboring blocks. Once. Twice. Three times. The area was quiet and motionless under the midday sun, with only the occasional screech of a vulture to disturb the peace.

And still no sign of a silver-eyed eagle, WindLord.

With a bat sigh, I returned to the pipe.

A quick mind-hop later and I was back in my own body, conscious again. Asher still held me against his chest, and for a moment I lingered in his embrace, listening to his heartbeat, savoring his strong arms, reveling in his musky odor.

"Kass," he murmured, sensing my return. His arms tightened as he gathered me closer.

38

"Ash!" whispered Willow, distressed. She moved to the front of the pipe. "Why are you hugging Kass? What's going on?"

Flustered, I straightened and reluctantly stepped away from him. Attempting to sound feeble, I quavered, "Thanks, Asher. I feel a bit better now. I thought I might faint from the smell, but I'm okay."

"Oh." Willow paused, then quietly said, "I'm glad you're feeling better, Kass."

The girl, a renowned actress, must've seen through my amateurish performance. Perhaps she was simply choosing to believe that I'd been queasy and that Asher, the love of her life, hadn't been hugging me.

"I'm glad you're feeling better too, Kass." Asher's voice held an underlying question as he continued, "Do you want to go outside for some fresh air? Or do you want to remain in here?"

"Let's go outside. It looks safe."

"Great." He swallowed guiltily as Willow stared at him. Clearly, he wanted to tell her that he'd been holding me because I was non-conscious; however, his orders from Commander Powell prevented him from revealing my mental powers to anyone.

I felt a twinge of satisfaction. *Ha. How does it feel to keep secrets from those you care about, Asher? Not much fun, eh?*

And then, surprisingly, a flare of longing pierced me. Had he enjoyed holding me as much as I'd enjoyed his embrace?

Were we really over each other?

These unanswerable questions lingered within me.

We hurried from the pipe, glad to be out of that dark, reeking place.

Booker grabbed up an old board half-buried in the dirt. "We can use this as a stretcher for Raj."

"Good," Asher said, flicking back to leader mode. "Yuki, wipe down Raj's back. It's covered in muck."

As we laid the middle-aged Indian on the board, I noted that Raj's dirty mechanic's coveralls were threadbare and patched. Strange. With all the clothes available in New York, why did he prefer these particular coveralls?

"How are you feeling, Raj?" asked Mr. Isaac, pressing two fingers to a spot on the man's neck. "Your pulse is rapid. Are you in pain?"

"Sure am, buddy."

"Let me check your injury." My ex-neighbor peeled off the dirty rag, revealing a pair of sticks tied to Raj's swollen leg. "Excellent. The splints have immobilized the bone."

Booker kneeled beside the makeshift stretcher, telling Raj, "We've found some ropes. They'll hold you in place while we carry you out of this sinkhole."

"Thanks, kid."

Mr. Isaac asked me, "Are you taking him back to your garrison, Mushroom Girl?"

"You know about our garrison?" I asked.

"Every survivor out here knows about it."

"Oh. Right."

"So, is that where you're taking Raj?"

Booker and Natalie began securing Raj to the board.

"Yes," I said. "We have an infirmary there—and a doctor."

"What kind of doctor?" Mr. Isaac asked.

"Family medicine."

"Do they have painkillers? Ice packs to reduce the swelling on Raj's leg?"

"Yes to both. Don't worry, we'll take good care of your friend."

Mr. Isaac motioned Asher and me aside. "Raj used to be a mechanic before the Mist. For twenty years he worked on engines and he loved it." He stared into the distance for a long moment, his eyes haunted. "Perhaps there's a position for him in your garrison? Once his leg is better?"

"Perhaps," Asher said. "He'll have to pass an interview first, but we can always use another mechanic."

"What about me, mister? Can I join your garrison too?"

My eyes widened in surprise. For months in the subway tunnels, Mr. Isaac had lived like a hermit, refusing to open his bunker door even when I'd brought him food every week.

He noticed my surprise. "I'm sick of living alone, Mushroom Girl. I thought, after watching thousands of people die from the Red Fever, that I'd failed both myself and society. I couldn't save anyone, no matter how hard I tried. And that despair broke something inside me. But that was over a year and a half ago. I'm better now. Plus since you left, the tunnel's been mighty lonely." He turned to Asher, his expression eager. "Can I join your garrison too?"

Asher eyed Mr. Isaac's gray hair, stooped posture, and skinny physique. From the dismay on his face, I guessed his thoughts: *this guy's too old and frail to be useful to the Weston Battalion; we can't accept him.*

Quickly, before Asher could shatter the man's hopes, I spoke up. "Mr. Isaac, you seem experienced at first aid. Do you have any medical training?"

The old man's shoulders straightened and his eyes glinted with bright memories. Twenty years fell away—and I suddenly realized he wasn't old. He was middle-aged, possibly late fifties.

"I have *lots* of medical training, Mushroom Girl," he said proudly. "I was a top trauma surgeon until the Mist. Why? Do you need a surgeon at the garrison?"

"Absolutely!" Asher's face was alive with excitement, as though he'd just found a priceless treasure—which he had. "Welcome to the Weston Battalion."

"Hang on." I held up a hand. "There's one condition, Mr. ... I mean, Dr. Isaac."

"Which is?" he asked.

"You gotta stop calling me Mushroom Girl."

"Agreed ... Kass Madison."

We hurried back to our Hummer, still scanning the streets for krols, still cautious, but overall in a jubilant mood. The Weston Battalion now had a doctor *and* a trauma surgeon. For once, things had gone our way. It was a small victory, but victories were scarce these days and we gladly took it.

39

Tension sizzled in the air, as alive as an electric current.

Two days after the incident with the bison at the sinkhole, I stood with Asher and Willow on the bank of the Hudson River. At least fifty members of the garrison had gathered here as well, all waiting for Lightning One to begin its test flight.

However, instead of focusing on the parked ship, most people were whispering and staring at Asher, Willow, and me.

A flush burned my cheeks. Why were they talking about us? Were they discussing my breakup with Asher? Or Willow's coolness toward me? Surely they had more important things to worry about.

With a bright smile, I said to Willow, "I hear you're lifting heavier weights each week, plus your target shooting has improved. That's great."

"We do what we must, for to do otherwise is against our fate." She cast me the briefest of glances. Then she studied the cloudless sky, as if Lightning One were flying up there instead of parked on the riverbank.

We do what we must, for to do otherwise is against our fate. Another famous line from her old show, *Pandora.*

A short distance away, Sergeant Thorne and two of his men watched us, their glares heavy with loathing. My flushed cheeks were joined by a shiver down my spine.

"Where's Lynxx?" Asher asked me.

I shifted position, turning my back on the three soldiers. "No idea."

"I thought he'd want to watch the test flight."

"He must have something else to do." Not unexpected. Since Lynxx's accusation that I'd betrayed him, he'd made a point of avoiding me. Maybe he was watching from afar.

I scanned the bank. No sign of him.

And no sign of any tumbleweeds, either. *Good.* I still had nightmares about the one that had carried Lynxx and me to the bottom of the shark-infested Hudson River.

At least I was still healthy.

It had been over fifty days since I'd drunk any Lazarus tonic, and I could finally relax. My leukemia was gone. I would've liked to celebrate my cure with Lynxx—and thank him again for all his help—but he kept avoiding me.

With a groan of engines, Lightning One rose a few feet into the air and hovered. To my relief, people returned their focus to the ship, *oohing* and *ahhing* in excitement while keeping well back. Since no one knew how safe the repaired ship was, the commander had decided its test flight would be over water instead of land.

Powell joined us. "I wanted to copilot with Nila," he said, brow furrowed, "but she insisted on going alone."

"No point in risking your life too, sir," Asher pointed out.

Willow waved to Soo-Yun on the other side of the crowd. "I'm going to say hi." She headed for her friend.

Inside Lightning One, Nila must've pushed something because the bullet-shaped ship suddenly expanded, becoming as long as three buses. This incredible "accordion" feature changed the ship from short and stumpy to long and thin—like the fuselage of a small commercial plane—and increased its internal space.

Lightning One's engine rose to a whine and the white ship trembled. Then, with breathtaking speed, it whooshed forward, creating wide ripples across the water. In the distance, it slowed and turned in a series of aerobatic moves, graceful as a bird.

People's gazes remained fixed on Lightning One, aware this ship could help save their lives.

Lightning One sped back across the river and reduced speed as it approached us. Engine humming, the ship suddenly dropped to the ground. Wings of dirt sprayed on either side as it slid toward a group of spectators, who screamed and scattered. With a groaning shudder, the ship stopped at the end of a long furrow. Silence hung like a guilty accusation in the air as Nila exited through the open hatch.

"Rough landing, folks," she called out. "It's still got a few glitches, but I'll fix them."

"Is anyone hurt?" Commander Powell shouted to the spectators.

A chorus of "We're okay" and "No" answered him.

Interesting, I thought. Nila's concern had been for the ship, while Commander Powell's concern was for his people.

She approached us. "The ship should be ready in two days, Lincoln. My team will be here by then."

"Your team?" Powell asked, raising his brows.

She lowered her voice to a whisper. "Other Sphere hybrids." So far, Nila's hybrid origin was still a secret, known only to Lynxx, Asher, the commander, and me. Talking at a normal volume again, she said, "A dozen will be coming on the mission with me. Two of them will remain at each location around the world, guarding the drums of Shimmer gas until Zero Hour."

Asher and I stayed silent, listening.

Powell frowned. "I planned on sending two squads from the Weston Battalion to guard the drums."

"We don't need them."

"I thought this was a joint operation."

"Be logical. We'll only have one shot at distributing the six Shimmer drums around the world. Each drum must release its contents at exactly Zero Hour. Nothing can go wrong. My team has been preparing for this mission for ages. They know what to do."

"Yes, they'll guard the drums, which will be programmed to go off at Zero Hour. It's not complicated, Nila. I'm sure my soldiers could handle it too."

"It's my plan and my Shimmer gas. I know my team and, with respect, I trust them. It's my decision."

She and Commander Powell moved away, still arguing. As they left, Willow rejoined us.

Sergeant Thorne and his two men glared after Powell and Nila, then turned their glares back on Asher, Willow, and me.

Fed up, I rolled my eyes. "What's with Thorne and his cronies? They keep staring at us."

"Not us," Willow muttered. "You, Kass."

"Me? Why?"

"Is it true that you're like the hybrids?"

My heart started pounding. "What do you mean?"

"Word is, you got some of Lynxx's blood in a cut on your hand or something." She paused for a long moment. "Apparently, you have special mental powers just like the hybrids."

40

Asher quietly asked, "Who told you this, Willow?"

"Everyone knows. It's all around the garrison."

Oh no. That was why people were whispering and staring. They were talking about *me*. And Sergeant Thorne and his pals were glaring at *me*.

For a moment, I felt a flash of panic. My old fears of being an outsider returned, along with terrible memories of rejection and loneliness.

And then a calm filled me.

I was different; I accepted that. Most of the Weston Battalion had known me since I'd joined the garrison. If they couldn't accept me for who I was, then that was their problem, not mine. If they wanted to turn against me through fear and ignorance and prejudice, let them.

I was tired of worrying about other people's opinions. As long as I didn't harm anyone, I had the right to be me.

Several people warily approached, their words tumbling in a jumble of questions.

"Is it true? Do you have some of *their* blood in you, Kass?"

"Are you now a hybrid?"

"Do you have their powers?"

"Can you read our minds?"

"What am I thinking right now?"

Dismayed, Asher muttered to me, "I'm beginning to understand why you kept your secrets for so long."

I remained calm. The people at the garrison had eventually accepted Lynxx, even though he was a hybrid. Hopefully, they'd accept me too.

"Mutant. Freak." Sergeant Thorne spat out the insults as he stomped across to me. "You don't belong with our kind."

Asher stepped forward, hands balled into fists. "What kind is that, Sergeant? Bigots? Narrow-minded idiots?"

"I have a right to my opinion," he snarled. "She's infected with their blood. We've got to protect the purity of humanity."

When Asher opened his mouth to argue, I silenced him with a gesture and stepped toward Thorne, my voice steady. "Yes, Sergeant, I do have hybrid blood in me, but I'm still human." Around us, more and more people moved forward, listening. "The blood's been in me since the day I joined the garrison over a year ago. And in all that time, even when I was sick or injured or felt like crap, I've worked toward the survival of the Weston Garrison and every person in it."

"That's true," Asher told the gathering. "Kass is an important part of our community. She's fought the terras and xans almost every day for a year."

"She's an incredible fighter," Harlem added loudly. "Plus she's saved my life a few times."

"Same here," Booker called out.

"Kass smart and brave," Yuki said in his precise manner.

"She's my role model," Natalie piped up. The ex-cheerleader waved invisible pompoms as she spelled out, "K-A-S-S. Yay, Kass!"

Moved, I swallowed a lump in my throat. "Thanks, guys."

One of our gardeners wove his way to the front of the crowd. "Hey, Kass, have you ever used your mental mojo?" His tone was friendly and interested.

I nodded. "I've used my ... er, mojo ... a few times, especially to keep my team and me alive. I'm not a big fan of terras, xans—or death."

People chuckled.

A thirteen-year-old from a scavenger team raised her hand. "I'm gonna be a resistance fighter just like Kass when I get older."

"Hopefully you won't have to," I said, thinking of the Shimmer gas. "It's dangerous work, but I do it for the same reason that every fighter in the Weston Battalion does. Because we have to. We know we can't win. But we still have to try."

A mechanic, Ben, yelled from the back, "We're lucky to have all of our resistance fighters, including Kass!"

"Ben's right," Asher said firmly. "Apart from fighting terras and xans and krols, we're going up against two even more dangerous enemies—the Outriders and the Chi'az. Kass's mental powers might give us an edge we can use."

I glanced at him, surprised. This was the first time he'd openly accepted my hybrid powers.

"I agree, son." Commander Powell strode through the crowd, his face grim. "I don't know who leaked the news about Kass's mental powers, but it doesn't matter. Secrets always leak out, sooner or later."

So true.

"You knew about Kass, Commander?" a woman asked. "And you're okay with her?"

"Yes to both questions." Powell's gaze swept the crowd. "It's a new world, folks. Recently, I've come to realize that we need to adapt or die. Kass never asked for her powers—she gained them by accident—but she uses them to save people's lives and to fight the good fight. We should be thankful she's on our side."

The crowd murmured their agreement, and people cried out variations of "He's right" and "Good on you, Kass!"

"Okay, folks," Powell said, "let's get back to the garrison. We've work to do."

The group disbanded, no longer whispering about me. Instead, they openly chatted about my powers, and their glances were supportive and approving rather than furtive.

Except for Sergeant Thorne and his men. They stood apart, arms folded, glowering at me.

The commander and Nila wandered back to Lightning One.

Asher relaxed. "That went okay, Kass."

"Yeah."

Harlem grinned at me. "I can't believe you've got superpowers. How cool is that?"

I laughed. "They're not superpowers."

"Close enough." Beaming, Harlem slung an arm over my shoulder and held up a digital camera. "Say cheese." *Snap.* He inspected the selfie. "Perfect. I gotta take one of you, me, and Soo-Yun when we get back to the garrison. I'm even going to print off the pictures in case we ever run out of electricity."

"I think we'll be fine for a while," I told him. Weston Tower's solar panels and wind turbines still produced huge amounts of electricity each day.

I smiled as he carefully pocketed his camera. At least Harlem was enthusiastic, and most of the other people seemed okay with me, including Asher. Perhaps having humanity in peril—again—had made them more accepting.

Except for Sergeant Thorne and his cronies.

They hated me.

To them, I was a freak.

A mutant.

Dangerous.

41

After I'd been "outed" at the test flight, word quickly spread about my mental powers. Fortunately, almost everyone at the garrison was enthusiastic about having another weapon—me—to use against the Outriders and the oncoming invasion.

The next day, when someone noticed two eagles coming and going through an upper-floor window, Commander Powell ordered the floor off-limits to the general population. He also posted soldiers there, pointedly choosing men loyal to him and not to Sergeant Thorne.

My next mission involved the eagles—and Lynxx's reluctant participation again. In the birds' room, he made sure the door to the Aerie was locked; we trusted Powell's soldiers, but with both our bodies vulnerable, we were taking extra precautions today.

Finishing our lesson, Lynxx coldly asked, "Agreed, Kassia?"

"Okay, okay. You're in charge."

"And you understand all our eagle sounds and wing gestures?"

"Locked away in my vault." I tapped my forehead, trying to inject a little lightness into our lesson.

It didn't work. Lynxx's face remained hard. "Good. Let's get this over and done with."

I sighed. Would he ever forgive me for telling the commander about our mental powers?

We moved to the separate couches that he had set up in the Aerie.

"Ready?" he asked the other person in the room.

"Yep." Harlem's face beamed with excitement and pride. He'd been chosen to place a warming blanket over the egg in the nest once WindLord and SkyLady left. "Good luck."

"Luck is a non-programmable variable," Lynxx stated. "Kassia and I are simply going to listen to the Wilders on the beach today. If they mention the Outriders, excellent. If not, we head back home. Either way, this will be a short, simple mission."

Within minutes, Lynxx and I had mind-blended with the two eagles and were flying south to Brighton Beach.

SkyLady-me scanned the streets and buildings below. As expected, the terra jungle was expanding each day, along with the numbers of xans and krols. The sooner the Shimmer gas was released, the better, I thought. But what if the Threads were released first?

Shaking off my fears, I followed WindLord-Lynxx on our "short, simple mission."

The reports were right. Three men stood on Brighton Beach, dwarfed by a dead whale on the sand. Circling far above, I scrutinized the trio with my sharp eagle vision. All wore biker gear, and I recognized the bald tattooed head of one of them.

Fang, the former leader of the Wilders.

So the thug was still alive. Plus he'd rustled up a couple of new biker buddies.

WindLord-Lynxx cocked his feathered head and gave three soft chirps that meant *Follow me.*

Quietly, we landed in a pine tree near the trio. We hoped the men would mention the Outriders and their possible location. It was a long shot, but it was all we had.

After our attack on Crendell Laboratories, Bone and his black canisters had disappeared. Many people believed that he and the Brethren had left Manhattan. Unconvinced, Commander Powell had organized for posters to be placed around the city, offering food rewards for any information about them.

So far, no one had come forward.

"This is a bad idea," said one of the men on Brighton Beach.

"It's a no-brainer." Fang slurred his words as he waved a long-bladed knife around. Was he drunk? On drugs? "We cut up the flesh. Dry it. Trade the meat with other survivors around the city. Make a killing."

"It stinks." The second man crinkled his bulbous nose.

"It won't stink after we dry it out," Fang said. "You gotta look at the bigger picture. We'll become whale meat barons and earn some respect."

"We can kill a deer for fresh meat."

"Too much work." Fang's bloodshot eyes peered at the carcass, and he waved his knife again. "We got a mountain of meat right here, ready for the cutting."

"Stinky meat."

I sniffed the air with my beak but could only detect a faint foul odor. Eagles had great vision, good hearing—and a poor sense of smell.

Fang staggered across to the whale. "Wimps. I'll do it myself."

WindLord-Lynxx turned his silver eyes to me. He shoved his beak forward, sniffed the air, then cocked his head in a silent question.

Huh? That series of gestures hadn't been in our lesson. What did—?

Oh. Got it. Lynxx was wondering how long the whale had been beached.

I shrugged my bird shoulders. *No idea.*

Through the mesh of leaves, I studied the whale, remembering an old internet video I'd seen years ago. In it, a man had started cutting up a beached dead whale bloated with methane gas.

Fang made a long ragged incision down the side of the decomposing whale—

—and a huge gush of guts and liquid exploded from the incision like a gigantic popped pimple.

Yep, that's what had happened in the internet video too.

The bikers staggered back, drenched in brown muck and draped with whale intestines.

Fang's two cronies rushed into the ocean, trying to wash off the putrid stuff. Their furious shouts rang out.

"You idiot, Fang!"

"I told you it stank."

"You always think you know best!"

"We've had enough of your loser ideas. Find yourself some new suckers."

Fang tried to follow the pair, but they yelled abuse and threw pieces of whale intestines at him. Swearing, he stumbled down the beach and washed himself, alone.

WindLord-Lynxx turned to me, and his eagle shoulders shook as though he was laughing inside. My feathered head bobbed up and down as I silently laughed too.

After a few moments, WindLord-Lynxx tilted his head at me. His silver gaze somehow seemed a little friendlier, and I sensed a slight easing of the strain between us. He gave a short whistle. *Time to go.*

Still inwardly laughing, we began flying back to Weston Tower. Lynxx had been right. Our mission had been short and easy—plus unexpectedly fun. I couldn't wait to share the story with Asher and the others.

Midway over Brooklyn, the silent streets below us were ripped by a sudden volley of gunshots.

42

Cautiously, we descended toward the gunfire.

Were some people battling krols? Or hunting animals?

The truth was much worse.

Below, SkyLady-me saw Roosevelt Plaza, an open area layered with velvet-vine terras. The plants carpeted the pavers and wallpapered the sides of adjoining buildings. They even blanketed the benches, kiosks, and vans in the plaza, creating a serene patchwork of greenery.

Except today the serenity had been shattered by a battle.

Two groups hunkered behind overgrown benches and kiosks, exchanging gunfire. The bodies of five strangers—four men and a woman—lay in dark pools of blood.

Three unfamiliar cars had mounted the curb, tires shredded. Spike-strips lay across the road.

Had this been an ambush?

WindLord-Lynxx jerked his head to the right and uttered three sharp chirps. *Follow me.*

We alighted in a thick tree in the sidewalk, its partial net of vines screening us from view.

I peered through the lattice of leaves—and stiffened in shock.

On one side, Sergeant Thorne and three of his men were crouching behind an old pretzel kiosk draped with vines. Shouting, they fired at a group of seven strangers across the wide plaza.

"... must protect purity of humanity ..."

"... this is *our* city for humans only ..."

"... not letting any more freaks into the garrison ..."

The strangers returned fire.

My gaze darted between the five bodies sprawled across the plaza and the seven strangers sheltering behind another kiosk. Twelve people in total.

Oh no. This must be the team that Nila had been expecting.

Somehow, Sergeant Thorne and his men had found out that these newcomers were Sphere hybrids, and they'd discovered their route to Weston Tower. I guessed they'd also found out that Nila was a hybrid too.

The commander was right: *Secrets always leak out, sooner or later.*

A metal canister thudded among the Sphere group, hissing out a furious gust of chemicals. Tear gas. The hybrids staggered into the open, coughing and doubled over, eyes streaming.

A smoke bomb followed close behind, spewing white clouds.

Chaos erupted.

Yelling like banshees, Sergeant Thorne and his men rushed across the plaza, shooting at the disoriented Sphere hybrids. A dark-haired teenage girl screamed, grasped her abdomen, and crumpled in a heap. A man fell backward, half his head blown off.

Beside me, WindLord-Lynxx uttered a furious screech and rocketed from the tree.

No, Lynxx!

Broad wings flapping, he flew through the thick smoke like a screeching feathered avenger. With his taloned feet, he kicked a rifle from Thorne's hands, then whirled on a soldier, Rogue, and raked his face.

SkyLady-me bolted after Lynxx, backing him up—but wishing we'd stayed hidden. Two eagles against four armed soldiers intent on protecting "the purity of humanity" was crazy.

As Thorne grabbed up his fallen rifle, I scraped my talons across his neck. He bellowed, spun around, and slammed the butt of his rifle into my small eagle head. Stars exploded before my eyes, and a surging brightness shoved me toward the edge of SkyLady's mind.

Desperately, I clung on.

Had to.

No other animal hosts nearby.

Eagle-me rolled across the pavers, a limp mass of feathers that flopped into a weed-filled garden bed. Stunned, I lay on some dead leaves, clinging to SkyLady's mind by a flimsy thread.

Noises raged in the plaza. Shouts and curses. Loud screeches. Moans. Pleas. More gunshots, harsh and brutal. Tires squealing as vehicles raced away.

Silence.

Lynxx?

The air was thick with smoke. Plus something else: death. It hung in a pungent stink of blood and voided bowels that even a weak, almost-knocked-senseless eagle like me could smell.

I uttered a soft chirp. *Lynxx?*

Nothing.

I peered around. No sign of Sergeant Thorne or his men. The kiosk that had sheltered the Sphere hybrids was now on fire and gushing brown smoke.

Crumpled bodies lay everywhere. Scattered guns. Empty tear gas canister. Smoke bomb trailing gray wisps. Bloodied velvet-vines. An old feather duster. Bullet casings—

What?

I staggered to my taloned feet. Still unsteady, I hopped to the out-of-place object.

Not an old feather duster.

WindLord.

Two yellow eyes stared sightlessly from a small, bloodied face with a snapped beak. WindLord's head had been bashed in and his dead body flung aside.

Noooo!

Where was Lynxx? Was he dead too? Had he died with his eagle host? Or had he managed to mind-leap into something else? Frantically I scanned the overgrown plaza. Still no animals or birds in sight. It was as empty as the surface of the moon.

SkyLady-me hurried around the area, searching for him. Too weak to fly, I used a rolling gait that was awkward and slow. At a low moan, I hopped over to the dark-haired teenager. She lay clutching her bleeding abdomen, eyes squeezed shut in agony.

Three weeks ago, I had mind-blended with a dying hybrid, Ethan Steel, to retrieve a formula we'd needed. Had Lynxx mind-blended with this dying hybrid girl?

I gave a sharp questioning chirp.

Her eyelids fluttered open. She stared at eagle-me, hope flickering across her face. I turned away, flooded with disappointment and guilt. Her eyes were brown, not silver. Lynxx wasn't in there.

Sorry, miss, I thought. I can't help you while I'm an eagle. Later, I can try—

Something thudded into my mind. I physically staggered forward, my talons scratching the pavers. Regained my balance. Felt weird. Crowded. Suffocating.

I need this host.

Shocked at the strange voice in SkyLady's mind with me, I mentally asked, *Who said that? Lynxx, are you trying to mind-blend with SkyLady?*

Get out.

No, not Lynxx. He'd never tell me to leave my animal host, especially with no other hosts around. Anyway, this presence felt feminine.

Heart racing, I stared down at the teenage girl. Once, she'd probably had delicate features, a slender body, and shiny dark hair. Now she looked like a dirty, crushed doll. Her hands had fallen from her bloodied abdomen, and her chest no longer rose and fell. Her hair was matted with leaves and dirt and blood. The pain in her brown eyes had evaporated, leaving them lifeless.

Get out. The voice was stronger this time. More insistent. The feminine presence swelled larger and harder, like a black rock crowding me against the side of SkyLady's mind.

Who are you? I asked.

Eva. I have to get to Nila. The Shimmer gas.

We're helping Nila at the Weston Battalion.

Must get to her.

The seconds were slipping past, each an eternity of not knowing if Lynxx was dead or alive.

I'm sorry, Eva, but you can't stay in SkyLady. I'm in here and I need to find my friend.

No other birds or animals around. All fled during battle.

Can't you wait in your own body? I'll get help after I find my friend.

Can't wait in a dead body. Need a living mind. You must leave. A cold blackness suddenly thrust me into a familiar spongy sensation: the thick gray wall that bordered SkyLady's mind.

Stop, Eva! There are no other animal hosts around. If you push me out of SkyLady, I'll die!

Get out. No room for us both.

The blackness swelled again, growing as solid as an upraised rock—and as threatening.

Desperately, using everything I'd learned, I tightened my focus into a single point and gave the cold blackness a massive shove that almost split my mind in half. I felt-heard a scream of despair as Eva's consciousness plunged backward, through the gray wall, and vanished.

SkyLady's mind suddenly had more space in it, and I could mentally breathe again. Fighting a massive headache, I studied the Sphere girl sprawled on her back. Her brown eyes were still frozen, and I sensed her temperature cooling.

Eva's body was definitely dead, and her consciousness was gone.

My relief held a tinge of guilt.

My overriding worry, though, was for Lynxx.

Where was he?

43

IN PAIN AND NEAR exhaustion, I continued my search, moving as fast as my awkward eagle gait would allow.

SkyLady-me hurried from body to body in Roosevelt Plaza. The Sphere hybrids' injuries were horrific. Brains blown out, mangled throats, gaping chest wounds.

A deep emptiness began to engulf me. How could Lynxx just be gone? I wanted to scream at the sky and fate, beg that he come back to me, that—

A low grunt. Then another.

Trembling with weariness and grief, I turned.

In a dead garden, two rabbits scurried from a burrow. One was white, the other brown. Both hopped toward SkyLady-me.

Hang on. Rabbits wouldn't hop toward an eagle. Eagles ate *rabbits.*

Unless ...

SkyLady-me studied the rabbits. Both had twitchy noses, quivering whiskers—and silver eyes.

Each rabbit was mind-blended with a hybrid.

They stopped a few feet away and peered at SkyLady-me with anxious, intelligent gazes.

Was Lynxx in one of these animals? If so, I needed to get both of us back to our bodies as soon as possible. But my mind-battle with Eva had left me too weak to carry two full-grown rabbits to the garrison several miles away. I barely had enough strength to carry one.

What if I brought the wrong animal back to the Aerie? What if I bought back a Sphere hybrid who then mind-leaped into Lynxx's body—and refused to leave? Lynxx would be left without a body—*his* body.

The white rabbit hopped forward and rose onto its hind legs. Its left ear was tattered but healed, as though it had been in a fight ages ago. Paws cutely held in front, it looked at me with a soft silver gaze that silently pleaded for my help.

This has to be Lynxx. No, wait. When has he ever acted ultra cute?

Maybe this was a Sphere hybrid trying to manipulate me. It might even be Eva, the dying girl who had tried to shove me out of SkyLady's mind. Eagle-me shuddered. I didn't want that ruthless girl anywhere near Lynxx's body.

How could I be certain?

Hmm.

Earlier today, before we'd mind-blended with the golden eagles, Lynxx and I had discussed signals. We'd agreed that a raised left wing or two chirps would mean *yes*, and a raised right wing or one chirp would mean *no*.

Rabbits couldn't chirp, but they could communicate in other ways.

Watching the white rabbit, I raised my left wing, the signal for *yes*.

Whitey blinked at me.

I raised my right wing, signaling *no*.

Whitey's pink nose twitched, and it brushed a fly away with a paw.

Not Lynxx.

My stomach knotted in panic.

Trembling, I shifted my gaze to the brown rabbit. *Please be him, please be him.* Slowly, barely breathing, I raised my left wing.

Brownie raised a hind foot, held it in the air, and then deliberately stomped the ground. Once. Twice. *Yes.*

Tiny heart thundering, I lifted my right wing.

Brownie stomped the ground once. *No.*

Lynxx!

The hybrid in Whitey must've sensed that it'd failed a test, because its silver eyes suddenly narrowed, going from cute and appealing to cold and hard. Growling, it glared at me, its tattered ear flicking in anger.

A sudden thought hit me. What if this Sphere hybrid leaped from Whitey's body into SkyLady's mind, like Eva had done? I wasn't strong enough to survive another mind-battle.

Fueled by fear, I swept forward and scooped up Brownie, taking care not to hurt rabbit-Lynxx with my talons.

SkyLady-me soared up, then headed toward the garrison, flying high to avoid being shot at by anyone on the ground.

Rabbit-Lynxx hung in my claws, calmly observing the empty city below. Trusting me. He was heavy for such a small animal, and I thought the flight to Weston Tower would be tiring and difficult.

But it wasn't.

As we flew home, my wings were strong and sure, and my grip on Lynxx never wavered.

44

Harlem's eyes widened as SkyLady-me flew into the Aerie carrying a brown rabbit in my eagle talons.

"Where's WindLord-Lynxx?" he cried.

Gently, SkyLady-me placed Brownie in Harlem's arms, and he cradled the furry animal, confused.

Seconds later, Lynxx's body stirred on the couch, his golden eyes haunted. "Thanks, Kassia. That was close."

When my human body remained unresponsive, Lynxx looked at SkyLady-me. I pointed my wing at Brownie, who was squirming in Harlem's arms. "Oh. Right." He turned to the black boy. "As soon as Kassia mind-leaps out of SkyLady, the eagle will try to eat the rabbit. You need to take it somewhere safe. Wrap it in the blanket that's covering the egg."

"Okay, but where's WindLord?"

"We'll explain everything later, Harlem. Hurry. Kassia needs to return to her body now."

Harlem grabbed the warming blanket and rushed from the room with the rabbit.

I mind-leaped into my own body. *Yes! I'm back!* I sat up, stretching my stiff muscles as SkyLady settled onto the egg in the nest.

For a long minute, Lynxx and I remained on the couches, numb, unable to verbalize the horror of the past half hour. Finally I stood. "We need to tell Commander Powell."

He nodded, then said, "Thanks for saving me." His voice was no longer cool and remote. It was normal, as though he'd finally forgiven me.

"You've saved me a stack of times, Lynxx. Glad to return the favor."

Lapsing into silence, we headed to Powell's office. When we saw the commander was alone, the floodgates opened. Talking quickly, tumbling over each other's sentences, Lynxx and I detailed the massacre at the plaza. Powell's face tightened, and he barked orders into his radio.

The three of us hurried down to the courtyard. At the main gates, Lieutenant Wu and a dozen soldiers had their weapons trained on Sergeant Thorne and his three men, who'd just returned to the garrison. Amid angry protests and scuffles, they were handcuffed and hustled across to us.

A small crowd gathered nearby.

"What's going on, Commander?" shouted Thorne.

Nila rushed across, crying out, "Is it true?"

Sergeant Thorne glared at her. "How did you find out so quickly?" As the commander's eyes flickered to Lynxx and me, Thorne turned his scowl on us. Fury reddened his skin. "So it was you two in those eagles at the plaza. I thought some of *them* were trying to do that mind-blending mojo as they died."

"Did you murder them all?" Nila asked him, pale and shaking.

"It's only murder if they're human," the sergeant snarled. "You *exterminate* cockroaches, rats, and hybrids."

Rogue spat on the ground. "We're just sorry we didn't kill more of your kind, freak."

"They were Sphere," she whispered. "We're on the same side."

"Not all of us." Thorne focused his beady eyes on me, and spittle sprayed the air as he went on, "You claim you're human, Kass, yet you tried to stop us. When you were in that eagle, you attacked *us*. You're worse than *them*. You're a filthy, hybrid-infected traitor."

Calmly, I met his furious gaze. However I remained silent. Why waste time arguing with someone who embraced such sick hatred and rage?

"Get them out of here," Commander Powell ordered Lieutenant Wu. "Post extra guards outside their cells. I'll deal with them later."

"Yes, sir." The lieutenant and his men pushed the swearing prisoners through the growing mass of spectators.

"Back to work, everyone." At Powell's words, the crowd reluctantly dispersed. He turned to a soldier. "Get Dr. Isaac, Nurse Ortiz, and Soo-Yun right away."

"Yes, sir." The soldier hurried off.

Since joining the Weston Battalion last week, my ex-neighbor from the subway tunnel had thrived. As our resident trauma surgeon, Dr. Isaac had already saved two lives, plus he and his mechanic friend, Raj, were a happy couple.

"What about Dr. Tran and the new medic, Juliet?" Nila demanded. "We'll need them both too."

"Tran and Juliet left an hour ago to deliver a baby." Sometimes the Weston Battalion loaned our medical personnel to outsiders who had refused to join our community.

"What's going on?" Asher asked, joining us.

Powell scowled. "Thorne and his men found out about Nila's Sphere colleagues. They ambushed them. No survivors."

Asher paled.

Powell sighed. "Soon everyone will know that Nila is a hybrid too. But I guess it doesn't matter anymore." He turned to Lynxx and me. "Meet us at the Hummers. We'll need you to show us exactly where it happened."

A short time later, we arrived at Roosevelt Plaza, along with ten armed soldiers. Nila raced toward the bloodied corpses, scattering feeding vultures. Dr. Isaac, Nurse Ortiz, and Soo-Yun hurried to the closest bodies. The rest of us followed, warily scanning the area for danger.

Wisps of acrid smoke trailed from the burned kiosk, and flecks of ash speckled the sprawled bodies like black tears. The reek of blood hung in the air, coppery and sour.

Kneeling, I opened the cardboard box that Harlem had given me. "Thanks for your help, Brownie." The brown rabbit scurried out, hopped across the death-quiet battlefield, and disappeared into his burrow.

Nila wove her way through the bloodied corpses. Most had freshly ripped flesh or gaping holes from the scavenging vultures. She stopped at a handsome middle-aged man with a chest wound, and her breaths grew faster, shallower. Tears trickled down her cheeks. "Teo." The name quivered with pain and grief; clearly, this man had been important to her.

Shuddering, she moved on. Finally, she reached the last body—the dark-haired teenager with the abdominal wound.

Eva. The girl who'd tried to kill me.

Nila sank to her knees like a broken marionette, and her shoulders slumped in despair. Gently she touched the girl's arm. "She's cold."

I turned away from her grief—and saw Lynxx dealing with his own.

"WindLord didn't deserve to die like this." His hands shook as he cradled the golden eagle's battered body. Gently, he wrapped the bird in a soft cloth he'd brought along.

"What are you going to do with him?" I quietly asked.

"Bury him near Olivia and Owlfred." After we'd returned from Florida, Lynxx had buried his pet owl between Olivia's and Charlotte's graves. "Do you think your sister will mind?"

I gave him a faint smile. "She'll be glad to have his company. She loved animals."

In the plaza, Dr. Isaac felt for a pulse on a slumped woman, then shook his head. Elsewhere, soldiers began wrapping the dead in black plastic. The Weston Battalion's cemetery, a few miles from the garrison, would be getting far more burials this week than just a golden eagle.

A familiar roar rang out. Lion. A few blocks away.

Closer, a pack of coyotes howled.

Asher cocked his head, listening. Then, unclipping his revolver's holster, he called out, "We need to move fast, guys. Sooner or later, those animals will head here, drawn by the scent of blood."

"We can deal with some wild animals, son," Commander Powell said. His hand rested on Nila's shoulder as she kneeled beside Eva's slender form.

"I'm not worried about the wild animals, sir. I'm worried about that thing calling its pack." Asher pointed across the plaza.

A krol with a wooden spear was crouching on the roof of a bus shelter, watching us.

Stiffening, Commander Powell called out, "Listen up, everyone. That krol's off-limits unless it attacks first. No sense in provoking it." He caught my eye and gestured me over. "Can you stay with Nila? I have to talk with Lieutenant Wu."

"Of course."

Awkwardly, I waited near the woman. Wiping her eyes, she stood and scanned the plaza.

"Are you looking for someone, Nila?"

"Not someone." She gestured to the dead girl at her feet. "She ... they ... would've tried to mind-leap into a bird or animal as they lay dying." She hesitated. "Kass, when you and Lynxx flew down here, did you see any animals?"

"By the time we arrived, most had been scared away by the battle."

"Most? So you *did* see some animals?"

Should I tell her the truth? Or would it be kinder not to give her false hope? I sighed. I was tired of secrets. Anyway, what right did I have to keep the truth from her?

"There were two rabbits with silver eyes." At her sharp intake of breath, I hurried on, "Lynxx was in the brown one, so I carried him back to the Aerie in my talons."

"What about the other rabbit?"

"The white one? Whitey? I couldn't carry him as well."

A gritty wind roamed the plaza. It gusted across the covered bodies and snapped the black plastic, creating a sound like bones clicking together.

"So you just left the other rabbit, Whitey, here?"

"I had no choice." I pointed to the garden bed. "Maybe he's in his burrow."

"If one of my people was mind-blended with a rabbit, he or she would've hopped over here as soon as our vehicles pulled up."

"I'm sorry."

"Not as sorry as me." As the wind ruffled the dead teenager's long dark hair, Nila's face crumpled. "She looks cold."

I scowled at the girl who'd tried to kill me. Yes, she had been cold—and ruthless. "I'll get a soldier to cover Eva with some black plastic. Then she won't be cold."

Nila's head snapped toward me, jaw rigid with shock. "I never told you her name."

I remained quiet.

"Did you talk to her before she died, Kass?"

"Sort of."

"What do you mean?"

"She tried to mind-blend with SkyLady-me. When there wasn't room for both of us in the eagle's mind, she tried pushing me out."

"And?"

"I told Eva that I was already in the eagle. I suggested she wait in her body until I could get some help."

"What did she say?" Tension edged Nila's voice, sharp as a razor. "Tell me her exact words."

"She told me that she couldn't wait in a dead body—"

"True."

"—and that she needed a living mind—"

"Also true."

"—and then she told me to leave."

"But you didn't."

I gaped at the woman. "Of course not. There were no other animal hosts around, and my own body was at Weston Tower miles away. If I'd left, I would've died."

"So you pushed Eva out of SkyLady's mind instead." Nila's brown eyes gleamed with a stony hatred. "You murdered my daughter."

45

During our drive back to the garrison, I again tried explaining to Nila what had happened with Eva.

The woman wouldn't look at me or listen. When we arrived at Weston Tower, she locked herself in her laboratory and refused to talk to anyone.

Thankfully, no one else blamed me for surviving. Still, I understood Nila's grief and fury. In her eyes, I had murdered her daughter, Eva. To me, it'd been self-defense.

I deeply regretted the woman's grief, but I didn't regret surviving. It had been Eva or me.

Face tight with grief, Nila drove off in a car, telling everyone she needed some time alone. When she returned to the garrison a while later, she worked in her lab for hours, refusing all help and company.

The next day, she called an urgent meeting with Commander Powell and the others. I stood at the back of the crowded room, wishing I wasn't there. She didn't look at me once.

By now, everyone knew Nila was a Sphere hybrid—but this time there was no flood of questions or debates about her origin. Instead, there was a swell of sympathy due to her personal tragedy: the death of her only child.

She stood at a podium at the front of the room. After clearing her throat a couple of times, the audience fell silent and she began speaking.

"My daughter's death has almost shattered me. However I know she'd want me to continue my work." Her voice trembled, and the audience murmured in sympathy. "The Shimmer formula is finished and the chemicals have been mixed." She paused. "I've managed to make enough Shimmer solution to fill seven metal drums, and at the moment it's going through a process of synthetization."

When people looked confused, she explained, "Putting it in non-scientific terms, the chemicals are kind of 'fermenting' in the drums, like beer fermenting." When the audience still looked confused, she tried again. "With beer, you put all the ingredients together, and over one or two weeks it ferments into a drinkable brew. The Shimmer chemicals are going through a similar but far more complex process."

People finally nodded in understanding.

"Why can't we just release the Shimmer gas now?" Sergeant Wu asked Nila.

"I wish we could. Unfortunately the gas isn't ready. As I just said, the chemicals need to synthesize—'ferment'—in the drums. And then all the drums have to release their gas at the same time."

"Why at the same time?" Commander Powell asked.

"Think of a pond with a single stone thrown into it. It will create ripples in only one part of the pond. Take that same pond, position seven people around it, and have them all throw their stone into the pond at the same moment. Those seven sets of ripples will hit each other, covering the entire surface."

"Okay. I get it." Powell paused. "How long will this 'fermentation' take?"

"Seven or eight days."

"We can't wait that long, Nila!"

"You have no choice. It'll be ready when it's ready."

"Can we start positioning the drums around the world now? We can set each timer to go off in a few days—at Zero Hour—when the gas has finished fermenting."

"That's exactly what I've decided to do. We'll leave one drum here in New York and position the other six at various release points around the world."

"Excellent. I'll have my men finish equipping Lightning One for departure. It should be ready to leave by tomorrow afternoon."

"Good," Nila said emotionlessly. "That'll give me time to bury my people."

Two hours later, I arrived at the small cemetery. Thankfully, the murdered Sphere hybrids—including Nila's daughter, Eva—were being buried on the far side. I hoped the woman wouldn't notice me over at Olivia's and Charlotte's graves, as I wanted to say goodbye to my sister and cousin in peace.

Following the latest meeting, Commander Powell had selected the participants of the oncoming five-day mission. Nila would be the main pilot, backed up by Carolyn, an ex-Air Force officer. Fourteen soldiers from the garrison would go on the mission; most would be left in pairs to guard the Shimmer drums at their various locations. Liberty Team would ensure that each location was free of dangerous terras and xans. Lastly, our resident terra expert, Lynxx, and a medic, Soo-Yun, would complete the group.

Twenty-four people in total.

Our mission would be underway tomorrow afternoon. Sooner than expected.

But maybe not soon enough.

Nila's latest intel had revealed that the Outriders were still racing to release their virus before us. No one knew if the Threads 2.0 would be ready in a day, a week, or even a month. This uncertainty left me feeling as if I were walking across a minefield, bracing for an explosion beneath my feet.

Shuddering, I pushed that bleak thought away.

Across the cemetery, four guys leaned on shovels, waiting for Nila to finish her eulogy. An old backhoe was parked nearby, used to dig today's graves. One of the diggers looked my way, then walked toward me.

I groaned.

Jase.

I turned my back, hoping he'd get the message that I wanted to be alone.

Nope. As he joined me, he whispered in an exaggerated conspiratorial tone, "If Nila tries to strangle you, I'll hold her while you run away."

So he'd heard about her daughter, Eva.

Disdainfully, I replied, "I don't run away. That's what you do."

His lips hardened into a thin line.

A small fresh grave lay near Owlfred's grave. Lynxx must've buried WindLord during the last hour, then weeded Olivia's and Charlotte's graves as well as Owlfred's. He'd placed armfuls of scented flowers on the two larger graves and stuffed toy mice on the two smaller ones.

His caring gestures brought a lump to my throat.

I placed a bunch of flowers on Olivia's grave, then another on Charlotte's. Their wooden grave markers had been freshly cleaned and were free of terra vines.

Lynxx again, I guessed.

Months ago, he'd carved a series of images into Olivia's grave marker that had represented parts of her life: Wind-Lord and Mousy, the Gapstow Bridge where Olivia and I had been reunited after the Mist, pill bottles and Lazarus flowers.

Jase studied my cousin Charlotte's grave. "So that's where she's buried." His tone was disinterested. Obviously, he hadn't crossed the cemetery to talk about his old girlfriend.

"Why are you bothering me?" I asked, annoyed. "Don't you have work to do?"

"Not until your great commander gives the signal. Then I'll have the honor of helping my talented workmates shovel dirt into a dozen graves."

"If you don't like your assignment, leave. No one's keeping you a prisoner at the Weston Garrison anymore. Everyone's too busy with other problems. Stay or go, it's your choice."

"Where am I supposed to go? Bone is probably long gone by now."

I stared at him in disbelief. "How could you even think about going back to that murderous hybrid?"

"At least he never put me on graveyard duty."

"Bone is trying to kill us! Are you insane, Jase? Or just a selfish idiot who doesn't care about anyone else?"

"Lighten up. I'm only joking."

"I don't believe you."

"I came over here to ask you a favor."

"Whatever it is, the answer's no. I don't owe you anything."

"C'mon, help me out. Put in a good word for me to the commander. Do it for Charlotte's sake."

"That's low, even for you."

"No, graveyard duty is low, the bottom of the bottom. I'm better than this. Before the Mist, I used to be class president and our school's star quarterback."

Willow and Asher wove their way through the headstones to us. She looked at Jase curiously. "You were class president? Really?"

"And my school's star quarterback," he boasted. "I was popular with the girls too. Even Kass here used to have a huge crush on me. Oh, she tried to hide it from my girlfriend, but I knew."

Flushing, I said, "That was a long time ago."

In a low, intimate tone, he murmured, "The memory of your crush, Kass, warms me in bed late at night. Perhaps someday I'll have more than your memory to keep me warm."

My stomach tightened. What was he doing? Was he trying to suggest that he and I could ever be lovers? The thought made me sick.

Scowling, Asher flicked his gaze between Jase and me. "I didn't realize you two knew each other before the Mist."

"Jase was my cousin's boyfriend," I told him.

"Your cousin?" Asher paused. "You mean CJ?" Charlotte's nickname in the Weston Battalion.

"Yes."

Willow tugged at Asher's sleeve. "We should get going. I promised Chef Einstein I'd help in the kitchen."

His scowl remained riveted on Jase. He almost looked jealous. Surely not. We were broken up. He was with Willow now.

"Hey, Kass," said Jase with fake concern, "how are you feeling these days, what with your leukemia and all?" He asked the question casually, but the way he watched Asher's face revealed his true intent. He was trying to cause problems between Asher and me. Payback, no doubt, for me refusing to help him with Commander Powell.

"Sorry to disappoint you," I replied, "but I'm cured."

"What?"

"Lynxx made a special tonic from the Lazarus terras. I drank it for months, and my leukemia eventually disappeared."

Asher gazed at me in wonder and relief. "Really? A while ago, you weren't sure if you were cured."

"I'm sure now. Lynxx is too. I haven't needed any meds or Lazarus tonic for the last couple of months. I'm perfectly healthy."

"Ash, we should get going." Willow shifted from foot to foot, as if eager to leave.

Jase arched a brow at me. "You were on death's doorstep when we were together after the Mist."

Asher flinched. "Together?"

"Not as a couple," I hastily explained. "Jase and I teamed up for a week after the Mist. Then, one day, he left me at Central Park and joined another group."

"Hey, it's not my fault the other people didn't want you." Jase fixed an innocent expression on his face. "What was I supposed to do? Hang around until you died? Then I would've been by myself."

Eyes darkening, Asher stepped toward the youth. "You left Kass alone?"

Jase bristled. "I had to, pal. Heck, you were there that day."

"What day?"

"That day in Central Park when Kass and I helped you burn some glow-lotus terras. You told us you were part of a group of resistance fighters. *You* didn't live alone, right? Since the Mist, people have had to band together to survive."

Asher turned to me, realization dawning on his face. "That girl at the field of glow-lotus terras was *you*? I had no idea."

Not surprising, I thought. I'd been wearing baggy clothes, huge sunglasses, and my hair had been tucked into my father's aviator hat.

"Maybe she was embarrassed," Jase suggested slyly. "She looked different back then. Skinny. Pale. Ill."

"I'm not embarrassed," I said. "I'm ashamed."

"Why?" Asher asked.

I struggled against the black memory that sometimes throbbed like an open wound at the back of my mind.

Locusts swarming up from the glow-lotus terras. Scores of insects crawling over me. Beating them off in a blind panic. Bumping into the young woman beside me.

My words emerged in a croak. "I knocked a woman, Sophie, into the glow-lotus terras."

Asher nodded. "I remember her lying on the flowers, pinned down."

"Yeah," Jase added grimly. "Screaming as she died."

"It was an accident," I whispered, guilt weighing each word. "My leukemia was getting worse. My meds had run out and I was getting sicker every day. Weaker."

Asher stared at me, a strange expression on his face.

Did he hate me now? Did I disgust him?

He murmured, "That was the day I played the 'Flower Duet' on the loudspeakers."

"I know," I said.

Jase rolled his eyes. "Kass was really weak and sick. I *had* to join the other group."

Face like thunder, Asher grabbed the boy by his shirt. "So you just left Kass in the middle of Central Park? Sick and alone and afraid? She almost killed herself that day."

I gasped in relief.

He didn't hate me.

Asher had remembered what I'd told him some months ago. How I'd sat on the edge of Gapstow Bridge, searching for a reason to live—and finding none. Below had floated some pink terra flowers, beautiful and deadly.

I had been about to throw myself onto them when two things had happened.

Music had started playing on a loudspeaker, and a silver-eyed squirrel had joined me on the bridge. A short time later, my sister, Olivia, had appeared—and I'd kept living.

Asher shoved Jase away. "You disgust me. Get out of my sight."

Swearing, Jase brushed down his shirt and stormed off.

Willow's beautiful face had grown strained during the argument. Her anxious gaze darted between Asher and me.

Was she worried that her boyfriend still had feelings for me?

46

A SCREECH RIPPED THE midday air.

Cradling a box of supplies, I looked up.

Beyond the garrison walls, a krol stood on the roof of a building, a spear gripped in its clawed hand. Since dawn, the animal had monitored the activity in this corner of the garrison, always watching in silence—

—until now.

Was its screech a territorial warning? An angry cry? Or a call for reinforcements?

"Where's Lynxx?" Harlem asked me, pausing near the open hatch of Lightning One. Around him, other people continued loading supplies into the ship, whose hull had been extended to its maximum length.

"He's getting some stuff from his old apartment at the Ferguson Complex," I replied. "He'll be back before we leave at four this afternoon."

"Good." Tiredness shadowed Harlem's face. Like everyone in the Weston Battalion, he was overworked and worried.

Stretching my aching muscles, I surveyed the busy garrison, wondering how things had gotten so bad. Every day since the Night of the Red Mist had felt slightly darker than the one before it as, helplessly, we'd watched our world break down. In the last eighteen months, we had slowly regressed to a pseudo twilight, no matter how bright or sunny the days actually were.

But now our twilight was darkening into midnight.

We knew the Outriders were determined to release their Threads first. If they succeeded, humanity could soon plunge into a darkness from which it would never emerge.

"I wish Soo-Yun wasn't going," Harlem fretted. "It's too dangerous."

"Good luck in trying to persuade her to stay behind." Soo-Yun looked delicate and petite, but she had an iron will once she'd made up her mind. "Besides, Commander Powell wants a medic on the mission. Juliet is too inexperienced, so Soo-Yun is going."

"Yeah." Harlem shifted his gaze to me. "Asher doesn't want you to go either."

"He told you that?"

A nod. "He's afraid you'll get hurt."

"Any of us can get hurt. It doesn't matter where we are."

"True." Sighing, Harlem carried a pile of sleeping bags into Lightning One.

Again, I glanced at the watching krol on the rooftop. The sooner we released our Shimmer gas, the better. By this time tomorrow, we'd be twenty hours into our five-day mission: depositing six drums of the "fermenting" gas across the planet in six different locations.

Two heavily armed soldiers would remain behind at each release point to protect their assigned drum. And even though Liberty Team would try to ensure that each point was free of dangerous terras and xans, I suspected that not everyone would survive.

The laughter of children interrupted my gloomy thoughts.

Nearby, an extensive vegetable garden occupied this distant part of the garrison. A dozen young children had finished their morning lessons and were now weeding the garden beds, supervised by their teacher. Our elderly head chef, Einstein, helped a trio of chatting kids fill baskets with carrots and potatoes.

Older children, also freed from their lessons, crossed to their chores in the converted buildings beyond the gardens. One structure contained horses, donkeys, and camels. A piggery housed dozens of hogs, and a coop contained hundreds of chickens. To their left, a large fenced area held sheep and cows.

At another screech, I looked up again.

Three krols now stood on the roof. All stared intently at this back area.

Were they interested in us—or our livestock?

In the past year, the garrison walls had been extended to include four main buildings and a park. Its high walls were patrolled by soldiers and dotted with skinned krols on upright wooden crosses. The soldiers and the dead krols were meant to deter anyone from attacking our community, and so far they'd worked. But for how long?

Weeks ago, Sergeant Thorne had suggested topping the walls with razor wire and explosives. Although the man was a hateful bigot, I had agreed with his suggestion. Commander Powell had not.

I sighed. In just a few hours, our mission would be underway and all events would be out of my control.

"Hey. They're back again." The little girl from the cruise ship, Zoey, pointed at half a dozen black vultures circling overhead.

"Back again?" I asked her. "You've seen them before?"

"Today and yesterday."

Weird. Usually, vultures circled above sick or injured animals, waiting for them to die. Why were these circling above our garrison? Were they mind-blended with Outrider hybrids?

Near the ship, Willow practiced throwing a spear at a straw-filled, krol-sized dummy. I watched her for a minute. Since Asher's argument with Jase at the cemetery yesterday, Willow had trained for extra hours. She seemed determined to become the actual embodiment of Pandora. She had even increased her dialogue quotes from the show.

Willow's spear hit the straw krol in the chest. She wiped her hands on her jeans and looked around for about the twentieth time. Over the past few hours, as I'd brought supplies to Lightning One, I'd seen her repeat the pattern time and again. Whenever she had hit the target on the dummy, she'd paused and looked around, as though hoping Asher had seen her bull's-eye.

Noticing me, she again asked, "Where's Ash?"

"He's in a meeting with Commander Powell and the councilors. They won't be finished until one o'clock, remember?"

"One o'clock?"

"Yes," I said. "I've told you this three times already." How could she have forgotten?

"Oh. Right," she replied vaguely. She picked up another spear, assessed its weight in her hand, and threw it at the straw krol. *Bull's-eye.*

Once again, her eyes swept the area for Asher.

Worried by her strange behavior, I had mentioned my concerns about Willow to Carolyn Wilson, Nila's backup pilot. She'd promised to talk to Commander Powell about getting Willow dropped from the mission.

Nila's cold tone cut through my thoughts. "Stop standing around like a slacker, Kass. Don't you have work to do?"

I flushed at her unfair accusation. I'd been loading supplies into Lightning One for three hours straight. Before I could answer, she swept past me, headed for Weston Tower.

"Don't take her comments personally, Kass," said Chef Einstein, a basket of carrots cradled in his arms. "She's still grieving her daughter's death."

"I know she blames me. But if I'd let Eva push me out of SkyLady's mind, I'd be dead instead of her daughter."

"Everyone here understands that, lass, including Nila. Logically, the woman is aware you had no choice. And eventually she'll accept it. But she's not there yet." The old man gently patted my shoulder. "Give her time, lass." Basket of vegetables in hand, he headed toward Weston Tower. "And good luck on your mission."

"Thanks."

A shadow flitted over me.

One vulture was still circling overhead but lower this time. Like the krols, its gaze was fixed on this back area of the garrison. The bird was too far away to see its eyes. Still, from the way it was intently watching us load the ship, I again suspected it was mind-blended with an Outrider hybrid.

Abruptly, the vulture veered away and disappeared.

Although relieved it was gone, I guessed it was off to report to Bone.

Along with the others, I continued loading Lightning One, supervised by Carolyn. Over the past few days, Nila had given the councilor a couple of lessons in flying the ship. Since Carolyn had flown Air Force planes before the Mist, she had quickly picked up the skills needed to pilot the ship.

An hour later, we had almost finished packing Lightning One. Its rear section was crammed with tents, weapons, tools, food, other supplies—and six drums of "fermenting" Shimmer gas.

"Good work, everyone," Carolyn said as Liberty Team took a brief break. "Have some lunch. Do your final packing. Then at 4 p.m. sharp, we take off." She paused. "What's that noise?"

A deep rumble came from the front of Weston Tower.

It grew louder, closer.

"What's going on?" Harlem asked Carolyn.

"No idea."

Blasts of gunfire rang out.

47

Confused, I glanced around. A low structure, Building B, blocked my view of the front courtyard.

A moment later, a thunderous explosion erupted from the area at the main gates. Another blast came from the eastern wall beyond Weston Tower. A third blast battered the western wall alongside Building C. Metal and concrete crashed down. Shouts. More gunfire. Screams.

Carolyn gasped, "I think our walls have been breached."

In the vegetable garden, the teacher shouted to her students, "Everyone to the barns. Now!" Screaming, the children scurried toward the far corner of the garrison.

The rumbling grew louder, a deep mechanical groan that I recognized from old war movies. It sounded like a tank. Was that possible?

Along with the others, I ran toward the front courtyard—but a massive blast stopped us midway. The ground shook and more chunks of concrete and metal crashed down. Black smoke billowed from Weston Tower.

Carolyn cried, "The tower's been hit!" She turned to us. "Stay back here. Take cover. I have to find my husband." She dashed away.

Harlem shouted, "Take cover, guys. We're under attack."

The concrete wall alongside the vegetable gardens disintegrated in a tremendous blast. Debris sprayed everywhere. A soldier plunged to the ground, vanishing beneath a waterfall of bricks and rubble. Other soldiers shouted as they ran along the wall's high walkway, toward the newborn hole.

Beyond the smoking gap, I saw a man holding a portable rocket launcher on his shoulder.

People in gray clothes and red armbands poured through the opening.

Brethren.

Some exchanged fire with the soldiers on the wall. Other Brethren ran toward Lightning One, pocketing their guns and raising swords and baseball bats.

Swords? Baseball bats?

Oh no.

I lunged at Lightning One and slammed my hand on a small exterior panel. The metal hatch hissed down, sealing the ship and preventing access to its interior. I could've sealed myself inside, but I couldn't abandon my friends.

Plus I had to stay outside to help protect Lightning One.

A group of Weston Battalion soldiers charged forward, firing at the Brethren, and a couple of the intruders slumped to the ground. Others sheltered behind benches, carts, compost bins, whatever they could find.

Harlem raced toward us, yelling at our soldiers, "Put your guns away. You'll damage the ship."

The Brethren weren't after Weston Tower, I realized. The tank attack at the front of the garrison, plus the rocket launcher breaches of the eastern and western walls, were all diversions. Their true target was in this area beside the vegetable gardens.

The Brethren wanted their ship back—intact.

Since bullets might damage the hull, they couldn't use their guns near it. Lightning One was their only means of distributing the Threads around the world—and our only means of spreading the Shimmer gas.

A spear whizzed past, missing me by inches.

I threw myself behind a huge water tank. Peered around the metal side. Fired at a charging Brethren. Watched the man clutch his chest and fall, blood spurting from his mouth.

Chaos everywhere.

Willow lunged at a muscled Brethren, dropping him with a sidekick to his stomach. She aimed another kick at his neck. He grabbed her leg, toppled her to the ground, and raised his baseball bat.

I darted forward, remote-pushing a broken brick off the ground. It arced through the air, struck the man's temple, and he slumped to the dirt.

"What are you doing, Willow?" I grabbed her hand and pulled her up. "That Brethren almost bashed in your face."

She cocked her head to the side, looking just like Pandora on her television series as she uttered a well-known line: "Victory belongs to the brave of heart."

"Maybe. But not to the dead of body."

"Triumph feeds on sacrifice." Another Pandorism.

She ran toward three Brethren who'd ganged up on a soldier, Ian. Frantically, he wielded his sword, backing away from his attackers.

Willow leaped onto an outdoor table, somersaulted through the air—her signature move from *Pandora*—and landed behind the trio of Brethren. She thrust her sword into the chest of one man, dropping him like a rock. Then, incredibly, she ignored the two Brethren still fighting Ian. Instead, she proudly stood over the man she'd stabbed and surveyed the area, her face alight with hope.

What the heck?

I raced toward her.

What? She's looking for Asher's approval—in the middle of a battle!

One of the Brethren turned away from Ian. Sword thrust forward, he lunged at Willow.

I remote-pushed the Brethren's sword from his hand and flung it high into the air. The man glanced up, following its flight. Eyes widening, he turned to run. I remote-pushed him back and guided the sword's descent—

—straight through his shoulder into his chest.

He fell. Killed between heartbeats.

By now the soldier, Ian, had dispatched the third Brethren. "Thanks, Kass." He raced to help another soldier battling two Brethren.

I pulled Willow behind the huge water tank. "What's wrong with you? You almost got yourself killed."

She cocked her head, her expression distant. "But I didn't die, did I? You saved me with your magical powers."

"What are you talking about? You know I don't have magical powers. I gained some hybrid mental powers by accident."

"Same thing. No matter how hard I train, I can never match you. And I can't get Ash to look at me the way he looks at you."

"I'm not interested in a relationship with anyone right now." Although eager to return to the fight, I couldn't leave Willow here alone, not when she was so emotionally unstable. "Don't you get it? Humans are on the brink of extermination. We could all be dead in a week."

"No, *I* can't match you. But Pandora can."

"Did you hear what I just said?"

She wiped her red-stained sword on the leg of her jeans, smearing blood on the material as though announcing her kill. "As within, it is without." Another Pandorism.

"What does that even mean, Willow?"

"Not Willow. *Pandora.*"

Sword in hand, she ran back into the battle.

I gaped after her. Willow's recklessness, along with her Pandorish behavior, could get her killed.

Unfortunately, I didn't have any more time to protect her today.

The mechanical rumbles grew louder from the front of Weston Tower. It sounded like the tank was trundling across the courtyard, smashing benches and rolling over tables. Shouts and screams were punctuated by gunshots.

Something exploded into the side of Building B, creating a jagged hole. Flames flickered within the building and black smoke spewed out.

Another diversion?

I turned toward Lightning One—

—and gasped as a baseball bat swung toward me. It caught me on the side of my head, exploding stars in my eyes. Crumpling to the ground, I struggled to see through the bright lights and crushing pain.

Sergeant Thorne crouched over me, grinning like a slavering maniac.

48

"What?" I mumbled. "How?"

"Fate, you traitorous bitch. That tank blasted a nice hole in the tower's prison cell. Bad news for those who died. Justice for me." He raised a hunting knife. "This payback will be as sweet as your spilled blood."

His arm swung down. Desperately, I grabbed his wrist with both hands. Tried to push him away. He swore. Punched me in the head. More starbursts, sharp and painful. But I tightened my grip on his wrist.

He wrestled for control of the knife, grunting and swearing. Slowly, the blade moved closer and closer to my breast.

I couldn't push his arm away. He was too strong. Rabidly determined.

Could I—?

Impossible. Hybrids couldn't mind-blend with normal humans, only with babies or weak-minded adults. Thorne was strong. Savage. And about to kill me.

I had only seconds left to live.

I can't—

I had to try.

But what if he kills me first, before I can—?

Do it.

I focused on Thorne. Threw my mind forward. Plunged into a mass of brilliant stars. Ripped through a soft gray wall. And then I was there. Inside a hideous blackness. Surrounded by shock and rage and hate. Thorne's mind felt like a steamy swamp, full of poisonous mists and dark waters. If I relaxed for even a moment, my consciousness would drown in this vile, sludgy mess.

Focus.

Through his eyes, I saw my body go limp beneath him, my face pale and lifeless. No, not lifeless. *Not conscious.*

Mind-blended with Thorne, I gripped the hunting knife, whose tip was about to plunge into my breast.

I squeezed Thorne's hand. Tight. Began to pull the knife back.

Get out of my head, bitch. *Thorne's mind smacked against my consciousness, trying to shove me toward that soft gray wall. If I pierced it, I'd be locked out of his mind forever—and dead a second later.

Somehow, I stayed in his murky swamp. I refocused on the fingers gripping the knife. Slowly, I twisted the hand around and, with a massive effort, thrust the blade upward, deep into the man's chest.

Agony blazed through Thorne-me, unbearable—

I threw myself out of there. Away.

Back into my own body.

Sergeant Thorne slumped on top of me, beady eyes frozen in death.

I shoved his body away, wincing at the warm blood that stained my clothes. His blood.

Dazed, I struggled to my knees. Stared at the knife sticking out of the man's chest. Waited for guilt to overwhelm me.

Somehow Thorne's death was different from the Brethren I'd killed today. His death felt more intense. More personal.

I'd just killed a former colleague, a human, in cold blood—

—a man who'd attacked me first, intent on murdering me.

Sure, I felt some guilt—

—but I felt more relief at surviving.

A dark shadow fell over me. Looking up, I jerked in shock, then hurriedly crawled behind the water tank again.

A large gray tumbleweed terra dropped toward the vegetable garden. A smaller tumbleweed, snagged on its rear branches, was being towed along by the first. The pair of rattling tumbleweeds landed in a garden near Lightning One and opened their curved woody branches.

A cadaverous man in gray clothes and a red armband stepped out.

Bone.

Gaunt face tight with urgency, he hurried toward Lightning One, moving awkwardly, as though his muscles were almost too weak to hold him upright.

Harlem rushed forward, sword in one hand, gun in the other.

Bone waved his fingers. The sword and gun flew from Harlem's hands, arced through the air, and landed on the far side of the vegetable garden. Swearing, Harlem bolted into the field, searching for his weapons.

Soldiers from the Weston Battalion ran toward Lightning One. Some Brethren members also rushed toward the ship. The two groups met in a fresh clash of swords and baseball bats and fists. No one used their guns.

Jase raced into the fight. He slammed a bat into a Weston Battalion soldier, dropping him to the ground, then felled another of our soldiers with a blow to the chest.

I gaped at him.

He was helping the Brethren! Jase actually believed that his chances of survival were greater with Bone than with us.

"This way, sir," he shouted to Bone, pointing at the ship. "Take me with you. I can help."

I knew my mental powers wouldn't work on Bone, who was stronger than me. But Jase wasn't. With a raise of one brow, I remote-slammed him to the ground and he lay there, groaning.

Two soldiers threw metal lances at Bone, but he deflected them with a wave of his hand and a quick one-two remote-push, and the lances clattered harmlessly against a bench. Turning, he gestured toward the tumbleweed terras. With a snap of branches, the rear one broke away and rolled toward the two soldiers. Shouting, the men scattered.

Was this why Bone had brought along the second tumbleweed? To use as a weapon?

At a series of shrieks, I glanced behind me.

What the—?

A dozen krols were scrabbling through the huge hole in the garrison wall. Screeching, they loped forward, brandishing swords and spears as they joined the battling soldiers and the Brethren. Claws slashed throats, teeth ripped flesh, swords and spears pierced bodies.

For a horrifying moment, I thought the krols were a part of the Brethren's attack, but as both soldiers and Brethren fell beneath the creatures' onslaught, I realized the krols had simply taken advantage of the breach in the wall. Perhaps they saw our conflict as a win-win situation. Kill some people and then steal our livestock—

Oh no.

"The kids are hiding in the barns!" I shouted. "Keep the krols away from them."

Four soldiers broke away from the fight and ran to protect the children.

The three-sided battle continued: Weston Garrison members, Brethren, and krols, all trying to kill each other. Shouts and screams. The clang of metal spears. The thwack of wooden bats. Snarls as sharp teeth and claws sank into flesh. Shrieks as swords skewered bodies.

I whirled like a tornado through the pandemonium. Remote-pushed a lance away from a soldier. Remote-shoved a

Brethren onto another soldier's sword. Plunged my own sword into the barrel chest of a krol.

Through it all, the sounds of the other battles shredded the smoky air. Gunshots from the front of the garrison. Rumbles of the tank. Exploding grenades. More shouts and screams. Amid the chaos, Dr. Isaac ran from the smoking tower and headed into the battle, medical bag in hand.

Nearby, the smaller tumbleweed rattled toward Harlem and Willow. They were focused on fighting two sword-wielding krols—*swords; the krols are using swords now; incredible*—and hadn't noticed the tumbleweed. It loomed behind them, branches shifting into an open mouth, ready to swallow them.

I threw a frantic remote-push at the thing.

Abruptly, the tumbleweed changed direction and rolled toward the two krols wielding the swords. Squealing, the xanimals disappeared inside the woody ball of branches and the tumbleweed shot upward. Long gray arms poked through the thorny branches, slashing at the air with their claws.

A child's cry came from the garden bed.

I spun around.

Zoey stumbled along a furrow, whimpering. A gray krol loped behind her, its ugly eyes fixed on the hybrid child.

I raced toward her.

If Zoey had been older, she could've remote-pushed the krol away, but she was only eight. She could wear a plastic princess tiara and wave a toy wand to make pigeons bow, but she couldn't remote-push with any strength yet.

A familiar voice yelled, "Help me, Kass!"

I glanced over.

Jase lay on the ground, struggling to hold off a large krol with a distinctive red scar across its snout. Scar Snout, the leader of this pack. Weeks ago, Lynxx and I had seen this xan and its pack kill a rhino in Central Park.

Further back, Bone remote-pushed away a clump of krols that had swarmed him. His body might be weak—

—but his mind was as powerful as ever.

"Help me, Kass," cried Jase again.

Save Zoey or Jase? It was a no-brainer.

I shouted at him, "Get Bone to help you, jerk!"

I ran across the garden bed toward Zoey. The krol leaped at her, its claws outstretched, ready to rip and shred flesh.

I was too far away. Couldn't help her—

—but I pushed with every bit of mental strength I had, anyway. My mind almost split apart and I staggered, blinded by piercing flashes of pain. My vision cleared. The pain remained.

The krol thudded to the ground near Zoey. It rolled for a few yards. Leaped to its skinny gray legs. Snarled at me, spittle spraying from its razor-toothed mouth.

Willow bolted across. She lunged at the krol with her sword, driving the blade into its fleshy stomach and spraying pale red blood everywhere. The creature fell in a screaming, writhing heap.

She grabbed up Zoey and ran toward the barn.

Scrambling to my feet, I staggered across to Jase.

49

Arms outflung, Jase lay faceup in a spreading puddle of blood. His shredded shirt revealed a chest crisscrossed with frenzied slashes. A deep gash had almost severed his neck, bleeding the life from him. His brown eyes—selfish and weak and traitorous—stared sightlessly at the smoky sky.

Jase Harris. Former class president and star quarterback. Once popular and charming. If he'd died during his reign in high school, countless female hearts would've been broken—including mine.

Today, his death would go unmourned. No one would miss him and no one would care—including me.

Had the apocalypse warped Jase's personality? Or had his ugly qualities always lurked beneath his smiles and charm?

Jerk.

I turned away from the useless body.

With a mechanical rumble of engines, Lightning One rose into the air, swaying slightly from side to side.

Oh no. Bone had the Chi'az ship.

Lightning One whirred into a turn. At the sight of Nila's somber face behind the slitted front window, I relaxed a little. Somehow, in all the pandemonium, she'd boarded the ship.

Bone threw off the last of his krol attackers and bolted to the remaining tumbleweed. I ran after him, remote-pushing away a Brethren who swung a sword at me, and the man tumbled backward, banging his head on the pavers.

I couldn't let Bone get away again.

The Outrider leaped into the tumbleweed. Branches snapped shut behind him. The woody ball launched into the air.

Trembling, I stood below the rising tumbleweed, pain blazing through my head like a rampaging chainsaw. Ignoring my agony, I stared upward and mentally focused on the woody terra.

Had to stop him.

The tumbleweed hovered in the air, caught between two opposing forces: Bone's and mine. Seconds later, the woody ball lunged upward and zipped after Lightning One.

Head on fire, body burning with agony, I crumpled to the ground. My muscles felt as shattered as if I'd been beaten with baseball bats. Every breath knifed fresh pain through my lungs, and I closed my eyes, blocking out the bright sunlight. Around me, the sounds of the battle began to fade away. Was I falling unconscious?

My agony was almost unbearable.

I almost welcomed the soothing eternity of death.

Almost.

My agony floated on a timeless flow, and eventually some of the pain drifted away.

Slowly, I became aware of my body again and my surroundings. *Dirt beneath my hands. Leaves scratching my face. Smoke in my nostrils.*

How long had I been lying here?

Was I dead?

My eyes flickered open. Thankfully, the smoke had dimmed the bright sunlight and I was able to scan the sky. No sign of Lightning One or the tumbleweeds.

I crawled to my knees. Looked around.

The ship was gone.

Bloodied bodies lay scattered like debris after a storm. Soldiers. Civilians. Brethren. Krols. Injured members of the garrison groaned in pain. Others wandered around, dazed.

Dr. Isaac ran across and helped me to my feet. "Are you okay, Mushroom Girl?"

"I'm fine," I lied. "Help the others."

"Call me if you feel faint." Gripping his medical bag, he rushed to a man with a bloodied head wound.

As Harlem and Willow ran to me, I asked, "Where are the Brethren?" Each word stabbed my brain. "Are they dead?"

Willow gestured to the huge hole in the garrison wall. "About a dozen Brethren retreated when Lightning One flew away." She sounded normal again. Like herself.

"And the krols?"

"They took off after the Brethren," said Harlem. He gave a grim smile. "Hey, let the krols eat every Brethren they can catch, right?"

"Right." I turned to Willow. "Where's Zoey?"

"In the barn with the other kids. They're all safe."

"You saved her, Willow. And me. Thanks."

"You're welcome."

Slowly, I moved across the garden beds. At least I didn't have to worry about Lynxx, who was at his Ferguson Complex apartment, gathering supplies. "What about Asher, the commander, Soo-Yun, the others?"

"Asher and Soo-Yun are okay," Harlem reassured me, glancing at the smoke gushing from Weston Tower. "I don't know about the others yet. Will you be okay by yourself? Willow and I need to help the wounded."

"I'll be fine."

He and Willow hurried off.

Smoke billowed from Building B and Weston Tower. Shouts multiplied in the front courtyard, but no longer in fear. People shouted instructions: "Aim the hose there" and "Get that fire engine over here."

Despite these distant cries, the battleground next to the vegetable gardens was quiet. The coppery smell of blood clung to the air, along with the acrid stench of smoke. Vultures circled soundlessly overhead, waiting to feed.

I stood among the dead bodies and gazed at the empty spot where Lightning One had stood. Silence smothered the area, thick and heavy as the breathless stillness of a graveyard.

We'd won this battle.

But had we just lost the war?

50

For long hours after the battle, we remained in an agony of uncertainty.

Nila had flown off with Lightning One, pursued by Bone in a tumbleweed. We knew the ship could easily outrun the tumbleweed. However, when she didn't return within an hour, people started worrying.

Finally, at 5 p.m., Lightning One descended onto the courtyard and parked next to the army tank abandoned by the Brethren.

"I had to hide the ship," Nila explained in a quick debrief. "If I'd brought it back here earlier, the Brethren could've attacked again. I also had to maintain radio silence in case Bone tried to track my signal."

The commander nodded, then turned to the rest of us. "Load the last items, folks. We need to get underway ASAP."

"We?" Nila looked at him sharply.

"Carolyn was killed in the battle today. Since I'm the only person left in the Weston Battalion with extensive flying experience, I'm your new copilot."

"You're needed here, Lincoln. The tower's badly damaged. I heard that twenty-three people died, with dozens injured."

"Lieutenant Wu and the council can handle things at the garrison."

"And I can handle the ship by myself for a few days. Asher can help me. Doesn't he have some flying hours?"

"Nowhere near as many as me." Powell folded his arms, his face set in hard lines. "If something happens to you, Nila, the mission will fail. Releasing the Shimmer is our top priority."

Reluctantly, Nila gave him a quick lesson in flying Lightning One. Then the last of the supplies were loaded.

She paused outside the ship. "Here." She handed a vial of pink liquid to Lynxx and another to me.

"What's this?" I asked.

"Your vaccine. All the Sphere hybrids are being vaccinated against the Shimmer. Plus you two."

"But I'm not a hybrid."

"You have hybrid blood in you, Kass. Best to be safe."

I was surprised she wanted to protect me. Two days ago, she'd wanted me dead—at least mentally—so her daughter, Eva, could take my place in SkyLady's eagle mind.

Weird.

Lynxx and I glanced at each other, shrugged, then drank the vaccine.

A crowd gathered in the courtyard to see us off.

Harlem paused in front of Chef Einstein, who was cradling a plump tuxedo cat. As the boy petted the silken black head, he told it, "You used up one of your nine lives in the battle today, Fluffy. But you're okay and I'll be back in a few days. Be good for Chef Einstein." Harlem anxiously studied the old man. "You promise to take good care of her?"

Einstein stroked the purring cat, his face crinkling with delight as he regarded his new charge. "Don't worry, son. Isabel and I plan on spoiling this furball with lots of pets and tasty treats."

"Good plan!"

Now, finally, we were about to start our mission.

Seven days.

The Bible claimed that God created our world in seven days.

The Chi'az's Red Mist had destroyed our world in seven days.

And now we, a ragged group of survivors, were trying to resurrect our world in seven days.

Could we do it? Could we position the drums of "fermenting" Shimmer chemicals across the planet in time?

If we didn't release the gas before the Outriders unleashed their Threads, humanity would be exterminated.

In the courtyard, people shouted "Good luck" and "Stay alive" as Lightning One rose into the air with a hum of engines.

At the front, Nila sat behind the controls. Beside her, Commander Powell studied a panel of lights, trying to remember everything from his brief lesson—along with the stern warnings of our engineers.

A couple of weeks ago, Lightning One's engine had been damaged during the explosion at Crendell Laboratories, with the damage made worse when the ship had crashed in Jersey City. Nila and our engineers had managed to fix the engine—sort of. The superfast hyperdrive remained broken. However, the slower "low-drive" would work, provided each lengthy leg of the trip was followed by a long rest period, allowing the engine to cool.

Earlier, Powell had asked Nila, "How long does the engine need for its cool-down?"

"I'm not sure. I think it can do short flights of less than thirty minutes without cool-downs. But after each longer flight—thousands of miles, like we'll be doing—the engine will almost certainly need nine hours to cool before heading on to our next destination."

The commander had blanched. "That's really going to slow us down."

"There's no way around it, Lincoln. We're lucky the ship works at all. At least this way we have a chance."

As the ship's speed increased, I peered through the narrow horizontal windows that ran down both sides of the hull. Manhattan passed below us, green and brown, and then we were over the blue-gray ocean. Although only in low-drive, the ship could still travel over five hundred miles an hour, about the speed of a commercial plane.

The real benefit was the ship's ability to cloak itself.

I glanced down the crowded cabin. Yesterday morning, Nila had pushed a button that had activated its "telescopic" feature, tripling the length of Lightning One. Only Powell and Nila sat at the front window, facing forward. Behind them, twelve people sat along the left wall, with eleven along the right.

The group on board was now twenty-five instead of twenty-four. It was made up of our two pilots, fourteen soldiers, the six members of Liberty Team, our senior medic Soo-Yun, our resident terra specialist Lynxx—and Harlem, a last-minute addition.

Kendra, the newest member of Liberty Team, regarded Harlem curiously. "How did you swing this sweet trip?"

"Because I'm special." He grinned like a delighted child. "I'm the only one who can drive that souped-up Zodiac in the back. Asher never got around to taking the lessons."

On the floor down the middle of the ship, mounds of supplies, tents, and weapons were secured beneath strong nets. At the rear, the six drums of Shimmer gas were bolted down. In front of them, our engineers' prototype of a large inflatable land-sea Zodiac was stored upright, acting like a wall. An airtight portable restroom was tucked in a back corner.

At first, people chatted or looked around in awe, excited at being in a spacecraft. However, as the hours uneventfully droned past, most people wedged pillows behind their heads and slept sitting up.

As usual, Booker had his nose buried in a paperback.

Beside him, Kendra Bothra read Sun Tzu's *The Art of War*. Although only sixteen, Kendra was a kick-ass fighter who was highly respected by her teammates. After work each day, the black girl trained for two hours. She lifted weights, did cardiovascular sessions, and practiced with a range of weapons. She also studied Lynxx's information sheets on the various terras and xans, memorizing their strengths and weaknesses. Once, I'd seen her offer to share her study notes with Willow, who'd merely gazed into the distance and repeated a Pandorism: "The will of the universe is greater than the wants of man."

"What?" Kendra had replied, her pretty face creasing in bewilderment. "What the heck does that mean?"

Willow had simply given her a vague smile and wandered away.

In the ship, I leaned back against the hull and stared at the ceiling. Although tired, I couldn't sleep. My head still ached from today's battle, and whenever I closed my eyes, I was either back in the hideous swamp of Sergeant Thorne's mind or standing over Jase's traitorous dead body.

Also, Nila's behavior this afternoon puzzled me.

My seat was near the front of the left row, in between Soo-Yun and Willow, who were both sleeping. From here I could hear Nila and Commander Powell talking. The woman seemed to be back to her cool, scientific self. Or was she simply relieved the Sphere's mission was finally underway?

Perhaps that explained her changed attitude toward me.

Before we took off this afternoon, she had directed Lynxx and me to seats near the front of the ship. To my surprise, she'd asked how we were feeling and then expressed concern at my cuts and bruises.

She'd turned to Lynxx. "You were fortunate you missed the battle today. It was a double-barreled attack. Brethren *and* krols."

"I was getting some stuff from my old apartment," he replied, giving me a guilty glance. "If I'd known—"

"It's fine." She smiled at me. "Kass and I both survived."

Although I found her smiling friendliness weird, it was still better than her recent hostility over her daughter's death.

Across the cabin, Lynxx, Asher, and the others slept in their seats, heads lolling on their pillows. My gaze rested on Asher. Before we'd left, I'd told him about Willow's strange behavior prior to and during the battle at the garrison. Busy with a dozen problems, he'd brushed off my worries. "She seems okay now."

"She's always okay when she's with you."

"Even more reason not to leave her behind. She'll feel abandoned."

"Maybe—"

"Willow will be fine."

Hopefully.

Head still throbbing from Sergeant Thorne's baseball bat, I squeezed past the mounds of supplies down the middle of the cabin. At the rear, I rummaged in my duffel bag, hoping a book would distract me from my pain.

Abruptly, the ship lurched from side to side, then bucked and rocked.

"Just a little turbulence, folks," Commander Powell called from the front. "Nothing to worry about."

Seconds later, the flight became smooth again.

Book tucked in my pocket, I zipped up my duffel bag and—

A wave of queasiness surged through me, sickening in its intensity. My head reeled. My vision blurred. The world swayed and swirled, and I fought an urge to vomit.

Oh no. My leukemia? *Please, no.*

I staggered back to my seat, hiding my terror behind a stony face. Hands shaking, I reached for one of the seatbelts we'd had installed and—

—my queasiness vanished.

I felt completely normal again.

Stunned, I shut my eyes, my thoughts racing. What had just happened? Was my old disease stirring to life again? *Please, no.* I couldn't lose everything I'd worked for and everything I'd become. If my disease was back, I'd wither into a sick dying girl, a burden to the Weston Battalion.

In seven days, if our Shimmer gas was successful, the terras, xans, Outrider hybrids, and Chi'az would be doomed. Earth would be ours once more, along with a hopeful future. But if I had leukemia again, I'd never be a part of this new future. I'd be dead.

I focused on my body. Except for my throbbing head, I felt fine. Normal.

Perhaps I'd just had a flash of airsickness, that's all.

Although worried, I finally surrendered to my exhaustion and slept.

Too soon, a loud voice rang through the cabin.

"Release Point One, folks," Commander Powell called out as Lightning One decelerated. "We'll be landing shortly."

People stirred in their seats, and I was surprised to find that I'd slept for hours.

"Engaging cloaking device," Nila said.

Along with my colleagues, I gasped as the hull suddenly transformed into a glasslike substance. This gave us an amazing 360-degree view—and, weirdly, made the ship invisible. A minute later, Nila switched to stealth mode, silencing the engine.

Outside, thick gray clouds filled a gloomy sky. As we descended, Rome sharpened into view—but not the Rome I had dreamed of visiting one day.

51

ROME WAS EVEN GRAYER than the overhanging sky. Thick gray terras covered most buildings and structures, and its streets had been transformed into gray-watered canals, similar to its famous sister city, Venice.

"Why's it flooded?" Willow asked, dismayed.

"Perhaps the Tiber River has broken its banks," the commander suggested. "It's happened twice in the past century. Not to this extent, though."

"I think the Tiber has flooded," Lynxx agreed. "Plus the electric pumps beneath the city have almost certainly failed; they would've removed millions of gallons of groundwater every day."

Below, a cruise ship had been carried by the flood to the outskirts of Rome and now lay wedged between two apartment buildings. Small riverboats bobbed against the blackened domes of old churches. The tip of an ancient obelisk poked from the waters. Further in, several hills rose above the waterways, their buildings and roads dry but overgrown with gray terras.

Nila circled the city, searching for a landing spot. She finally brought Lightning One down on a large flat roof that stood like a bare island in the bleak floodwaters.

Liberty Team spread across the flat roof, searching for terras and xans.

"All clear," Booker announced after two sweeps of the area. "Just a few crabbens and glow-lotus terras, all now dead."

Commander Powell supervised the unloading of the first Shimmer drum, along with tents, weapons, and supplies for the two soldiers assigned to remain behind with the drum.

After the camp was set up, Asher and Harlem brought out the land-sea Zodiac. They attached a long rope to it, tied one end to a pole, then dropped the twelve-man inflatable boat onto the gray waters that lapped the building a foot below.

"Anyone up for a boat ride?" Asher asked. "We'll be back in a few hours."

Booker glanced up from his paranormal novel, incredulous. "You want to go sightseeing, boss? Now?"

"It's actually a rescue mission," Asher replied. "Lightning One's nine-hour cool-down means that we're stuck here until evening, so we might as well do some good. It's better than sitting around here worrying about the Threads."

"Yeah, but a rescue mission?" I surveyed the empty, flooded streets around our rooftop. "Who are we saving, Asher? This place looks deserted."

"I know. That's why I want to rescue some paintings." He consulted a map of Rome and pointed north. "A month before the Night of the Red Mist, a new art museum, the Radenia, opened a couple of miles from here. It had an amazing collection of Rembrandts, Picassos, Monets, even a da Vinci."

Booker pocketed his novel. "Hey, I'm always up for an adventure."

"Great," Asher said. "I've already cleared it with the commander. Any more volunteers? We need to leave room for the paintings, so I can only take four people, apart from Harl, who'll be driving the Zodiac."

He soon had his team: Booker, Willow, me—and Lynxx who, as our resident terra expert, was conscripted into joining us. Annoyed, he asked Asher, "Is this an efficient use of our time? The museum's probably underwater."

"Not necessarily. The ones built on hills should be okay for now as long as the terras and xans haven't damaged them."

Willow rested her hand on a large knife clipped to her hip, the same kind her character used on *Pandora*. "This could be a useless trip, Ash. The Radenia may be empty of artwork. Some survivors might've moved the paintings to safe locations."

"Yes," I told Asher. "After all, that's what you've been doing for over a year." Weston Tower now had twelve floors crammed with paintings, sculptures, and old books that he and the Cultural Team had rescued.

He nodded. "Hopefully, survivors have done the same thing here. But I doubt it."

"Why?" I asked.

"Where are they? Lightning One was silent and invisible as it flew over Rome before landing. No one knew we were in the sky, so I expected to see a few survivors on the rooftops, digging in gardens or whatever. Instead, I didn't see a single person."

It was true. The rooftops visible around us were bare and empty. Only terra plants fluttered in the wind.

As the Zodiac headed toward the Radenia, Harlem sat at the back, handling the motor's tiller. The rest of us sat on the inflatable sides, holding on via handles or black ropes.

On either side of the canal, rows of four-story buildings lay semi-submerged, with only their top floors visible above the water. Darkened windows stared deadly at the changed city, and I imagined restless spirits peering through lace curtains, searching for a world forever lost.

The Zodiac's engine purred. Water gushed past us. Elsewhere, silence reigned. No birds cawed or wheeled overhead. No animals—Earth or xans—chittered or roared or howled.

The city's ominous silence felt drenched with muted warnings.

Shivering, I rubbed my goose-bumped arms.

52

To my surprise, the Radenia was high and dry, and its art collection mainly intact.

As Asher helped the others swaddle the most valuable paintings in waterproof wrappings, I muttered to Lynxx, "I need to talk to you."

Puzzled, he followed me to the far side of the main gallery.

I hesitated, unwilling to voice my fears. Finally, I whispered, "Did you bring along any Lazarus tonic?"

"Why? Are you feeling sick again?"

Quietly, I explained about my sudden attack of queasiness back in Lightning One, finishing with my shaky hope: "Maybe I was just airsick."

"I was positive your leukemia was cured months ago, so I didn't bring any tonic. And I didn't pack any equipment to make a new batch." Lynxx raked his fingers through his dark hair. "We'll have to tell the commander to go back."

"To the Weston Garrison?" My voice emerged in a loud squeak, drawing Asher's attention. He stared across the marble floor at us, curious. With a flush of guilt, I turned away. How many times had I promised him that there'd be no more secrets between us? And yet I was once again hiding a potential illness.

"Impossible," I whispered to Lynxx. "We can't go back. It'll throw off the whole schedule with the Shimmer drums. You know they all have to release their gas at the same time around the world."

"Your life is more important."

"No! I'm only one person. There are four hundred thousand survivors' lives at stake. Even a delay of one day might be enough for the Outriders to release their Threads first. We have to keep going." When he remained unconvinced, I wrapped my words with soft persuasion. "It's probably just a false alarm. I feel fine now. Even my headache is getting better. Please promise you won't mention my queasiness to anyone, Lynxx."

"What if—?"

"*Promise.*"

"Fine. I promise." His brow knotted in concern. "Let me know if you feel sick again, right?"

I nodded.

Asher frowned as Lynxx and I guiltily rejoined the others.

An hour later, our laden Zodiac began heading back to our camp. We'd only gone a few blocks when we heard a familiar trumpeting sound. Harlem switched off the motor, and as the Zodiac drifted down the canal, we listened.

Silence.

"Did anyone else hear an elephant?" I asked.

"I think so," Asher replied. "But how can an elephant survive in this flooded city?" A deep whoop echoed in the distance. "Is that a howler monkey?" He paused, his blue eyes glittering with interest. "Maybe we should have a look."

Harlem and Booker quickly agreed. Willow shrugged. Lynxx grunted as he peered through his binoculars at the surrounding buildings, and I guessed he was searching for Lazarus terras.

We followed the elephant's trumpeting and the monkey's hoots to an open area of floodwaters. In the middle, a famous Roman structure stood in solitary splendor. Although the bottom level was submerged, I recognized the soaring curved walls and the upper levels of distinctive arches.

"Incredible," I breathed.

"The Colosseum." Booker stared at the massive stone amphitheater, his eyes round behind his glasses. "I never thought I'd see it in real life." The trumpeting sounded again, closer this time. "Hey, I think the elephant is inside the Colosseum."

Cautiously, Harlem drove the Zodiac closer to the structure.

"This could be dangerous," Asher said. "It's an unnecessary risk—"

Inside the Colosseum, a baby wailed.

We fell silent.

Harlem cut the motor again. We listened.

The baby's wails rose to a high pitch of distress.

"A baby wouldn't be in there alone," Willow cried. "Someone must be with it."

"Maybe someone *was* with the baby," I suggested, "but they died. And now the baby's alone, hungry, and afraid."

Harlem restarted the engine, and our Zodiac slowly passed through a large gate in the looming wall.

"Everyone be careful." Asher withdrew his revolver. "Stay alert and stay alive."

We checked our guns and swords.

Booker glanced at the sky behind him. "This gate faces west. I think it's the Gate of Death."

"Charming name," I muttered dryly.

"After a fight or hunt in the arena," Booker explained, "the dead bodies were taken out through the west exit, toward the setting sun."

Our Zodiac cruised down a long arched corridor about twenty feet high and fifteen feet wide. A vile smell hung in the air, diluted in spots with lavender-like whiffs from the velvet-vines on the stone walls.

Our inflatable stopped at the edge of an enormous gray lake that filled the arena.

Booker's voice quivered with excitement. "And this is the Arena of Death. Over five hundred thousand people died here, plus a million animals."

We paused in the shadows of the arched passageway, surveying the place.

The sloping stone stands that ringed the arena had once held thousands of spectators, eager to applaud death in all its gory carnage.

The lake that covered the arena had also submerged the first few levels of seating. On one side, a broken speedboat protruded from a stone wall like a cork. Debris floated everywhere—bottles, plastic bags, pieces of wood.

We jumped as a racket abruptly rang through the Colosseum. Loud trumpeting. Whooping noises. A baby's screams.

Then we saw them.

A yellow xan bird landed on the broken speedboat, trumpeting like an elephant; eagle-sized, it had a football-shaped neck and four skinny wings. In the spectator stands, another yellow xan bird threw back its thick neck and released a whoop like the cry of a howler monkey. To our left, a third xan bird wailed like a baby.

"Mimic xans," Lynxx said, fascinated. "I've heard they're experts at imitating noises. They're amazing."

Asher shrugged. "Sure, but not unique. Australia's lyrebirds can mimic dozens of sounds, including chainsaws, car alarms, even revving engines. Plus Earth parrots can speak like people."

Booker pulled out his digital camera and eagerly snapped photos of the arena. I wondered if he'd ever get the chance to enjoy his photos. Even if we made it back to Weston Tower, would any of us be alive in a week or so?

I stifled my worries. Fretting about the Outriders and their Threads wouldn't change a thing or make our mission go faster.

Tiller in hand, Harlem scrutinized the tiered stands. "So, no baby?"

A yellow mimic xan flew overhead, its four wings whirring as it wailed like a distressed infant. Its cry rose to the exact pitch we'd heard earlier.

"No baby," Asher confirmed.

"Okay, then." Relaxing, Harlem holstered his gun. "Let's get out of here."

Lynxx lowered his binoculars. "Not yet." He pointed to a large door floating in the middle of the lake. A clump of plants with familiar green leaves and purple flowers grew on the rotting wood. "I need those Lazarus-vine terras."

"Why?" Asher asked. "You've got a stack of them in your lab at Weston Towers."

"Um ... these are a different strain."

Asher paused, then nodded to Harlem, who drove the inflatable toward the floating door.

"The plants look the same to me," Asher said, squinting at them.

"These petals are a lighter purple." Lynxx began filling a burlap sack with the flowers and leaves. "I need a variety of Lazarus specimens. Different ones may have different medical uses."

"Fine."

Willow shifted restlessly in her seat. "We must proceed with haste, my friends. The fate of the world hangs in the balance. We are the chosen few, destined to save humanity."

This time, even Asher looked surprised at her blatant use of dialogue from *Pandora*.

"What's the rush?" Booker asked, still snapping photos. "We're not leaving until evening."

She shook her head. "We should stand guard at the ship until it sweeps us into the heavens again."

"It's okay," Asher told her gently. "There are lots of people with Lightning One right now. It's safe."

"Of this you are certain?" she asked, still Pandora.

"Promise."

I caught his concerned expression and resisted the impulse to mouth, *I told you so.*

Booker gestured at the arena. "Over there, the Roman general, Paulus, had a group of army deserters crushed to death by a horde of elephants. Sometimes this arena was filled with water, and ships had sea battles; of course, they added packs of hungry crocodiles and threw naked Christians overboard, just to liven things up a bit."

Harlem's eyes widened. "Sick!"

As Booker detailed more atrocities from the Colosseum's history, I trailed my fingers in the water, waiting for Lynxx to finish bagging his Lazarus "specimens."

I knew he wasn't gathering the flowers for research. He was getting them for me. If my leukemia was back, their pollen might suppress my symptoms until we returned to the garrison in five days—

Bubbles broke the surface of the water, scalding my fingertips.

"Oww!" I jerked my hand out. Red blisters covered my fingers. Alongside the Zodiac, dozens more bubbles belched a putrid stench that stung my eyes and scraped my throat. "Watch out," I croaked between coughs. "Those bubbles might be toxic."

A long shape flashed beneath the boat.

"Hey!" I cried. "There's something in the water!"

"Shark?" Booker gasped.

"Worse. I think it's an enormous xan."

"Time to go." Harlem began turning the Zodiac.

Too late.

A gush of huge bubbles exploded upward around our boat.

53

THE BUBBLES BURST, RELEASING a stinging gas that scratched like cactus prickles. I grasped my burning throat, struggling to breathe.

The others grabbed at their throats as well, choking, eyes watering.

Tears streaming down his cheeks, Harlem gunned the Zodiac, and it plunged across the arena lake like a panicked horse. We streaked down the arched corridor, through the Gate of Death, and burst onto the floodwaters beyond.

Fresh air gusted past, easing my burning throat.

Glancing back, I saw something following us. The long dark shape resembled an enormous eel, at least fifteen feet long and as thick as a man's thigh.

"The thing's ... getting closer," Booker cried amid deep gulps of air.

An ugly head burst from the water. It had a pointed face resembling a dragon. Black scales. Bony spikes flanking large nostrils. Longer bony spikes that swept back from fierce scarlet eyes.

Its gaping mouth revealed rows of needle-sharp teeth as—

—it spat at us.

Globs of green spit splattered Willow and Booker in the rear, just missing Harlem. Asher grabbed two bottles of water and shoved them at the shocked pair. "Don't touch the stuff. Wash it off." As they drenched their faces, Asher emptied the contents of another bottle over some green spit on his sleeve.

I sat at the front of the Zodiac opposite Lynxx, relieved the green globs had missed us.

"What's with all the spitting?" Harlem cried, handling the tiller.

Lynxx went into lecture mode. "In India, spitting cobras spray venom at people and animals."

"Did you hear that, bro?" Harlem asked Asher. "That spit could be poisonous. You could die."

"It only got my sleeve." Asher passed more water bottles to Willow and Booker. "Wash your faces again, guys, just to be sure." They did.

Engine roaring, Harlem powered the Zodiac down a canal lined with partially submerged buildings. The apartments flashed by on either side, only their top floors visible.

The dragon xan continued the chase, six large fins fanning along its eel-like body as it serpentined behind us. Further back, a sharp claw sliced the surface, leaving white froth in its wake; I guessed this claw was on the tip of the creature's tail.

"I'm going left, bro," Harlem shouted. "We can lose it in a side street."

"What if the side street is blocked?" Asher shouted back. "We could be trapped."

"Good point." Harlem continued down the main canal, swerving past a half-sunken tank and an old rowboat. Here and there, patches of gold leaves floated like lily pads, their size and shape very familiar.

"Watch out for the Hades terras," I called out.

Harlem groaned. "Those things burst into flames on land. No way can they burn on water, right?"

"Let's not find out," Asher said.

Harlem swerved around the floating plants.

Bright red splotches marred Booker's cheeks, and he winced in pain. Looking over his shoulder, he shouted, "It's still coming."

Willow huddled on the rubber floor amid the paintings we'd recovered from the Radenia. She clasped her knees to her chest and buried her face in her folded arms.

Our Zodiac charged from the end of the canal and zigzagged across an open flooded area, avoiding the tops of tourist buses and signposts.

"It's not as deep here," I said. "Maybe that'll slow it down." A glance back showed the dark shape still chasing us. "Nope."

"Hang on, guys." Harlem swung the Zodiac into a sharp turn that almost sent me flying over the side. I grasped the rope tighter, hoping we'd outrun the dragon xan. But it wheeled around and shot after us down another canal. This new channel had lower buildings, which were almost completely submerged, with only their sloped roofs visible.

The dragon xan narrowed the gap between us to twenty feet.

I glimpsed a dark shape leaping from a rooftop on our left. "Incoming nine o'clock!"

Harlem swerved the Zodiac right.

A large brown creature splashed into the frothy wake, missing our vessel by inches. A moment later, the water boiled and churned, and bubbles burst on the surface. In the murky depths, the dragon xan and the creature writhed and snapped as they fought a frantic life-and-death battle.

Blood gushed upward.

Which one had won?

A long black form serpentined toward us again, tipped at the rear with a curved claw. *The dragon xan.*

Harlem had increased our gap to seventy feet—

—but I feared it wouldn't be enough.

Lynxx peered through his binoculars. "Bad news. There's a huge patch of floating Hades terras dead ahead. Too wide to go around."

"Is there a side street coming up?" Asher cried.

"Negative."

As the Zodiac zoomed forward, we scanned for a turnoff, a gap between the submerged houses, a miracle.

Nothing.

"Maybe Hades terras don't burn on water," Harlem again suggested.

Booker added, "Or we race through the blazing plants and only get a little burned."

"Everyone hang on tight," Harlem shouted. "I've got a crazy idea."

54

WE GRASPED THE SIDE ropes of the inflatable boat—except for Willow.

The patch of Hades leaves loomed closer.

Only thirty yards away.

"Willow," yelled Asher. "Hold on. Now!"

Twenty yards.

Reluctantly, she stirred from her huddled position and held on to a side rope.

Fifteen yards.

I braced, turning my face away from the Hades plants. We would be smashing through them any second now. Would they ignite into an inferno? Or remain inactive?

Five yards.

Harlem suddenly angled the land-sea Zodiac toward the sloping rooftops on our left. Grasping the tiller with one hand, he flicked two switches. As the motor and propeller swung upward, I felt two sets of wheels unfurl beneath the rigid base. The inflatable boat drove across the row of rooftops parallel to the canal, the small wheels scattering dozens of small crabbens that had been resting on a black plant with long fat tentacles.

Oh no. Tentacle terra.

The black tentacles grabbed at us—

—then pulled back, snapping shut around a square wrapped painting that had thudded onto it.

"Sorry, bro," Harlem shouted, one hand on the tiller. "I had to distract that awful tentacle somehow."

"I hope it wasn't the da Vinci," Asher cried.

The Zodiac continued racing along the rooftops.

"Crabbens," Booker shouted, pointing to the other side of our boat.

A dozen crabbens scuttled forward on the roof, sharp claws clicking. These baseball-sized xans wouldn't kill us, but their painful bites could lead to serious infections.

Quickly, Lynxx and I joined hands. As the crabbens began leaping toward our Zodiac, we brutally remote-pushed them back, sweeping our combined focus from left to right. The hard-shelled xans arced into the air. They landed on the far side of the concrete rooftop—and I heard the satisfactory sounds of their shells cracking on impact.

In the canal, the long patch of gold Hades leaves rose and fell as the dragon xan swam beneath it.

"It's still coming," Booker yelled.

"And the plants aren't bursting into flames," Harlem added.

"Interesting," Lynxx said. "Maybe swimming through their roots doesn't ignite them. Perhaps you have to physically break their stems and leaves."

A short distance ahead, the roofs suddenly stopped at a tall building that rose from the canal.

Asher gaped at the looming obstruction. "We have to get off these roofs. Now!"

I glanced at the Hades leaves below. "We're almost past the plants."

"Hang on." Harlem angled the Zodiac toward the canal again and clicked a couple of buttons. The motor and propeller descended as the boat dropped onto the water with a spine-jarring thud, just missing the floating patch.

"We need to break those Hades leaves." Asher grabbed the sack of Lazarus flowers and heaved it into the water behind us.

"*No!*" Lynxx shouted, rising from his seat.

Too late.

The sack landed on the floating plants, instantly igniting them into an inferno.

Huge gold flames whooshed across the Hades terras with incredible speed. The dragon xan shrieked and writhed, trapped by the fire. Even the water burned as though mixed with oil, and foul black smoke roiled in all directions. The dragon xan tried to crawl onto an adjoining rooftop, long pieces of burned skin peeling from its scaly body. Shuddering, it uttered a final dying shriek and slumped back into the blazing canal.

"Let's get out of here." Harlem increased the Zodiac's speed.

Lynxx whirled on Asher. "Why'd you throw that sack overboard?"

"I had to throw something," Asher responded. "Be glad it wasn't you."

Lynxx glared at him, then said, "There are more Lazarus flowers in the Colosseum—"

"And probably more of those creatures. Forget it. No one's going back there."

Lynxx clenched his hands, clearly fighting an urge to punch Asher.

Hurriedly, I tugged Lynxx's sleeve, murmuring, "I feel fine. Truly. I was airsick earlier, that's all."

Willow stirred from her huddled position and raised her head. "Is the monster dead?"

I choked back a gasp. Angry red splotches stained both cheeks of her beautiful face, the marks far larger than the ones on Booker's cheeks. Willow had caught the worst of the dragon xan's spit.

"It's dead, Willow," replied Asher, carefully not reacting to her marred skin. "We'll be back at camp soon. And then we'll fix your injuries and Booker's." He glanced at me. "And your blistered fingers too, Kass."

"It hurts." Willow huddled amid the paintings, knees to her chest, face hidden again.

We returned to camp, where Lynxx and Soo-Yun treated Willow's and Booker's wounds. As I smeared a terra ointment on my blistered fingers, easing the pain, Asher debriefed the commander and Nila about the dragon xan.

Harlem and I began loading the wrapped paintings into Lightning One, storing them in the rear—but after five minutes, I let Harlem finish the job without me.

As evening fell, we said goodbye to the two soldiers, Mark and Abdul, who'd been assigned to stay with the Shimmer drum in Rome. The men stood next to their tents, surrounded by weapons and supplies. Behind them, the drum was secured to the rooftop and camouflaged by a brown tarpaulin.

Abdul, a wiry Afghan in his early thirties, rubbed his bearded chin, worried. "Are you sure we do not have to press any buttons?"

"Absolutely," the commander told him. "All six drums have been programmed to release their gas at the same time: Zero Hour. You and Mark are just here to protect this drum from Outrider hybrids or other threats. That's why we're leaving a stack of weapons with you."

Mark squared his broad shoulders, echoing the police officer he'd been before the Mist. "We won't let you down, sir."

"I know you won't."

"We will be okay," Abdul told us, reading the uncertainty on some of our faces. "We are staying up on this rooftop, though, far above those ugly spitting xans."

"Don't forget to pick us up in eight days," Mark said.

"We'll be here," Powell assured him.

We'll be here.

The commander's words lingered in my mind as Lightning One rose over Rome and set off on the second leg of our mission. Powell handled the controls as Nila napped. Most of the others slept upright in their seats. Even Willow and Booker slept, their faces bandaged and their pain eased by terra meds.

We'll be here.

I gazed at my sleeping colleagues, at Nila napping down the back, and at the commander at the controls.

They'd be here.

But would I?

A few hours ago, five minutes into helping Harlem load the priceless artworks into Lightning One, I'd been swept by another wave of nausea. Muttering an excuse, I'd rushed outside, struggling not to throw up in front of anyone.

Fortunately, the cold air had eased my nausea, and no one had noticed my pale face.

Now, as our ship raced toward our next release point, I stared through the narrow window, seeing only an endless blackness. Was this my fate? I wondered bleakly. Was the blackness of death finally catching up with me again?

This time, my second batch of nausea couldn't be explained away as "airsickness," since the ship had been parked on a rooftop in Rome.

That left only one possibility.

My leukemia was back.

55

Hours later, Lightning One approached our next stop. At the controls, Nila decreased speed to stealth mode and engaged the cloaking device.

Pushing aside my worries about my leukemia, I stared through the transparent hull as we descended.

Release Point Two was in the wilderness of Lower Mongolia, where green grasslands and clumps of scrubby trees had once swept to the horizon. The scrubby trees remained, but the long green grasses had been replaced by endless waves of ice-white grass terras. Beneath a morning sky as white as an Arctic glacier, a wind gusted across the grass terras, bending their stalks almost flat to the ground.

A single structure dominated the landscape, stretching for miles east to west.

The Great Wall of China.

We landed near its southern side, below one of the many towers that punctuated its length. As we unclipped our seatbelts and stood, Willow remained seated. Face covered in bandages, she told Asher, "I'm staying here. I need to sleep."

"I'll keep you company," he said.

"I'm fine." She closed her eyes.

I resisted offering my sympathy. Knew she didn't want it.

Outside the ship, I folded my arms against a wind that was unusually cold for August. Its chill numbed my skin and seeped into my bones, and my breaths emerged as visible puffs.

Thankfully, the terra ointment had healed my blistered fingers, allowing me to easily slip them into gloves.

Nearby, the Great Wall of China was both awe-inspiring and depressing. This man-made wonder of the world stretched from horizon to horizon, an impossibly long and formidable sight—once. Built over two thousand years ago, the structure had stood firm and strong against screaming hordes of Mongol invaders.

However, it had been helpless against the tiny, silent invaders brought by the Mist.

In many sections, the twenty-five-foot-high stone wall appeared solid and bare; in other places, white vines draped the sides, their leaves trembling in the wintry conditions.

"Angel-vine terras," Harlem said. "Harmless."

"Not harmless." Lynxx studied the tall structure. "Their extensive root systems will slowly weaken the wall until it crumbles. In a decade or so, all this"—he waved his arm at the ancient construction—"will be a pile of rubble."

"Not if the Shimmer works," Asher reminded him.

"Correct."

"Okay, folks," Commander Powell said as we gathered before him, "we're here for nine hours while the engine cools." He paused, hands on his hips as he surveyed our surroundings. "This place appears uninhabited by humans or large xans. But keep your voices low anyway. And let's avoid the locals."

Yuki raised his hand. In precise, clipped tones, the Japanese youth asked, "Excuse, please, why avoid locals?"

"We don't know if they're harmless or dangerous, Yuki. And they don't know if we're harmless or dangerous. If some locals saw Lightning One, they'd probably think we were aliens, the enemy. They could attack us or try to destroy the drum of Shimmer gas we leave behind."

Camera slung over his shoulder on a strap, Booker studied the Great Wall. Above his bandaged cheeks, his bespectacled eyes gleamed. "Isn't it fantastic? It's over thirteen thousand miles long—combined length, of course."

"Combined?" Harlem shoved his hands into his pockets to warm them.

"Most people think the Great Wall is a single construction," Booker said, cleaning his glasses. "But it's not. It's a series of long walls."

Ignoring the cold, the commander supervised the unloading of the tents, supplies, and weapons for the two soldiers assigned to remain with the second drum of Shimmer gas.

After Liberty Team searched the area for dangerous terras and xans, Asher reported to Powell, "It seems clear, sir."

Booker added, "But maybe we should go up and look around the top of the wall, sir. Just to be sure." He shifted restlessly from foot to foot, eager to explore this latest historical wonder.

Commander Powell nodded, then gestured to a soldier. "Bramwell, you go with them."

Booker and several of us hurried to the ramp of stairs that rose alongside the southern wall. The rest of the soldiers remained at the camp, protecting the ship and drums of Shimmer gas.

"This is unreal," Booker enthused, leading the way up the stone steps. "We're about to walk on the world's longest cemetery."

"Is cemetery?" Soo-Yun gasped.

"Sure. Almost five hundred thousand workers died during its construction. Their bodies are buried in the wall."

"Yuck." Soo-Yun screwed up her delicate face as though she'd eaten a slug.

Inside the watchtower, we passed through four rooms, their corners thick with dust.

"The soldiers would've cooked and slept here," Booker said, pocketing a broken shard of pottery. "And see those stalls over there? That's where they stabled their horses."

Soo-Yun crinkled her pert nose. "Much stinky in here. Is dead bone of many worker?"

Harlem took a deep sniff. "I don't think so, Soo. It smells old and musty, plus a bit flowery."

"Jasmine." Lynxx pointed to the angel-vines on its brick floor.

We passed from the watchtower onto the Great Wall. A twenty-foot-wide carriageway was edged by parapets over six feet high, similar to the ones found on the battlements of English castles. A quick scan revealed more patches of angel-vines. No xans.

Relaxing, we spread out along the carriageway, chatting softly as we admired or photographed the view. A chill wind blew through the spaces between the parapets, chilling me, and I hastily buttoned up my denim jacket.

"Are you okay, Kassia?" asked Lynxx.

Making sure no one was close by, I quietly told him about the second wave of nausea I'd experienced on the rooftop in Rome.

Dismayed, he muttered, "So your leukemia *could* be back."

"I'm pretty sure it is. I have to tell Asher and Commander Powell."

"Hold off until we're certain."

"I promised Asher that I wouldn't keep any more secrets from him."

Lynxx gave me a curious look. "That was when you were a couple. You're not together anymore, are you?"

"No. But he's still my team leader. If I'm sick, he needs to know. Otherwise I could endanger the others."

We fell silent as Nila approached us. Behind her, Natalie giggled as she assumed a model pose for Yuki, who was snapping photos with a digital camera.

"This is amazing," Nila gushed. "I've always wanted to visit the Great Wall of China." She winced at a patch of terra vines. "Although not under these circumstances."

"Yes. Very unfortunate," Lynxx agreed. He gestured to a structure with a pointed roof a short distance away. "Kassia, I'm heading to that beacon tower. It might have some Lazarus flowers. Coming?"

I saw Asher watching us, his face tight with curiosity—plus a wisp of jealousy. "I think I should stay here and have that chat with Asher."

Lynxx's eye caught mine. He nodded. "All right."

"Be careful."

"Always." He headed off.

As Booker and Yuki took photos of the Great Wall, Nila asked me, "Is Lynxx still searching for Lazarus flowers?"

"Yes." I kept my voice light, reluctant to discuss my leukemia with her. "He lost the ones he'd gathered in Rome."

"I thought I saw some in there." She pointed to the watchtower a hundred feet behind us.

"Really?" I asked, surprised. "We were just in there a while ago. I didn't see any."

"They were in a little room in the rear." When I looked unconvinced, she said, "Come. I'll show you."

My spidey sense started tingling. "I'll radio Lynxx to turn back."

"Let's make sure they're actually Lazarus flowers first. Otherwise, he'll have walked back here for nothing."

"He wouldn't care."

She fixed a smile on her face, super friendly. "Let's go find those flowers in the watchtower now."

The hairs prickled at the nape of my neck. She seemed eager to get me into that tower. *Why?* "Maybe later."

I could feel her eyes on my back as I crossed to Asher. He stood at the northern battlement wall, peering at the landscape through his binoculars.

"Asher, I have to talk to you."

"Hold on." He refocused the lenses, stared through them again, then lowered his binoculars. Voice low yet urgent, he said, "Everyone, take cover!"

56

Hurriedly, I pressed my back against a six-foot-tall parapet. Nila and the others also ducked out of sight.

Asher quietly told us, "There are two Mongols in the distance, north of the wall."

When Soo-Yun gasped, Harlem softly said, "Don't worry, Soo. Lightning One is parked beside the southern side of the wall. They can't see the ship."

"Is much good," she whispered, relieved.

Asher radioed the commander and told him about the two Mongols.

"Are they on foot?" Powell asked.

"Yes, sir."

"Okay, son. I'll make sure everyone down here remains quiet. Are you and the others coming back?"

"Not yet, sir. The spaces between the parapets are wide and low. There's no way we can move without the Mongols seeing us. Best to wait until they leave."

"They might head in your direction."

"We're still safe up here, sir. There aren't any stairs on the northern side of the wall, just on the southern side."

"Right. Call me if you have any problems, son."

"Yes, sir. Out." Asher clicked off.

Quickly, I radioed Lynxx with the same information, advising him to keep out of sight. He agreed.

On the Great Wall, each parapet was separated by a lower section of brickwork—a crenel—which was about three feet tall. Keeping out of sight, Asher kneeled behind a low crenel and peered over its top with his binoculars. I did the same thing at another crenel.

Shivering in the wind, I focused my binoculars on the pair in the distance.

The two Mongol men sharpened into view. They had long wild hair, thick beards, and mustaches. Both wore tunics and pants made from animal skins, pointed cloth hats edged with thick fur, and leather boots. Each man also carried a longbow and spear, plus a clutch of dead rabbits.

"Hunters," Asher said quietly.

The two men were too far away to be a problem.

Relaxing a little, I watched my breath emerge in cloudy gusts.

"Look," Nila whispered, peering around her parapet. "To the right. Closer to the wall."

I shifted my binoculars—and suddenly forgot about the chilly weather.

Asher swore. Harlem and the others gaped in disbelief.

A group of Mongols emerged from a grove of scraggy trees a short distance away. Four men, two women, three teenage boys, and a teenage girl. All had round faces, brown skin, dark hair, and almond-shaped eyes. Like the pair further back, they wore clothes made from skins and carried longbows and spears. Most had bulging skin bags hanging from their shoulders.

Six of the Mongols held leashes attached to—

I squinted through my binoculars, unable to believe my eyes. *Are those leashed—?*

"Krols," Harlem breathed, staring through his binoculars.

At two feet tall, the krols were half the size of the ones in New York and Florida. These also had other differences. Much larger heads proportionate to their bodies. White hairless skin, not mottled black or gray. Short thick limbs instead of long skinny ones. Also, they didn't walk upright on two legs but moved on all fours like dogs. Even their behavior was different. When the group of Mongols paused, the small xans wrestled and played with each other.

"Pups." Asher kept his voice low. "They're krol pups."

"Why are you calling them pups?" I whispered. "Dog pups are cute. These aren't."

"I was thinking of sharks. Their offspring are also called pups."

Below, one of the men held up a hand. The Mongol had long black hair tied with beaded string, and a thin black mustache that dangled from either side of his lips, hanging a few inches below his chin. He reminded me of Fu Manchu, a character from an old movie I'd once watched with my father.

Fu Manchu pointed to a patch of white grass terras where three slender antelopes grazed. The six Mongol handlers reached down to their krol pups' collars.

Fu Manchu pursed his lips in a short whistle.

Unleashed, the krol pups bolted through the grass, emitting sharp yips. The antelopes streaked away, hooves barely touching the ground.

We watched the chase through our binoculars.

In the field, the krol pups caught up with their prey. One jumped at the neck of the slowest antelope and clawed its throat. As the animal slumped to the ground, the krol grabbed the mutilated throat in its jaws, and three others latched their teeth onto the antelope's body. The two remaining pups yipped and howled in excitement as the krols hurried back to the awaiting Mongols, carrying the dead antelope in their jaws.

"Well," Nila muttered, "they might be pups, but they're still deadly."

One handler was a teenage girl whose long dark hair was adorned with beads. When she reached for the dead antelope, the largest krol pup lifted its head, its black eyes glaring as though angry at surrendering its kill. Lips peeling back from its sharklike teeth, it seemed to snarl at her.

Yep, I thought grimly, *that's definitely like the krols back home.*

Fu Manchu scowled. With one swift movement, he unhooked a bone club from his hip and slammed it onto the head of the snarling krol pup. The xan dropped in a bloodied heap. Dead.

The five remaining pups huddled on the ground as their handlers clipped leashes to their collars again.

"Whoa." Harlem lowered his binoculars. "Brutal."

"But efficient," Asher said. "When the pups grow up and start becoming as aggressive as the adults, I'll bet they're killed before they can turn on their handlers."

Soo-Yun asked, "How Mongrel get pup?"

"Mongols," Asher corrected. "Maybe they breed them from adult krols kept in cages or something."

As the Mongol girl blew a whistle, the huddled krol pups covered their bat-like ears with their paws. She tossed the dead one in a sack, slung it over her shoulder, then pocketed her whistle. The krol pups looked around sheepishly, like puppy dogs caught misbehaving.

One sniffed the air. Stiffening, it leaned forward on all four legs like a hunting dog locating its prey. It lifted a clawed front paw and pointed—

—straight at the Great Wall where we hid behind the parapets.

57

ASHER JERKED BEHIND THE parapet again, out of sight. "Cripes! It's picked up our scent."

On my left was a small spyhole in the bricks. Cautiously, I peered through it.

Down below, the group of Mongols stared at the watchtower near us.

"We're safe, guys," Asher said softly. "They can't get up here. There aren't any steps on the northern side of the wall."

The Mongols conferred, then checked the arrows in their quivers. The krol pups braced themselves on all fours. At a short whistle, the pack of Mongols and krol pups charged at the Great Wall.

"Stay where you are, everyone," Asher ordered, peering through another spyhole. "Keep out of sight. Those Mongols might suspect there are people or animals up on the wall. But since they can't get up here, they'll eventually give up and leave."

Along with the others, I sat on the carriageway, back pressed against a parapet as I considered Asher's claim. If the Mongols knew they couldn't access the top of the wall from their side, why were they racing toward it?

Opposite me, two pigeons pecked at a terra vine.

Time for a quick scout around.

I rested against the parapet wall, focused on the larger pigeon—

—and threw my mind into it.

Pigeon-me flew past my non-conscious body and over the northern battlement. High in the air, my pigeon eyes saw a frightening sight. The Mongols and krol pups were scrabbling up the terra vines that laced the wall below the watchtower. They climbed with fast, practiced movements, the krol pups pulling on their leashes as they surged ahead.

I mind-leaped back into my own body.

Regaining consciousness with a gasp, I cried, "They're scaling the wall beneath the watchtower. And they're fast. They'll be here any moment."

Asher gaped at me. "How do you know?" His gaze flickered to the pigeons across the carriageway. "Oh. Right." He gripped the sword at his waist. "Guys, we need to get out of here. Now." As the others grabbed at their weapons, he pointed toward the watchtower a hundred feet behind us. "Kass, do we have time to—?"

The Mongols poured from the watchtower onto the carriageway. Seeing us, they jerked to a halt, shocked. The adults raised their longbows, arrows poised for release, and the five krol pups yipped and strained at their leashes.

The teenage Mongol girl crossed to the southern wall.

"Qara." The long-mustached Mongol, Fu Manchu, gestured for her to rejoin them.

Ignoring him, the girl peered over the parapet, uttered an alarmed cry, and stepped back. She'd seen the Chi'az ship parked below. Jabbering and pointing at the southern wall, she rushed back to her companions.

"Great," Asher muttered. "Now they'll think we're aliens."

"What do we do?" Harlem asked.

I knew the answer even before Asher replied. The facts were obvious. Eight of us versus ten of them. We might've stood a chance, since we had swords and guns and they only appeared to have bows and clubs and spears—but they also had five vicious krol pups eager to rip our throats to shreds.

No way could we break through the group of Mongols, enter the watchtower, descend the ramp of stairs, and reach Lightning One without any casualties.

Only one choice remained.

Staring at the line of Mongols, Asher spoke in a calm, flat voice. "At my signal, guys, we turn and bolt to that beacon tower further along the wall."

Yep, my thoughts exactly.

"Lynxx went there earlier," I said, eager to back up his plan.

"Good," he said. "We can use his help. That beacon tower will have steps down to the ground. Defend yourself if the Mongols attack us. But first ..."

Huh? First?

Alarmed, I watched Asher raise his hands and step toward the Mongols. Speaking slowly and clearly, he said, "We're friends. Friends. Do any of you speak English?" When they stared at him blankly, he swallowed. With growing desperation, he repeated the questions in another language.

Harlem looked confused. "Asher speaks Chinese?"

"Mandarin," Soo-Yun said, impressed.

I remembered Asher's stories of his life before the Mist, and how his father had demanded that he become bilingual for business reasons.

As Asher continued speaking in Mandarin, the Mongols scowled and their lips curled in sneers.

Uh-oh. Maybe these Mongols didn't like their Chinese neighbors.

Fu Manchu raised his club—still bloodied from bashing in the rebellious krol pup's skull—and gave a fierce yell.

Asher swung back to us, shouting, "*Run.*"

As we bolted toward the distant beacon tower, Asher babbled something into the radio attached to his shoulder. Feet thudded behind us. Claws scratched the stone pavers. A spear whizzed past, headed straight for Nila's back—

—but I instinctively remote-pushed it aside, and it clattered harmlessly to the pavers.

The chilly wind picked up strength, howling as it barreled down the carriageway. More spears and arrows hissed around us as we ran, but the wind pushed them off course.

How far to the beacon tower?

I looked ahead—

—and saw Lynxx racing toward us, waving his arms as he shouted, "Go back! Go back!"

Was he blind? Couldn't he see the Mongols chasing us?

Asher yelled, "Harl, I need backup."

"I've got you covered, bro." Harlem slowed a little, joining Asher at the rear of our group.

"Kendra," Asher shouted. "How's your aim while running?"

"Eager to find out." The girl turned and, running backward, fired a series of shots at the pursuing Mongols. Asher and Harlem fired as well. One man tumbled into a heap. Another clutched his stomach and dropped to his knees. The rest faltered.

We raced on and met Lynxx a short distance from the beacon tower.

Lynxx eyed the Mongols, now cautiously advancing along the carriageway. Further back, two men sprawled on the pavers in bloodied puddles.

"We can't get out through that beacon tower," Lynxx said. In the building behind him, thick black tentacles twitched and waved at the windows. "It's infested with tentacle terras."

We groaned.

"What do we do now, boss?" Booker cried.

The Mongols suddenly shrieked and charged forward.

"We fight," Asher yelled.

58

Our two groups met in a clash of swords and spears and slashing teeth.

The krol pups, freed from their leashes, threw themselves into the battle with savage eagerness. Lynxx and I remote-pushed Mongol spears aside and remote-pushed krol pups as they leaped at throats. Gunshots rang out. Two more Mongols dropped. People shouted. Dodged clubs. Slashed swords.

I glimpsed Bramwell, one of our soldiers, slumping to the ground, an arrow through his throat.

The vicious little krol pups were everywhere. Jumping from person to person. Clawing at legs. Growling and snarling. One leaped at Booker's throat, but I remote-pushed it over the wall, and it squealed as it plummeted to the ground. Harlem shot another one in the stomach.

The three remaining krol pups skittered forward, teeth bared, claws bloodied.

"Qara." A Mongol boy tossed a club to the teenage girl with the beaded hair. She caught it in a confident hand and swung it at Soo-Yun. The Korean girl jumped back, whirled around, and slammed a fierce karate kick into the Mongol girl's stomach. The girl—Qara?—fell.

Way to go, Soo-Yun.

A krol pup charged our ex-cheerleader, Natalie. As I ran to help her, I glimpsed a club swinging down toward my head—

I jerked back.

—and it missed me by a hair.

"Oops. Sorry, Kass." Nila swung the club again, this time onto a Mongol's skull.

I turned back to Natalie.

She lay on the stone pavers, blood gushing from her ripped throat as the pup shook it. Uttering a gurgling sound, she tried to push the growling beast off her. More blood gushed, and her body spasmed as though electrocuted.

"*No*," I screamed, remote-pushing the krol pup over the side of the wall. Shrieking, it disappeared from sight. "Natalie!" I raced across the red pavers to her bloodied, motionless body.

No need to check her throat for a pulse. There was no throat. Just a bloodied gaping wound.

I felt sick.

A deafening roar sounded overhead, along with a strong downdraft of air.

Startled, everyone stopped fighting, covered their ears, and looked up.

Lightning One hovered above us, its hull as black as night. Gold zaps of energy shot from its undercarriage, sizzling like miniature lightning bolts in a showy display of ominous, threatening power.

Is this how Lightning One got its name?

The surviving Mongols shouted in terror. Whistling to their remaining pups, they turned and scurried over the northern side of the Great Wall, descending the trellis of terra vines with amazing speed.

I glanced over the southern parapet. All signs of our camp had vanished.

Slowly, Lightning One descended onto the carriageway, its long narrow hull fitting on the pavers with only a narrow gap to spare on one side. The roar of its engine abruptly changed to a hum as its metal hatch slid open.

"Get in," yelled Commander Powell from inside.

One by one, my colleagues squeezed down the gap between the hull and the southern wall. Those with injuries went first; Yuki had a broken arm, others had cuts and lacerations.

Asher shouted, "Commander, Bramwell and Natalie are dead."

"Leave them, son. No time."

Near the beacon tower, Nila stood over the body of the Mongol teenager. The woman held a bloodied club, and she had a strange expression on her face.

Blood trickled from a long gash on the unconscious girl's forehead. I ran across and pressed two fingers to her throat. "She's alive. Don't worry, Nila. Her people will come back for her after we've gone."

"We can't just abandon her," she cried. "Those savages won't know how to treat her injury. I did this. I have to help her."

"What are you talking about?"

"I thought this girl ... Qara? ... was knocked out. But when Lightning One appeared overhead, she woke up. She called out to her friends. I guess I reacted automatically because I just swung around and hit her in the head. *I* did this."

I stared at Nila. "You heard her call out? Over the noise of Lightning One's engine?" How was that possible?

"Hey," she cried out to Booker, "help me get Qara into the ship. Hurry."

I watched them carry the girl into the ship.

As I followed them inside, I saw Commander Powell at the controls. The drum of Shimmer gas had been rebolted to the floor, and the remaining soldiers were already seated. Tents and boxes of supplies from the camp lay jumbled in the middle, obviously thrown into the ship in their haste to leave. As Nila and Booker laid the limp Mongol girl on a bench down the back, the commander called out, "What the heck are you doing, Nila?"

"I didn't mean to hit her so hard on the head," she replied. "I did this. Now I have to help her."

"She and her people tried to kill us."

"They thought we were the enemy. She's just a kid. A *human* kid."

"We don't have time to nurse her. We're on a tight schedule. The Shimmer gas is our priority. Unfortunately, she's collateral damage. Leave her behind."

"I won't." Nila glanced at her watch. "We still have several more hours in Mongolia. By the time we set up camp in another spot, I'll have her patched up. Then we can let her go."

"You're jeopardizing our mission."

"Do you want to argue or get out of here?" Nila gestured to the side window, which overlooked the top of the wall. Below, a dozen Mongols on horses rounded a hillock. Seeing the ship, they charged toward the wall, accompanied by a large pack of snarling krol pups.

Swearing, Commander Powell closed the hatch.

As Lightning One rose above the Great Wall, the Mongols on horseback raised their longbows and unleashed a rain of arrows. All fell short.

Our ship zipped away in a shower of gold flashes.

Asher sat beside the commander at the controls. "I thought we couldn't use the engine until it cooled down."

"That's if we're setting off for several hours of flying, son," Powell replied. "There's no problem if we're airborne for less than thirty minutes."

"Oh. Right."

Lightning One reduced speed over a windswept plain hundreds of miles to the south of the Great Wall. Commander Powell cruised at a low altitude, carefully scanning the terrain below. Lots of scrubby trees. More sweeps of white grass terras. Antelopes. Goats. No signs of any humans—or krols.

When the ship landed, Nila remained in the cabin tending the Mongol girl. Our medic, Soo-Yun, put a cast on Yuki's broken arm and patched up the others' injuries.

Outside, Commander Powell posted extra guards, then supervised setting up the Release Point Two camp again. This time, no one from Liberty Team wandered away on a sightseeing jaunt. We remained at the camp with the soldiers, subdued by Bramwell's and Natalie's horrific deaths and the near-disaster of our mission.

By the time the engine had cooled down hours later, Qara was still unconscious.

"We have to take her with us, Lincoln," insisted Nila, checking the stitched gash on the girl's forehead. "We can't leave an injured, unconscious kid alone in the middle of this wilderness. It'd be murder."

Grimly, Commander Powell took the controls again.

Minutes later, we were airborne. Since our next leg would take ten hours, people slept in their seats or read. Willow stretched out on a bench, sedated by a terra powder Lynxx had given her. Blood splotched her bandaged cheeks.

I stared into the distance, lost in thought. For a while, I relived the battle with the Mongols, wondering what I could've done better, how I could've saved Natalie. But I had no answers.

Eventually my thoughts drifted to a different topic: my old enemy.

For the past few hours, I'd felt fine. Even after that fight on the Great Wall, after remote-pushing again and again, all I had was a bad headache. No nausea.

Was my leukemia back or not? *Please, please, please, let me be well.*

Eventually, worn out by worry and exhaustion, I fell asleep.

Hours later, I woke up as Lynxx sat down next to me. Rubbing the sleep from my eyes, I glanced down the cabin. At the rear of the ship, Nila remained by the unconscious Mongol girl's side, whose gashed forehead was now bandaged.

"How's Qara?" I asked.

"No change." Lynxx glanced around as he lowered his voice. "I was just in back getting a book from my duffel bag." Moving his head closer to mine, he whispered, "You don't have leukemia again."

My heart pounded. "I don't?"

He shook his head.

"How do you know, Lynxx? That nausea I felt twice—"

"—was when you were in the rear of Lightning One, right?"

"Yes."

"I felt that same nausea too."

"What? When?"

"A few minutes ago. And also a minute ago when I went down the back again, just to make sure."

"It's not leukemia?" I whispered, both relieved and confused. "Then what is it?"

"I don't know. Maybe there's a substance on the ship that hybrids—and humans with hybrid blood like you, Kassia—are sensitive to."

"What kind of substance? Is it dangerous?"

"I've no idea." Eyes narrowed, he looked around the cabin as he murmured, "Or maybe there's a mind-blended hybrid on this ship. An Outrider spy."

59

"Is that possible, Lynxx?" I whispered.

"I don't know. If there *is* a mind-blended hybrid on board, it's not one of our people. We've been near each of them during this mission. It must be Qara."

The unconscious Mongol girl stirred on the rear bench, groaning.

I shook my head. "The sensations started before we'd even landed in Mongolia. It can't be her." I paused. "Or it could be her *and* there's another mind-blended hybrid on board as well."

"Highly unlikely. First, let's clear Qara."

We waited until Nila rejoined Commander Powell at the controls. Casually, Lynxx and I wandered past our snoozing companions to the rear of the ship. "Operation Qara" only took a few seconds. Lynxx pried her eyelids open and I aimed a penlight into her eyes. Deep brown, not silver.

Back in our seats, we bent our heads together again.

"It's not her," Lynxx whispered.

"Then who is it?"

"I could be wrong. Maybe there's no spy after all." His brow furrowed. "The whole thing's impossible anyway."

"What do you mean?"

"A hybrid can only mind-blend for around three hours before its mind is drawn back into its living body. But we've been traveling for days. A hybrid can't stay mind-blended away from its own body for that long."

"So we're back to the idea of a substance making us nauseous?"

"Maybe."

Commander Powell called out, "We'll be landing shortly, folks."

People awoke as Lightning One descended and circled for a suitable landing spot.

I stared through the transparent hull, dismayed. Release Point Three—the desert of Central Australia—was a bright red expanse dotted with rocky outcrops.

"Oh no, the terras are everywhere," I cried. "Look at the land. It's an ugly blood-red color."

Asher gazed fondly at his homeland. "That's the natural color of the dirt in this area. That's why it's nicknamed 'the Red Centre.'"

"Oops. Sorry."

Amid this arid redness was a circle darker and redder than its surroundings. The size of four football fields, its scattered shrubs suggested an underground water source.

Bewildered, Booker squinted at the spot. "Can you have a red oasis?"

"The Outback," said Asher, "doesn't have any oases, red or green." He frowned. "At least, it never used to."

At the controls, Nila took the ship down for a closer look.

The red circle turned out to be a large area of crimson grass dotted with orange bushes. The place appeared as hot as the surrounding barren landscape, but the orange bushes threw off patches of shade, and the crimson grass looked softer and cooler than the red sands of the desert.

"Your thoughts, Lynxx?" asked Powell.

He lowered his binoculars. "The vegetation looks like *Nirvaneous exTerrus* and *Lanisonia exTerrus*. I've only studied small patches back in New York. Both are harmless."

"Good."

Lightning One landed in the middle of the red circle, and people disembarked.

As Asher and I reached for our weapons, Harlem held up a hand. "It's okay, guys. This oasis is fairly open. Kendra and I can do a sweep. You take a break, bro." Harlem's eyes flickered to Willow, still huddled in her seat.

"Thanks," Asher said. "Radio me if you have any problems."

Soo-Yun asked Lynxx, "I take bandage off Booker, yes?"

He nodded.

When Booker's bandages were removed, the boy peered into a small mirror. Three red scars crisscrossed his left cheek, each long and thin. He studied them for a minute, then grinned. "Cool. Harry Potter, step aside. There's a new bad boy in town."

I hid a smile at the thought of our resident bookworm coveting an adventurous, roguish image.

He hurried outside to show the others his battle wounds. "Hey, guys, take a look at these bad boy scars."

Willow held her breath as Soo-Yun removed the bandages on her cheeks. I kept my expression neutral, carefully not reacting to the half dozen angry splotches that marred her previous porcelain skin.

With a horrified gasp, she stared at her reflection in a mirror. "When will these marks go away?"

"I've no idea," Lynxx gently replied. "I don't know what that xan in Rome spat at you and Booker."

"But Kass's hand is unscarred from that buckshot-pod terra last year. She told me that you used some special powder."

"I've used that on you too. Some wounds heal completely. Others take time. Some scars never disappear."

At her anguished whimper, Asher drew her into a gentle embrace. "No one cares about your scars. You're still beautiful."

She buried her face in his chest and sobbed.

My heart ached for her. Willow's beauty was an important part of her identity, and without it she seemed even more broken than before. I wanted to tell her that looks and charm and talent were precious, yes, but in this new world, courage and quick thinking and resilience were more important.

Somehow, I doubted my words would comfort her, so I remained silent.

I watched her clutch Asher with the desperation of a shattered soul. Softly, he stroked her silken blond hair, murmuring reassurances.

Will her injuries bring them closer together again? I wondered. *Or is their relationship doomed by our changed world?*

Silently, Lynxx, Soo-Yun, and I left the ship, giving Asher and the distraught Willow their privacy.

60

IT WAS ONLY MORNING, but the air outside was as hot and thick as the breath of hell, and I suddenly longed for the chill of Mongolia.

"Isn't August winter in Australia?" I asked Lynxx.

He nodded. "The seasons seem warped. It's abnormally hot here, despite it being winter. And it was abnormally cold in Mongolia, even though it was summer there."

The burning sun had leached all the color from the sky, leaving it almost white. Around us, the oasis shimmered in a mid-morning haze as though underwater. The crimson terra grass rippled, and the orange terra bushes writhed beneath invisible flames.

To my surprise, a variety of native birds pecked at the crimson grass or nibbled at small terra flowers, unbothered by the scorching conditions.

"I pity the two soldiers assigned here," I said to Lynxx. Beyond the oasis, the red desert extended to the horizon. "Although it looks even hotter in the actual desert."

"This is hot enough." Wiping his sweating forehead, he peered at a patch of flowers. Small as eggs, their splayed red petals glinted like rubies, and their stamens resembled gold threads. "*Aginsatia exTerrus*."

"In English."

"Jewel terras." He picked one and presented it to me with a faint smile. "Beautiful but not deadly—just like you."

I took the flower, unsure whether to be pleased he thought I was beautiful or insulted that he didn't think I could be dangerous. "I'm a resistance fighter. Killing is my job. That means I'm a badass."

"You kill alien animals and plants. You're not exactly a deadly assassin."

People started setting up camp, moving slowly through the oppressive heat. Nila supervised two soldiers who were securing a drum of Shimmer gas near a clump of bushes, and I was relieved the gas wasn't flammable even under extreme temperatures.

"I'm going back into the ship." Nila shaded her eyes from the glary sunlight. "I need to see how Qara is."

As she entered Lightning One, Asher exited. Lynxx and I joined him as he headed to the commander at the edge of the camp.

"How's Willow?" I asked him.

"Heartbroken. Soo-Yun's taking her for a short walk." He shoved a sun-streaked lock off his sweaty forehead.

Commander Powell surveyed the terrain, radio in hand, listening to Harlem's voice crackle from it: *"All clear so far, sir."*

"Good. Let me know if you have any problems, Harlem. Out." Powell clicked off, muttering, "I really don't want any problems in this place. It's way too hot."

Lynxx stepped forward. "Sir, we might have a problem."

Rolling his eyes, Powell swore under his breath.

Quickly, leaving out all mention of leukemia, Lynxx told the commander and Asher about the nausea that he and I had felt when in the rear of the ship. He finished with, "It could be nothing. Just a substance that Kassia and I are more sensitive to." He paused. "Or our nausea could be caused by an Outrider hybrid stowaway."

A muscle twitched in Powell's heat-flushed face. "Are you saying that you can sense an Outrider on Lightning One, Lynxx?"

"Maybe. Sometimes a mind-blended hybrid gives off vibrations which feel like a change in the air . . . a current. But in this case, Kassia and I felt nauseous, which is not the usual sensation."

"So who is it?" Asher asked.

"It may be a *what*, not a *who*." Lynxx rubbed his chin in thought. "There's no indication that any human in our group is mind-blended with a hybrid. Still, an Outrider could be mind-blended with an animal that's hiding among the boxes and drums down the back."

"An animal?" Powell said, skeptical.

"It can be any size, Commander. When Kassia lived in the subway bunker, I used to mind-blend with a white mouse so I could keep her company."

Asher's face tightened, as if remembering my stories of those months underground. "Mousy? She loved that pet mouse. That was you, Lynxx?"

"Yes."

"Focus, son," Powell told Asher. "We could have a spy on board."

"Sorry, sir."

Beneath our feet, the ground trembled and the leaves of the orange bushes rustled and shook. After a few seconds, the land settled into stillness again.

We glanced at each other.

Powell asked Asher, "Does Australia have earthquakes?"

"Only minor ones, sir."

"Good." Powell turned back to Lynxx and me. "Have you told anyone else about this stowaway?"

Lynxx shook his head. "No. It's only a suspicion, not a fact."

A sudden thought struck me. "Maybe Nila's involved."

Powell scowled. "Involved how?"

"I'm not sure, sir. The way she insisted on bringing Qara on board seemed out of character. Normally she's one hundred percent focused on the mission. Now, she's constantly fussing over a Mongol girl she accidentally injured. It just seems odd."

Powell considered my words. "I'll take your comments under advisement." He shoved his gun into his waistband, within easy reach. "Let's go."

Back at Lightning One, Powell ordered three soldiers to wait outside. When we entered, Nila was bending over Qara, checking the unconscious girl's pulse.

"What's going on, Lincoln?" she asked.

"There might be a mind-blended Outrider hybrid on this ship."

"That's ridiculous."

Lynxx told her, "Kassia and I sensed . . . something."

Powell added, "Apparently the Outrider could be in a rat or another small critter. I have three soldiers ready to search every inch of this vessel. It would be best if you waited outside, Nila."

On the bench, Qara stirred. Her brown eyes fluttered, and she mumbled something in her native Mongol tongue.

Nila checked the girl's pulse again. "She's getting a little stronger. I can't leave her. She might regain consciousness at any moment."

"We'll let you know if her condition changes," Powell said. "Now please wait outside."

Nila started to argue again but saw the commander's set expression and gave an annoyed sigh. "Very well. Wait a moment." She hurried into the cluttered rear area, squeezed behind the remaining Shimmer drums, and emerged with a cardboard box with airholes in its sides.

"This is what you're looking for." Nila opened the lid and withdrew a large white rabbit—with silver eyes.

A wave of nausea swept me, stronger than the earlier two times but mercifully brief. Was I getting used to the sensation?

I recognized the animal's tattered left ear. "That's Whitey."

"Who?" Powell asked.

"The rabbit from Roosevelt Plaza. After the massacre, I had to choose between it and a brown rabbit. They both had silver eyes, and I had to figure out if one held Lynxx's mind." Fortunately, I'd picked the right rabbit.

"This is what Kass and Lynxx sensed." Nila sank onto the bench, cradling Whitey like a baby. "We don't have an Outrider spy on board. It's my daughter, Eva."

Powell gawked at Whitey. "This is your daughter? How? When?"

"I went back to the plaza a couple of times." Nila stroked the furry head. "I hoped that, somehow, Eva had mind-blended with an animal before her human body died. While I was there the last time, this rabbit emerged from a burrow. It was sick and weak, but I knew it was Eva."

"How could you know?" Powell asked.

"White rabbits normally have pink or red eyes. This one had silver eyes. I realized it could've been a Sphere hybrid, so I had it spell out her human name."

"How did she do that?"

"I recited the alphabet, and she lifted a paw as I reached each letter. E-V-A." She appealed to Powell, blinking back tears. "I couldn't go on this mission and leave my daughter behind. After losing my only child and grieving her death, by some miracle I had her back. I wanted her with me. Surely you understand, Lincoln. You were a father once."

"I do understand. But you still should've told me. Trusted me."

"You're right. I'm sorry." Her apology rang hollow, and I knew she didn't regret her deception at all.

Lynxx folded his arms. "It all makes sense now."

"What does?" I asked.

"I couldn't figure out how a hybrid could mind-blend with an animal for days on end. Normally, a hybrid can only mind-blend for around three hours before it's drawn back into its human body. But Eva's body had died, so there was no connection pulling her back into it. With this connection severed, she can easily mind-blend with an animal for weeks or months—or even years."

On the bench, Qara stirred and mumbled something in Mongolian.

Cradling the white rabbit, Nila leaned toward the girl. "She's regaining consciousness."

The air in the cabin abruptly shifted.

My body tingled from head to toe as though chilled by a winter wind. Puzzled, I turned to Lynxx. "What—?" His shiver indicated that he'd felt the same bone-chilling tingle.

Powell's brows rose as Whitey's silver eyes suddenly turned red. "What just happened?"

Qara sat up, her eyes now silver instead of brown. The Mongol girl gazed around with a slow, satisfied expression.

"Hi, Mom," she said in crystal clear English.

Nila thrust the rabbit at Powell and gathered Qara into her arms. "Are you okay, Eva?"

The silver-eyed girl wriggled from her mother's embrace. She flicked her beaded dark hair behind her shoulders, then stretched her arms above her head, as though awakening from a long sleep. "This body will do—for now."

61

COMMANDER POWELL GAPED AT the Mongol girl. "What's going on, Nila?"

Before she could answer, Lightning One shook as though flying through turbulence—except the ship was parked on the ground.

Asher rushed to the open hatch. "It's another tremor."

Powell gestured to Nila and Mongol-Eva. "Remain inside the ship. It's safer in here."

"Certainly," Nila said, distracted. She seemed so focused on her "reborn" daughter that nothing else mattered right now.

Lynxx gave an exaggerated yawn. "I think I'll stay inside too. I could use a nap."

I looked at him, bewildered. He never napped. He caught my eye and flicked a meaningful glance at Nila and Mongol-Eva. *Oh. Right.* I nodded and followed the others from the ship.

Outside, a low ripping noise filled the air, along with a series of faint pops.

"That doesn't sound like an earthquake," Asher said.

"And it doesn't look like one," I added. Beneath my feet, the land felt unsteady, almost trembling. But no cracks appeared in the earth, and the bushes and grass were undisturbed.

"We're moving." Powell stood with his legs astride, studying the ground. "Slowly." He addressed the three soldiers who accompanied him. "Stand guard outside the hatch. Don't let Nila or that Mongol girl out of the ship." When I looked surprised at the orders, he explained, "Just a precaution."

At the campsite, worried people asked Powell what was going on.

"I'm looking into it now, folks." He gestured to Asher and me. "Let's take a walk."

The oppressive heat engulfed us as we headed toward a grove of bushes beyond the campsite. The land kept trembling like a feverish dog, and the branches of the terra bushes scraped and clacked. Finally, the ripping-popping noises faded away—yet the ground continued to move.

Quietly, Powell said to Asher and me, "I'm not sure this is a tremor."

"Why do you say that, sir?"

"Look at the grass, son. There's not a single crack in it. And look at those birds." He pointed. In some nearby bushes, pigeons perched on the branches, sheltering from the overhead sun. Nearby, half a dozen sparrows pecked at grass seeds, and white cockatoos chewed on jewel terra flowers.

"That's strange," Asher said. "Birds usually fly away before a tremor. These are ignoring it."

Powell nodded. "These birds are behaving as if the moving ground is a common occurrence and not dangerous. Nevertheless, I'm reluctant to base my decision on a bunch of bird brains. That's where you come in, Kass."

"Me?" I asked, surprised. "How can I help, sir?"

"Are you able to mind-blend with a bird and fly beyond the oasis, checking things out?"

"Sure, but ..." I hesitated, still uneasy at the Nila and Eva situation. However, the pair was confined to the ship. Nila would be concentrating on her daughter, and Eva would be getting used to her new body. Besides, Lynxx was also in the cabin, keeping an eye on them. "Okay. I'll mind-blend, sir, as long as someone guards my non-conscious body."

"I'll stay here." As Asher took my hand, a familiar warmth swept me. "I won't let anything happen to you." His eyes held a deep concern, very different from the gentle soothing he'd offered Willow earlier.

Powell added, "Asher and I will both guard your body."

"Thanks." I sat behind a thick bush, hiding myself from Nila and Mongol-Eva in Lightning One. Asher and the commander stood a couple of feet in front of the bush, their postures deliberately relaxed as if having a casual chat.

Nearby, a white cockatoo was nibbling on a jewel terra flower. Focusing on the bird, I closed my eyes, leaned against the bush for support, then mind-leaped.

Starbursts. Gray spongy mass. Claustrophobia.

And then I was inside the cockatoo's mind. The taste of the jewel terra flower lingered in my throat. *Yum. Delicious. A sweet honey blend, topped with tasty ants.*

On strong white wings, I launched myself upward, seeking the proverbial bird's-eye view. Below, the round oasis was slowly moving, ringed by driftings of red dust at its edges. Beyond it, the red landscape baked beneath the heat-bleached sky, undisturbed and motionless.

Weird. What the heck's going on here?

Cockatoo-me flew a few feet beyond the edge of the oasis and landed on the hot ground.

Whoa! The entire oasis was raised a few inches above the red dirt. Thousands of tiny black millipede-like legs skittered underneath, and it took a few seconds before my stunned mind accepted the truth. This "oasis" was actually an enormous flat xan.

The oasis xan had moved away from its original position, leaving a large gray circle behind. Had it absorbed all the nutrients from its previous spot? Was it now looking for a new feeding ground? I flew high into the air and saw other gray circles scattered across the plain, possibly previous feeding spots.

Landing again, cockatoo-me walked alongside the raised edge of the oasis xan and watched as it lowered itself onto a patch of fresh red dirt. Underneath it, the countless tiny black legs burrowed into the soil as though securing the xan into its new position.

Ultra weird. Lynxx would've loved seeing this.

I flew back and mind-hopped into my own body. With an annoyed flutter of wings, my cockatoo host flew off. Standing, I brushed the red dirt off the back of my jeans and told Asher and the commander about the oasis xan. They listened, as astounded as I'd been.

Powell surveyed the area, uneasy. "We're camping on the back of a huge flat xan?"

"Yes, Commander. I think we're safe, though. The xan has stopped moving. It's settled into a new feeding spot."

"What about all the grasses and bushes?" he asked, still struggling with the bizarre concept. "How can they grow on its back?"

"Nature is opportunistic, sir," I replied, channeling one of Lynxx's lectures. "It takes advantage of everything and anything. Lichen and mollusks can grow on whales, and seaweed can grow on the shells of sea turtles. Lynxx calls them symbiotic relationships. Both sides benefit."

"What's the benefit for this oasis xan, Kass?" asked Asher.

"Maybe the grasses keep the xan cool, insulating its back from the hot sun."

"Where's its head?"

"No idea. Perhaps it doesn't have one."

Powell groaned in frustration. "Well, we can't leave two soldiers and a drum of our Shimmer gas on the back of a giant xan!" Asher and I accompanied him to the camp as he spoke briefly into his radio: "Sorry, folks. We have to move again. Start packing up." He clicked off and glanced at his watch. "We have about fifteen minutes. Time for another chat with Nila."

Inside Lightning One, Nila and Mongol-Eva held hands and quietly talked. As we moved down the cabin aisle, Lynxx sat up with a fake yawn. "Wow, I needed that nap."

Commander Powell took a seat. "How are you feeling?" he asked the Mongol girl.

Eva shrugged, then shifted her cool gaze to me. "You were in the eagle at the plaza, after the massacre, right?" When I nodded, her silver eyes glittered with hatred. "You pushed me out of that bird and flew away. You left me to die."

"Sorry. I had no choice. SkyLady was my host, not yours."

"Whatever." She swung her gaze to Lynxx. "We've met before, haven't we?"

"Sort of," he said. "That day at the plaza, I was mind-blended with a brown rabbit."

"Yeah, I remember. Your friend here saved you instead of me." Her glare flickered between Lynxx and me, heavy with loathing.

Quickly, Commander Powell said, "That was a dreadful day, Qara … er, Eva … but we're all trying to move past it."

"That's easy for you to say, Gramps. You weren't the one living in a flea-ridden rabbit for days."

Asher bristled at her sour attitude. "You didn't have to stay in the rabbit, Eva. You could've mind-leaped into any animal close by. Tiger. Horse. Eagle."

"I didn't want to live in an animal."

"Fair enough. But hey, you're human again."

"I want to be a *hybrid* again. This human body is too weak and inefficient. No rapid healing for a start. Worse, there's something seriously wrong with it. I think it's got a brain tumor."

Powell asked her, "Why do you say that?"

"I'm in this human's mind, and it feels … sickly … with a pulsing darkness, like a cancer that's slowly growing."

Frowning, the commander turned to Nila. "How long can Eva inhabit Qara's body?"

"I'm not sure. Since Eva's own body is dead, there's nothing pulling her mind out of her new body. But obviously she can't stay in a cancerous body for too long."

"What about Qara?" Powell asked. "What happened to *her* mind?"

"It's still in there," Nila replied. "But Eva's hybrid mind is stronger, and eventually Qara's mind will die."

"So Eva doesn't have to return to the rabbit?"

"Technically, no," she replied. "Qara's concussion provided Eva with a non-animal body."

"What a stroke of luck," Asher said, his voice reflecting the skepticism we both felt. "It was lucky that you only knocked a human girl unconscious with a club, Nila, and didn't kill her. It was lucky that you insisted on bringing Qara's injured body on board Lightning One. And it was lucky that you just happened to be holding Whitey close to Qara as she began regaining consciousness."

"Knocking Qara on the head was an accident." Nila's claim had the hollow ring of a lie. "But, yes, I took advantage of the incident. My daughter's been stuck in a rabbit's body for days. I was worried she'd sink into depression or become mentally unstable. Surely any normal person would understand why I wanted to get her out of ... what was that name again? ... Whitey?"

I looked around. "Where *is* Whitey?"

"In its box," Nila answered, "eating vegetables."

Must keep Eva's host animal healthy, I thought cynically.

Booker poked this head through the hatch. "Commander, can we reload the Shimmer drum into Lightning One, sir?"

"Yes." When Nila looked at Powell, surprised, he said, "I'll explain later." He left the ship with Asher, and I heard him ordering the three soldiers outside to maintain their positions.

Uncomfortable under Mongol-Eva's hostile gaze, Lynxx and I hurriedly left as well.

We crossed the crimson grass to a quiet spot, watching as people reloaded supplies into the cabin.

"I don't trust Nila—or Eva," muttered Lynxx. "That girl wants a better body."

"But who?" I waved off some flies drawn to my sweat-beaded skin. "Everyone on board is mentally healthy, except for Willow. She's been a little off-center lately." I jerked toward Lynxx, alarmed. "You don't think she's after Willow, do you?"

"Doubtful. Willow's human. She doesn't fit the ideal criteria: injured, teen, female, *hybrid*."

"Hybrid?"

"You heard Eva. She's not happy living in a human body, Kassia, especially one that's got brain cancer."

"Can't Nila cut her hand and blend her blood with Qara's? Nila knows that's how I got your hybrid abilities. Couldn't Nila's blood make Qara stronger?"

"To a degree. But even hybrid powers can't cure cancer. Xavian's cancer—and your own previous cancer—have proven that."

I considered his words. "So Eva needs *another* body. One without cancer."

"And a more powerful one. She wants to be a hybrid again, with a hybrid's rapid healing properties and enhanced mental powers."

"You're a teenage hybrid," I pointed out.

"I'm male. Eva might object to spending the rest of her life in a boy's body. She needs an injured female hybrid, someone whose mind she can enter and then occupy indefinitely."

"Indefinitely?"

He nodded.

My mind flashed to two incidents. On the Great Wall of China, Nila—club in hand—had eagerly encouraged me to go into the empty watchtower with her. And later, while fighting the Mongols, Nila's club had swung down, just missing my head.

I gasped at a sudden realization. "How about me? Am I a good fit for Eva?"

"Sure. You're like a pseudo-hybrid teenage girl. But you're mentally healthy, so that rules you out. She can only take over a weak or injured mind."

"I'm mentally healthy *at the moment*. But Nila's already tried to change that." Quickly, I detailed the two incidents up on the Great Wall.

When I finished, Lynxx stared at me for a long moment, stunned. "You're right. Sometime on this trip, Nila is going to injure you."

I swallowed. "And then Eva will take over my mind and body forever."

62

Fear. Worry. Dread.

They gnawed at my stomach with tiny sharp teeth.

I couldn't talk about the issue near Nila and Eva in case they overheard me. I couldn't relax. All I could do was watch and wait for them to try to injure me.

Outside Lightning One, the sky was a cloudless white as we zipped away from the moving oasis xan. We landed in another spot three hundred miles away, its terrain rocky and heat-soaked but stable.

As usual, the ship was allowed to cool for nine hours—although I wondered how anything could cool down in this hellish place.

When the commander and Asher were alone outside, Lynxx and I shared our suspicions about Nila with them.

As expected, a furious Asher immediately wanted to confront Nila and Mongol-Eva. Lynxx calmed him down, saying, "We need to behave normally. We can't let them know we've guessed their plans."

Also as expected, Commander Powell resisted the idea that Nila was planning to harm me. "She's one of the good hybrids," he insisted. "Committed. Brave. Humanized. She protected that group of people in Florida. And remember, her brilliant Shimmer gas is humanity's only hope for survival."

"She's also a mother, sir," I reminded him. "Mothers will do anything to save their children." Well, mine wouldn't. But my father would've given his life for Olivia and me.

Powell paced the hot ground. "I think you and Lynxx are wrong about Nila. But we'll keep an eye on them both, anyway. And, Kass, make sure you're never alone with them."

Despite his words, his guarded tone left me anxious. If he had to make a choice, would he choose the woman he clearly cared for over me?

The tiny teeth of worry continued their gnawing.

From Australia, we traveled to Release Point Four. Antarctica.

Just as the Shimmer drum was bolted onto a massive ice field, a fierce storm struck. Everyone was confined to Lightning One for the entire layover.

"No need to set up a camp or leave any soldiers with this drum," Powell told us, raising his voice over the howling wind that buffeted the ship. "We can set the timer and leave. There are no signs of life within hundreds of miles of this spot."

The wild storm persisted for several hours beyond the cool-down period. Eventually, though, it fizzled out and we took off.

From Antarctica, we headed to South America.

As Nila landed Lightning One in an enormous Peruvian field, Harlem beamed at Soo-Yun. "We're at Release Point Five. Just one more stop after this one, then we can go home. I can't wait to see my Fluffy again, Soo!"

"Fluffy now infirmary cat," she replied with a teasing smile. "Anyway, home good. No like sitting up to sleep."

"Same here. I'm counting the hours until I'm back in my own bed."

I was counting the hours too. Nervously. With growing apprehension.

Eva had been in Qara's body for over two days—but the Mongol girl had developed a fever, possibly from her cancer. Qara-Eva's sweaty forehead, labored breathing, and pained groans were becoming more frequent as the fever raged in her stolen human body.

The commander paused in the aisle beside her. "Are you okay, miss?"

The mind-blended Mongol girl wiped her damp brow. "I don't feel well."

"Do you want me to get the white rabbit?" Powell asked, concerned.

Yes. Get Whitey, I thought. *Make Eva return to her animal host. Maybe then I'd feel a little safer.*

Nila joined us. "My daughter needs some fresh air." When Powell remained silent, she huffed, "Eva's been cooped up in this smelly ship since Mongolia, Lincoln. You didn't let her outside once in Australia. Why not?"

"Qara ... Eva ... doesn't look well. I thought she'd be better off resting inside instead of out in that awful Aussie furnace." He caught Asher's startled look. "No offense to your homeland, son."

"Um, none taken, sir."

"I appreciate your concern, Lincoln," said Nila. "But this new location has milder weather. Eva needs fresh air. Now."

"Very well. But once you're outside, my soldiers won't allow anyone back into this ship without my permission."

"Are you worried about someone hijacking Lightning One?"

Ignoring Nila's question, he headed for the hatch. "Oh, and stay close to the camp. Liberty Team hasn't cleared the area for dangerous terras and xans yet."

As Nila and Eva left the ship, I breathed a little easier. Several times during the last flight, I'd caught the pair looking at me with the slyness of hungry mutts eyeing a juicy steak.

"I'll watch them, Kassia," said Lynxx. He hurried from the ship.

Asher turned to Willow, who was still seated. She averted her face, trying to hide her scarred cheeks as she muttered, "I'm staying inside."

When he hesitated, Soo-Yun told him, "I stay too. With Willow."

"Thanks."

Asher and I gathered our weapons and left.

"How's Willow?" I asked him.

"Devastated. She won't talk to me. She just wanders up and down the cabin like a zombie. I don't think she cares whether she lives or dies."

I guessed that Willow already felt dead inside.

Desperately, I wished I could ease her pain.

A year and a half ago, she'd been living the dream. She'd been a beautiful, world-famous actress with a devoted boyfriend. Overnight, everything had changed with the Mist. And even though she'd remained sweet and kind, she had struggled—physically, mentally, and emotionally—to survive in this brutal new world. Xavian had been her bedrock, and now he was dead. Her wondrous reunion with Asher had soured when she'd realized his feelings for her had changed.

And now her incredible beauty—the rare attribute that had once made her special and adored by millions of fans—had been ruined.

No wonder she was wandering around like a zombie.

Glumly, Asher and I joined the rest of the team outside.

Booker surveyed the place with his usual excitement. Harlem scowled at the massive field, wary. Our newest recruit, Kendra, narrowed her eyes as she assessed the threats in this latest environment; quick-witted and brave, the black girl from South Africa would make an excellent team leader one day.

If we weren't killed by the Threads.

If the Shimmer gas worked.

If we survived this mission.

So many *ifs*.

Near the center of the field, the others began setting up camp and securing the second-to-last drum of Shimmer gas. Four soldiers guarded Lightning One. Nila and Eva strolled the grounds together, staying close to the camp. Across the field, Lynxx alternated writing in a notebook with frequent sideways glances at Nila and Eva.

Asher moved us away from the two female hybrids; I'd once told him that hybrids could only mind-leap twenty yards, but he put a gap of fifty yards between us, just to be safe.

Finally, the tiny teeth of worry stopped gnawing at me. Relaxing a little, I looked around.

In school, I'd learned that Peru was a beautiful country of lush rainforests with colorful birds, snowcapped peaks, and windswept plains of yellow grass.

Maybe snippets of that beauty still existed in other parts of Peru.

But not here.

Lightning One had landed in an open area that reeked of death and darkness and menace.

63

Overhead, swollen gray clouds smothered the land with shadows that somehow felt bleak and mournful.

A gloomy jungle, thick with silence, surrounded the blackened field.

I scuffed the ground with my boot. The grass had been burned, leaving dead leaves that crackled and snapped with each step I took. Scattered across the field were scorched trees whose twisted black branches resembled grotesque skeletons.

At the far end of the clearing, an ancient pyramid-like temple rose hundreds of feet upward. Somber and foreboding, it towered like a sinister threat, watching us.

"An Incan temple," Booker breathed in wonder. "Or Aztec. I'm not sure."

The stone pyramid was blackened and netted in burned terra vines. Looming against the gray skies, its terraced sides led to an altar at the top.

"Up there, the priests made their sacrifices," Booker eagerly informed us, pointing to the altar. "They would slaughter hundreds of young men and women in lengthy ceremonies, cutting open their chests and ripping out their still-beating hearts. They also sacrificed children and animals. Blood would run down the sides of the temple like red rivers." He paused. "I'd better stop before I freak anyone out."

"Too late," I muttered, grimacing.

"Weapons ready, guys." Ever practical, Asher launched into the role of Liberty Team leader. "Let's make sure this area is safe."

"What about that temple?" Harlem asked, grimacing at the death-drenched structure. "Are we going to search that too?"

"Only from the ground and through our binoculars, Harl. Those dead terra vines make it too unsafe to climb."

Good. No climbing the blood-soaked pyramid today.

Swords and guns drawn, we began our sweep of the huge field.

Forty minutes later, Asher spoke into the radio clipped to his shoulder. "All clear, Commander. No dangerous terras or xans. Just lots of dead grass and trees, and that butt-ugly temple of doom."

"Roger. Are you heading back to the ship, son?"

"Yes, sir, after we do a quick scan of the perimeter's trees."

"Be careful."

"We will."

Nervously, I looked around. Senses alert for vibrations in the air, I scanned for any silver-eyed animals or birds sneaking up on me.

Nothing.

This blackened place was as dead as a cemetery.

Through my binoculars, I could see Nila and Qara-Eva still walking near Lightning One. My tension eased a little. They were both moving around. Good. If either of them had been sitting motionless and with her eyes closed, I would've been worried.

Warily, my colleagues and I entered the shadowy jungle to the east of the field. As the clouds parted, weak shafts of sunlight diluted the darkness, silhouetting the trees and vines.

I glanced over my shoulder. We'd only gone a hundred feet into the jungle, yet it had already swallowed all sight of the field and our ship. The trees engulfed us, tall, lush, unburned.

I should've glimpsed birds and small animals. Heard wingbeats or chirps. Smelled life.

Yet the jungle felt strangely wrong.

Eyes narrowed, Asher raised a hand, halting us. When he glanced at me, I gave him a hesitant thumbs-up. *I'm okay.* He nodded and returned to scrutinizing our surroundings.

A branch snapped.

We froze, listening.

I scanned for movement. Faint beams of sunlight seeped through gaps in the overhanging branches, creating a gray haze. Nothing moved. No sounds brought life to the deathly stillness around us.

And then—

—small egg-sized pods arced downward.

They thudded around us, bursting on impact. A fine powder misted the air with a yellow hue, and I tasted a bitter substance. Seconds later, a gust of dizziness swept through me and I swayed, unsteady on my feet. The others also stumbled around, disoriented.

"Wh ... what? Wha ...?" Asher's words were slurred and confused.

Nila? Had she doused us with something so she could attack me?

Clutching a thick vine, a dark shape swung down from the trees. The creature swept past me and, through my daze, I glimpsed its hairy arm grabbing up Kendra. It soared upward with the yelling, struggling girl and vanished into the treetops.

That wasn't Nila.

A second shape swung down toward us, its arm outstretched for another victim. Booker had his back to the creature and didn't see death approaching through the yellow mist. As the hairy arm reached out for him, I tried to focus my blurry mind and remote-push the creature away. I intended to slam it into a tree trunk and—

Abruptly, Booker thudded to the ground and lay on his back, groaning.

Oops. Missed. My bad.

The creature swept past on its vine, arced upward—hairy arm empty—and disappeared into the canopy.

Asher clasped a handkerchief over his mouth, yelling, "Cover your mouths and noses, guys. Move. Get out of here." He grabbed Booker's arm and hauled him to his feet. "Let's go."

Faces buried in shirt bandannas or handkerchiefs, we stumbled through the thick forest into a small clearing dimmed with morning shadows.

No yellow mist.

Bending over, we gulped in the fresh air and babbled our panic and confusion.

"What?"

"Did you see—?"

"Krols?"

"Too big."

"Too hairy."

"They looked human, sort of."

Asher was shouting into his radio, "One got Kendra, Commander! We need to go after her."

From the radio, Powell's tinny voice replied, "Where are you, son?"

"South-east quadrant, sir. In the jungle."

"Got it. We'll be there ASAP."

"If you see a yellow mist, avoid it at all costs. And watch out for Tarzan-like creatures swinging on vines through the trees."

"Roger. Wait for us."

"Negative, sir. We have to go after Kendra now before they kill her."

If they haven't already, I thought grimly.

"Understood. Be careful, son."

"Will do." Asher clicked off. His worried eyes sought me out as he asked, "Everyone okay?"

I nodded, and the others mumbled that they were fine. Except Booker. He swore as he rubbed his sore butt. "Some jerk slammed me to the ground."

"Sorry, Booker," I muttered. "One of those things tried to grab you."

"Really? *Shoot!* Thanks, Kass."

Asher lifted his gun. "Quick weapons check, guys, before we head off."

As Harlem and Booker checked their guns, I gripped my sword. My head no longer felt fuzzy, so my most valuable weapon—my mental powers—seemed to be working again.

"Okay, guys," Asher said. "Stay alert and stay alive." Quietly, we crossed the small clearing and entered the shadowy forest again. "Kass, keep close to me."

At his special treatment, I bit back my annoyance. I wasn't the leukemia girl anymore. And Asher was no longer my boyfriend.

A sharp cry rang through the forest, filled with fear and pain. *Kendra.*

64

Asher pointed left. "She's over there."

We raced through the forest, scanning for danger from all sides. A few minutes later, we trailed to a halt and sniffed the air. A familiar smell stirred up memories of cookouts, picnics, and Fourth of July celebrations.

"Does anyone else smell that?" Harlem warily took another sniff. "Roasting meat?"

"It's coming from there," Asher whispered, gesturing with his gun. Smoke drifted like wraiths through the trees to our right.

On cat-soft feet, we crept forward, following the smoke. I braced myself, expecting to see human survivors sitting around a campfire—

—or maybe some krols. A couple of months ago, Lynxx and I had watched a pack of krols use fire at Central Park, after they'd driven a rhinoceros into a field of glow-lotus terras.

Something moved up ahead.

We took cover behind bushes and trees. Screened by thick branches, I gaped at the creatures in the large clearing.

Not human.

Not krols.

Were they Chi'az? No way. These creatures were far too primitive to be associated with spacecraft and terraforming and invasions.

Only one possibility remained.

Mutant humans.

For months, Commander Powell had forbidden people in the Weston Battalion from eating terra plants, saying, "We don't know what effect the non-terrestrial plants will have on us. People could become mutated."

Lately, he'd relaxed his rules.

Maybe he shouldn't have.

In front of us, five mutant humans had set up a campfire. Naked except for tattered loincloths, all appeared to be adult males. Grunting and growling like savages, they used gestures to aid their communication.

Have they lost their ability to speak? I wondered.

One turned the handle of a rough spit that held a hindquarter of roasting meat, and as fat dripped into the fire, the flames writhed and crackled. Another used a sharp blade to peel back the skin of a dead krol. A third hacked a joint of cooked meat into small pieces and dumped them in wooden bowls. The remaining two were tying a struggling krol along a log, immobilizing its body, arms, and legs with rope. The bloodied krol twisted and jerked its head, snapping at them with its pointed teeth.

I studied the nearest mutant human.

Wisps of long hair sprouted from its bald head, topping a face that looked melted. Its cheeks drooped in thick waves of flesh that pulled its eyes downward. A sunken nose had nostrils turned outward like a pig's. Ears were shriveled and rotting, about to drop off. Thin lips were peeled back from ragged teeth in a slobbering mouth. Unnaturally thick mats of hair covered its torso and limbs, and long yellowing nails curved like claws from its fingertips.

Had these humans been mutated by eating terra plants?

I glanced at the roasting hindquarter of krol and the nearby partially skinned dead krol.

A strong suspicion gripped me.

Their mutations had been caused by eating krol meat.

Grunting, a mutant kneeled beside the krol tied to the log. With savage force, it plunged a huge knife into the xan's chest. The krol shrieked. Ignoring its screams, the mutant sawed through its ribs, wrenched them apart, and ripped out its beating heart.

Whooping, it waved the bloody organ high in the air.

Gross. They were mimicking parts of the Aztec-Incan human sacrifices.

The mutant sank its teeth into the heart and ripped off a piece. Thin lips rimmed with red, it shoved the organ at the others, one by one. All eagerly bit off chunks, grunting with pleasure as they chewed.

After untying the dead krol from the log, they dragged its carcass toward the campfire.

Two more mutants emerged from the trees beyond the clearing. One carried a long wooden spear. The other triumphantly waved Kendra's sword, its metal blade glinting in a stray sunbeam. Between them, they half-dragged, half-carried the sixteen-year-old girl. Blood ran from a deep cut on her cheek, and her hands were tied together with vines.

They threw her on the dirt, kicking her when she tried to roll away. One creature slammed her sword into the ground, only missing her by a couple of inches.

The mutant at the campfire rose. Hunched shoulders knotted with muscles, arms like small tree trunks, the thing grabbed Kendra and shoved her onto the bloodstained log. She struggled to sit up, but it shoved her down again. Another mutant hurried forward with ropes.

Gunshots boomed from next to me.

The hunch-shouldered mutant roared, then collapsed on top of Kendra.

"Come on, guys," Asher cried, waving the revolver he'd just fired.

He charged into the clearing, shouting and firing again. We charged after him, hollering wildly, our loud calls fueled by anger and fear and an urgent need to save our teammate. As we got nearer, we swapped our guns for swords, since stray bullets were dangerous in close battles.

The mutants grabbed up spears and clubs and rushed to meet us.

Chaos.

Screams. Shouts. Slashing swords. Swinging clubs.

Remote-pushing away a mutant, I raced to the campfire. Kendra had already crawled from beneath the groaning beast that Asher had shot. Hands still bound, she wrenched her sword from the earth and plunged it into the hunch-shouldered mutant's back, yelling, "I am *not* your dinner, freak!" The creature convulsed, then lay still.

"Glad to see you're okay, Kendra," I cried, cutting the vines around her wrists.

"Never better." Sword in hand, she rushed into the battle.

Across the clearing, Harlem jumped aside, avoiding a spear. He stumbled over a large rock, fell, and lay stunned on the dirt. As a hulking mutant lumbered toward him, I recognized the one who'd ripped out the krol's heart. Snarling, it raised its club, preparing to smash Harlem's head.

I raced toward the fallen boy, focusing my mental energies on his attacker's weapon. The bone club veered away from Harlem's face, missing him by inches. The heart-ripper mutant was still gripping the club as it swerved upward and smashed into the mutant's own head with a satisfying *crack!* of bone.

Groaning, Heart Ripper stumbled away, blood streaming from its split scalp.

Harlem scrambled to his feet. "Thanks, Kass."

From beyond the clearing, a flood of new mutants charged into the battle. Their screeches and snarls reminded me of demons unleashed from hell, and my pulse raced.

Three to one. Not good.

At the corner of my eye, I glimpsed Commander Powell and others brandishing weapons as they also rushed into the fray. Their shouts sounded sweeter than the singing of angels.

Phew. Much better odds.

Amid the clash of steel and bone and wood, I saw Asher battling one of the newly arrived mutants. The male had semi-human features, thinning hair, and wore tattered shorts.

I stared at the newcomer. Was he a mutant or a man? Or somewhere in between?

As he raised a bone club, preparing to strike Asher, I decided I didn't care what he was. I remote-pushed Mutant Man away with enough force to fling him across the clearing—except Mutant Man only staggered back a few feet. Shaking his head, he growled and rushed at Asher again, bone club raised.

This time I tried to remote-push him into the campfire—

—but he crashed beside the flames, not on top of them.

Why couldn't I remote-push Mutant Man as easily as I'd remote-pushed the other creatures?

I suspected the answer was because he was still more human than animal.

Mutant Man grabbed up a flaming branch from the fire. He loped toward Asher, who had turned to fight off another attacker. As the creature swung his burning branch toward Asher's blond head, desperation shot through me, fierce and hot as a lightning bolt.

Could I remote-kill him?

Visualizing the base of Mutant Man's brain, I mentally shot out and used fingers of energy to pull at his spinal cord. And even though I was fifteen yards away, I *felt* his life force fading as he dropped the branch and sank to the ground.

Memories of Mutant Man's life flashed through me in a blaze of light—

—his pride at his college graduation; nervousness while watching his bride walk down the aisle; pure love as he cradled his baby son—

—and then his darker emotions surged through me in a scorching mass.

Terror. Pain. Loss. Grief.

Each intense feeling scraped a layer from my soul and, as Mutant Man collapsed onto the dirt, I lived his death. It was far worse than my mind-blend with the dying Sphere hybrid, Ethan Steel. This semi-human's death screamed its horror through my mind, melding with the yells and screeches of the battlefield.

My head throbbed as if it were splitting apart, about to shatter into a hundred pieces.

Noise and death all around me.

Grabbing my head with both hands, holding it together, I stumbled into the black jungle, welcoming its soothing shadows, its coolness, its—

Something slammed into my head.

Bright lights exploded in front of my eyes.

I fell.

65

Groaning, I lay on the ground, engulfed in a star-studded blackness. Seconds later it dissolved and, squinting, I peered up at my attacker.

A familiar figure stood over me, blood dripping from a bone club in her hand.

"What?" My muttered single word punched through my brain.

"Sorry, Kass. Nothing personal." Nila raised the dripping club above her head. "One more blow should do it. I need to leave your body alive but your mind weak." Behind her, Eva anxiously watched from Qara's feverish body.

"*Stop!*" Commander Powell staggered through the trees, his face blood-spattered and his shirt stained red. He pointed his gun at Nila, voice and weapon both wavering. "Drop your club. *Now.*"

Scowling, she lowered her club but didn't drop it. She gripped it tightly before her like a golfer ready to tee off, and I knew she'd slam the bone into my head at the first chance she got.

Head aching, I gazed beyond Eva, looking for Lynxx. He'd promised to keep an eye on Nila and her daughter. If they were here, he had to be nearby.

Or had he been caught up in the battle with the mutants? Was he lying injured somewhere? Or dead? The last possibility washed me in fresh despair, and my heart tightened in my chest.

I had to find him. Help him.

With an effort, I focused on Nila and mentally tried to shove her away, but my mind—traumatized and pummeled from Mutant Man's death—barely had the strength of a fly's kick. She didn't even flinch.

"You can't use Kass's body for your daughter," Powell shakily said. His chest bore a long slash that streamed blood, with another slash on his thigh.

"Lincoln, listen to me," she begged, voice thick with urgency. "It's just us here. No one will ever know what happened. We'll tell people that Kass was injured in the battle. We'll blame those mutated humans."

"Step away from her."

"I know you care about me, Lincoln. And I care for you, more than I should. If the Shimmer gas works, we'll have the chance of a life together. You, me, and Eva."

"At what cost? Kass's life?"

"What about my daughter's life? She and eleven of my people were massacred by your soldiers. You owe me this one body."

Groaning, I tried another remote-push. It was stronger this time, with maybe the strength of *two* flies kicking Nila.

She tossed me a glance, then returned her pleading eyes to the commander. "I've sacrificed so much. And I'm saving four hundred thousand people. Kass is just a single casualty. Walk away. Please."

The commander's gaze flickered from Nila to me. "It's murder."

Oh no. He's hesitating.

A faint moan sounded on my left.

Lynxx?

Slowly, I looked over, the movement shooting fresh pain through me.

Not Lynxx.

Bleeding from a scalp wound, an injured mutant lay near some bushes. It was Heart Ripper. A short while ago, I'd remote-slammed a bone club onto its head.

My mind could survive in its non-human body.

Any second now, Nila could club me again—and I'd be gone. Should I mind-blend with Heart Ripper now, before I died? It might be my only hope of survival. I didn't have enough mental energy to push away a strong, healthy hybrid like Nila, but maybe I could manage a single, desperate mind-hop.

I stared at the creature's ugly molten face, remembering how it had ripped the krol's still-beating heart from its chest. The gorge rose in my throat and I gagged. No way could I live in that mutant's body, even short-term.

Shuddering, I turned away from Heart Ripper.

For a moment, my thoughts drifted. *Please please please let Lynxx be okay.*

Eva uttered a drawn-out moan of pain. She wiped her damp brow, her skin flushed with fever.

Nila rushed across to her daughter. "What's wrong?"

"Mom, the Mongol girl is really sick." Silver eyes filled with pain, she sank to her knees, her hands still pressed to the sides of her head. "I think I'm dying again."

"Hold on tighter, Eva."

"I can't. I need another body." She pointed at me. "*Her* body."

Nila whipped toward the commander and lifted her club. "I have to do it."

Fear shot through me, scorching, and I sensed the approach of my old shadow, Death.

"No," he snapped.

"It's just one girl."

"*No.*"

Eva whimpered, tears sliding down her cheeks. "Hurry, Mom."

Gripping her club, Nila ignored Powell's shouts and moved toward me.

Shoot her, Commander, I mentally begged.

No gunshot.

Powell aimed his revolver in a trembling hand. "I can't let you kill her, Nila."

Shoot her, Commander.

Still no gunshot—

—as the woman raised her club.

Shoot her, Commander.

A single shot boomed out.

With a shocked cry, Nila stared at her chest. A red patch bloomed across her white top and blood bubbled from her lips. She crumpled to the ground.

Thank you, thank you, thank—

Sudden horror sliced through my relief. Had I actually remote-pushed the commander into shooting Nila?

Powell dropped to his knees and bent over the dying woman. Blood dripped from his slashed chest, blending with her own. "I'm so sorry, Nila. I had no choice."

Had I forced him? Guilt burned through me in a cold fire.

"Help us," she croaked, clutching his arm. "Get medic."

He shook his head. "By the time Soo-Yun gets here, you'll both be dead. And maybe that's for the best. I can't let either of you on my ship again. You're too dangerous."

I heaved a relieved sigh as my guilt dissolved. It had been the commander's decision to shoot Nila, not mine.

"Please, Lincoln ..."

He gestured to the groaning mutant, Heart Ripper, lying nearby. "That thing's scalp wound doesn't look fatal. But it's dazed, maybe concussed. One of you could live in it."

"Mom." Mongol-Eva's silver eyes stared at Heart Ripper. She gave a despairing wail. "I can't live in that monster, Mom."

"Me neither," Nila croaked, blood trickling from her mouth.

A monster for a monster, I thought bitterly.

Powell limped toward me, favoring his slashed leg. "I'm sorry, Nila. Maybe some birds or animals will wander by within the next minute or two. If not, you'll both die here, along with the sick Mongol girl, Qara."

The noise of the battle had faded away, and Asher's voice rang from the clearing. "Kass. Commander. Where are you?" He sounded fine. Unhurt.

Good.

But where was Lynxx?

Powell slung an arm around my waist, helping me to stand. "Let's go."

He turned his back on the begging Nila, the whimpering Eva, and the groaning mutant.

Together, injured and weak, the commander and I limped away.

Was Lynxx okay?

66

The following hours passed in a blur of pain.

I vaguely remember Lynxx stumbling from the jungle, blood streaming from his temple. "Nila caught me off guard."

Dazed, I glimpsed the others gathering our injured and helping them back to the ship.

More glimpsed snippets: Soo-Yun's hasty triage at Lightning One. Asher treating my split scalp with medicinal terras. Soo-Yun stitching the commander's slashed chest and thigh, then the cut on Kendra's cheek. Lynxx, forehead bandaged, withdrawing a plastic specimen bottle from his pocket and scrutinizing the intact yellow terra pod inside.

Willingly, I slipped into the merciful oblivion of sleep.

I awoke hours later, lying on a bench in Lightning One. My head still ached, but I could sit up without feeling woozy.

Soo-Yun inspected my scalp. "Much healed. Is good. No need bandage now."

"How long was I out for?" I asked.

Seated opposite me, Lynxx gently replied, "Almost a day. How are you feeling?"

"Better," I lied, trying to ignore my throbbing head.

"Release Point Six, guys," Asher called from the front as he reduced speed. "Preparing to land."

I was surprised to see him at the controls, with Commander Powell issuing instructions from the copilot's seat. It made sense, though. With Nila gone, Powell needed a backup pilot. And Asher was the only one among us with flying experience.

Powell's chest and thigh were now free of bandages. When I looked around the cabin, I saw that no one else was bandaged either—except for Yuki, whose arm remained broken from the fight on the Great Wall.

In the day since our battle with the mutants, Lynxx's medicinal terras had healed most of our injuries with amazing speed. I frowned at the prospect of these valuable terras being destroyed by the Shimmer gas. What did the military call it? Collateral damage?

As Lightning One dropped from a cloudless sky, I gazed through the transparent walls.

Kenya, Africa.

Terra bushes and Earth plants stretched for miles to the horizon. My binoculars picked up herds of giraffe, elephants, buffalo, gazelles, and other wild animals. They roamed the flat African landscape, coexisting with the mixed vegetation.

And then an astonishing scene came into view as our ship descended.

Below us, an enormous lake contained a large island covered in neat rows of plants and small shrubs. From the rim of the island, a series of wooden walkways extended in all directions, like spokes from a wheel. These walkways led to smaller islands—

—and to almost a hundred floating huts.

The huts resembled giant beehives with their rounded thatched roofs and curved walls made from branches and dried grasses. These huts floated on platforms interconnected with dozens of narrow walkways. Rowboats and speedboats bobbed at the edge of the floating village, tied to poles.

On the lake's western shore, at least fifty huge cargo trucks stood in neat lines. All were partially covered in green terra vines, suggesting they'd been parked there for months.

People were everywhere. Dozens worked on the islands that had been turned into farms. Others repaired huts, cooked on large stone fireplaces, or played with children. Many waved as Lightning One landed on a long, bare pontoon edged with three-foot-high walls of dried branches.

"It looks like they're expecting us, sir," Asher said to Powell.

"They are, son. Nila and I ..." The commander's voice wavered as if still grieving the woman he had cared about—and still mourning her terrible fate in Peru. He drew in a deep breath. "I've been in contact with their leader, Wanjala, ever since they sent out a radio signal some months ago."

As we exited Lightning One, excited people surrounded the Chi'az ship, awestruck and babbling questions as they touched the hull. The noisy jumble of English and foreign languages made my head throb even more, but I tried to ignore the pain.

Lynxx appeared at my elbow. "You don't look well. Perhaps you should rest inside the ship."

I forced a smile. "And miss out on seeing this incredible place? No, thanks."

The crowd was almost fifty percent black. The other half was made up of Caucasians, Asians, and Arabs. *Tourists*, I guessed. *Probably stuck in Kenya when the Mist arrived.*

All wore brightly colored clothes. Some had bare feet, others favored flip-flops or grass sandals. A smattering of wide-brimmed hats offset the hot sun for many people. Everyone looked happy and relaxed, free of the worried expressions that had usually shrouded us back at Weston Tower.

The crowd parted for a black man in his forties, his wild Afro hairstyle held off his beaming face by a beaded headband. His bloodshot eyes were bordered by purple-rimmed glasses, his green board shorts were loose and old, and his tie-dyed T-shirt rioted with colors. I almost expected him to raise two fingers in the peace sign that hippies had used decades ago.

"Much welcome to New Eden," he said, vigorously shaking Powell's outstretched hand. "I am Wanjala, leader of community. We meet finally, Commander."

"Thank you for building the pontoon," Powell said. "Our ship fits it perfectly."

"Pleasure is ours." Wanjala's grin revealed yellowing teeth. "Visitors very much few these days."

Powell's gaze shifted to the bushy shores of the lake, where lions and hyenas drank at the water's edge. "This pontoon looks safer than setting down on the land over there."

"Is true. Not safe in lake, also." Wanjala gestured to several pairs of pebble-rimmed eyes that floated near the pontoon.

Gasping, I stepped back. *Dragon xans?*

"Many crocodiles," Wanjala advised us. "We safe here. Huts and thorny walkways above water and crocodiles."

The pontoon and all the huts had hip-high walls of dried branches along their edges. Lynxx and I peered at a nearby branch. Dozens of ten-inch thorns protruded in all directions, with tips that looked strong enough to pierce steel.

"Are these terras, Wanjala?" asked Lynxx.

"Thorn terras. Grow many places on land. Much good to keep crocodiles away from walkways, huts, islands. They very hate thorn terras."

Powell's gaze swept the sprawling settlement. "This place is astonishing."

"Very much more than you realize, Commander," said Wanjala cryptically. "You here for some hours, I think, while waiting for ship to cool. You like tour? We much eager for visitors. Your people break into small groups; my people show around. Plus excellent food later in new hall." He pointed to a domed building larger than the rest of the huts.

"Thank you. We'd enjoy that." Powell's voice grew wistful. "A friend of mine, Nila, would've loved this place." He shook his head as if throwing off painful memories. After assigning four soldiers to stay with Lightning One, he said, "Asher, Kass, and Lynxx, you're with me. The rest of you break into small groups for your tours."

To my surprise, Willow stepped forward. "Commander, I'd like to be in your group too." She looked down as she spoke, clearly embarrassed by her scarred cheeks.

"Of course," Powell said gently. "Good to see you out and about."

She gave a tiny shrug and kept her head down.

We followed Wanjala, Powell, and the others along a series of walkways that dipped and swayed above the water. Smooth planks provided the bases, and the reed sidewalls had thorn terras tied to their exteriors.

Every hut we passed had bright murals on its outside walls. "Scenes from home countries of some here," Wanjala explained. Mixed with African images were the windmills of Holland, the Eiffel Tower, a Japanese temple, even an Egyptian pyramid.

Singing drifted from various beehive-shaped huts, the notes off-key but happy. Scores of large earthen pots with bright flowers added another layer of beauty to the vibrant, color-drenched community.

Lynxx bent his head to a huge orange blossom.

"Careful," Asher cried. "That might be a spitter." He shuddered as if remembering his encounter with a spitter on an abandoned cruise ship some months ago.

"It's okay," Lynxx said. "This is a perfume-globe terra." He turned to Wanjala. "All the potted flowers we've passed have been terras."

"Harmless but good terras," the New Eden leader said enthusiastically.

"How are perfume-globes good?" Asher asked.

"Is it not obvious? They beautiful and have wonderful smells."

"So do roses," Asher pointed out.

"Roses much difficult to grow. We live in new world, yes? We enjoy good terras, kill bad ones."

Chatting constantly, he led us to a smaller island where laden fruit trees grew between rows of vegetables. "We grow sweet potatoes, cabbages, beans, eggplants, peppers. Also bananas, peanuts, cassava, and very much more."

"So, no terra plants," Commander Powell noted.

"We not eat terra plants." Wanjala beamed at the farm. "Only eat Earth plants."

"Are your people vegetarians?" I asked.

"No. We ... how you say it? ... farm fish in pens. Not writing pens. Pens made from wire nets." He pointed to three fish farms on the huge lake. "Also eat fresh meat. Big teams with very much weapons go on land. Hunt gazelles, antelopes, warthogs, others."

"Big teams with very much weapons?" Powell frowned. "Just to hunt wild animals?"

"No. Is protection from xanimals you call krols."

"Krols?" Powell said sharply. "You have krols in this area?"

Wanjala nodded. "Is why community in middle of lake. Krols hate water; cannot swim. Safer we are on water than land."

"So far. But the krols are evolving. Fast."

"Explain, please."

"Six months ago," Powell told him, "the krols back home were savage animals. Now they fight with spears and shields and use fire. They live in packs and behave cooperatively. They're getting smarter every month."

"Krols around New Eden very much mean but still dumb."

"Are you sure, Wanjala? If they're evolving like the krols in other places, your community could be in serious trouble one day." At a sudden thought, Powell stiffened. "Do your people eat krol meat?"

I winced, thinking of the krol-eating mutants in Peru. Had either Nila or Eva mind-blended with the injured mutant lying near them? Or had they chosen to die together in that dark, savage place?

"Eat krols?" Wanjala's bloodshot eyes widened as if Powell was insane. "Never."

"Good."

We crossed the next walkway to the main island. Nervously, I stared at a huge cathedral-dome terra in its center. During my one and only encounter with these trees, some cones had almost killed Lynxx.

Wanjala followed the direction of my gaze. "Beautiful, is it not?"

"Yes," I replied, keeping my voice low. If I spoke too loudly, my headache pulsed in protest. "But its cones are dangerous once they turn red."

Wryly Lynxx added, "Kassia and I found that out the hard way."

"Agree." Wanjala giggled like a kid. "Cones dangerous. Is why we remove soon as they start buds."

Curious, Powell asked, "Why do you have a cathedral-dome terra in the middle of your garden?"

"We make terra tree harmless. In return, it gives beauty and joy each day."

I stared at the rows of plants. "These aren't Earth vegetables like on the smaller islands. You're growing terra plants. But you told us that you don't eat terras."

"We do not," he declared firmly.

Lynxx bent and examined the leaves of a nearby yellow plant. "These are dope terras, Wanjala. They're like our mari-juana."

"Dopes very much good. Relaxing. No stress."

"But dope terras could affect humans," Powell gruffly told him.

Wanjala shrugged. He withdrew a homemade reefer, lit it, and inhaled deeply.

A faint strawberry scent wafted around us.

"I smoke weed for very many years," he said. "Dope terras smell very better."

Frowning, Powell fell silent.

Lynxx surveyed the rest of the gardens. "Incredible. You're not just growing dope terras. You've got Lazarus plants, crimson-sun terras, eye-wings, and zero terras. They're all extremely useful for a range of diseases and injuries."

"True," Wanjala said. "One by one, very valuable. Together ... priceless."

"What do you mean?"

The African leader paused before announcing, "They make cancer cure."

67

We stared at him, stunned.

Puffing on his reefer, Wanjala proudly surveyed the thriving medicinal terra plants. "You think New Eden is primitive community, yes? Not true. Behold much important building." He pointed to a midsize wooden structure made from planks, with glass windows and solid doors. "Is more than hospital. Is also medical research facility."

"You have doctors here?" Powell asked, studying the distant building.

"Yes. Two ... how do you say it? ... geniuses. Before Mist, each work on breast cancer. Then terra plants arrived. Many are bad plants. But some good. Some very much good."

"Are you saying these plants can cure breast cancer?" I asked.

"Not breast cancer only. *All* cancers."

We gaped at him, speechless.

"Our community large," Wanjala continued. "Three hundred and more people. Fifty-three with cancer. Brain tumors, lung cancers, leukemia, melanomas, more. Twenty-two types. This year, all people with cancers completely cured—easily, quickly."

"How easily?" Lynxx asked.

"How quickly?" I gasped, thinking of the gallons of disgusting Lazarus tonic I'd drunk for months and months.

"Fourteen pills. Two weeks."

Incredible! "It's the Holy Grail of medicine," I breathed.

"And the results are conclusive?" Powell asked, astonished.

"Very many documents. I myself am living proof."

"You had cancer?"

"My throat, Commander, it had tumor big as flamingo egg." He gestured to his smooth, normal throat. "Now nothing."

Powell struggled with Wanjala's incredible claim. "But surely your doctors would've needed high-tech medical equipment."

"Done." Wanjala pointed to the line of cargo trucks on the western shore. "Teams bring very much stuff from empty cities. Clothes, medical equipment, tools, plus more we need for New Eden."

"What about electricity?" Powell asked.

"Also done." The African pointed to three huge tanks on a pontoon. "Oil good, yes?"

"Well, yes. But how do you protect your community?"

Wanjala grinned like a proud child. "Much special security force. Help protect from bad people, bad xans."

Powell shook his head in awe.

Willow looked at Wanjala. Above her scarred cheeks, her beautiful violet eyes glimmered with hope. "Can you help me?"

"Familiar you are, miss." The man's eyebrows rose. "We have met, yes?"

"No. I'm Willow Grace. I'm an actress. I mean, I used to be an actress."

A sharp intake of breath. "Ah. *Pandora*. Much good show."

"Thank you. Can you fix my face?"

He studied the ugly red marks on her cheeks. "These are from what?"

"A xan in Rome. It spat at me. Its saliva ... spit ... whatever, burned my skin."

"Water xan?"

"Yes."

"Long, scaly, no legs? Face like dragon in *Game of Thrones*?"

"Yes," she cried.

Lynxx added, "We called it a dragon xan."

"We know as water xan. One in lake when first we arrived. It eat three people. Four others received spit before we killed it."

"Can you help me?" Willow whispered, desperate.

Wanjala lit another reefer. "We tried for very much months. Nothing heal four people scarred by water xan. I am sorry, Willow Grace."

Her distressed sigh trembled in the air. Blinking back tears, she turned away, hiding her face again.

Wanjala inhaled deeply, held his breath, then exhaled a cloud of strawberry-scented smoke. Behind his purple-rimmed glasses, his bloodshot eyes grew hazy for a few seconds before refocusing. "Commander, you and I speak six times on radio. Each time, you not mention why you want visit us."

"I couldn't. Our conversations weren't secured."

"Understood. Not get me wrong. Guests are good. But you fly alien ship. Stolen from Chi'az, I think. Very dangerous. Your mission very much important, yes?"

"The fate of humanity depends on our success." Commander Powell paused as a laughing, chatting group approached. Harlem, Soo-Yun, Booker, and Kendra had five New Eden guides, each one noisily vying for the newcomers' attention.

"Come." Wanjala gestured to the commander. "You and I go my office. Quiet place for talk."

Quickly, Lynxx asked, "Wanjala, I'd like to have a look at your hospital and research facility."

"Very welcome."

Soo-Yun overheard them and veered away from Harlem and the noisy group. "Hospital? I look also." She gave a wave to Harlem as she accompanied Lynxx to the wooden building.

Willow called out, "I'm coming too. They might have some new ointment." She hurried to catch up with the pair, determined to fix her face. I didn't know whether to applaud her stubbornness or worry about her refusal to accept her condition.

As Commander Powell and Wanjala headed to the community hall, I noticed that the Kenyan wasn't walking as steadily as when he'd first met us. Were his dope terra reefers affecting him physically and mentally?

The others and I chatted with the inquisitive New Eden guides, answering their questions, asking our own. Gradually my headache intensified, made worse by the harsh African sun and our noisy hosts.

After twenty minutes, I murmured to Asher, "I'm going for a walk."

"I'll come with you."

"Not necessary. I'll be back soon."

I desperately needed to be alone.

68

CRAVING SHADOWS AND PEACE, I wandered across to the glittering cathedral-dome.

Triple the size of the one back in Manhattan, it was shaped like a massive open umbrella, with its bottom edge supported by five-foot-tall roots.

For a long moment, I hesitated. *Cones dangerous*, Wanjala had said. *Is why we remove soon as they start buds.*

Taking a deep breath, I slipped between the thin roots and entered the hollow domed interior.

A wave of wonder swept me.

Outside, sunlight drenched the terra's dome, transforming the leaves into translucent shapes. The cathedral-dome in Manhattan had leaves that glowed green, blue, red, and purple, like stained glass windows.

This Kenyan terra tree had gold, yellow, and red leaves—and as a breeze caressed them, they flickered like living flames.

Dozens of iridescent gold butterflies rose from the soft yellow grass below the dome. Large wings catching the light, they swirled around me like fractured sunbeams.

On a whim, I remote-pulled twenty or so butterflies toward me. Gently, I settled them around my head in a wreath of flickering wings—and, strangely, I felt my throbbing headache start to ease.

As the living gold wreath fluttered soothingly against my skin and hair, I realized that my headache hadn't been caused by Nila's blow to my head back in Peru. Lynxx's medicinal terras had healed my split scalp within hours, and my hybrid-given powers had repaired me internally.

My headache had been a cumulation of stress.

In the past few days, I'd remote-pushed crabben xans in flooded Rome, and the Mongols and krol pups on the Great Wall. I'd mind-blended with a cockatoo to investigate a moving oasis xan in Central Australia. I'd almost been killed by Nila in Peru. Most traumatic of all, I'd remote-killed a mutated human, also in Peru.

Today, inside this glorious cathedral-dome terra, I wasn't using my hybrid powers in life-and-death battles that sometimes threatened to split my mind apart.

As I gently controlled these butterflies, my traumatized mind finally relaxed. It released its stress—and peace flowed through my soul.

"Kass!" Asher's hushed voice interrupted my thoughts. Staring in awe, he moved into the hollowed, domed interior. "You look like you're on fire."

I glanced down at my top and jeans. The overhanging translucent leaves had dappled me in flickering gold and red and yellow lights that shifted in the breeze. My clothes and skin glowed with dancing flames as if I were made of fire, and as I released my hold on the wreath of butterflies on my hair, they scattered around me in gold sparks.

His eyes caressed me. "I'll remember this forever. You looked extraordinary. A girl of fire, wearing a crown of gold butterflies."

"Thanks." I smiled. "You've changed."

"Me?"

"You used to be strongly opposed to all terra plants and hybrids. Yet here you are, happily standing beneath a terra tree—"

"An amazing and beautiful terra tree."

"—watching a girl use her hybrid powers."

"An amazing and beautiful girl." Gently, he took my hands. "One I've tried to catch alone for days."

My heart started beating faster. "Oh?"

A gold-red leaf drifted from the dome above us. As it swayed past, I reached out and touched it. It disintegrated into fiery specks, and a glorious fragrance filled the air.

He hesitated. "I loved Willow for years. When I thought she was dead, something within me died as well. Yet I went through all the motions of living. I helped build a community at Weston Tower. I threw myself into the fight against the terras. I made friends and surrounded myself with a new family. But it wasn't until I met you, Kass, that I was truly happy again."

Where was this going? "Asher, this is not the place."

"I disagree. Here, in this cathedral of beauty, with you covered in firelight, it's the perfect place and time."

"Willow's not dead. She still loves you. She needs you."

"And I still care about her. I guess I always will. But she's known for weeks that we're not a couple anymore. The world has changed. She's changed. And so have I."

"But—"

He drew me closer, his voice dropping to a husky whisper. "I'm in love with you, Kass." Tenderly he stroked my cheek. "And I will never stop loving you."

Stunned, I stood in the circle of his arms, struggling to find a response.

During Lightning One's flights between the continents, my primary focus had been on the success of our mission. I'd tried to push aside my confused feelings for Asher and Lynxx. Focus on the now. Delay thoughts of a future, aware that all my hopes and dreams would vanish if the Outriders' Threads were released first.

Nothing had changed.

"We're in the middle of a mission," I told him. "I can barely get through each day in one piece. I don't have time to think about love—"

He smothered my protests with a kiss—long, slow, and passionate. Stiffening, I began to pull away from him.

A strangled gasp came from behind us.

Jerking apart, we turned.

A few yards away, Willow held a trembling hand to her lips. Lovely eyes raw with pain, she stared at us, too shocked to speak. Her heartbroken expression suggested an agony of betrayal, as though we'd plunged a knife into her heart.

Next to her, Lynxx's face was frozen in blank lines—and yet, I sensed a riot of emotions behind his flat expression. Voice carefully neutral, he said, "Willow was looking for you, Asher."

Awkwardly, Asher cleared his throat. "We—"

Four men in gray uniforms pushed their way into the domed space, each carrying a rifle. They spread out and surrounded us, weapons raised.

"What's going on?" Asher asked, stepping forward and shielding me.

I stepped out from behind him, hands open to show the soldiers that I was physically unarmed. However, my headache had vanished, so I was once again mentally armed. "Who are you people?"

Gray clothes. Were they Brethren?

One soldier moved forward. Skin jet-black, with hair cropped close to his scalp, the man's posture and handling of his weapon suggested a military background. "I'm Corporal Egebe, part of the New Eden Security Forces."

Good. Not Brethren.

Lynxx calmly regarded the soldier. "Is there a problem, Corporal?"

The man growled, "You're all under arrest."

69

At gunpoint, the soldiers marched us onto a flat pontoon edged with five-foot walls of lethal thorn terras. *An effective jail*, I thought grimly.

The rest of Liberty Team had already been herded into the open-air "prison"—including the soldiers who'd been guarding the ship.

Willow ran across to Soo-Yun, tears streaming down her red-splotched cheeks. My heart ached for her devastation, and I wished I could ease her pain. Beside me, a worried Asher watched his former girlfriend turn to his friends for comfort.

Harlem patted Willow's shoulder, while Soo-Yun tried to soothe her, saying, "We be okay. Is misunderstanding with Wanjala."

I knew Willow's tears were for Asher, not our detention. And she hadn't misunderstood him kissing me.

As Lynxx, Asher, and I joined Commander Powell, the black man quietly told us, "I ordered our soldiers to surrender. I can't risk a gun battle. If Lightning One is damaged again, we won't be able to complete our mission."

Lynxx said, "It looks like we're not going anywhere, anyway." Calmly, he turned to me. "Mission-wise or relationship-wise."

My heart twisted in pain, but I remained silent. This wasn't the time or place to discuss relationships.

"What's going on, sir?" Asher asked Powell. "Didn't you explain to Wanjala how important our mission is?"

"I did, son. He won't listen. I think his years of smoking marijuana—and now dope terras—have addled his brain. I've seen it before. Drug addicts who lose the ability to think rationally. They cling to what they want to believe, even if it's illogical and false."

"What can we say to change his mind, sir?" I asked, trying to focus on the immediate crisis, not my personal life.

"Nothing, Kass. I've tried again and again. He won't budge."

"What's his problem?" Asher asked. "Why's he holding us?"

Wanjala approached, flanked by two soldiers wielding rifles. His smiles had been replaced by scowls. "You stay here, Commander. Change Shimmer gas. Make it not kill Lazarus terras, crimson-suns, eye-wings, or zeros. Then you go."

Powell shook his head. "Nila, the scientist who developed the Shimmer, is no longer with us. Besides, we don't have time to change the formula. We have to release the Shimmer before the Outriders release their Threads."

"I not help destroy only cancer cure."

"You mean our only *current* cancer cure. Once we rid our planet of the terras and xans and Chi'az, humanity can start rebuilding our world, Wanjala. Down the road, our scientists might find another cure for cancer."

"'Might find'? Here certain cure."

Frustrated, Powell asked, "Don't you get it? When all the non-terrestrials are dead, you and your people won't have to live in reed huts on a lake. You won't have to worry about the krols anymore."

"We safe here. And healthy. Is good life."

In despair, I listened to the pair argue. We'd been so close to completing our mission. We'd just had to place the last Shimmer drum in Kenya. Then, at Zero Hour in two days' time, the "fermentation" would be finished. All the drums would release their gas—and we would be safe. Alive.

Now, a stoned man was jeopardizing everything.

"If the Outriders release their Threads first," Commander Powell explained, "every human on Earth will die, Wanjala. I've told you this many times."

"My people survived Red Mist," came the stubborn reply. "We will survive Threads also."

"No one will survive the Threads."

Wanjala puffed on a reefer. "Maybe you make up Threads. Scare us. Maybe Threads not exist." He turned to talk with his soldiers.

Powell, Asher, Lynxx, and I moved away from Wanjala, out of his earshot.

"Perhaps we don't need to worry about the seventh drum," the commander quietly said. "We've already got five drums in position, plus the one in New York. They're all timed to go off in two days."

"So you think the six drums can do the job, sir?" Asher asked.

"They should. The Shimmer is self-replicating. As long as it's released before the Threads, we can still win and—"

At a distant roar, people looked up.

In the sky, a cigar-shaped ship suddenly appeared. It circled a spot several miles away and descended. A minute later it rose into the air, hovered, then flashed to the horizon and vanished.

We stared at the empty sky, stunned.

"The Outriders have a Lightning ship!" Powell gasped.

Wanjala stalked across, pointing to the horizon. "Ship was yours?"

"No," Powell replied. "It belongs to the Outriders."

"What mean that?"

Powell swallowed. "The end of the world."

70

"WHAT YOU MEAN?" WANJALA demanded.

"The Outriders have a Lightning ship," Powell replied. "And it looks faster than our ship. I think they're depositing containers of their Threads around the world, with their timers probably set to go off before ours."

"More lies." But Wanjala's words weren't as hostile as earlier. Clearly, the unexpected sight of a second Chi'az ship had shaken him. "You and I go, Powell. See if Outriders real. See if Threads real. Then talk."

"Go where?"

"Think ship land near Janella. Is fifteen kilometers away."

"That's about nine miles," the commander said. "How are we going to get there? Drive one of your big-ass trucks?"

Wanjala rolled his bloodshot eyes. "We not ... how you say it? ... truckers. Very much noisy. Attract krols. We take silent Hogs so not be 'meals on wheels.'" He giggled at his joke. "Hogs charged just yesterday."

"They're electric?"

"Yes. Generators. I bring Corporal Egebe and Private Mullin with us. Much good soldiers."

"Fine. But I want to bring two people as well," Powell insisted. "They'll help protect us from terras and xans."

"No point. They no allowed weapons."

"Okay, they'll be unarmed. But they're still experts at identifying dangerous terras and xans before it's too late. The more eyes the better, right?"

Wanjala hesitated, then shrugged.

Asher immediately stepped forward. "I'll come, sir."

"Sorry, son. If something happens to me, you'll be the only person left who can fly Lightning One. You need to remain here." With deliberate casualness, Powell's gaze swept our group. "O-kaaay. I'll take Lynxx and Kass."

Wanjala grinned at the choice of a teenage girl and boy instead of two burly soldiers. "Is good decision."

I hid a smile. Powell had chosen the two people in our group who didn't need physical strength—or physical weapons.

Ten minutes later, the six of us stepped from a speedboat onto a small ramp at the lakeshore. Nervously, I looked around. Where were the lions and hyenas we'd seen drinking at the water's edge earlier? No sign of them.

Was that good or bad?

Suspiciously, I peered at a patch of tall grass.

As five electric motorcycles were wheeled from a nearby wooden shed, Commander Powell glanced back at the floating pontoon where the others waited. "You guarantee, Wanjala, that my people will be unharmed while we're gone?"

"No problem, Commander. My soldiers no harm anyone unless ordered." Wanjala tapped a radio clipped to his belt. "You no do anything make me angry."

"Hey, you're the boss." Powell spread his hands in a placating gesture.

And we're still your unarmed prisoners, Wanjala, I thought bitterly.

I studied the two armed Kenyan soldiers with us. Each straddled a Hog, wore sunglasses, and had a rifle slung across his back, ready for use at a moment's notice. Corporal Egebe continued to behave with military efficiency, but Private Mullin was more awkward and unsure, and I suspected he was there to boost numbers.

Wanjala and Powell took a motorcycle each.

I shared the last Harley-Davidson with Lynxx. He stiffened as I sat behind him, my arms awkwardly wrapped around his waist. "Sorry," I muttered. "There's nothing else to hold on to back here." I flushed, remembering Asher's arms around me in the gold cathedral-dome.

Lynxx shrugged, and I felt his muscles ripple beneath his white T-shirt. The heat of his body radiated through my own, and his skin smelled like a forest after rain—strong and elemental. I resisted an impulse to stroke his black hair, which gleamed in the sunshine.

"Keep watch, everyone," Powell ordered.

We set off, riding single file through a patch of jungle. Corporal Egebe led the way, with Private Mullin bringing up the rear.

To my surprise, the Hogs were as silent as shadows. *Good.* Although Wanjala was a dope-smoking stoner, even he knew better than to ride noisy bikes through the wilds of Kenya.

I scanned the trees for danger but saw only monkeys, birds, crabben xans, and the occasional click xan.

After a few miles, the jungle opened onto a flat savanna. Clumps of scrubby native bushes and terra trees dotted the earth. A scattering of huge onion terras and colossus-trees added an otherworldly element to the landscape.

The hot sun heated my skin and the air, and the drone of insects lent a lazy summer feel to the day.

My thoughts drifted to Asher ... the gold cathedral-dome terra ... his kiss ...

I'm in love with you, Kass.

"Kassia?"

"Huh?" I jerked back to the present. "What did you say?"

Lynxx pointed to three tall palmlike trees on our left. Quietly, he said, "Palm terras." Since the Hogs' engines were silent, we could speak at a normal volume, but everyone kept their voices low anyway. Danger lurked in many forms in this wilderness; no sense in announcing ourselves to it.

Palm terras. I shivered. *Horrible, nasty things.*

Last year in Central Park, we'd come across a battle between palm terras and Alien-egg terras. The palms' blood-red innard-balls had smashed onto the ground near us, and we'd flinched as the Alien-eggs had flung their sharp petals in retaliation.

Ahh, what wonderful memories, I thought sourly. *My grandkids will revel in these stories one day, assuming I live long enough to have grandkids.*

On the horizon, anvil clouds warned of an approaching storm, still some hours away.

Unbidden, Asher's voice echoed through my mind again. *I will never stop loving you.*

Guilt tinged my thoughts. Would Asher still love me if he knew I'd remote-killed a mutant human back in Peru?

"Lynxx." I leaned close to his ear so the others wouldn't hear. "You still haven't remote-killed, have you?"

His body tensed and I felt his surprise. "No. Have you?"

"Twice. The first time, I remote-killed an attacking eel xan. It was an accident. I'd only meant to remote-push it away."

"And the other time?"

"Deliberate. Back in Peru. I had to stop one of those mutant humans from killing again."

"Killing who?"

"Asher."

"Of course."

"He's not the point," I stressed. "I *remote-killed* someone, Lynxx."

"Not a person. A mutant. To save someone you—"

"Not the point," I interrupted, reluctant to let him finish that sentence. "I have to tell them."

"Who?"

"The commander. And Asher. I promised no more secrets."

"So tell them."

"But what if he ... they ... look at me differently?"

"It won't change the way Asher feels about you. He loves you."

Once again, Asher's words echoed through my mind. *I will never stop loving you.*

"Do you love him, Kassia?" asked Lynxx quietly.

His question hung in the languid, heated air. Waiting.

"Back under that cathedral-dome," I insisted, "I didn't kiss him. *He* kissed me."

"That wasn't my question."

Up ahead, Corporal Egebe raised a hand.

We braked to a halt.

Not moving a muscle, we watched a pride of lions emerge from the yellow grass and pad across a trail in front of us. One male lion, three lionesses, four cubs. The male was twice the size of Asher's fur-brother, Zimba, back in New York. Dried blood speckled its thick mane, and its amber eyes glinted coldly as it stopped and stared at us, assessing the five "meals on wheels."

Slowly, Corporal Egebe reached for the rifle slung across his back.

I tensed, preparing to—

Lynxx whispered, "Move along, furball." My arms were still wrapped around him, and I felt his chest muscles tighten as he remote-pushed.

The huge lion jerked and angrily shook its mane. Snarling, it hurried to catch up with the others.

Corporal Egebe relaxed and dropped his hand from the rifle.

Do you love him, Kassia?

"You beat me to the lion," I murmured in Lynxx's ear.

Brushing hair out of his eyes, he pointed to a pack of dirty yellow hyenas slinking through the grass. "Remember those hyenas in Feral Tower?"

"Yes. Gross!"

"Remember what I told you about them?"

"That hyenas are savage and efficient hunters, not just scavengers?"

"Exactly." His voice hardened. "We need to focus on our surroundings right now. Everything else can wait."

Do you love him, Kassia?

Lynxx's question evaporated beneath the need to survive this hot and hostile environment.

Thunder rumbled as the distant storm gathered its forces. A gust of cool air swept across us, laden with the scent of ozone and the promise of rain.

Wanjala studied the cloud-studded horizon. "Is storm in four, five hours."

Enough time to sort out this situation—I hoped.

Continuing toward Janella, we crossed a plain where pungent earthy smells rose from mounds of dung.

"Elephant droppings," Lynxx murmured to me. "Fresh."

"Charming."

Herds of antelopes loped away at our approach. Giraffes paused in grazing treetops and stared at us with suspicious eyes. Bull and cow elephants shuffled their calves behind them as they warily watched us ride by. I understood their caution. The world hadn't just changed for humans. It had changed for the Earth animals too.

Corporal Egebe raised his hand again, halting our convoy. He pointed to wisps of smoke coming from a grove of trees alongside a river.

"Is that Janella?" Powell asked Wanjala.

"No. Is north bit more. But smoke not supposed to be here. We see."

Quietly we rode to the edge of the forest. Leaving the Hogs under Private Mullin's guard, we crept through the trees.

A familiar sound made my flesh crawl. Hurriedly, we ducked behind some thick bushes and peered through their branches.

My heart sank.

No way.

71

A GROUP OF KROLS had set up camp on the bank of the narrow river.

They were as ugly as every other krol we'd seen, with the same overlarge heads, huge ebony eyes, bat-like ears, and shark-toothed jaws. However, their pus-yellow skin with orange blotches meant they'd blend in perfectly with the yellow African wheatgrass, allowing them to become invisible hunters. No wonder the elephants and giraffes had watched us so warily.

A full-grown krol and two krol pups tended a fire ringed by stones. Six more pups yipped and snarled as they mock-battled each other with wooden swords and bark shields. More primitive weapons were piled at the edge of the camp, enough to arm a hundred krols.

In the stockpile, I also saw clubs studded with enormous terra thorns, capable of piercing a skull with one blow; large innard-balls, ready for throwing; and vine-net bags filled with lethal razor-edged petals from Alien-egg terras.

Nearby, three adult krols worked on a fallen log with V-shaped ends. Grunting, they used metal axes, hammers, and iron chisels to hollow out the center of the log.

I didn't know what was more worrying—the fact that the krols were using man's metal tools, or the fact that they'd stockpiled so many homemade weapons, suggesting their pack was much larger than the dozen xanimals here—

—or the fact that they were hollowing out a log to use as a boat.

Beside me, Wanjala gawked at the busy krols and stifled a gasp. He shifted his gaze to the river. Tied to trees, five completed log boats bobbed in the shallows, each large enough to carry a dozen krols.

Commander Powell waved us back.

We retreated, moving cautiously and avoiding sticks on the ground as we returned to our bikes. Then, thankful for silent motors, we sped away from the krol camp.

A few miles later, far enough across the savanna to be safe, we halted.

Wanjala gripped the handles of his Hog, his face drawn in downsloping lines of shock. Wordlessly, he stared at the outspread plain where terra trees grew alongside Earth trees and bushes. He scrutinized the high wheatgrass as though expecting a pack of krols to rise from it, their clawed hands clutching metal tools.

He pulled out a reefer. Stopped. Stared at the scraggy cigarette. With a muttered curse, he threw it on the dirt and crushed it beneath his beaded moccasin. "You right, Commander." Anger and shock darkened his words. "Krols evolving. Planning attack."

"We can't be sure—"

"Can. River with wooden boats, it flows into New Eden Lake."

"Oh. Right." Powell folded his arms as if resisting an urge to say, *I warned you.*

Somberly, we rode on.

A little while later, we parked our Hogs at the edge of a deserted luxury resort.

Before the Mist, Janella had catered to high-end travelers, providing comfortable beds, gourmet meals, and cool swimming pools, all in safari country. Now, terra vines netted the lodge, a young colossus-tree grew through the roof of its reception area, and its doors hung askew. The lodge's forlorn air held a trio of trembling questions: *What happened? Where did you go? Why did you abandon me?*

After a stealthy reconnaissance, we arrived at the back of the resort. Two bare-chested men in gray cargo pants were stretched out on sun loungers beside an empty pool.

Idiots! Don't these Brethren recruits realize they're in Africa? Helllooo. Lions. Snakes. Terras. Krols.

A two-foot-long metal canister rested on the pavers between the pair.

I guessed the canister contained the Threads. Death encased in metal.

Powell motioned us back around behind the main building. He whispered, "Okay, Wanjala, now do you believe—?"

Screaming with rage, Wanjala flung himself around the corner, firing his gun. "Bastards. Ruin New Eden! I kill." His two soldiers raced after him, scrabbling to keep up with their leader.

In seconds, it was over.

One Brethren recruit lay dead, his blood glistening on the pavers. The second recruit crouched behind a huge ceramic pot with a leafless tree. Futilely eying his revolver on a side table, he shouted, "*Nyet! Nyet!*"

Corporal Egebe held a shouting Wanjala back as Private Mullin gestured with his gun to the Brethren recruit. "Get out here."

Hands raised, the man staggered forward, bleeding from a bullet wound in his shoulder.

Powell tied the man's wrists with a plastic cable. In his fifties, the recruit had a pudgy figure like an inflated balloon. His bare chest was a smooth mound of flesh and his arms were sausages. His white skin suggested too much time spent indoors, explaining his desire to sunbathe.

Private Mullin gathered the Brethren's radios and guns.

As Wanjala's shouts fizzled away, Powell shoved the recruit onto a lounge chair and stood over him. "When are the Threads being released?"

A stream of Russian answered him.

Powell raised his voice—and his fist—as he spoke slower. "When are the Threads being released?"

More Russian.

"Maybe he doesn't speak English, Commander," I suggested.

"Possibly not," Powell acknowledged. "One way to be sure." Leaning down, he dug his thumb into the bullet wound in the man's shoulder. Ignoring the shrieks of pain, he yelled, "*When are the Threads being released?*"

The answering babble was Russian mixed with sobs.

Powell wiped his bloodied hand on a handkerchief. "Anyone here speak Russian?" When we shook our heads, he focused on Lynxx and me. "What about mind-blending with Russki here?"

"It won't work," Lynxx replied, voice sharp with frustration. "He's human, wounded and in pain. But his mind is still whole and intact. We can only mind-blend with mentally unstable humans."

"What talk about?" Wanjala snapped. "What mind-blend?"

Powell waved off the man's questions and continued our conversation. "How about I hit Russki in the head? That might leave him mentally unstable for a bit."

"Or kill him," I said dryly. "Then he'd be useless."

"True. Still, it's worth a shot."

"I've got a better idea." From his jacket, Lynxx withdrew a plastic bottle holding a yellow terra pod the size of a chicken egg. "Let's use this specimen from Peru."

I grinned, guessing his plan. "Brilliant."

Lynxx told Corporal Egebe to tie Russki to a lounge chair. Once the prisoner was immobilized, Lynxx moved us upwind. "Are your questions ready, Commander? Good. Ask them loudly and slowly once Kassia gives you the signal."

"But Russki doesn't understand English," said Powell.

"It doesn't matter. I can't really explain how mind-blending works. I just know that when I repeat your questions in Russki's mind, I'll somehow be able to sense his answers."

"That's true," I said. "When I mind-blended with that dying Sphere hybrid, Ethan Steel, I didn't have a scientific background. But when I asked him about the Shimmer formula, it automatically flashed through his thoughts. And I understood the formula so clearly that I was able to write it down."

Carefully, Lynxx handed me the yellow terra pod. "I can only mind-blend with Russki for a few minutes, so we'll need to be quick." He stretched out on a lounge chair a short distance away and focused on Russki. "Ready."

I hurled the pod at the pavers beside the bound man. He shrieked as it burst and released a fine yellow powder. Seconds later, Russki's brown eyes glazed over and he slumped in the chair, head lolling from side to side.

A moment later, the man's eyes turned silver as Lynxx mind-blended with him.

"Now, sir!" I said.

Keeping away from the yellow mist, Powell slowly called out a series of questions about the Threads, the Outriders, and the Chi'az.

Wanjala and the soldiers watched in confusion.

Two minutes later, Russki's eyes turned brown again.

With a shudder, Lynxx sat up.

"Are you okay?" I cried.

"Yes."

"Did you get the answers?" Powell asked him urgently.

"Yes," Lynxx replied, face haunted. "And we're in serious trouble."

72

Lynxx's mind-blend with Russki had revealed some devastating news.

As Lightning One raced toward our only hope of survival, I sat back on the cabin bench, trying to ease my cramped muscles. This extra twenty-one-hour flight had been almost torture. Long and uncomfortable and drenched in worry. Despite this, the half-empty cabin had allowed people to snatch a few hours of sleep on the benches and the floor.

Now, this endless flight was almost at an end.

I checked my watch. Our Shimmer gas was due to be released in fourteen hours.

But according to Russki, the Outriders' Threads would be released in eight hours—six whole hours *before* our Shimmer gas.

Shortly after that, every last human on Earth would be dead.

I looked around the cabin as people rolled up their sleeping bags and took their seats again.

Grim-faced, Commander Powell sat at the controls, with Asher in the copilot's seat. Our three remaining soldiers glumly cleaned their weapons. Harlem and Soo-Yun held hands tightly, as though trying to hold on to their dreams of a future together. Booker and Kendra pretended to read their paperbacks. Yuki adjusted the sling holding his broken arm. Willow stared into space, occasionally touching her scarred cheeks. Lynxx examined a plastic bottle of priceless pills. Me.

Thirteen people.

Unlucky thirteen.

"How long until we get there, boss?" Booker asked, trying to hide his dread.

Asher did a quick calculation. "Thirteen minutes."

Unlucky thirteen again.

Desperately, I tried to think of seven positive things. Wasn't seven supposed to be a lucky number?

One: Wanjala had allowed us to leave New Eden. "Very much hurry, please. Must wipe out krols before they logboat into our lake."

Two: our final drum and two soldiers were positioned in New Eden, the timer manually adjusted to release hours earlier than planned.

Three: Wanjala had given us two large bottles of his precious cancer-curing pills. "Please ... how you say it? ... make copy pills. Best hope for sick people everywhere."

Four: we had a black canister of Threads—confirmed by Russki—in the rear of our cabin. At the first opportunity, we'd destroy it.

Five: we knew the location of the Chi'az scouts. Instead of returning home to New York, we were reluctantly on our way to Hawaii.

Six ...

I scrabbled to find more positives.

Six: Russki had been imprisoned in New Eden. Not exactly a positive for us, but definitely a positive for him, since the Brethren recruit could've been executed.

Seven ...

Come on, one more positive.

Got it.

Seven: the rabbit, Whitey, had a new home with some adoring children in New Eden.

"Honolulu below," Powell called from the front. "Switching to stealth mode. I'm taking her down for a quick recce."

Reducing speed, our ship slowly descended.

As the hull became transparent, I scanned the early-morning scene. Long, green-tinted beaches. Gray waves crashing on the shore. Tall buildings almost covered in terra vegetation. Wide streets, overgrown and deserted—

I leaned forward, peering through my binoculars.

No, not deserted.

On a wide avenue, twenty or so adults and children cowered behind abandoned cars. A couple fired at a pack of spear-throwing krols; others attempted to shepherd the children into the safety of a once-grand hotel. Bodies from both sides lay on the street.

"Hey," Harlem cried. "There are people down there. Kids too. They're under attack by krols."

"Sorry. We can't help them." The commander kept his focus on his controls. "Our mission is top priority."

"Sir," Harlem objected, "I need to do something, not sit around."

"You know why I have to keep my team small. Half a dozen at the most."

"Yeah, sir. And Lynxx and Kass should definitely go with you, what with their mind-mojo and all."

"But?"

"But I can't just stay inside Lightning One, waiting for you guys. If I'm going to die today, I'd rather die fighting the good fight."

A chorus of voices from the others echoed Harlem's sentiments.

The commander hesitated. "I'll circle back. Determine the viability. But we have to make it quick. And no soldiers; we might need them at the Chi'az site." He swung the ship into a turn.

I stared at a distant mountain—our destination. Even now, hours later, I still couldn't believe how wrong we'd been.

When we had started this mission, we'd thought we had the only remaining Chi'az ship, which meant the Outrider hybrids couldn't distribute their Threads around the world.

Back in Kenya, the sight of the second ship had been a massive shock.

Under Lynxx's mental questioning, Russki had revealed that, a few days ago, a group of Outriders had finally finished re-pairing Lightning Two, the ship sabotaged months ago by the Sphere hybrids. Like our own ship, Lightning Two's superfast hyperdrive remained broken and it could only use the slower low-drive.

But—*big but*—it didn't need a lengthy cool-down between each long destination.

Subsequently, the Outriders could distribute their canisters of Threads around the world in three days, much faster than the five days it had taken us.

Only one hope remained.

From Lynxx's mind-blend with Russki, he'd learned that some Chi'az scouts were living in a cavern in Hawaii.

And they had a third ship, Lightning Three. *Fully functional.*

Back in Kenya, as we'd hurriedly taken our seats in Lightning One again, I had asked Lynxx, "Why aren't the Outriders using Lightning Three to distribute their canisters of Threads around the world? Its hyperdrive would do the job in a few hours, not days."

He'd shook his head. "I've got no idea. Russki didn't know either."

In the cabin, Commander Powell had asked Lynxx, "So where does that leave us?"

"Well, the Shimmer's synthetization might be done by now. If we steal Lightning Three, we can zip back to each of our release points and reset the timers; the entire trip should only take three hours with its superfast hyperdrive. We can bring our Zero Hour forward so that it beats the Threads' release by an hour."

"What if the fermentation of the Shimmer chemicals isn't finished?" Powell asked.

"At the time we left New York," Lynxx said, "the fermentation was due to take six or seven days. That's why the drums were programmed to release in seven days, just to be completely sure the gas was ready. Today is the fifth day. By the time we get to Hawaii, it'll be the sixth day. The gas might be ready."

"Or it might not," Asher argued.

"Lynxx's plan is a good one," Commander Powell decided. "It's a risk, but it's one we have to take." He sighed. "It'll be neck and neck which is released first: the Shimmer gas or the Threads. But at least we'll have a chance."

Booker raised a skeptical brow. "Not if we're dead, sir. Steal the Chi'az's ship? That's suicide."

"Not necessarily," Lynxx said. "According to Russki, it's parked near the Chi'az's cavern on Oahu. No guards or alarms."

"Are you sure about the location, Lynxx?" asked Powell.

"Yes. People can't lie in a mind-blend."

It sounded like a simple mission.

Now that we were almost there, I was starting to feel cautiously optimistic, almost hopeful.

Commander Powell circled Ainahau Stadium, a couple of blocks from the battling humans and krols. Its huge open-air arena held a clump of boulder terras about thirty feet tall, with smaller boulders scattered here and there. The ground around them was dotted with patches of eight-foot-long tentacle terras.

Carefully, Powell parked Lightning One on the flat top of the largest boulder terra in the outdoor arena.

"Why are you landing here, Commander?" asked Harlem nervously.

"Look around. This deserted stadium is the perfect place to land a ship. When we descend in stealth mode, the ship is silent and invisible. But as soon as I switch off the engine, it becomes visible and can attract unwelcome attention from krols, thugs, whatever."

"But aren't boulder terras hollow inside? Won't our ship be too heavy for it?"

"Actually," Lynxx explained to Harlem, "smaller boulder terras like these are like living rock. They're solid and strong. It's only when they reach heights of fifty feet or more that they become hollow so they can store their seeds."

Asher added, "And landing on top of the boulder terra keeps the ship far above the ground, out of the tentacle terras' reach."

"Exactly, son. Now move it!" Powell pointed to half a dozen abandoned trucks in the arena. "Use one of them to drive to that battle, Harlem. Load up the survivors and drive back here. Then wait for us."

"Yes, sir." Harlem pulled a bottle of ReVive from his backpack, ready to pour it into a fuel tank.

"And keep your radio on," Powell said. "Once we have Lightning Three, I'll use it to go and manually reset all the timers. Asher will fly back here in Lightning One to pick up you guys, plus any survivors you rescue." He glanced at his watch. "It's 7 a.m. now. Hopefully, he'll be back to pick you up in an hour."

"Copy that, sir." Harlem turned to a teenage boy with the broken arm. "Sorry, Yuki, you can't come with us. You'll have to stay with the ship."

Yuki's nod held both disappointment and relief.

Asher watched Willow grimly clip a knife to her thigh. "You should stay on the ship, Willow. We'll need someone to help guard Lightning One."

"Find someone else, Ash," she snapped. "You're good at that." She flicked a glare at me, obviously remembering him kissing me in the cathedral-dome.

He turned to the commander in appeal. "Sir—"

"No time for arguments, son." Powell pressed a button.

As the hatch whooshed open, a tropical breeze gusted inside, thick with exotic scents.

Suddenly apprehensive, I called out, "Good luck, guys."

"Ditto," Harlem cried as he stepped through the hatch, onto the boulder terra.

Weapons drawn, Harlem, Soo-Yun, Booker, Kendra, and Willow hurried across the top of the boulder, then down the sloping side. Dodging patches of tentacle terras, they ran to the closest truck. As Booker climbed into the cabin, Harlem turned and, bottle of ReVive in one hand and mini-charger in the other, waved us off.

My heart clenched.

How many of my friends would survive the next hour?

Once again in stealth mode, our ship rose above the boulders and headed toward a thickly forested mountain range on Oahu. As we approached, we saw a ship land in a clearing ringed by Earth trees and terra trees.

Commander Powell kept the stealth mode engaged as he hovered our silent ship at a distance, anxious to keep our presence a secret. After several minutes, he cautiously brought the ship above the clearing.

In the middle of the dirt stood our target—and possible salvation.

73

A WHITE SPACECRAFT GLEAMED a short distance from the base of the mountain.

The parked vessel was in a clearing partially screened by trees and impossible to access, except by air. No wonder the Chi'az hadn't bothered posting guards around Lightning Three.

We landed in silence.

Commander Powell ordered one of our soldiers—and the injured Yuki—to guard our ship. The other two soldiers came with us.

Powell, Asher, Lynxx, the two soldiers, and I hurried toward Lightning Three. There was no sign of an entrance to a cave system, I noted. Perhaps it was further along.

A brittle clinking sound grew louder as we approached the ship, and a foul stench saturated the air. Nose crinkling, I glanced around uneasily. The surrounding forest contained a variety of lush Earth trees and ferns. Mixed among them were skinny black trees about seven feet tall, their stubby leaves clinking like countless tiny teeth.

Teeth-tree terras.

One of the soldiers, Jasper, jerked to a halt and stared at the ground where two holes belched green smoke. "Oh my gawd. Is this island about to erupt?"

"That's not smoke," Asher said. "They're terra seeds."

"You sure?"

"Positive. I've seen them before."

I swallowed, remembering Armstrong Stadium back in New York. My sister, Olivia, had died in that hellish place. "Asher's right, Jasper. They're just seeds. Harmless."

We stopped beside Lightning Three, straining to hear non-human footsteps over the brittle clink of the teeth-trees.

Nothing. Yet.

The white ship appeared similar to our own but with a smoother, pristine hull.

My pulse quickened with excitement.

We had made it.

In a few minutes, we'd be zipping around the world via Lightning Three's superfast hyperdrive. We would reset the Shimmer timers so they'd release earlier and—

The other soldier, Hakeem, reached for the ship's hull. The air around the exterior shifted slightly, and I glimpsed a faint flicker of movement. "Wait, Hakeem! Don't touch it."

A bright gold flash—strangely familiar—shot from the hull. It crackled like metal shavings in a current, sharp and ominous. Hakeem flew backward as though struck by lightning and thudded to the ground a few feet away.

We rushed to help him.

"What the heck?"

"Are you okay?"

"What happened?"

Hakeem moaned as we pulled him to his feet and led him to a fallen log. He sank onto it, waving his singed palms. At the faint smell of burned flesh, I rummaged in my backpack for a first aid kit.

Powell turned to Jasper. "Treat his injured hands and keep an eye on him."

"Yes, sir." Jasper took my first aid kit and pulled out a jar of terra cream.

The rest of us returned to Lightning Three, keeping a safe distance back. The air around the ship continued to waver.

The commander groaned, "I think it's a force field."

With a disappointed sigh, Lynxx nodded. "I guess the Chi'az aren't as slack as we'd hoped."

"When Hakeem touched it," Asher said, "he might've set off a silent alarm."

"Doubtful." Lynxx folded his arms, studying the ship. "According to Russki, Lightning Three doesn't have any guards or alarms protecting it."

"He could've been lying. He didn't tell us about the force field."

"Obviously he didn't know. It's impossible to lie in a mind-blend."

"I guess we'll have to take your word for it."

Lynxx bristled. "Exactly."

"So, how do we deactivate this force field?"

"Why are you asking me, Asher?" came Lynxx's terse reply. "Do I look like a Chi'az?"

"You often know things that the rest of us don't."

"Yes, about terra plants and xans. That's because I study them. But I've never studied a Chi'az ship."

"Nila never mentioned the force fields?"

"Not to me," Lynxx snapped.

Powell stepped forward, his words low but whip-sharp. "Whatever's going on between you two boys, it can wait until later."

Both Asher and Lynxx glanced at me and fell silent.

Flushing, I looked away.

Asher and I hadn't spoken privately since our kiss in the cathedral-dome terra back in New Eden. His words lingered in my mind, though. *I'm in love with you, Kass. I will never stop loving you.*

I would never forget Lynxx's face when he'd seen us kissing, his frozen expression hiding ... what? What had he been feeling?

Powell surveyed the forest. "We need to make sure the Chi'az aren't around before we try to deactivate that force field. Kass and Lynxx, you go left. Asher and I will go right."

When we opened out mouths to argue about the pairings, Powell scowled and raised a hand. "That's an order."

In an awkward silence, Lynxx and I hurried into the shadow-draped forest. Dried teeth-tree leaves splintered beneath our boots, and an earthy smell mingled with the stench of the green seed-geysers.

We moved cautiously, alert for dangerous terra plants, xans, krols, Outriders, erupting seed-geysers, mutant humans, Chi'az scouts ... heck, alert for everything.

A short time later, we paused at the edge of a large vegetable garden. Keeping to the shadowy forest, we peered in disbelief at the neat rows of terra plants.

"Is some lunatic growing tentacle terras?" I whispered. These plants, with their long black tentacles, were deadly. Before we had wiped them out in Manhattan, six Weston Battalion members had been killed by them.

Fortunately, the tentacle terras in this clearing were only a couple of feet long. Since full-grown tentacles were fifteen feet long, I guessed these smaller ones were juveniles.

"Lynxx, we should—"

He stiffened. Clasped a hand over my mouth. Held me against him as we edged deeper into the shadows. At the alarm glinting in his golden eyes, I nodded my understanding.

Wordlessly, he released me.

Huddled behind a shrub, we watched a creature wander across the tilled garden. Its physique matched the size and shape of the burned body found after a fiery battle at Crendell Laboratories, the building where we'd first seen Lightning One.

Although this creature wasn't burned, it was still hideous.

Moving upright on two legs, the eight-foot-tall Chi'az scout resembled a Grim Reaper but with a long spear instead of a scythe.

Fighting down my rising panic, I tried to study the creature objectively.

Gray skin like dried leather. Overlarge bald head. Huge pitch-black eyes that glinted with the coldness of deep space. A naked, skeletal body with jutting ribs on a narrow torso. Two long skinny arms. A pair of legs that moved with stiff jerks. Clawed fingers and toes that looked capable of slicing through flesh with a single flick.

A dead krol was slung over the Chi'az's angular shoulder. Blood dripped from a wound in the krol's back, and the Chi'az's metal spear glistened red in the sunlight. I noted the krol's dark green skin, a perfect color for blending into the Hawaiian rainforests.

Midway across the tilled field, the Chi'az paused and snarled at some plants. Using the clawed toes of one foot, it yanked a weed from the dirt and threw it aside. Then it stretched its clawed foot toward a writhing terra and snapped off a piece. Balanced on one leg, it swung the other up and popped the tentacle into its teeth-crammed mouth. Crunching the tentacle like a carrot, the Chi'az disappeared through a crack at the base of the mountain.

Lynxx and I remained frozen to the spot. When no more Chi'az scouts appeared after a minute, he muttered, "Hideous."

"Yeah." I shivered. "Talk about a killing machine. Soulless. Deadly."

"Agreed."

"It seems to hunt krols for food," I whispered, sickened. "Plus it eats those disgusting tentacle terras."

"That explains a lot."

"It does?"

"I've often wondered why the Chi'az would terraform Earth with dangerous xans and terras. Clearly, they have a different relationship with them compared to ours."

"Those tentacles didn't even try to attack that Chi'az," I murmured. "They just lay there, waiting to be picked like turnips or carrots."

"Most interesting. Especially considering that all tentacles—juvenile and adult—can inject their attackers with poison."

"Those ones didn't even attempt to poison that Chi'az."

"As I said, they must have a different relationship to them. It's possible the Chi'az also eat other dangerous terra plants. Those innard-balls from the palm terras might be like mangoes to them. And the strangler terras could be their spaghetti."

"Gross." I grimaced. "If they hunt krols for food, why are the krols evolving?"

"Maybe the Chi'az also hunt them for sport and they prefer their prey to be challenging." Lynxx rubbed his chin, thinking. "Or maybe the krols' evolution is an unexpected glitch. I don't know."

I glanced at my watch. The Threads would be released in seven hours, according to Russki. But maybe the man had been wrong. "If—"

We froze again as a familiar figure emerged from the crack at the base of the mountain. Cadaver-thin body, gray shirt and pants, red armband.

Bone.

My heart sank.

The Outrider leader had been inside the Chi'az's cave system, probably reporting to them. Did that mean his canisters were already positioned around the world?

Lynxx drew me closer again. Lips near my ear, breath hot on my skin, his whispered words sent a fresh sliver of fear down my spine. "We need to capture Bone. Alive."

Appalled, I gaped at him. "I'd rather pet a cobra with my bare hands."

"Probably safer," he dryly acknowledged. "Still, we need him." Briefly, he told me his idea.

When he finished, I stood there in stunned silence. His plan was brilliant—and horrific on several levels.

Shuddering, I took a deep breath. "Count me in."

74

Crouched behind a thick bush, Lynxx and I watched from the shadows. As long as we remained in our own bodies—and stayed quiet—Bone couldn't sense our presence.

We needed him closer.

Twenty yards.

Distracted, Bone awkwardly moved across the tilled field, ignoring the juvenile terras that waved their tentacles above the dirt. His gray shirt and pants flapped on a body whose muscles seemed to be withering away, leaving only skin and bones. His thinning hair hung limp and greasy—

—but his dark eyes were still as hard and cold as a snake's.

Fifteen yards.

When a couple of tentacles grabbed at his ankles, he booted them away and continued on, still lost in his thoughts.

Ten yards.

I glanced at Lynxx. His tight face reflected the same anxiety I felt. Would our plan work? Bone might be physically sick, but we knew his formidable mental powers could crush us both if we made the slightest mistake.

Five yards.

Lynxx gave me a nod. *Now!*

I focused on the ugly tentacle terras to Bone's left. Eyes narrowed, I remote-pushed the largest one from the earth. Trailing bits of dirt, it arced toward the man with the accuracy of a heat-seeking missile. He yelped as it landed on his face, tentacles outstretched like an octopus. Swearing, he dragged it off and slammed it to the ground—but Lynxx quickly remote-pushed another terra into its spot. Working together, we bombarded the man with tentacle plant after tentacle plant. They writhed and squirmed as they gripped his head and neck and hands, each one stinging his exposed skin.

Gasping for air, Bone staggered around, blinded by one tentacle masking his eyes and partially smothered by another covering his nose and mouth. His movements grew weaker as their poison burned through his body. Finally, moaning, he crumpled to the dirt.

"Good," Lynxx whispered. "We have about four minutes."

I hesitated, my worries bubbling up. "Have you ever done this before?"

"No. It won't be easy. We have to do it anyway."

"I know. But what if you can read my private thoughts and feelings?" About him. And Asher. My cheeks burned at the possible emotional violation.

"That won't happen," he assured me. "Both of us will leave our privacy barriers up. We won't be able to read the other's mind. You and I are only mind-blending with Bone, not each other."

"Good." I moved on to my next worry. "Can he kill us while we're blended with his mind?"

"Probably."

"How about a small lie here, just to make me feel better?"

Desperately, I tried to sear this patch of forest into a final snatch of memory. Pale red sky. Sunshine. Green palms rustling in a warm breeze. Birds chirping. Color. Life.

I'd always wanted to visit Hawaii. I'd never wanted to die here, though.

"Okay," I whispered. "Let's do it."

Lynxx and I lay on some soft Earth grass. Holding hands, we drew in deep breaths and threw our minds forward—

—into Bone.

We landed in a frigid blackness, deep and evil. Amid the icy darkness, Bone's anger and pain twisted together, mixed with a whirling confusion and a swelling fear.

Tentacles cannot leap from ground. How? Poison burnsss. * Then, as the man felt our arrival, the soulless chasm of his mind was lit by a flash of fury. *You two! Get out of head.*

Enraged, he shoved me back and, for a terrifying moment, I was pushed toward an invisible barrier that led to the eternal emptiness of oblivion.

Lynxx mentally grabbed me in an embrace that somehow felt warm and secure. *We've got about three minutes, Kassia. Hurry.*

United, we focused our minds and pushed back. Hard.

We felt Bone falter. Spasms of hot tentacle poison continued to shoot through his body, killing swathes of cells in their passage. We sensed a growing coldness as death hovered outside the hybrid's body, waiting to move in.

Lynxx launched into his first mental question for Bone. *Have your canisters released their Threads yet?*

Bone hardened his mind against the mental interrogation and tried not to answer. But, unable to lie or evade, he finally replied, *No.*

Relief flashed through me, brief and sharp.

When will they be released? Lynxx asked.

Again, Bone struggled to suppress his answer. Couldn't. *Seven hours.*

So Russki had been telling the truth. The Threads would be released six hours before the Shimmer gas.

Why aren't you in Lightning Two? Shouldn't you be distributing the canisters of Threads around the world?

No need. Sssimple job. My people handle it.

A question had been bothering me since I'd found out about Lightning Three's existence, and I mentally asked it now.

Why aren't your people using Lightning Three to distribute the Threads around the world? It's got a hyperdrive, so it'd do the job in a few hours.

Couldn't. Lightning Three unavailable. Chi'az had meeting with main fleet at edge of galaxy. Needed fast ship. It return only short while ago.

What was the meeting about? I asked, trying to suppress a quiver of fear.

Invasion tomorrow, after all humansss *dead today.*

At his words, my fear began to rise, but I firmly pushed it back down. The battle wasn't over yet.

Lynxx mentally told Bone, *You thought the Red Mist would kill everyone, but it didn't. There's no guarantee the Threads will kill every human either.*

It will kill most survivors. Is all we need.

I asked, *Why are you in Hawaii?*

Reporting to Chi'az.

Yep, just as we'd thought. I felt a twinge of satisfaction—and I also felt Lynxx's urgency as he mentally told me, *Two minutes left. That should give us time to ... time to ...* His words stumbled as though suddenly weakened by ... what?

Panic sparked through me. *Are you okay?*

Head hurts. Take over. Be quick.

I dragged my focus away from him and back onto Bone. *Do the Chi'az know we're here? That we're trying to steal their ship?*

No, Bone responded.

Good. Do they have alarms or guards anywhere near Lightning Three?

No. Not need them.

Why not?

Force field impenetrable.

How do we turn off the force field?

Cannot, he replied.

Within me, dread flared like a midnight flame. Without Lightning Three, our mission would fail. I hesitated. Perhaps I wasn't asking Bone the right questions. *Can the Chi'az turn off the force field?*

Yes.

How?

Button on xanatron.

An image flashed through his mind, and I latched onto it: a brick-sized piece of metal with a black hexagonal button. Relieved, I asked, *Where is this xanatron?*

Sssafe in cave with Chi'az.

My relief turned into alarm. *How many Chi'az are on Earth?*

Five.

How can we steal the xanatron from these Chi'az?

Cannot.

Why not?

Seared with pain, Bone replied, *Chi'az mentally stronger than humans. Stronger than you and Lynxx combined.*

The raw truth of his thoughts hit me like acid. I wavered, struggling to stay in his dying mind. Sensing my despair, sharing it, Lynxx tightened his hold on me. *I've got you.*

Are you feeling better? I asked him.

No. Hurry. He'll be dead in a minute.

Rallying, I aimed my thoughts at Bone again. *Can the Chi'az be killed?*

Not by you. Not by Lynxx. Not by anyone.

I sensed an omission in his answer. *What about the Shimmer gas? Can that kill them? Nila swore it would. Was she right?*

Reluctantly, Bone replied, *Yes. We got small sample ... Shimmer gas. Tested it. Shimmer gas will kill Chi'az.*

My mental sigh of relief was cut short by a grim realization. If we couldn't release the force field, we wouldn't be able to use

Lightning Three. Without Lightning Three, the lethal Threads would be released first and the Shimmer would be useless.

Bone heard my worries. The tentacles' burning poison reduced his glee to a short, weak response. *Exactly.*

I sensed his life force thinning. We had only seconds left. If Lynxx and I were inside Bone's mind when he died, we'd die too.

Through his agony, Bone struggled to deliver his final, triumphant message. *You cannot win. Even mentally combined, you and Lynxx cannot win. Ssstupid to try.* His mind began to disintegrate into nothingness.

I heard Lynxx's mental voice: *Come on, Kassia. We have to get out of here.*

Together, we leaped from that frigid blackness, through Bone's dissolving mind, back into our bodies.

With a gasp, I sat up on the grass. "Lynxx?"

"Here." He gave my hand a squeeze, then dabbed a handkerchief at the blood trickling from his nose.

"You're injured," I gasped.

A slight shrug. "My head still hurts from when Nila clubbed me."

"Why haven't the terra meds healed your injury?"

"Nila fractured my skull, and bone heals slower than flesh, even with the terra meds. That's why I couldn't fix Yuki's broken arm overnight."

"But you'll be okay?"

"Eventually, yes."

Carefully avoiding the tentacle terras, we crossed to the hybrid, Bone. Half a dozen plants remained attached to the man's body, suckered onto him. Disgusted, I remote-pushed most of them across the field—but left two on Bone. If the Chi'az discovered his body, it'd look like he'd accidentally died after being stung by the tentacles.

Bone's deep-set eyes were open and lifeless. Hundreds of red dots covered his face and neck, each an injection point of the tentacles' poison.

Lynxx checked the hybrid's pulse three times. "Nothing. He's definitely dead."

My eyes met his, and I read the bleak despair in them.

"Bone told us the truth, didn't he?" I croaked.

"Yes. It's impossible to lie in a mind-blend."

"That means ..." My voice trailed away.

Somehow, Lynxx found the strength to say the words I couldn't.

Taking my hand, he softly told me, "We can't win, Kassia."

75

W E C A N'T W I N.

The grim realization hung in the air as Lynxx and I rejoined Commander Powell and Asher at Lightning One. It hovered like a toxic cloud as we told them about our mind-blend with Bone.

Stunned, they stared at us, too shocked to speak.

Only the clinking of the teeth-trees broke the silence.

"We can't just give up," Powell finally growled. "We need that ship." He frowned, thinking. "Maybe *our* Lightning ship has its own xanatron that we can use to bring down that force field." Then he shook his head. "I know every inch of that ship. There's no black brick-sized xanatron in it."

"I've never seen one in there either, sir." Asher turned to Lynxx, his antagonism shelved in the face of looming obliteration. "You've told us that people can't lie in a mind-blend, but Bone wasn't a person. He was a hybrid. Maybe he *could* lie."

"He couldn't," Lynxx assured him.

"Bone claimed the force field was impenetrable. Have you and Kass tried combining your powers to bring it down?"

Hope stirred and I turned to Lynxx. "Can we do that?"

"Not individually. But I guess we could try together."

Hands linked, we faced Lightning Three. Narrowing our eyes, we focused. *Hard.*

We pictured the quivering force field.

Harder.

Visualized it growing weaker.

A vein throbbed in my temple, threatening to burst.

Imagined the force field evaporating into ...

Nothing.

Lynxx heaved a defeated sigh and dropped my hand. "We're not strong enough." He swiped away a fresh trickle of blood from his nostrils.

"Does your head still hurt?" I asked.

"Yes."

"Take a break, guys," Commander Powell said, stepping forward. "Let Asher and me have a go."

Wearily, Lynxx gave another shrug. "You won't be able to bring it down."

Powell and Asher tried anyway. Together, they heaved a large boulder at the force field—and Powell almost got flattened when the boulder bounced back, triggering more glittering gold sparks.

Why do the sparks seem so familiar?

Powell withdrew his gun and aimed it at Lightning Three. Then he lowered his weapon. "Bad idea." He scowled at the boulder that had bounced off the force field, nearly hitting him. "Real bad."

"Let me try this." Asher shoved a flaming log toward the ship, but it couldn't penetrate the field. More gold sparks flew out, vivid and sizzling.

Where have I seen these sparks before?

I stifled a gasp as a memory slammed into me.

Nila's zap terra. For months, she had supercharged her hybrid brain by touching a zap terra a few times a day.

Lynxx had been right. We weren't strong enough, but maybe we *could* be. All we needed was a zap terra. I glanced at him. He sat slumped against a large boulder, eyes squeezed shut in pain as he pressed a blood-soaked handkerchief to his nose.

My heart fluttered. Lynxx wasn't well enough to deal with another mental trauma—and zap terras were definitely traumatic. I winced, remembering the pain I'd felt after touching an aquatic zap terra in the Hudson River. Even though I'd only grasped that orange plant for a couple of seconds, I'd felt sore for hours.

I searched for another solution.

Came up with none.

Knew I'd have to handle this by myself.

Carefully, I scanned the nearby trees and bushes. No signs of gold plants with long thin leaves. I searched the far side of the ship. Teeth-tree terras. Yellow pod terras like the ones in Peru. Even a creepy palm terra.

No zap terras.

My gaze rested on Lightning Three. Its force field had given off gold sparks, just like the zap terras.

What if I touched it?

Nope. Bad idea. A soldier, Hakeem, had been flung across the ground after touching the force field with both hands.

But what if I only use one hand? I would need to keep it in place for at least ten seconds. That was how long Nila had grasped the leaves of her zap terra.

I glanced at my watch. We were running out of time. I had to do it—

Now.

I stepped forward. Pressed my left hand against the hull.

Gold sparks zapped out. Pain shot up my arm and blazed through my body, jolting my heart and—

I jumped back, breaking free. Sweat beaded on my forehead. My body screamed with pain as if I'd stepped on a live cable, and my head reverberated with the intensity of being slammed by a two-by-four plank.

Worst of all, I didn't feel smarter.

Perhaps I need to touch the force field for more than ten seconds.

Shaking my arm, trying to flick away the pain, I glanced around. No one could see me. They were still on the other side of Lightning Three.

Throat dry with fear, heart racing, I pressed my hand against the hull again.

A shaft of gold electricity splintered through me, blisteringly cold. It twisted like lightning as it flashed through my arms, legs, torso, and brain. Gold flames flared through my mind, leaving it ablaze with a cold fire.

And then—

—I was thrown through the air. I thudded to the ground, winded. I couldn't move, couldn't think. My brain felt fried, my mind burned.

Shocked cries shredded my daze, each one tinny as though coming from the bottom of a metal well.

"Kassia!"

"What happened, Kass?"

Hands lifted me. Carried me to a patch of grass. Nauseous, I closed my eyes, letting the voices slide past, unable to identify anyone. They all sounded weirdly alike, only this time they bubbled as though fish were talking.

Fish talking? How brain-damaged am I?

"Did she touch the hull?"

"Don't think so. Her palms look fine."

"I think it was a pod terra."

"What?"

"One of those yellow pod terras, like in Peru."

"Right. I saw a broken pod on the ground beside Lightning Three."

"One must've burst near her. She probably got a full dose of that powder."

"So she's just disoriented?"

"Yes. She should be fine in a little while."

Eyes still closed, I heard more snippets of conversation, and I struggled to identify the voices. Couldn't. The words continued to bubble as though spoken underwater.

"I'm going into that cave. Get the xanatron."

"It's suicide."

"No choice. We need that force field down."

"Then I'll go. You wait here."

"Forget it."

Who was arguing? Asher? Lynxx? Commander Powell?

"Listen to me. If you get yourself killed, it'll destroy her. She loves you."

"I'm not letting you take my place."

"I'm trying to keep you alive. For her."

"Forget it."

A weird crackle interrupted their argument. Our radio. It screeched through the paper-thin fragility of my mind. "*We need Lightning One to pick us up.*"

The clink of the teeth-trees pounded like war drums. Through my swirling nausea, I heard footsteps thunder as they hurried off. Other sounds slammed into me, each a blow of pain. Desperately, I tightened my mind against the aural assault. I floated on nothing. Drifted through emptiness. Endured.

An eternity passed. Or maybe just minutes.

Gradually, my nausea began to dissolve as though evaporated by the sunshine.

Can sunshine dissolve nausea? Probably not.

Seconds flowed into minutes. Blade by blade, I became aware of the grass beneath me. Smelled the stench of the smoky green seed terras. Heard the teeth-trees cease their pounding and instead clink and tinkle once again.

Gingerly, I sat up. Streams of gold pain fell from me, smooth as water pouring off my skin. The former strident sounds became chirping birds and rustling leaves.

Trembling, I held my head and focused.

Nope, I still didn't feel smarter.

Commander Powell squatted beside me. "How are you feeling?"

"Better, sir." Blinking at the bright sunshine, I looked around. Lightning Three remained protected by the almost-invisible force field. There was no sign of our battered Lightning One.

"Where's Lynxx?" I asked. "And Asher?"

"Asher and a soldier took Lightning One into Honolulu. They've gone to collect our people and some survivors."

I began to nod. Stopped. My head hurt too much to move.

Throat dry, I asked, "Where's Lynxx?"

"He's trying to get that xanatron."

"What?" I gaped at the commander. "He's gone into the Chi'az cave? That's suicide."

"He and Asher argued about who was going to get the xanatron. Lynxx won by default when Harlem radioed for help."

"You could've flown Lightning One to Honolulu, sir, instead of Asher. You could've helped Harlem and the others."

The commander shook his head firmly. "Our mission has to come first. Humanity's survival depends upon it. If Lynxx gets that force field down, I'll need to fly Lightning Three around the world ASAP. Our priority is to reprogram the Shimmer drums, then—"

"Don't you get it, sir? Lynxx is injured. He won't be able to get the force field down. Bone warned us. Even with our combined mental powers, Lynxx and I aren't strong enough to face the Chi'az."

"What? Lynxx didn't appear injured."

"Was his nose bleeding?"

"Well, yes."

"Exactly. He can't mentally handle those Chi'az. They'll kill him. When did he leave?"

Commander Powell wiped his damp forehead, his eyes glazed with anguish at our looming defeat. "Ten minutes ago."

I tried to stand, but a sudden surge of blackness forced me back onto the grass.

"You should rest," muttered Powell, his thoughts elsewhere. "Asher and the others will be back soon."

"What about Lynxx? What if he dies in that Chi'az cave system? Alone? Without me?"

"He's not alone. I sent Jasper and Hakeem with him." The remaining two soldiers. "They're armed."

I groaned. The soldiers' presence would be meaningless to the Chi'az—and their rifles useless.

As I struggled to my feet, the commander asked, "Where are you going?"

"To help Lynxx." The blackness receded like a wave pulling away from a rocky shore. I remained behind, calm in my decision. "I can't let him face the Chi'az without me."

76

SOMETHING WAS WRONG WITH me.

By the time I reached the opening to the Chi'az cave system, hot sweat slicked my face. My hair hurt and I longed to rip off my helmet, but I didn't, aware that falling rocks were common in caves. My muscles quivered like Jell-O, and my head boomed with every step.

Earlier, I'd felt fine when I'd taken a caver's helmet from Lightning One. I'd also felt okay when the commander had wished me luck as I'd swapped my sword for a gun.

However, during my trek to the cave entrance, my senses had become twisted and distorted.

The pale red sky smelled of emptiness. The trees exhaled sour rainbows. And the chirps of birds wrapped me like ropes.

Worst of all, I didn't feel smarter. Nila's zap terra had supercharged her intelligence for an hour after she'd gripped it, and I'd hoped for a similar result.

$E=mc^2$. Nope, I still didn't understand the famous equation.

Agitated, I entered the rock passage but only managed a few yards before I sank to my knees in the dank darkness.

How could I've been so stupid?

I should never have grasped Lightning Three's force field—twice. Instead of making me smarter, those gold sparks had physically and mentally damaged me. Right now, I couldn't even remote-push an ant, let alone a powerful Chi'az scout.

Logically, I knew I should retreat. Emotionally, I had to go on.

Holding my breath, I listened for sounds in the rock passage.

No echo of footsteps from Lynxx and the two soldiers. No gunfire or shouts of battle. Were they lying in the darkness ahead, injured or—?

No! Lynxx couldn't be dead.

Heart pounding, I edged down the wide passage. The light of my caver's helmet, switched to its lowest setting, barely penetrated the darkness. Moments later, I halted.

Was I now hallucinating?

The walls and roof were covered in thousands of tiny gold stars that transformed the dark passage into a magical wonderland. Clicking off my headlamp, I squinted at the rock. *Please be glowworms, not a hallucination.*

Wiping my sweaty face, I peered even closer—

—then froze. They weren't stars or glowworms or hallucinations. They were small gold Hades terras. Highly dangerous, they'd burst into flames if their stems or leaves were broken.

Staying away from the walls, I crept down the wide passage as it twisted and plunged deeper into the mountain. Its entire length was lit by the glowing Hades terras, creating the illusion of walking through golden starlight.

The air was cold and yet I began to bake in my jacket and helmet, and sweat trickled down my back. My black pants felt like they were suffocating my legs. Step by step, the heat became more unbearable. No longer caring about safety, I removed my helmet, clipped it to my belt, and wrapped my jacket around my waist. I should've felt cooler in my sleeveless black top, but I didn't. Sighing, I pushed on.

Eventually, the passage opened into a huge cavern dotted with metal tables. Gun drawn, keeping to the shadows, I scanned for Lynxx and the two soldiers. No sign of them. Were they hiding behind some of the large boulders scattered along the rock walls?

And where were the Chi'az? Had they heard my footsteps in the passage? Were *they* hiding in here, waiting for me?

Ducking behind a boulder, I placed my jacket and helmet on the floor, then studied the cave.

Thousands of small Hades plants covered the soaring roof and walls. Their gold glow diluted the darkness and illuminated the stalactites that hung down like giant incisors. Fallen rocks dotted the floor, and the place reeked of rotting meat and powdered bones.

Below the roof, floating rods cast downfalls of amber light here and there.

About ten shiny metal tables were positioned across the floor. Half held strange scientific equipment that hummed and clicked. One bore metallic objects that blinked multicolored lights. Nearby, a small screen flickered with strange symbols.

In the furthest corner, five enormous egg-shaped objects puzzled me until I realized they were sleep pods. Each had a raised, curved cover that, presumably, could be closed. All were open and empty.

I wondered why the Chi'az were living in this cave. With humanity almost wiped out, they could've set up anywhere on Earth: On a beach in Bora Bora. In the spectacular Canadian Rockies. Or in any of the many palaces left empty around the world.

For some reason, the scouts preferred this dim, dank hideaway. Perhaps it suited something in their alien psychology.

At a shuffling sound, I withdrew deeper into the shadows.

77

THREE GRAY CHI'AZ SCOUTS emerged from an adjoining passage. Thin and ashen-skinned, they had large bald heads and oversized dark eyes. Their height varied from seven to nine feet tall, and each scout had a glowing white crystal embedded in its left palm.

Their smooth naked bodies seemed devoid of sex organs, making it impossible to tell if they were male or female—or neither.

I recalled a snippet of my earlier mind-blend with Bone, when I'd asked, *Can the Chi'az be killed?* He had replied, *Not by you or Lynxx or anyone else.*

Why couldn't they be killed? I now wondered. Was their skin invulnerable like Superman's?

One Chi'az bent over a clicking piece of equipment and tapped a tablet-sized screen. I winced as the creature peeled a piece of skin from its chest, revealing a moist patch underneath. Holding up the removed piece, it gave a brief sniff—then shoved it into its teeth-crowded mouth and chewed.

I clasped a hand to my mouth, smothering my gag.

Dis-gust-ing!

Did these creatures shed their skins like snakes? And why the heck would they eat pieces of it?

The krol hunter I'd seen in the garden crossed to a blood-stained table. Wielding a small, laser-like object, it began skinning a dead krol sprawled on the metal surface. A pile of tentacle plants lay nearby, twitching.

Skin Eater and Krol Hunter worked in silence. Occasionally, they'd tilt their heads as if listening to something. But the only sounds came from their science equipment, the squeak of unseen bats—and snarls.

Snarls?

In a shadowy corner, a krol snarled as it rattled its cage. Krol Hunter strode across and shoved a sharp stick through the bars, poking the xan. Hissing, the krol grabbed at the stick and missed.

I held my breath as the third Chi'az passed my boulder, trailing a foul stench like skunk spray. *Sheesh.* Did they all stink like this? My eyes watered and I pressed my hand over my mouth again, trying not to throw up.

Skunk Stink crossed to a wall and adjusted a vine slung like a garland. I winced. Two human skulls—an adult and a child—stared in dead horror from a line of animal skulls. I also recognized a horse, tusked boar, wolf, and bear. Were they trophies? Did the Chi'az hunt other creatures besides krols? And—*double dis-gust-ing!*—did they eat them too?

Back at the metal table, Skin Eater looked up from an instrument. It pressed a clawed hand to its bulbous forehead, as though concentrating.

Still hunched behind a boulder, I stifled a gasp as something stirred in the nearby shadows. Scales faintly rasping the rock floor, an enormous rattlesnake uncoiled and slithered past me. Its muscled length rubbed along my right calf for endless seconds, and I braced for venom-filled fangs to impale my leg.

The rattler wriggled across to Skin Eater, who grabbed it up, bit off its fanged head, and spat it to the floor. Next, the Chi'az scout ripped a chunk of flesh from the snake's twitching body and chewed.

I sank back behind the boulder, feeling faint again—

—but not from the revolting sight I'd just witnessed. My skin tingled as though swept by flames. My muscles locked up, hard and hot. I couldn't stand. Even my voice caught in my throat, muted and useless.

What was happening?

78

THE QUIET OF THE cavern was suddenly shredded a fierce burst of gunfire. Male voices yelled, one achingly familiar.

Lynxx.

Unable to cry out or even stand, I could only numbly peer around the boulder.

The two soldiers, Jasper and Hakeem, had charged into the open. Shouting, they blasted their rifles—

—and, incredibly, holes exploded in the chests of Krol Hunter and Skunk Stink. The two scouts collapsed, each twitching like the headless snake earlier. The glowing crystals embedded in their clawed hands faded from white to black as their bodies fell still.

Hot sweat dripped into my eyes as I studied the pair of bullet-ridden Chi'az scouts. They were supposed to be unkillable. Were they really dead? Or would they reanimate like unstoppable zombies?

Skin Eater rose from behind a shiny metal table that had fallen on its side. Black eyes fierce with anger, it pointed a gaunt arm at Jasper and Hakeem.

With a soundless cry, I tried to remote-push the Chi'az away. My brain burned and pulsed. Heat flared through my body, but nothing happened. My remote-pushing didn't work. Skin Eater didn't even glance in my direction.

However, I remained scorched, unable to move or shout.

Shrieking, the two soldiers clutched their eyes. Blood flowed from their sockets and poured down their cheeks in gory waves. They dropped to the ground, twitching and jerking. Abruptly, both men fell still.

Fear blazed through me. Skin Eater had remote-killed the two soldiers at the same time, indicating a mental power far greater than anything I'd seen.

Poor guys. What an awful way to die.

This mission had failed—and I'd been useless. All I could do was gape at the dead Chi'az scouts, still expecting them to spring up, whole and unhurt.

A sudden flash of understanding struck me.

Can the Chi'az be killed? I had asked Bone.

He had answered, *Not by you or Lynxx or anyone else.*

Bone hadn't lied. He'd just omitted a few details. Yes, a human or hybrid couldn't kill a Chi'az in a *physical* hand-to-hand conflict; the alien scouts were much stronger than humans.

But bullets could kill them—as well as fire, I thought, suddenly remembering the burned body at Crendell Laboratories; its height and shape matched the Chi'az in this cave.

Russki had said there were originally five Chi'az scouts on Earth, a figure confirmed by Bone. With one scout dead at Crendell Laboratories and two dead here, that left two still alive.

Movement flickered on my right.

Lynxx was creeping through the shadows along the far wall, cradling his gun. As Skin Eater noticed him, it raised a clawed hand. Stopping, Lynxx aimed his rifle at the Chi'az scout, but before he could pull the trigger, the scout made a slow twisting gesture.

Lynxx's face paled and muscles twitched at his temple as he mentally fought back. His finger trembled on the trigger, trying to squeeze it. Blood trickled from the corners of his eyes. As Skin Eater clenched its fist, the trickles became red streams—

—and I knew Lynxx was dying.

Have to help him. Desperately, I struggled to unlock my burning muscles. I needed to break the Chi'az's mental hold on Lynxx. Save him.

But I still couldn't move.

Forcing a smile, Lynxx stared at an empty spot just beyond Skin Eater. "Shoot him, Jasper!" he shouted, using an old trick known to most humans—but not to the Chi'az.

Startled, Skin Eater glanced around, momentarily breaking its mental hold.

It was enough.

Lynxx pulled his trigger again and again, firing until his rifle clicked on the empty barrel.

Skin Eater jerked as bullets exploded in its chest. Dark blood spraying, it staggered back and slumped to the floor. The glowing crystal in its palm dimmed to black.

Four down, one to go.

Released from Skin Eater's mental hold, Lynxx crumpled to his knees. Chest heaving, breaths labored, he ignored the blood dripping from his eyes. Instead, he clutched his head with the desperation of someone trying to stop it from exploding.

I trembled as though I'd been saved from stepping into an abyss. *Lynxx!* The Chi'az scout had almost killed him.

And then my trembling disappeared. Deep within me, something shifted.

A bat flew across to its roost, and as it flapped overhead, I sensed its tiredness and need to sleep. In a dark corner, a scuttling rat threw off waves of panic as it raced back to its nest.

Weird.

Gradually, my muscles unlocked. My body still felt hot, but it no longer burned. Instead, it seemed heated by the breath of an unseen fire.

Weirder and weirder.

$E=mc^2$? Still meaningless.

I scanned the cave for the fifth and last Chi'az. Empty. I listened. Nothing. Maybe the remaining one was out hunting or something.

I hurried forward, whispering, "Lynxx."

His head whipped around and he gasped, "Kassia! Get out of here."

"Not without you." I squatted beside him. "Are you okay?"

"Not really. But I'm alive. You need to leave."

"We'll both leave after we release the force field."

"The xanatron's over there." Weakly, he pointed to the furthest table. "While Jasper and Hakeem were battling the Chi'az, I crept closer to it." He gave a guilty shudder. "And while those poor guys were dying, I remote-pressed the xanatron's button, switching off the force field."

"Do you know if it worked?"

"It did." He gestured to a small military device strapped to his wrist. These were used to transmit text messages, their signals capable of penetrating rocks and mountains. "Commander Powell texted me that the field was down and he was in Lightning Three. By now, he's thousands of miles away in the ship."

"Good!" Grasping his arm, I tried pulling him to his feet. "Let's get out of this place."

He struggled to stand. Failed. After several unsuccessful attempts, he sank back on his heels, breaths shallow and shaky. "I just need to recover a bit. That Chi'az almost remote-killed me. It was brutal."

"I'm so sorry."

He glanced around, making sure we were still alone. "You shouldn't be here."

"Hey, we're the Dynamic Duo," I gently reminded him. "We're supposed to have each other's back, aren't we?"

For a moment his anxiety faded. Face softening, he stared into the past. "Always."

As the white mouse, Mousy, he'd been my close companion when I'd been living in the subway tunnels. As the Dynamic Duo, we'd shared books, pieces of cheese, and treks along the dark tunnels.

Gingerly, Lynxx touched his head, then wiped away the blood trickling from his eyes and nose. "I don't feel dynamic right now. I need a few minutes." Wincing with pain, he leaned against a boulder.

"Why did you volunteer for this mission, Lynxx? You were already badly injured from Nila's blow to your head."

A weak shrug. "Someone had to turn off the force field."

"I heard that Asher had volunteered to do it. Yet you insisted on taking his place, even before he received Harlem's radio call for help. Why?"

His golden eyes met mine, his expression raw with longing. "I want you to be happy. If Asher had been killed on this mission, your heart would've broken. I couldn't let that happen."

"Let me get this straight. You were prepared to die so Asher could live and I'd be happy?"

"Of course."

I fell silent. There was so much I wanted to say to him. So many feelings I wanted to finally acknowledge. But now wasn't the time or the place.

"Kassia, I—" His words trailed away as he stared over my shoulder. Dread flooded his face. "Oh no."

79

ON THE NAPE OF my neck, I felt a stir of coldness. As a foul stench drifted through the air, my skin prickled at the approach of death.

My heart raced, fueled by fear. I knew the last Chi'az was behind me.

Slowly, I turned.

The approaching Chi'az was taller and uglier than its colleagues. Head like a large skull, thinly covered by gray skin. Huge cold eyes. Ridged cheekbones.

At the sight of its three dead companions, its lipless mouth stretched in a soundless snarl. It raised a skinny arm, ready to decapitate me with a single swipe of its clawed fingers.

"*No!*" I tried remote-pushing the creature back.

The Chi'az swayed but didn't move an inch. Instead, it stared at me in shock. *You are not hybrid.*

I tried to hide my own shock. This thing had easily resisted my mental shove—and I'd understood its thoughts.

The Chi'az seemed to telepathically communicate with each other and, probably, with hybrids. Since I shared Lynxx's mental powers, I could hear its telepathic thoughts too.

"No," I said aloud. "I'm not a hybrid."

What are you?

Skull Head's words moved through my mind, not just in sound but almost physically. Its words wriggled like slimy, squirming worms. *Gross!*

"I'm human."

Lynxx struggled to stand. With a supreme effort, he moved his leg a little. Then, dripping sweat, he slumped against the boulder again, exhausted.

I needed to stall Skull Head. Buy some time for Lynxx to get a bit stronger.

When the Chi'az turned to him, I snapped, "Leave him alone."

Skull Head blinked at me, angry. *Someone must pay for deaths of my colleagues.*

"We killed four of you. You killed billions of us."

Irrelevant.

The single word felt cold and twisting, like a viper slithering through my brain.

"Irrelevant?" Hot anger surged through me. "Your species murdered almost every human on Earth. And you think that's irrelevant?"

Humans in our way.

"This is *our* home."

Now one of our homes.

"So you have multiple homes? Other planets you've invaded?"

Colonized. As humans have colonized lands not theirs for centuries.

I was surprised that Skull Head knew anything about man's history. "We don't destroy entire species just to take their lands."

Not true, human.

I needed to keep Skull Head distracted so that Lynxx—

A gunshot echoed through the cave in a thunderclap of sound.

Skull Head jerked as black blood gushed from a hole in its stomach. Eyes bulging with rage and pain, it remote-pushed the revolver from Lynxx's shaking hand.

The gun flew through the air and hit a rock wall, igniting a patch of Hades terras into gold flames.

With a silent wail that I felt rather than heard, Skull Head clutched its bleeding stomach. *My death will be your death.* The cryptic sentence moved through my mind like brittle bones, dry and sharp with shards.

I sniffed in disdain. "You're the one with a bullet hole in your stomach, pal, not me."

On our left, the Hades terras' golden flames raced across the rock wall and onto the roof, glimmering and spectacular in their deadly beauty. The cave was large, but the air already felt warmer. As usual, the smoke from the Hades terras reminded me of burned sugar.

"Get out of here, Kassia," croaked Lynxx, sweat layering his face. "Save yourself."

"I'm not leaving without you."

"I can't leave. Someone has to stay here." He gestured to the injured Chi'az. "Someone has to make sure this thing dies without contacting any of its kind in space."

"I'll help." Grimly, I reached for the revolver in my waistband.

Skull Head remote-pushed the weapon from my hand and flung it across the cave, into a fire-filled corner. *My death will be your death.*

Around us, smoke gushed in coiling waves as the flames grew larger and fiercer. They now covered the entire roof and all the walls, trapping us in an enormous bubble of fire.

Panic burned within me. The flames weren't physically close enough to burn us—and yet I felt hot, so hot.

"How can I save us, Lynxx?" I cried, sweat running down my spine.

You cannot, Skull Head telepathically told me, pain and glee intermingled. *My death will be your death.*

Why did it keep repeating that phrase?

Frantic, my skin on the point of sizzling, I searched for an exit. Both passageways that led from this cave were blocked by crackling fire. If we tried to run down either of them, Lynxx and I would be incinerated.

And then, abruptly—

—my panic and fear and terror dissolved. Calmness flowed through me, along with a strange sensation that I couldn't identify. My body remained hot, but the burning sensation had gone. Now a curious golden lightness filled me.

What was happening?

Skull Head clutched its stomach. Black blood poured through its clawed fingers, and its skinny body slumped as it grew weaker. *You cannot escape. None of us can. Flames too fierce.*

Every inch of my body tingled as though covered by golden starlight.

"The flames are fierce, aren't they?" I replied, strangely unafraid.

Finally, I identified the strange sensation that had flowed through me moments ago. The gold sparks from Lightning Three's force field hadn't made me smarter as I'd hoped. They had affected me differently from Nila's zap terras.

The strange internal heat I'd been feeling had been my mental powers intensifying far beyond my usual hybrid levels.

Would my mental boost last an hour, like Nila's enhancements? Or would it disappear in minutes?

No way of knowing.

However long it lasted, I intended to wield my newfound golden power like a weapon.

Skull Head glared at me. *We will all die here, human.*

Calmly, I shook my head. "Not Lynxx. Not me."

You are not strong enough to survive the fire.

I gave the creature a cold smile. "Today, I *am* the fire."

80

STANDING IN THE MIDDLE of the floor, with Lynxx a safe distance away, I stretched my bare arms above me. Heated air gusted through the cavern, flaring my long auburn hair behind me.

Glittering streams of gold flames poured down from the burning roof in brilliant torrents, engulfing me.

Skull Head's telepathic shout held a vicious glee. *Human girl is on fire.*

"Kassia!" Lynxx's anguished cry rang out, sharp with grief and despair.

I caught my reflection in a shiny metal table lying on its side.

Ribbons of fire covered my face and body in a living layer of gold flames. They wavered in the hot air and merged for a moment, turning me into a single brilliant flame. Then they fractured into separate pieces of brightness that glimmered on my skin, my clothes, my hair. A glow radiated from me, so bright that Lynxx raised a hand to shield his eyes.

Flames streamed with my hair in the wind, blurring into a gold halo around my head. My fiery body exhaled waves of heat that scorched nearby rocks but left me cool. Powerful fingers of fire ran across my skin and clothes, brutal and terrifying.

And yet I remained calm. In control. Unburned.

With a flick of my hands, I transformed my coating of thick flames into a glittering haze. I wanted Lynxx—and the Chi'az—to see I was unharmed. I felt Skull Head's astonishment. Saw Lynxx's face shift from despair to wonder. Remembered his earlier words about the Chi'az: *I can't leave. Someone has to stay here and make sure this thing dies without contacting any of its kind in space.*

Fine, I thought.

I waved my hands through the air, gathering long skeins of flames from the roof. They encircled my hands, large and burning. With a series of quick movements, I flung the flaming balls around the cavern. Gathered more fireballs. Flung them too.

The fireballs smashed into the Chi'az's scientific equipment, exploding the items into tiny pieces. Others reduced the sleep pods and meal areas into glowing ashes that were swept up by the hot wind. More smoke curled and billowed.

As the caged krol screeched and shook its cage, trying to escape, I incinerated the creature with a gold burst of flames.

Grimly, I turned back to the stunned Chi'az.

"Do you practice cremations on your home world, Skull Head? Or do you just eat the dead bodies? No matter. I prefer cremations."

I hurled a series of fireballs at Skin Eater, Krol Hunter, and Skunk Stink. Their skinny, skeletal bodies flashed into crackling black-flamed infernos.

"Interesting," I said, raising my voice over the roaring blazes. "The caged krol burned with gold flames. But your friends burned as black as hellfire." I fixed my fiery gaze on Skull Head, who was now gaping at me with terror. "I wonder what color your flames will be?"

Rolling my flaming hands, I created a spinning ball and heaved it at the Chi'az. Instantly, Skull Head was consumed by a black firestorm. Its telepathic words skittered through my mind like hairy spiders— **Help me. Please. I beg you. **—but I silenced the creature with a flick of my fingers. Skull Head had coldly watched as billions of humans had died. It had shown them no mercy. And it would receive none from me.

A minute later, Skull Head's skeletal body collapsed into a pile of ashes licked by black flames.

My relief at its death was cut short as the rock floor gave a brief tremble. A longer tremble followed.

Startled, I glanced around. Did Hawaii have earthquakes?

With a circular gesture, I extinguished the fires covering me. Not one of my hairs was singed. Not an inch of my skin or clothing was scorched.

I kneeled beside Lynxx. "We need to get out of here."

Coughing at the thickening smoke, he weakly gestured to the flames on the walls, the roof, even extending down the passageway that led outside. "How?"

"I don't know yet."

He tried to stand, but his legs buckled under him. Fresh blood trickled from his eyes and nose. "You go. I can't walk."

"Then we both die here. Together."

"No." His gaze firmed with determination. "I won't let you die. We have to think of something, anything—"

An idea flashed through me. "I've got it!"

"What? Already?"

"I can't believe I didn't think of it earlier." I sat on the floor. "Hurry. Take my hands. Close your eyes."

"Why? What—?"

"Do you trust me?"

Softly, he replied, "Always."

We sat facing each other on the rock floor, holding hands, our eyes shut. Quickly, I cast a domed force field around us that blocked the heat from the approaching flames and silenced their terrifying roar.

Enclosed in this temporary dome of peace, I focused on creating a stream of warm invisible flames. They flowed from me, through Lynxx's hands, into his damaged body and mind.

Seconds whispered past.

The ground beneath us trembled again, stronger this time. Eyes still closed, I squeezed Lynxx's hands, hoping he wouldn't break the bond between us.

His hands remained in mine, trusting me.

Gently, I flowed the invisible warm flames across his injuries like water washing away dirt and grit. His bleeding wounds stopped seeping blood. His split flesh and his fractured skull fused together. The fragments of his battered mind melded into a whole again.

Smiling, I looked at Lynxx. "How do you feel?" Even before he replied, I could see the answer. His cuts, bruises, and trails of blood had vanished. His skin was clear and healthy, his golden eyes bright and pain-free.

He sprang to his feet, pulling me up against his strong body. "I feel great. How did you do it?"

I laughed in relief and delight. "I'll explain later. First, let's get out of here."

A flick of my wrist removed the peaceful dome around us—

—and the inferno suddenly returned, whirling in a fury of flames.

As the cavern began to shake, Lynxx stared at the piles of incinerated Chi'az. "I think I know what's happening."

"What?"

"This mountain is about to explode."

81

OVERHEAD, THE ROOF CRACKED.

Chunks of rock began falling, trailing flames behind them, but I remote-shattered the dropping rocks into hundreds of glowing specks that lit the air like fireflies.

Lynxx grabbed my hand and pulled me toward the passage that led outside. As a stalactite snapped from the roof and plunged toward me, he gestured impatiently, remote-exploding it into harmless tiny particles. "Hopefully, the passage isn't completely filled with fire."

It was.

The long passage no longer glowed like a magical wonderland. Flames howled from every side, their fiery fingers fusing in the center. Smoke billowed, hot with the promise of death.

My skin tingled from head to toe—but not from fear or heat or the threat of death.

Power.

I waved a hand at the passage—

—and the flames instantly shrank against the walls and roof, creating a clear channel wide enough for us both.

Lit by firelight, we ran down the passage, watching the fire retreat before us.

Lynxx threw me a stunned glance. "You're amazing."

"It's only temporary," I said with a twinge of worry. "I'm hoping it lasts for at least an hour."

His smile faded and he glanced around uneasily. "You mean it could be shorter?"

"Yes." For a horrific moment, I pictured the flames swelling and grabbing Lynxx and me in a burning embrace.

We ran faster, working as a team. I carved a passage through the inferno, and Lynxx remote-pushed away falling rocks. Behind us, the flames surged together in our wake, seething at our escape.

As new tremors shook the passage, I cried, "How do you know this mountain is about to explode? This could be an earthquake."

"Perhaps." He remote-pushed back a crumbling wall until we safely passed, then he let it crash down behind us. "But remember those glowing white crystals in the palms of the Chi'az? When each one died, its crystal turned black."

"I remember."

Around us, the burning Hades plants swirled like scorched snowflakes in a blizzard from hell.

"I think those white crystals transmitted signals to an explosive device," he said. "When the device no longer received any signals, a doomsday sequence was triggered."

I remembered Skull Head's words: *My death will be your death.*

It made perfect, terrible sense. "How long do we have?"

"I don't know. Probably not long."

We plunged from the burning passage into the open. Gulping in the fresh air, we bolted past Bone's body and across the garden of tentacle terras, crushing them beneath our boots. Birds catapulted from trees into the sky, fleeing something.

What was happening?

We headed toward the clearing where our ship had landed earlier. The ground shook violently as we wove around bushes and dodged falling trees. The sky was filled with billowing brown smoke, far too thick to have only come from the Chi'az cave.

"There must be more fires nearby, Lynxx."

"I agree. I really hope Asher's picked up the others and is waiting for us in Lightning One." We both knew the ship was our only chance of survival.

The mountain rumbled and shook, and we leaped over widening cracks in the ground.

Finally, we reached the clearing.

It was empty. No ship. No people from our group. No hope of us surviving.

As the land cracked and broke around us, our hands entwined, seeking a shred of comfort. Despite the destruction around us, my feelings for Lynxx burned within me, their heat more intense than I'd realized.

"I'm sorry," he said.

"For what?"

"I wanted you to have a long and happy life. I failed."

"You didn't fail. You brought down the force field with the xanatron. You gave the others a chance to live."

"But not us."

"I'm okay with dying like this," I replied, still holding his hand.

At least we would die together.

The ground trembled as a deafening roar sounded overhead.

82

WITH A ROAR OF engines, Lightning One descended like a mechanical angel from the heavens. It hovered a foot above the cracking land.

Nearby, the mountain's rumblings grew deeper, and the ground shook with the ferocity of a moderate earthquake.

"Get in," Asher shouted through the open hatch.

Lynxx and I raced across the clearing, which began splintering around us. We jumped over small sinkholes, remote-pushed away falling trees, and leaped inside. The hatch hissed shut and Lightning One darted upward.

I gasped, "We thought you were in Honolulu."

"I was," Asher replied, seated at the controls. "But before Commander Powell took off in Lightning Three, he radioed me that you'd followed Lynxx into the Chi'az cave. So I came back."

I sank onto a seat next to Lynxx. "Thanks for saving us."

As Lightning One rose far above the forested mountain range, I peered through the narrow window behind me—

—just as the mountain exploded in a deafening thunderclap. Rocks and dirt hurled in all directions, obliterating every trace of the Chi'az cave.

Cries came from further down the ship.

Startled, I saw Yuki and a group of strangers huddled in the rear. Three men, two women, five children. Yuki still had his broken arm in a sling. Some of the civilians had bandaged heads; a woman had burns on her face; the others had bleeding wounds.

Lynxx scanned the frightened group. "Where's the rest of our people?"

"They're okay. We're going to get them now." Asher turned the ship toward Honolulu and raced across the mountain range. To my surprise, smoke gushed from several peaks, not just the crater that had once held the Chi'az cave.

We began to descend into Honolulu.

"Cripes!" Asher peered through the front windshield. On a wide boulevard below, a battle raged between krols and humans. "When I left a little while ago, there were only a couple of krols alive. Now there are lots more. Where'd they all come from?"

At Ainahau Stadium, he again landed Lightning One on the largest boulder terra. Across the outdoor arena, the scattered patches of tentacle terras sensed the ship's vibrations and quivered in anticipation.

Hurriedly locking the controls, Asher told the survivors, "You kids and the woman with the facial burns, you all need to stay down the back." As the children whimpered in relief, he shoved spare guns and ammunition at Yuki and the other adults. "I know you guys are injured and afraid, but you need to guard this ship with your lives. It's our only hope of getting back to New York."

An elderly Hawaiian with an age-spotted face stepped forward. Blood seeping from his bandaged temple, he gripped his gun firmly. "You can count on me, son."

"And me," Yuki added.

The other adults loudly agreed.

"Good," Asher said. "Everyone remain inside the ship. You're safe up here from those tentacle terras."

Sword drawn, he hurried down the side of the boulder and paused at a nearby truck, frowning.

Lynxx and I joined him. "What's wrong?" I asked.

Asher pointed to the open fuel cap on the side of the truck. A yellowed plastic hose hung limply from it. "This was the truck that Harl and the others were planning to drive." He hurried along the row of parked trucks. All had open fuel caps. "I think these gas tanks are empty."

It made sense. After the Mist, survivors would've siphoned gas from abandoned vehicles. And these trucks would've held large amounts.

"They're all empty?" Lynxx asked. "So how did Harlem and the others get to the boulevard?"

"I'm guessing they simply ran the couple of blocks, like I'm about to do." He hurried toward an exit, swerving around the tentacle terras in the arena.

"Asher, you should stay with Lightning One," I cried as Lynxx and I caught up with him. "You're the only one who can pilot it."

He didn't slow down. "And I'd prefer that you remain with the ship too, where you'll be safe." He slashed his sword at a tentacle that tried to grab him. "But you won't do that, will you? Not even for me."

He picked up the pace, and our conversation became punctuated with puffing as the three of us rushed from the stadium.

"How can I remain behind?" I cried. "My friends are in trouble."

"If you're joining the battle, then so am I. I can't hang back, worrying about you, imagining you bleeding out from a fatal injury."

"You don't need to worry about Kassia," Lynxx said quietly. "She can take care of herself. Especially today."

At Asher's confused expression, I explained how I'd touched Lightning Three's force field—and its powerful mental effect on me.

He jumped over a fallen trash can and continued running. "I feel better about you going into battle, Kass. At least you'll be able to protect yourself."

"So you'll wait in the ship?"

"Not a chance. Harl and Willow and the others still need help."

Beyond the stadium, the streets were carpeted with angel terras. We ran across the feathery white leaves, and for once their jasmine-like scent didn't calm me.

"Have you heard from Powell?" Lynxx asked Asher.

"I lost contact with him when Lightning Three went into hyperdrive."

"The Threads are due to be released in a few hours. Is Powell coming back when he's finished reprogramming our timers?"

"No." Asher booted away a crabben xan that lunged at us. "He'll wait until the Shimmer gas is released. Then he'll use the hyperdrive to return to all the release points and pick up our soldiers. And *then* he'll head home. We're all meeting back at the Weston Garrison."

We rounded the corner of a hotel and found ourselves on the wide boulevard we'd seen from the air. Overgrown buildings flanked the street on one side, and a muddy canal ran along the other. A vine-bridge stretched from a hotel rooftop, across the canal, and stopped at a distant colossus-tree terra.

The battle raged further down the street.

Liberty Team members and survivors fought green krols that were armed with iron rods, clubs, and axes. Civilians huddled behind vehicles covered with terra plants. Krols crouched on an overhanging vine-bridge.

At a strange smell, I sniffed the air ... and gasped.

83

"WHAT'S WRONG?" LYNXX ASKED me.

"Can't you smell it?" My heart hammered against my rib cage.

Asher inhaled. "Yeah. Gunpowder."

I nodded. "Plus human fear. Animal rage. And something much worse. Something I can't identify."

"Is this linked with your special powers today?" Asher asked, bewildered.

"Possibly." Or perhaps my senses were messed up again, like they'd been before I'd entered the Chi'az cave. At that time, I'd thought the sky had smelled of emptiness and the trees were exhaling sour rainbows.

Then again, maybe my recently heightened mental powers allowed me to sense things that others couldn't.

I drew in a deep breath, trying to calm my heartbeat. "Let's go."

My skin tingled beneath the invisible fire I'd felt earlier, and I welcomed the boost to my mental powers. But the strange, unidentified smell still worried me.

What was it?

We charged into the battle. Wielding his sword, Asher stabbed a green krol as it grabbed a pregnant woman, and the xanimal slumped in a heap. Lynxx remote-pushed another krol onto a snapped post, impaling it on the splintered concrete. Both dead krols wore necklaces of animal and human teeth. They also wore bandoliers slung across their chests, with lengths of rope looped through the bullet holders.

They're still evolving.

Skin tingling, I strode through the chaos, remote-pushing two krols into a patch of tentacle terras, which dragged them into the earth. I mentally shoved two more krols through a large glass window, shattering the pane into lethal shards.

Further down the boulevard, a pack of krol pups ripped and clawed at the body of a bloodied man. Kendra and Booker fought off adult krols, their swords clanging against shields hammered from pieces of metal. Soo-Yun bandaged a girl with deep slashes on her chest and arm. Harlem karate-kicked a krol to the ground, then repeatedly stomped its head.

A krol lassoed a young boy, knocked him flat, and began tying his hands and feet with pieces of ropes from its bandolier.

Weird. Why didn't it just kill the kid?

With surprising ease, I remote-snapped the krol's neck, dropping it to the ground. The little boy pulled off the ropes and ran across to a blood-smeared woman.

"Jimmy!" she cried, hugging him.

I called out to them, "Do you know where Ainahau Stadium is?" Frightened, they nodded. "Good. Go there now and wait inside the Chi'az ship that's parked in the arena. It's safe. Tell your friends to go there too."

A krol charged at us, swinging a metal spike.

The blood-smeared woman hurled a homemade Molotov cocktail at a nearby tourist bus draped in pink terra vines. As the leaves burst into flames, a stench of rotten potatoes gusted forth. The charging krol gagged and hastily retreated. The woman threw me a "Thanks," grabbed Jimmy's hand, and raced away.

That's new, I thought. The krols were repelled by certain odors. A bit late learning this now, though. In a few hours, the Shimmer gas or the Threads would decide whether humans or krols survived.

A krol—the one that had gagged at the rotten pota-to stench—heaved its metal spike at me. Casually, I re-mote-pushed the spike and it boomeranged back, piercing the creature's chest.

On an overhanging vine-bridge, two animals peered at Harlem below. As he poured ReVive into the gas tank of a minibus, they began emptying a bag of crawlers over the side. I winced, remembering the agony that crawlers could inflict. These pieces of terra plants would wrap their victims in thorny lengths and slowly poison them.

As the thorny terras plopped onto the ground, Harlem jumped back in horror. "Crawlers!"

"Don't worry, Harlem." With a wave of my hand, I re-mote-pushed the crawlers high into the air. With another wave, I drew flames from the blazing tourist bus and hurled them at the floating crawlers, setting them alight. They landed on the vine-bridge, scattering patches of flames along its length. The krols on the vine bolted away, uttering ear-piercing howls. *Noisy!* I threw flames at the retreating animals, transforming them into shrieking fireballs.

Power. So heady, intoxicating—and darn useful.

The ground trembled like a dragon stirring in its sleep. *An-other tremor?* Palm trees swayed, their dead branches scratching the air. The vines blanketing the buildings and cars whispered uneasily to each other.

The boulevard fell still.

And then—

—scores of click xans and crabbens poured from storm drains and manholes. Humans and krols alike froze in shock as the critters flooded onto the street.

I felt my face pale.

Although smaller than baseballs, the click xans had scor-pion-like stingers that could paralyze or kill small prey, as I'd discovered when I had mind-blended with a frog, Hopalong.

And the painful bite of the larger crabbens could lead to fatal infections in humans.

Like the others, I stood frozen as the xans scuttled past, their high-pitched clicks ominous and threatening. My muscles braced for multiple bites and stings.

Was I powerful enough to remote-push them all away? But they were everywhere, still gushing out, now in their hundreds. So far, the crabbens and click xans were ignoring everyone. What if my remote-pushing triggered them into attack mode?

I glanced down the road at Lynxx, who stood statue-still in the middle of the streaming xans. He caught my eye, read the question on my face, and slowly shook his head.

I frowned. Why were the crabbens and click xans fleeing their subterranean homes? What were they running from?

The flood of small xans became a trickle. As the last ones disappeared around corners or inside buildings, the krols and humans snapped out of their shock and launched back into battle. Shouts and screeches mixed with the clash of swords and metal.

Again I sniffed the air.

The strange unidentified smell had grown stronger.

Tension filled me, a dark tightness that I couldn't dismiss.

Something was coming. Was it the Threads? Had the Outriders won? Were we about to die?

"Wait, Willow," Kendra cried as Willow ran past me and darted around a corner. The South African girl swore, then resumed hacking and slashing at a trio of krols; Booker ran to help her, his sword dripping blood. Further away, Asher lifted a wounded man off the road, leaving a red smear behind.

Where was Lynxx?

I scanned the boulevard and saw him remote-pushing a krol into the canal. Screeching, the xan floundered in the murky water.

Relieved he was okay, I rushed around the corner after Willow.

Where was she going?

84

"Kass." Willow pulled me into the shadows. Her scarred cheeks were inches from mine as she whispered, "Have you come to assist me in my quest?"

Not this Pandora nonsense again.

"What quest are you talking about?" I muttered, my skin still tingling in warning.

She pointed down the street. A dozen civilians—men, women, and children—had been tied up and stacked like cords of wood on the sidewalk. Four of the biggest, fiercest, and ugliest krols I'd ever seen stood guard over them, clawed hands grasping huge machetes.

And I suddenly understood why the krol earlier had started tying up that little boy, Jimmy.

Evolution could be a bitch, I thought.

Once the battle was over, I guessed that the krols would take these bound humans to a hole or cage where they'd be untied and imprisoned. If the captives were lucky, they'd be fed scraps of food to keep them alive. And then, over a few days or weeks, one by one, they'd be slaughtered.

Fresh meat.

The tingle on my skin flared into an invisible blaze, fueled by outrage and horror. "Stay here, Willow. I'll handle this."

"My name's Pandora. And this is my rescue."

"Whatever. Stay here."

Senses on fire, I sheathed my sword and ran toward the captives. Despite my order, I heard Willow's footsteps behind me. *Great. One more person to protect.*

Waving their bloodied machetes, two krol guards rushed at us, shark-teeth bared. Their black eyes quivered in savage anticipation as they loped along the sidewalk, muscled bodies strong with power.

But I was more powerful.

"Eww! You're so scary," I mocked. Then I remote-snapped their necks in a quick one-two gesture.

Another krol guard charged at me, yanking a gun from its bandolier. The fourth guard turned to the bound prisoners and swung up its machete.

These creatures were smart. And ruthless.

But I was smarter and more ruthless.

I remote-pushed Gun Krol into the air, impaling the xan on Machete Krol's upraised blade. Screaming, they both crumpled to the sidewalk and I remote-snapped their necks, just to be sure.

Silence ...

... broken by the cries of battle back around the corner.

A flock of birds launched from a banyan tree in a loud flap of wings, and my skewed senses saw orange waves of panic streaming behind them.

What were they fleeing?

Willow began cutting the ropes binding a little girl's ankles.

"Stand back, Willow." At her stony glare, I hastily corrected myself. "Er, Pandora." Her mental instability glimmered around her, eggshell-pink and just as fragile. Best to play along with her delusion. "With your permission, Pandora, I shall release the prisoners."

She gave a regal nod. "Proceed."

Quickly, I remote-snapped the civilians' ropes. They scrambled to their feet, gaped at me in terror, then fled down the street—

—away from me.

"Wait!" I cried after them. "I'm not a hybrid. I'm human." When they didn't stop, I yelled, "Get to Ainahau Stadium. You'll be safer there."

They dashed around a corner and disappeared.

Willow shrugged her delicate shoulders. "Such poor manners. They didn't even say goodbye." We returned to the boulevard, where she rushed to comfort a frightened toddler sobbing on the sidewalk.

I ran toward the battling krols—and stopped, my knees almost buckling. A tremendous weight pressed on me, as though the sky had dropped to the ground.

Yet when I looked up, the pale red sky was still above us, hazed with brown smoke and crowded with flocks of fleeing birds.

Something's coming.

85

A FEW BLOCKS AWAY, a skyscraper suddenly crumbled and disappeared below some shorter buildings. A tremendous crash shook the ground. Debris billowed upward in a thick gray cloud.

I gaped in astonishment. What was happening?

The boulevard trembled as though frightened by the same unseen threat I'd sensed. And then—

—rocks and concrete snapped as cracks crisscrossed the road like landlocked lightning.

Humans and krols stopped fighting and gawked at the street.

"Tremor?" cried Willow, cradling the weeping toddler.

"Maybe," I replied.

Was Lynxx okay? I scanned the area. No sign of him.

"Moana!" A young Hawaiian woman grabbed the toddler from Willow's arms and rushed away.

The water in a nearby canal quivered and turned an inky black. Thousands of bubbles broke the surface, belching a gut-churning stench. Steam rose from the boiling water.

Deep within me, a dark tightness stretched almost to breaking point.

Something terrible was coming. And I was powerless to stop it.

The distant mountain range beyond Honolulu rumbled. Trying to keep my balance on the moving road, I gasped as one of the mountain peaks exploded. Red-orange lava sprayed high into the air like a monstrous Roman candle firework.

"It's erupting!" Asher shouted.

More explosions shook the mountain range as other peaks hurled brilliant streams of molten rock upward. They arced in red-gold falls that flowed down the slopes and blazed through forests. The sky dimmed under the spreading clouds of black smoke.

I gaped at the terrifying sight. A single erupting mountain was rare. Multiple eruptions were almost impossible. Had the death of the Chi'az scouts triggered all these eruptions—accidentally or deliberately?

Along the boulevard, steam spurted from the cracked road, hissing furiously. The krols staggered back, black eyes bulging, bat-like ears quivering in fear. Screeching, they grabbed up their pups and scurried away.

Hot water droplets rained down, stinging my skin, and I almost dashed for cover. An idea flashed through me.

Would it work?

I made a wide, swirling gesture with my hand. An instant later, the stinging droplets slid off an invisible shield that encased me head to toe. I could see the droplets quivering on my bare arms; I could even smell their stench, but they remained a fraction above my skin, unable to sting or burn.

Asher yelled, "Gather whatever survivors you can, guys. Get to Ainahau Stadium. Now. No heroics."

I turned to the others, wondering if I could create invisible shields around each of them too.

Seconds later, the hot rain stopped and the hissing steam fizzled into an ominous silence.

I sensed that something worse was coming.

Nervously eyeing the distant eruptions, my friends sprang into action. Some helped the injured civilians into the minibus that Harlem had managed to get started. Others reassured the children, telling them everything was going to be all right—and their lies hung in the air, calming the kids but tasting sour and bitter to me.

I suspected that the silent roads were only a lull before an oncoming hurricane.

Lynxx had disappeared again. Fear gripped my heart so tightly I couldn't breathe. Where was he?

I moved forward and peered down a side street—

—and my breaths returned.

He was bending over a bloodied civilian, checking the man's pulse. With a regretful shake of his head, he turned and hurried to another crumpled man. Another check for a pulse. Another headshake.

Seeing me, he hurried across as the ground shivered again. "We need to get out of here."

Overhead, thousands of bats squeaked in panic. Delicate wings beating in frantic flight, they arrowed through the smoke-dimmed sky.

The dark tightness stretched even further within me.

The ground's shivers grew stronger, heralding the approach of something unseen. By the time Lynxx and I returned to the main boulevard, my heightened senses were screaming another silent warning.

Down the street, I saw the minibus—crammed with survivors—chugging back to the stadium. At least Harlem, Soo-Yun, and their civilian passengers would soon be safely on Lightning One.

Only a few of us remained on the boulevard: Lynxx, Asher, Willow, Kendra, Booker, plus a middle-aged man in a Hawaiian shirt, a twentyish woman in a flowery dress, and a youth in purple shorts. Nine people, including me.

Asher asked, "Has anyone got another vehicle working?" No one had. "Okay, we'll have to hotfoot it back to the stadium."

I glanced at the darkening sky. It no longer felt empty, even though the birds and bats had vanished. The sky now felt afraid. Or was that my enhanced-but-distorted senses talking?

The far end of the boulevard began to rumble.

86

THE SOUND GREW LOUDER and louder, a deep wordless threat that promised death and destruction. Pulse racing, I instinctively reached for Lynxx's hand. And despite the invisible shield over my body, I felt the warmth of his skin.

A heartbeat later—

—the far end of the boulevard erupted.

Lava fountained from the road, spraying upward in glittering fat droplets. As they fell, they ignited trees, benches, and vehicles, and turned roads into ribbons of fire.

"Go!" Asher yelled.

Releasing hands, Lynxx and I bolted with the others down Rayley Boulevard, leaping over wide cracks and dodging terra shrubs in the concrete.

Booker yelled, "What if steam shoots out of these cracks, boss? We'll be cooked alive."

"We have to risk it. We don't have time to zigzag around each one."

Elsewhere in the city, more explosions sounded, and several blocks away, bright lava streamed high into the air.

Kendra cried, "These cracks are getting wider and brighter." She pointed ahead to a three-foot-wide crevice that threw up a gold glow. Stopping, we cautiously edged forward and peered down. Orange lava flowed below, rising fast.

"Get off the street," Asher shouted.

We ran into an enormous park. No grass. Just dirt dotted with dead palm trees—and patches of large tentacle terras.

Booker yelled, "I'm definitely zigzagging around those tentacles, boss."

"Same here," Asher cried.

Smoke filled the sky. The vivid blues and greens and pinks of Hawaiian daylight vanished as an artificial twilight fell. The only color in the dimness was the burning red-gold of lava fountains.

Overhead, a fireball arced down with a drawn-out shriek. We stopped, staring in confusion.

"What's that?" yelled the man in the Hawaiian shirt .

"Lava bomb," Lynxx cried. "Don't move. It'll just miss us."

The flaming ball slammed into the park, flinging burning drops through the air. I remote-pushed away as many as possible, sweeping my focus outward.

Booker yelled and jumped back, grasping his leg. A large black wound smoldered on his thigh.

"Lava burn." Lynxx hastily wrapped a bandage around Booker's thigh, telling him, "You'll be okay once we get to the ship. Soo-Yun will treat you with terra creams."

"I can't walk."

Lynxx slung Booker's arm over his shoulder. "I'll help you."

More lava bombs screamed across the sky. They exploded into shops and hotels, flaring massive fires that spread with alarming speed. One struck the ground near a patch of tentacle terras, and the flaming tentacles writhed and twisted in the unnatural dusk.

The land around us cracked as though a monstrous claw had slashed the earth, cutting the park in two. We scattered as orange-gold lava bled from an enormous crevice, gushing a bright river that incinerated everything it touched.

"Lynxx!" I screamed.

"I'm fine, Kassia."

The river of lava had divided our group. Asher, Willow, and I were on one side. Lynxx, Booker, and the rest were on the other.

The crevice widened. More lava vomited from the earth, forcing us to retreat before the burning streams.

Asher yelled to Lynxx, "Get Booker and the others to the ship. We'll take a detour and meet you there."

"I won't leave Kassia."

"I'll be okay," I assured him. "I'm Super Kassia today, remember?"

He hesitated. Frowned at Booker, whose arm was still slung around his shoulder. Sighed at his colleague's pain and injured thigh. "Okay. I'll see you back at the ship." His anguished eyes met mine across the burning river. "Take care of yourself, Super Kassia."

"You too." My voice shook, worried about him, and Asher threw me a sharp glance.

Lynxx and Booker joined the others. They turned west and headed down a road that led to the stadium.

Asher, Willow, and I ran east.

We left the park and started down a street that looked clear. With any luck, it would connect with a road that would take us to the stadium.

"Willow," shouted Asher. "Where are you going?"

I turned.

Willow had run across to a figure crumpled on the sidewalk. It was the young Hawaiian woman from the boulevard earlier, the one who'd grabbed the crying toddler and fled. Her left arm bore an ugly black burn.

"Please, save Moana. I can't walk. I sprained my ankle." Her long black hair almost covered an embroidered name on her shirt. *Tracie.*

Asher slung the woman's right arm around his shoulders. "I'll help you walk, Tracie."

"I found this shirt. My name's Ona." She scoured the sidewalk with panic. "Where's Moana?"

Willow stepped forward, brandishing her sword, her scarred face filled with determination. "Fear not, m'lady. I vow to find your daughter."

Pandora again.

As Willow ran back into the park, I said, "Asher, bandage Ona's arm. I'll get Willow."

"Are you sure?"

"I'm Super Kass today, remember? I'll remote-pull Willow to safety if I have to."

"Okay." He dug in his backpack for a first aid kit.

In the park, Willow was bending over a little girl. The toddler, Moana, sat on a huge patch of dirt that was almost surrounded by a thick circle of glowing cracks. Willow grabbed the sobbing child—

—just as the glowing cracks joined up, stranding the pair on an island fifty feet wide.

I stopped at the edge of the glowing "moat." The circle of cracked earth was too wide to jump.

Below, lava bubbled and flowed, and heat gusted my face like a blowtorch.

87

"WILLOW!" ASHER RACED UP. "Wait there. I'll leap across and get you."

"No, Asher." I grabbed his arm as he started to run toward the glowing moat. By now the crack had grown to a burning ring at least fifteen feet wide. Too wide to leap across. "You'll die."

He faltered at the edge of the circle. "I have to do something."

I glanced back at Ona. She struggled to stand on her sprained ankle but crumpled to the ground again.

On the lava island, Willow hurried forward, carrying Moana. She stopped a few feet from the fiery crack.

"Kass is right, Ash," she said to him. "It's too wide. Besides, you're the only one left who can fly Lightning One. If you die, everyone we've saved today will die too. Plus Harlem, Booker, Soo-Yun, even Kass here." She cast me a sad smile. "You might be Super Kass today, but no one can win against an eruption."

Asher's face crumpled beneath the brutal truth of her words. "Willow—"

"Hang on," I interrupted. "As Super Kass, maybe I can help."

Hope flashed through his eyes.

Mentally, I focused on Willow and the little girl. Drawing energy from around me, I channeled my thoughts on the trapped pair. Lights sparked across my vision and my head began to throb. I pushed on, picturing the two of them rising high into the air. Floating across the flaming moat. Landing safely on the other side.

More lights exploded in my mind, brilliant and sharp and—

—black. Flat. Dead.

I slumped forward, breathing heavily. "I can't do it."

"It's okay, Kass," said Willow, surprisingly calm. "Save Moana." She held the sobbing child. "I'll throw her to you."

"No! Don't!" Asher cried. "You can't throw her that far. She'll fall into the lava."

"*I* can't throw that far. But Pandora can." She swung the child back and hurled her through the air. Moana flew a few feet forward, then began to fall—

—toward the glowing crack.

My horrified gasp sparked a brief flare of lights in my brain. Somehow, I managed to remote-pull Moana across the chasm and into my arms. Blood trickled from my nose as I sank to my knees, cradling the screaming child.

Asher squatted down and put his arm around my shoulders. "You're bleeding."

Without thinking, I shrugged him off.

He stood, hurt clouding his eyes.

"Sorry, Asher. I'll be fine. I just need a minute to recover." I wiped away the blood with a handkerchief. "Where's Lynxx?"

The hurt in his eyes deepened. "He's meeting us back at the stadium, remember?"

"Oh. Right." In my arms, Moana screamed and struggled. Using some scraps of mental energy, I remote-soothed the infant, then put her in a deep sleep. Cradling her, I joined Asher. The lava moat was now twenty feet wide, surrounding an island that had shrunk to the size of a garage floor. Flames flickered upward as the lava slowly rose.

"Willow." Helpless, Asher stared at the trapped girl.

"It's okay," she said, voice gentle and unafraid. "I'm ready. This isn't my world anymore." Her gaze swept from the lava flowing in the park to the burning hotels beyond. "This hasn't been my world for a very long time."

She paused as a fireball struck some nearby palm trees, transforming them into torches.

"I'm not like you, Ash," she continued. "I've struggled every day since the Mist. Some days, I could only get through them by pretending to be Pandora. But even that's not enough anymore. Xavian's death devastated me. He was like the father I never had. Losing him was deeply painful." She shuddered. "Losing you, Ash, was even worse."

"You never lost me, Willow. I still care about you."

"But you love Kass."

As I shifted uncomfortably on the spot, Asher looked at me. "Yes, I love Kass." His face held a silent question. *But does she love me?*

Willow sighed. "You've changed since the Mist. Before, we were a perfect fit. These days, you need a warrior who's strong, independent, and passionate about the good fight. Someone like Kass." She touched her scarred cheek. "Someone who's not me."

"Willow ..."

"I'm so very, very tired." Beautiful face soft with acceptance, she gazed at Asher and me. "I wish you both long and happy lives."

As the island began to break up, she straightened her shoulders and cocked her head to the side, just like Pandora used to do. Calmly gripping her sword, she disappeared into the lake of lava.

Asher stood there, dazed by pain.

Gray flakes fluttered down, as though the sky shared his anguish and wept dry tears.

I stared at a gray flake on my arm. "Oh no! This stuff is ash. We need to get to the stadium. Now."

He stared into space, locked in his grief.

In the park, a gardener's truck exploded into flames. A split second later, two cars on the street exploded as fireballs struck them.

"What?" Asher snapped back to the present with its blazing vehicles and falling ash. "Cripes! Let's go."

We ran to Ona, who had crawled into the park. A large bloodstained bandage covered her injured arm. As I bent down, she grabbed her sleeping daughter and hugged her tightly. "What's wrong with Moana? Why is she so quiet?"

"I put her to sleep. She'll wake up in an hour or so."

My body began to tingle from head to toe once more. My golden power was growing stronger again, like a dead cell phone being recharged. I placed my hand on Ona's sprained ankle—and a warm energy flowed from me, shrinking her swollen flesh and erasing the purple bruise.

Stunned, she gingerly stood. "It's all better. You fixed it."

"Your power's incredible, Kass," said Asher.

"It's only temporary. It could disappear at any moment."

More cars exploded into flames, and the ashfall grew heavier.

"I'll carry Moana." Asher lifted the sleeping child from Ona's arms. "We need to go. Now."

We ran, dodging burning vehicles and blazing palm trees. The ground rumbled and shook, and endless lava oozed from the broken earth.

Effortlessly, I remote-pushed a stone wall as it began to fall on us. Bricks and concrete and chunks of furniture hung suspended in the air as we passed by; when I released my mental hold, the debris smashed down behind us.

The unnaturally hot air stank of sulfur, as though the gates of hell had been flung open. By the time we reached the car park outside Ainahau Stadium, we were drenched in sweat.

Our frantic flight trailed to a halt. We stared, open-mouthed.

A massive gold glow streamed upward from the center of the structure.

I gasped, "I think there's lava in the arena."

"So why are we heading for it?" Ona asked.

"Our people are in there." Asher nudged me. "Look, Kass. There's the minibus." Doors open, it stood empty. "Maybe Harl and the others made it to the ship in time."

Could we?

We entered the stadium and raced through a series of corridors and stairwells. Eventually, we emerged onto a section of tiered seating that overlooked the outdoor arena below.

Puffing, we paused.

Lightning One was still parked on top of the boulder terra—which had become an island in a lake of lava. Faces peered through the ship's narrow band of windows, searching for an escape.

There was none.

88

ONA'S ANXIOUS GAZE FLICKED from her sleeping child to Lightning One. "We need to get into that ship, don't we?"

"Yes," Asher replied. "Especially since I'm the pilot."

Cautiously, we descended to a lower level of seating.

The boiling gold lake was several feet deep, confined by the ten-foot-high walls that encircled the arena. At the far end, a trio of fountains spewed glittering sprays high into the air, adding more lava. Soon, the liquid lake would become deep enough to swallow the tiered seats, the boulders, and Lightning One.

Below, the top of a single boulder terra grew against the ten-foot wall. Four people stood on it, staring at the ship.

"Hey," Asher shouted to the small group.

We hurried past the tiered seating, stepped from the bottom landing, and joined them on the boulder.

Two civilians—Hawaiian Shirt man and Purple Shorts youth—had Booker slung between them, his injured leg wrapped in a bloodied bandage. Kendra stood at the front of the group, studying the expanse of lava.

My heart stuttered in panic. "Where's Lynxx?" I cried. "He was with you guys earlier."

Asher swallowed and looked away.

"He waited here for a while," Kendra replied. "Then he went looking for you."

I scoured the tiered seating but couldn't see him. Was he outside the stadium, in that growing hell? Should I go looking for him? Or wait for him here?

Asher asked, "Where's the woman in the flowery dress?"

"She didn't make it." Kendra's gaze swept us. "Where's Willow?"

Numbly, Asher shook his head.

"You there, bro?" Harlem's voice crackled from a radio.

"Harl." Asher grabbed his radio. "You okay? Where are you?"

"Standing outside Lightning One." We looked across and saw Harlem waving from the top of the boulder where Lightning One was parked. "I have forty-three people crammed inside and no pilot."

"Sorry, Harl. I'd truly like to help. But I can't walk on water, let alone lava."

"Think of a Plan B, bro. Meanwhile, I want to get rid of this thing." Harlem held up a long metal canister. It was the container of Threads we'd taken from the two Brethren recruits in Kenya.

"Throw it in the lava lake, Harl. The extreme heat will totally incinerate it."

"Good!" Harlem hurled the canister into the lava. It floated for a second, then sank into the burning liquid.

I scanned the stadium again, aware of the screams of lava bombs and explosions beyond it. Fear flowered within me like a black rose. "I need to find Lynxx."

Asher drew in a shaky breath. "He could be anywhere, Kass. *Anywhere.* You're better off waiting for him here."

"Do you think he'll come back?"

"Totally. He'll return, hoping you made it here." He paused, then asked in a flat voice, "Isn't that what you'd do if you were looking for him?"

"Of course." My fear eased. "He'll be back."

I wouldn't—couldn't—think of him dying. I needed to focus on something else, otherwise I'd break down from worry and fear.

Lightning One was a hundred feet away. So close. If only we had a bridge to the ship. Or a passage. Of course, we didn't have the time or equipment to make either. Unless …

My mind prickled and whirled. Could I do it? Was it possible, even with my superpowers today?

I stepped forward. "I have an idea."

"What?" Asher asked, handing the sleeping Moana back to her anxious mother.

I addressed the people on the rock with me. "If we stay here, we'll die. And so will everyone in the ship. But I might be able to create a path through the lava to Lightning One."

They stared at me as if I was crazy.

"That's impossible," Asher said.

"Is it?" I waved my hand. A large lava ball rose from the glowing lake. It hovered for a few seconds, burning bright, flames licking its sides. Slowly, I lowered it into the liquid again.

The civilians gaped at me.

"How did you do that?" Hawaiian Shirt croaked.

"She's got superpowers," Ona said with the smugness of an insider. "She flew my baby through the air. And she healed my sprained ankle."

"It's only a temporary boost of power," I told them. "That's the problem. I have no idea when it will vanish. It drained away a while ago." I gave Asher an apologetic look, remembering Willow's death. "But the power's recharged now. I don't know how long it'll last, though."

"Are you saying," Kendra asked, "that your power might switch off while we're halfway along the lava passage?"

"Exactly. You should only go if you're willing to take that risk."

She shrugged. "It sure beats waiting here to die."

"Can we talk about this first, Kass?" asked Asher.

"No time. We do this now, or not at all." My gaze swept the stadium again.

Asher saw me looking around, and he quietly repeated, "Lynxx will be back."

"I know. But he might return too late." Reluctantly, I turned my attention to the others. "If you're prepared to take the risk, guys, follow me."

89

Slowly, I moved down the slope of the boulder terra and stopped a few feet from the lava lake. I glanced behind me. Everyone was there, including Ona and her sleeping toddler.

"Asher," I said softly so the others couldn't hear, "you lead the group. You're the pilot."

"Aren't you going first?"

"I'll be last. I need to focus on carving out a passage between this boulder and the larger one holding Lightning One. I can't do that if I'm in front."

"What about the heat from the lava? Won't it burn people as they walk through the passage?"

"I'll suppress the heat. It'll be bearable."

"What happens if you can only clear the path for a few minutes, and we all get across except you?" he asked. "You could die back here."

When I'd first joined the Weston Battalion, Commander Powell had told me something that I'd angrily rejected. And now, a lifetime later, I realized he'd been right.

"The needs of the many outweigh the needs of the one," I murmured.

"What?"

"Forget it. You have to go first. You're the pilot. If you don't make it, none of us will."

"I won't leave you." His vow held an underlying intensity.

"Don't die for me, Asher. I'm not worth your sacrifice."

"Why do you say that?"

Gently, I told him, "You're not the love of my life."

He stumbled back a step as though physically struck. "Are you sure it's Lynxx?"

"Positive." Thinking back over the last year, I had no idea when my feelings for Lynxx had changed so dramatically. Like a spectacular sunrise, my love for him had started out as a tiny light on the dark horizon. Slowly, my love had grown brighter and brighter until its glorious golden brilliance now filled my heart and soul.

Asher turned away, struggling with his emotions. Then, with an infinitely sad sigh, he kissed my cheek. "Good luck. I hope you make it across."

"So do I." *With Lynxx.*

Clearing his throat, he turned to the others. "Line up, guys. I'll go first. Ona and her daughter are behind me. Then Booker and his two helpers." He gave Kendra a regretful look. "Sorry, Kendra, you're last."

Ever feisty, the girl lifted her chin. "Last but definitely not least."

I edged forward and focused on the lava flowing below like liquid fire. A tingle swept my body.

Not enough.

Eyes narrowed, I pushed my mind harder. Colors and sparks blurred in a whirlpool of light. My heart pounded, and energy surged through my brain in a swell of power. The lava below shimmered. A hollow formed on the surface, deep enough to cradle a car—

—then it flowed together, level again.

Abruptly, my power vanished.

Gasping, body shaking, I turned to my companions. "I'm sorry. I can't do it."

They murmured in disappointment and relief.

Quietly, Asher asked me, "Have your superpowers gone again?"

"No. They're still there. But they're not enough. I'm not powerful enough."

"It's okay," he said softly. "You tried."

My brow furrowed at a sudden wild idea. "But maybe, together, we can be powerful enough."

"Excuse me?"

A screaming lava bomb dropped from the heavens, trailing fire. It landed in the far side of the gold-black lake, splashing molten rock over the rows of seating. Fresh fires flared and more smoke billowed.

The civilians cried out and huddled together on the boulder. Ona muttered a prayer.

"It's okay," Hawaiian Shirt told them. "We're safe here."

"Yeah, for now," said Purple Shorts. "But what if the next lava bomb smacks into this rock?"

"Or what if it hits Lightning One?" Booker added, face strained with pain. He shifted uneasily, trying to keep the weight off his bandaged leg.

I grabbed my radio and clicked it on. "Can you hear me, Harlem?"

"Yes," came his reply.

"Okay. Get inside the ship. Leave the hatch open. And put your radio on the loudest setting so that everyone in there can hear me."

"Roger." A few seconds of muffled sounds. Then, "Ready, Kass."

"Good." I turned to the crowd on the boulder. Radio near my mouth, I raised my voice. "Listen carefully, guys. I don't have time for explanations or questions. When I give you the signal, everyone near me—and everyone in the ship—hold hands and close your eyes. Focus on creating a wide path in that lava lake. Visualize the liquid parting. Imagine a passage connecting the two boulders. Focus as intensely as if your life depends on it, because it does. Okay? Get ready."

Nearby, people gawked at me in stunned silence—

—then they fumbled and rushed to hold hands.

"Right," I shouted at them and into the radio. "*Start now. Hold hands, close your eyes, and focus. Visualize the lava parting and creating a path.*"

I moved to the front of the boulder and stood there.

Alone.

Arms outstretched, I faced the ship.

When I'd tried to save Willow back in the park, my enhanced powers had allowed me to draw energy from the people around me. I'd been able to boost my power, but there'd only been four people in that park, not counting the toddler, and the boost hadn't been enough.

This time, there were fifty people in this stadium.

Skin tingling as though swept by a cold fire, I opened my mind. Sparks pulsed outward, invisible to everyone—except me. They whirled and pulled at the air, craving energy.

For a long moment, nothing happened.

And then the air wavered as skeins of energy began to flow from the ship. Curling like breakers at a beach, they surged in glittering gold waves toward my boulder. From the people behind me, other currents rolled forward.

Arms outspread, I gathered the energy skeins and mentally wove them together. More and more came. Threads of gold, bright as life.

The woven energy skeins exploded through my mind like starbursts, infusing me with their power.

Hands stretched forward, I made a slow, outward movement as though physically pushing the lava apart. My brain throbbed with pain, but I kept pushing—

—and the lava shrank away from the boulder, leaving it bare and dry.

Slowly, I walked down the slope, still pushing outward.

Below, the lava began to divide and retreat before me, creating a wide passage between two burning walls. Some blackened tentacle terras lay shriveled and dead on the arena floor. The rest of the path was clear. Not a single drop of lava blemished the ground.

Still focusing, I stood to the side.

After a long, wistful look at me, Asher began to descend the sloping boulder, shouting, "Eyes open, guys. Form a line. Let's go."

They followed, too frightened to speak.

Everyone hurried along the newly formed passage, which radiated heatwaves upward, away from them. I could feel their fear as they stared at the towering walls of lava on either side. And I could taste their relief as they reached the high boulder terra at the far end of the path.

One by one, they scrambled up the dry slope. Harlem and others hauled them up the final few feet and shoved them through the open hatch, into the ship.

Asher stood with Harlem, gazing at me across the shifting lava lake. His voice crackled from my radio. "Come on, Kass. Your turn."

I didn't move. "Kendra's still in the passage." If I relaxed my hold for even an instant, the walls of lava would smash together, incinerating her.

My brain ached as if actually splitting apart. My golden power flickered—and the lava walls quivered eagerly. Sweat poured down my face. My muscles trembled, on the verge of cramping.

I knew I couldn't hold the lava apart any longer.

Please no! I'm about to kill Kendra.

And then, a warm hand slipped into mine.

My heart leaped—yet somehow I continued to focus on the trembling walls, keeping them apart. "Lynxx? You found me."

"Always." From the corner of my eye, I saw him nod at the lava. "Together, Kassia."

Together, hand in hand, we pushed the walls back. Our minds fused in a kaleidoscope of colors and sensations that pulsed like an expanding universe. Power filled me, extraordinary and brilliant—and then flickered again, becoming a little weaker.

As Kendra scampered up the boulder to Lightning One, I struggled to maintain my focus.

"Go, Lynxx," I cried. "Get to the ship. I can only hold the passage open for another minute or so. Go."

His hand tightened around mine. "We go together."

Heartsick at the thought of him dying, I said, "I need to stay here and hold back the lava. I'm not strong enough to control it while I'm running."

"Then we walk quickly. If we die together, I'm fine with that," he said. "But let's die trying to live."

I sighed. Knew he wouldn't change his mind. "Okay, let's try."

90

Holding hands, focusing together, Lynxx and I hurried along the passage.

The burning walls towered on either side of us, monsters breathing waves of heat. Flames flickered and grew, eager to grab us. Huge bubbles formed in the walls, swelling larger and larger. My heart raced. If those lava bubbles burst, Lynxx would be burned alive and—

Bubbles.

Desperately, I expanded my invisible shield, throwing it around Lynxx as well.

The bubbles popped, vomiting burning lava over us. Sizzling globs slid off the enlarged force field—*force bubble*—that I'd created.

He squeezed my hand. "Thanks."

Every foot we traveled felt like a mile. We were only halfway across the passage. Still fifty endless feet to go.

Keep walking, keep walking, keep walking.

The ground began to shake like the trembling boulevard earlier. Rocks snapped as a narrow crack zigzagged along the passage, all the way to the boulder holding the ship. Far below, the bottom of the crack gleamed bright yellow.

Molten death.

I longed to flee, pulling Lynxx along with me. Couldn't.

"If we run," I told him, "we won't be able to hold the passage open."

"I know." He squeezed my hand again. "We keep walk-ing—and focusing—together."

On either side, the tall lava walls quivered, straining to break free and smash down on us.

Forty feet to go.

In front of the boulder, lava slowly bled from the crack in the ground and flowed into our passage. It spread between the two lava walls. To get to the boulder and the ship, we'd have to cross that burning pool.

Speaking quickly, still moving forward, I said, "Lynxx, we need to split our focus. We have to keep holding the walls back—and harden that fresh lava so we can walk on it. Even with my extra powers today, that's impossible, right?"

"Maybe not. We might be able to create a super-mind."

"What's that?"

Thirty feet to the lava.

His words emerged in a rush. "Two separate torches can create two pools of light in the darkness. If you combine them, you get a larger and more powerful torch."

"How do we become this single, larger torch?"

"When we've mind-blended before, we've always respected each other's private thoughts. We've been those two separate pools of light in a dark room. Your extra powers today might allow us to *briefly* become one powerful light. To do that, we'll have to deliberately remove our privacy barriers. Are you game to try?"

No time to think about it. "It's that or die, right?"

"Right."

Twenty feet to the lava.

"This super mind-blend might feel like a long time," he said, "but it'll only be a couple of seconds."

"Okay."

We stopped.

Fifteen feet to the lava.

"Now, Kassia!"

Lynxx and I mentally held the towering walls back. At the same time, we thrust our minds closer and consciously dissolved our privacy barriers.

Our emotions and thoughts torrented into each other's mind.

I rocketed through fragmented memories of his childhood, sharp as broken glass. His pleasure in science. His fear of his albino guardian, Frost. Confusion and wonder as his humanity stirred. Brotherly love for Olivia. Platonic love for his friends in the Weston Battalion ...

... and a pure golden love for me. A love that would remain strong as we grew older. Shining bright with passion on many days. Steady and warming at other times. Always there. Always for me.

I felt Lynxx moving through my own emotions and memories, and his presence was intimate and unnerving and right. I sensed his surprise, wonder, and relief as he experienced the depth of my feelings for him. He discovered how he'd become a part of my heart and how he'd lightened my soul. He realized how the fire of my love for him would burn until death and beyond.

For a brief second, our intimately fused minds glowed white-hot. Diamond-sharp sparks shot outward, ricocheting off each other, faster and faster. With a blinding flash, our minds produced a single burst of pure energy—

—and the seeping pool of molten death in front of us turned black and hard.

We sagged as our fused minds parted and became separate again. Pain screamed through my body.

No time to talk about the raw emotions of our super mind-blend. That could come later.

If we survived.

Exhausted and battling to stay upright, we forced ourselves to hurry across the hardened pool. Despite my boots, I could feel heat radiating through the black shell, but it wasn't enough to burn.

Ten feet to the boulder.

Our new, lumpy path felt hot and brittle, as if it might crack at any moment and plunge us into the molten rock beneath.

Five feet to the boulder.

The trek felt endless, every step heavier and more difficult, like wading through wet concrete. Lynxx's sweating ash-gray face showed he was struggling too.

We staggered to the boulder terra. Sweat slicked my aching body, and it hurt to move or breathe or think. Lynxx appeared as drained and sore as me.

The ship rested on top of the boulder and, logically, I knew it was only thirty feet above us, but it seemed as high as Mount Everest.

Shaking with fatigue, we started to crawl up the boulder's sloped side—which suddenly began shaking.

91

SNAPS SOUNDED, BRITTLE AND ominous. Thin cracks crazed the boulder's surface, as though a giant hammer had struck it with enormous force.

"The heat," Lynxx gasped. "It's starting to shatter the boulder terra."

Still twenty feet to the top. In our weakened condition, it was an impossible distance to crawl.

There were forty-nine people on that ship. Two of us out here.

The needs of the many outweigh the needs of the one ... or the two.

Lynxx looked into my anguished eyes, and he read my despair. He nodded as though I'd spoken.

"We tried," he said wearily. "Do you want me to tell them?"

"I'll do it."

Harlem and Kendra and some others waited at the open hatch, anxiously watching us.

"Go," I yelled at them. "The boulder is about to break apart. Tell Asher to take off now."

"What about you guys?" Kendra yelled back.

"We can't make it. We're too exhausted."

Lynxx gestured to the people at the hatch. "Go. Leave us."

"No way," Harlem cried. "You two are family. We don't abandon family, no matter what."

He and Kendra ran down the cracking slope. Lynxx and I shouted at them to return to the ship, but they ignored us. Hawaiian Shirt and Purple Shorts rushed to join them.

"No!" I cried weakly. "You have to go."

Kendra and Hawaiian Shirt grabbed Lynxx, while Harlem and Purple Shorts slung me between them. Our rescuers turned and staggered back toward the ship, almost carrying us.

Large blobs of red-hot lava flew through the air, headed straight for our small group, about to hit us all—

—but from deep inside I managed to dredge up a scrap of golden power, and I remote-pushed with everything I had left.

The force bubble protecting Lynxx and me suddenly expanded, covering all six of us. The burning globs splattered harmlessly against the invisible sides, sizzling as they slid off.

Our rescuers gasped in awe.

A heartbeat later, the cracks on the boulder terra widened as parts began breaking away. A piece splashed into the lake, and orange waves rippled outward in growing rings.

"Pick up the pace, guys!" Harlem shouted.

Moments later, we reached the ship. Eager hands pushed and pulled us inside, and our rescuers piled in behind us. Just before the hatch hissed shut, I glimpsed the walls of the lava passage unfreeze and lurch forward, smashing together and flinging burning waves high in the air.

The boulder terra made a deep, moaning sound like the drawn-out wail of a dying brontosaurus. It began to tilt to the side.

"Go, bro!" yelled Harlem to Asher at the controls.

Still supported by Purple Shorts, I peered through a side window at the arena.

The ship arrowed upward. A split second later, the boulder broke apart and toppled into the lava lake. The thick waves gulped down the pieces, erasing the boulder terra's existence.

As Lightning One rose above the burning stadium, the crammed passengers cheered and clapped and hugged each other.

"Make the hull clear, Asher," cried Kendra, slipping into the copilot's seat at the front. "I want to see what's happening."

"Okay." He activated stealth mode.

Abruptly, my body sagged and I clung to my rescuers, struggling to stand.

"Here, Kass." Harlem motioned a couple of men off the seats along the wall, telling them, "She saved our lives. Again. Lynxx too."

The two men happily joined the crowd of passengers sitting on the floor.

Lynxx and I squeezed into the vacated spots.

"Actually," I said, gazing at my colleagues and the civilians, "when we created that lava passage, it was a team effort. We all mentally did it together."

People beamed proudly, and their deafening cheers briefly muted the explosions outside. As the racket simmered down, Lynxx and I thanked the four rescuers who'd risked their lives for us.

Wearily, I leaned against Lynxx's shoulder, noticing that his dark hair smelled of ash and sulfur. "The golden power is gone. Completely. I can sense its absence."

"How do you feel, Not-So-Super-Kassia?" he gently asked.

"Super-super-tired. Grateful to be alive." I squeezed his hand. "And happy we both survived."

We flew over Honolulu. Even in the unnatural twilight, we could see skyscrapers collapsing and hotels exploding. Lava flowed through the streets in endless waves. Scattered fires joined up, creating mega-fires and masses of black smoke.

Further away, red-gold rivers flooded from the distant erupting volcanoes. More forests flared into raging infernos.

Lava bombs screamed as they crashed into the land, triggering multiple blazes.

The beautiful island paradise of Oahu had turned into hell.

Booker winced as Soo-Yun treated his burned thigh with terra powder. "Have you heard from Commander Powell, boss? What's the status of the Threads and the Shimmer gas?"

I slumped in my seat. For a little while there, I'd almost forgotten about our oncoming doom ...

... due to the more imminent oncoming doom in Honolulu.

The civilians grew quiet and looked at Asher. From their worried expressions, most clearly knew about the race between the Threads and Shimmer gas. Bad news traveled fast.

"No word yet," Asher said. "We're meeting back in New York. By the time we get home, we should—"

Lightning One gave a shudder.

"What's happening, bro?" Harlem called out.

"*Cripes!* I forgot about the cool-down." Asher fiddled with the controls. "I need to put her down."

"Ultra-bad idea," Kendra cried beside him.

"I'm not landing her in Oahu. I think we can cruise for a few minutes without any problems—I hope. We need to reach another island. If we get lucky, it won't have an eruption ripping it apart."

Lynxx and I exchanged worried glances.

Everyone fell silent as Asher turned the ship south.

92

We got lucky.

Lightning One's low-drive transported us two hundred miles south, and Asher landed the shuddering ship on an uninhabited isle half a mile off Hawaii's Big Island.

Here, it was sunny and the pale red sky was clear. We couldn't see Oahu or the billowing black smoke. We could almost pretend that the eruptions hadn't happened and that Honolulu hadn't been buried in lava. We could almost believe it had all been a nightmare.

Almost.

"We'll head back to New York once the engine's cooled," Asher announced to the passengers after we landed.

"How long will we be here, boss?" Booker asked, pulling out a paperback as everyone exited the ship.

"Most of the day. The ship's already had a few hours' cool-down back in the stadium, but I'm giving it ten hours total, just to be safe." He glanced at his watch. "We should be ready to leave by late afternoon."

"Excellent." Booker opened his adventure novel with a contented sigh and headed for a spot beneath a sprawling banyan tree.

For a while, everyone sat around dazed and tired, recovering from the ordeal in Honolulu.

Eventually, people began to wander around the small isle. Some walked along the green-tinted sand, watching the kids splashing in the waves. Others lingered near the ship, reluctant to let it out of their sight. Soo-Yun and Harlem treated the injured, assisted by Asher and Kendra.

Our super mind-blend had initially left Lynxx and me physically exhausted, but it had also brought us emotionally closer. In a private spot on the island, we spent a few precious hours together—two flames merged into one fire.

Eventually, the remaining members of the Weston Battalion drifted back together, and we sat in the shade of the banyan tree.

"How's your arm, Yuki?" I asked.

The boy regarded his broken arm in its sling. "Good. Soo-Yun gave me blue terra drink. Very good for pain."

Another score for Lynxx's terra meds.

I turned to Booker. "Sorry I didn't have time to heal your lava burn when I was Super Kassia."

"No problem." He touched his bandaged thigh. "It doesn't hurt anymore, thanks to the terra cream. I guess it's another battle wound to impress the girls. Not as dashing as my scarred cheek, though."

Beside me, Lynxx told him, "The cream should heal your leg within a day, Booker."

"Excellent."

But would we still be alive in a day?

Our adjusted Zero Hour for the Shimmer had passed. Nila and her team had designed the gas to replicate with stunning speed, which meant it would spread around the world in a matter of hours—unless the Threads had been released first.

Asher watched the horizon, his face tight with grief and pain. I knew his grief was for Willow. And from the way he avoided looking at Lynxx and me, I guessed I was the cause of his pain.

Kendra spat on her sword, then polished it with a soft terra leaf. "If the Shimmer works, what then?"

"What do you mean?" Harlem asked, his arm around Soo-Yun's shoulder. The Korean girl snuggled against him, happy and secure in their relationship and pretending not to be worried about the Threads. For the first time on this mission, she wore her satin ballet slippers instead of her bloodstained combat boots, and I silently acknowledged her gesture of hope.

"If the Shimmer kills all the terras and xans and hybrids"—Kendra grinned at Lynxx—"the *evil, unvaccinated* hybrids, what then? What about those coldhearted Chi'az creeps lurking out there in space? Will they hang around and try again?"

Lynxx shook his head. "Nila told me that the Shimmer will remain in the air for a few thousand years. If any Chi'az try to invade Earth during that time, they'll die too."

"Good." She spat on her blade again and rubbed at a bloodstain. "So what do we do if we win?"

Lynxx pulled a bottle of pills from his jacket pocket. "I'm going to try to reverse engineer the pills Wanjala gave me. Hopefully, we can use them to cure cancer, like he's done. And maybe other diseases too." He tucked the precious bottle of pills safely away again.

"Great. *You* have a mission," Kendra said. "But I can't go back to being a farmhand at Weston Tower. I ultra-hate digging in dirt and yanking out weeds."

Asher stirred and his dull eyes finally gleamed with a dawning idea. "I'm going to use one of our Lightning ships to zip around the world. There'll be groups of survivors who'll need training in how to protect themselves from thugs like the Wilders."

"And from those mutant humans in Peru," Kendra added enthusiastically. "They're like Morlocks. If they survive the Shimmer gas, we'll need to deal with them too."

"We?" Asher tilted his head at her.

"You'll want a partner, won't you?"

A smile twitched the corner of his lips. "Definitely."

I relaxed a little. With time, Asher would recover from the wounds of Willow's death and my rejection.

As long as the Shimmer gave us that time.

Kendra turned to me. "What about you, Kass? What are your plans? Work with Lynxx on his pills?"

I shook my head. "That's his project. I want to carve my own path. Help repair the world." *But how?*

Swords sheathed, Lynxx and I wandered off again.

Ten minutes before we were scheduled to leave, we sat on a hillock overlooking the beach.

"How are you feeling now, Kassia?"

"Even better than when you asked me an hour ago." I rested my head on his shoulder. "The golden power is gone. Forever."

"Will you miss it?"

"Yes." If the Shimmer won the time countdown, the zap terras and their power-enhancing zaps would soon be dead. In addition, the destruction of the Chi'az cave had destroyed the xanatron, which had controlled Lightning Three's force field. With the xanatron gone, the force field was permanently off. No force field meant no enhanced abilities to—

I sat upright. "Lightning Two!"

"What?"

"The Brethren's ship, the one they were using to transport the canisters of Threads. It could have a xanatron!"

Lynxx's golden eyes widened in excitement. "We could turn on Lightning Two's force field—"

"—zap ourselves, enhance our mental abilities—"

"—and maybe I could create another batch of cancer-curing pills in months instead of years."

"Hang on. It's a random power," I reminded him. "Nila was affected differently to me. In fact, we've no idea how it'll affect us each time we use it."

"You're right. We'll have to be careful."

"I'd really like to use it to help people," I said, my enthusiasm tempered by caution. "But I've no idea how. Yet."

"First we need to get the xanatron. Hopefully Lightning Two is still in Kenya. Those Russkies parked it near that abandoned resort, remember?"

I nodded. "I'm sure Commander Powell will let us take Lightning One or Three to Africa, to recover the ship. It could be dangerous, so we'll need to take a team as well."

And I suddenly had a purpose again. A role to play in the new world. My work wasn't done. In fact, it was just beginning.

Sighing with relief, glad I still had my hybrid powers, I turned to a clump of shrubs covered with hibiscus flowers. Remote-picking a dozen blossoms, I floated them across to us. Lynxx added frangipanis, and we laughed as the flowers circled us. Orange. Pink. Lime. Purple. The sunlit blossoms swirled like pieces of a rainbow and my stress faded a little more.

"Oh no!" My heart jolted.

The floating flowers dropped to the ground.

Standing, we stared at the ocean.

Black threads appeared in the distance—

—and our dreams and plans and futures shattered into oblivion.

Lynxx put his arm around my waist, and his voice shook with immense sadness. "It's okay. Hopefully, our deaths will be quick and painless."

The black threads approached, relentless and ugly against the cloudless sky.

"I wanted a lifetime with you," I whispered, already grieving our stolen years.

"So did I. Still, it was worth it."

"What was worth it?"

"Everything I went through to be at your side." He drew me against his chest and I could feel his heart racing.

I wished I could stop time and stay in his arms forever. His golden eyes gazed at me, intense and brilliant but no longer haunted by his past. Instead, they glistened with love.

"You're not just at my side, Lynxx," I whispered. "You're in my heart. I love you, in all ways and for always."

The thin lines of death rushed to our isle—

—long black wings flapping. The blackbird xans wheeled overhead, settled into some palm trees, and began singing.

Lynxx and I released trembling sighs of relief.

The kids paddling in the water screamed. Adults grabbed them from the waves and bolted off the beach.

"It's okay," I called out to them. "It's not the Threads. They're just blackbird xans. Harmless."

"Shh!" Lynxx pulled me into the shadow of a palm tree.

I drew in a sharp breath. A double-hulled war canoe was plowing toward the shore, its wooden sides adorned with Hawaiian carvings. Ten green krols paddled each hull, their oars rising and falling in unison. At the sight of the fleeing humans, they shook their machetes and axes, and screeched.

Wearily, I withdrew my sword, preparing for yet another life-and-death battle.

With a bloodthirsty cry, a white-nosed krol brandished a rifle above its head, the shiny barrel flashing in the sunlight. It shouted a brief order, the words crystal clear: "*Kill every human!*"

The order was taken up by others in the war canoe. "*Kill every human!*"

Lynxx and I exchanged horrified glances.

"The krols can speak!" I gasped.

"And they've got rifles!"

The white-nosed krol fired at a woman running down the beach, but the shot missed her by inches, pinging off a piece of driftwood. Shrieking, the krols powered the war canoe through the shallow waves.

And then something moved on the horizon. A dazzling mist raced forward, expanding in all directions with breathtaking speed.

Seconds later, the mist draped our isle.

The blackbird xans' singing abruptly ceased.

Hesitantly, Lynxx and I emerged from the shadows and stood in the sunlight.

Whirling iridescent colors engulfed us, as wondrous as the famous Northern Lights. The Shimmer danced across the sky, shifting and twisting as though alive. Silvers and golds cascaded in weightless waterfalls that splashed us with glitter. Violets and blues rippled and flowed like airborne streams. A soft pink breeze caressed me, and a gold-tinted wind blew away the last of my stress.

Voice hushed with awe, Lynxx murmured, "I can feel my soul soaring, Kassia."

"Me too," I whispered. "It's like being inside music."

On the beach, the krols leaped from the war canoe and swung their weapons. As the swirling lights touched them, they fell to the sand, whimpering. Moments later, they collapsed into piles of decomp-dust. The palm trees with the blackbird xans now rained dust from their empty branches. Everywhere we looked, terra plants and xanimals and xan bugs were turning into gray piles of dust.

These piles of decomp-dust seemed to deliberately echo the deaths of billions of people following the Night of the Red Mist.

"Nice touch, Nila," I murmured.

Cheers erupted from my colleagues—*my family*—and the forty or so civilians we'd rescued.

The Shimmer passed over us and moved on, leaving a faint sparkle in the air. On the island, the plants and animals native to Earth continued their lives, unharmed.

I looked around, marveling as the pale red sky began to turn blue. Even the green-tinted sand was fading to yellow again. And already, the gray piles were being blown away by the wind and washed away by waves. In time, the decomp-dust would only belong to a dark yesterday.

Today, a new world was being born from the ashes of two lost ones.

In the distance, Asher called out, "Okay, everyone, let's go home."

Together, Lynxx and I turned toward a hopeful future.

Thank You

Thank you for reading *Phoenix Rising*. I hope you enjoyed the book. If you did, I would be very grateful if you would tell your friends and consider leaving a review online—it can be as short or long as you wish.

Not a fan of writing reviews? That's okay. A rating (where you just leave stars) online is also much appreciated.

Reviews and star ratings are like life buoys. They help my book float on the surface of a gigantic ocean of books. From there, other readers can see it.

Without reviews and star ratings, my book will sink out of sight, dropping to the pitch-black bottom of the ocean. This is a graveyard for books.

Please help save a book today.

Happy reading!

Eden Hart

ALSO BY EDEN HART

The complete *Girl on Fire* Series:

Girl on Fire Book 1

Ashes Falling Book 2

Embers Burning Book 3

Phoenix Rising Book 4

About the Author

There are several authors named Eden Hart, who write in a wide variety of genres.

So far, the only books I've written are the 4 books in the *Girl on Fire* series.

My dystopian post-apocalyptic novels focus on compelling characters caught up in extraordinary events. They are laced with romance, action, sci-fi, and suspense, and aim to create immersive worlds that stir the imagination and enthrall the reader.

Along with writing, I'm passionate about travel. I've explored the crater of a mildly active volcano in Hawaii, abseiled down cliffs in Australia, trod the ruins of Pompeii, breakfasted with an orangutan in Asia, and crawled through the tunnels of an ancient subterranean city in Turkey.

Some of my less enjoyable experiences include flying on a broomstick-like ultra-light, having a ten-foot snake draped around my neck, and traveling in a plane whose engine burst into flames over the Indian Ocean.

Books are now my preferred way of adventuring!

I love hearing from my readers and can be found at:
Facebook Page: "Eden Hart - Author"
Email: EdenHart77@outlook.com
Website: www.edenhart.com.au